A Valediction

[a novel]

Ellis Friedman

Produced by:

FriesenPress
Suite 300 – 852 Fort Street
Victoria, BC, Canada V8W 1H8
www.friesenpress.com

Distributed to the trade by The Ingram Book Company

TABLE OF CONTENTS

For Papa,
who made me publish this

If they be two, they are two so
As stiff twin compasses are two;
Thy soul, the fixed foot, makes no show
To move, but doth, if the other do.

John Donne

1

An oreo.

The sound of the copy machines was like an Oreo, the mechanical soprano buzz sandwiching the sound of a train clacking by.

"Daddy, I want a hot dog."

Or maybe it was like a hot dog, the fluffy, squealing hum cradling the clicking shutter button. With extra mustard.

"Daddy, I'm hungry."

"Of course you are."

The whir of the Xerox machines had done nothing to lull Chloe into a meditative trance. Back when she was a baby, Toby used to go out to the garage, sit in the car with her and turn on the windshield wipers to get her to fall asleep. Too bad he hadn't thought of Kinko's all those years ago; it would have been like infant Ambien.

"Daddy, this is boring."

"I know, Chloe, but Daddy has to get this done."

"Why?"

"Because it's important."

"For what?"

"Where are you going to get a hot dog?" he asked, changing the subject.

"Can we go to Spike's?"

"Daddy's busy, Chloe."

"It's right next door."

"Maybe when Daddy's finished."

"But I'm hungry now."

"Well you'll just have to wait. I'm sure you'll still be hungry in fifteen minutes."

"I'm ten, Dad. I can go by myself."

Toby looked up and out the window. It was the middle of the afternoon—he had just picked Chloe up from school on his way back from his lawyer's office. He hoped it was too early for child predators.

"All right," he sighed, reaching into his pocket for his wallet. "Get me one, too. The one with honey mustard and Swiss."

"Can I get fries, too?"

Toby sighed. Might as well enjoy childhood while she could.

"Sure."

He handed her a twenty and she bounced out. Toby turned back to the rocking whiz of the machines and thought of his father's hairy legs. Like they were covered with a thousand spiders each. Toby had been standing next to his father at a barbeque—it must have been Labor Day or Independence Day, because his father was wearing shorts. His hairy legs tickled Toby's arms. Being only three or four at the time, Toby had an especially intimate knowledge of people's legs. He preferred his mother's, because they were soft and smooth.

He was sitting at a white plastic patio table with his father. It was hot and Toby's legs stuck to the plastic chair. His father had cooked a hot dog fresh from the grill, but Toby, still in toddler taste buds, had requested a microwaved hot dog, no bun. The hot dog sat pink and naked on his plastic plate. He picked up the limp stick of meat by one end, dipped the other in ketchup and lifted it to his mouth. But before it got there, his sad nuked hot dog drooped and broke in half.

Toby was horrified. Hot dogs could break? But that was his hot dog! His lunch was broken, so he cried.

"Don't cry, Toby, it's just a hot dog."

"Fix it, Daddy," he cried. "Fix it. Glue it back together. Make it better."

"I can't fix it, Toby," said his father reasonably.

Toby cried harder, "Fix it, Daddy!"

"I can't fix it, Toby," his father repeated with a bit more impatience.

Toby screamed and howled, "Fix it! Put it back together!"

Toby's father stood up and walked around to Toby and crouched down, putting one hand on Toby's shoulder and the other grabbing Toby's chin.

"Toby," he said, looking straight into Toby's face. "There are some things that cannot be fixed."

Toby found it strange that he thought of this memory now, looking at the bright scanning light of a Xerox machine at Kinko's forty years later as he made photocopies of his joint tax returns for the past three years. Was he really still in the same body? Why was it that he had ever wished he were a grown-up when he was a kid? When you're a kid you think being an adult is staying up late, driving cars, and buying candy. What they don't tell you is that really, you spend most of your time doing shit like this, proving your existence through paper, because no one takes you at your word.

He didn't shut the machine lid because he liked to watch the light move side to side. He could pretend he was in some future space movie where machines did face scans to let you into the room with the top secret, state-of-the-art computer. He might as well get a little fun out of copying his joint tax returns.

This is so stupid. Shouldn't my lawyer be doing this? Isn't this what I pay him for? thought Toby as the robot scanned him into the room for the fiftieth time.

Right. Because you're the only person Howard is helping get divorced.

He slid a new piece of paper on the glass.

Well then, isn't this something Howard's summer intern should be doing?

Maybe this was punishment, something the state made you do to punish you for making the wrong choice. You married the wrong person? Go photocopy your joint tax returns, your house deeds, your life insurance policies and every paper record you have of the time you've been with your spouse.

There are some things that cannot be fixed.

Like broken hot dogs and Toby's marriage.

As Toby was paying, Chloe came back in, cradling a paper bag from Spike's in one hand and digging inside for French fries with the other.

"Okay, sweetie, Daddy's done. Let's go."

They ate their hot dogs in the parking lot, sitting in the car with the windows down. It was a heavy, cloudy day, a cool breeze cutting deceitfully beneath the heat; a steely reprieve from September summer. As he was digesting and driving, Toby had the sudden, overwhelming urge for caffeine. Tax forms had a way of doing that.

"Daddy's going to stop for some coffee," he said, pulling into the Starbucks by his house.

"I'll stay here," said Chloe.

"Lock the doors," said Toby.

"Leave the keys so I can listen to the radio. Please."

He walked across the parking lot. The absence of his keys jingling in his pocket felt almost like a missing limb, and twice he had to remind himself that he had left them in the car with Chloe.

The smell of coffee and warm milk exacerbated his caffeine anticipation. The coffee shop, overwhelmed by the orange wood counters and tables, seemed more crowded than it was. It was far too narrow to be a coffee shop; the pick-up counter was jutted almost to the opposite wall, and nowhere in the small café could two people walk abreast. Toby wondered how many coffees got spilled there each day.

He recognized pretty much everyone who worked here at every shift. It was so close to his house and his caffeine addiction so strong that he was here a bit more than he'd care to admit. Some days when he came in twice, a barista who had been working during his first visit was still working during his second and he'd feel a bit sheepish.

Today there was a new employee at the cash register, and as he approached he noticed her fingers first. They seemed so fascinatingly long, like they could wrap themselves endlessly around anything. Her hands were eerily elegant. Then he noticed the spot where her earlobe met her jaw line and had the startling vision of putting his mouth around it as though eating a grape from a vine.

What startled him more than the beautiful woman beneath the tacky green apron was the fact that he noticed her at all—almost two years prior, he had concluded he could never like a woman again. He had slept with a few after Jenny, of course, but that wasn't the same as liking them. There had been plenty of beautiful women around, but usually the coffee was of more interest to him than their earlobes.

"Hello sir, what can I get for you?" she asked him.

All his attention focused on a small section of hair that had adhered itself to her cheek near the corner of her mouth; he pictured pushing it away with his lips. After a pause only marginally longer than appropriate, he recovered his wits enough to give her his order.

"And your name?"

"Toby," he said. "And, uh, what's your name? I haven't seen you here before, and I'm a regular."

"Funny, I would have pegged you as a decaf this late in the day," she said.

He laughed as she wrote his name on a cup. When he handed her his money, her long pinkie grazed one of his knuckles. He should have made a witty reply, but there was a line forming behind him, and her lips had smiled and thanked him and moved on.

As he walked back to the car, he looked at the loopy, lower-case swirls that spelled out Toby. He thought of her earlobe, her pinkie, her lips, and then he stopped in the middle of the parking lot. He didn't know her at all, not even her name, and yet, he was stunned to realize he was intrigued. A girl who could make a joke about coffee deserved further thought.

He meant to return to the Starbucks the very next day to discover her name, but Grace got sick. As he crouched on the kitchen floor, mopping up half-digested Froot Loops, he wondered to himself if by chance Gracie could take a nap. Then he might be able to pop out just for a second and run to Starbucks for a coffee he could just as easily make right in that very kitchen. Even if Gracie had taken a nap, and even if she hadn't thrown up twice more and if he hadn't decided to take her to the doctor, he wouldn't have gone. He might like the girl with long pinkies, but he loved his daughters, even when they upchucked rainbow sugar onto his hardwood floor.

Gracie turned out to have the flu. She was out of school for three days and on the couch watching movies, eating toast and chicken soup and drinking Coke. Then it was the weekend and he was driving all three girls to nine different places and fixing three or four different dinners each night. When it was finally Monday, and the girls were with their mother, he slept until one in the afternoon, and by the time he got to Starbucks, the girl with long pinkies wasn't there.

On Tuesday he took great care to go at the exact same time he had gone before. The day was steamy and reverberated with the deafening buzz of cicadas, so after the two minutes between his house and Starbucks, he was dusted in fine beads of sweat. He tried to look through the glass when he got to the door, to see if it was worth his three dollars to buy coffee, but the glaring reflection of the world around him obscured everything in front of him. So he opened the door and stepped into the jolt of air conditioning. His eyes drowned with the green light left over from outside.

When he regained his sight, he saw that she was there. There was only one person in line, a woman, middle-aged like him, dyed hair, small calculated waist, skin glowing with a tinge of tellingly artificial orange. She was trying desperately to uphold the fading façade of youthful beauty, but it didn't stay up too well in the presence of his long-fingered barista.

"Hello sir, what can I get for you?" asked the ivy-fingered girl as the other woman moved to the end of the counter. She didn't remember him.

Toby's throat fell backwards a little bit as he gave his usual order.

The girl reached for a cup, "And what's your name?"

"Toby."

She wrote out t-o-b-y and set the cup on the ledge. She paused for a moment, then looked at him.

"I was right, you are a decaf," she said.

"What?"

"You said you were a regular, and I said you seemed more like a decaf. You haven't been in for a while, so you are a decaf," she tried to explain.

He laughed awkwardly as his throat crawled back up behind his mouth.

"I remember because *I* thought it was clever," she said, her cheeks turning pink. "And there's been no one else named Toby."

"Well from now on I'll be regular," he said.

She arched an eyebrow and suppressed a smile.

"I mean *a* regular," he stressed hastily. "I just had a lot to deal with this past week."

"Make it a double, then?" she asked.

He was supposed to be the witty one. Had forty-three years taught him nothing?

"There aren't enough shots of espresso in the world," he said. She politely chuckled and smiled.

Now or never, buddy.

"What's your name?" he asked, throwing decades of practiced nonchalance into those three words. "I at least want to know the name of my daily drug dealer," he added, perhaps a bit lamely.

She smiled, "Oh, so I'm an enabler?" She raised an eyebrow.

His mind was blank. *Shit.* He did not want to start driving to another Starbucks.

"I'm July," she said. "But you gotta pay for your fix."

He had never felt so glad to pay three dollars for a cup of coffee.

He went back every day that week. On Friday, he got to the coffee shop just as she was coming out the front door. She was in a breezy skirt and a tank top. He had never seen her without a green apron.

"Hi Toby," she said, stopping and smiling.

"Hi July," he replied in surprise.

"You're going to have to get your fix from someone else now." She ran her hand through her hair, "I quit."

"You quit?"

"They were having trouble scheduling around my classes."

"Your classes?" he said a bit too dubiously, hardly believing that he was hearing himself say completely nonchalantly, "You want to give me your number and maybe we can meet up for drinks sometime?"

Somehow, he walked away with her phone number. Caught completely off guard by his forwardness, she had given it gladly, and he hadn't even planned to ask her out that day. Or really any day. He never thought he would actually do it—the old guy who made bad jokes asking out the college student barista would probably seem creepy to almost anyone. But she had seemed completely *not* creeped out as she gave it to him.

At least he wouldn't have to go to Starbucks every day from now on and pay for his coffee.

He called her the same day. Actually, he called her three hours later. At forty-three years old, he had already spent too many years trying to play the game with women, with Jenny, and look where that had gotten him. He wasn't about to screw around—at least not in *that* way—with the first person he seemed to like in over two years.

Like that, he had a date tomorrow.

July sat at a table in the campus dining hall with her friends Emily and Rachel. Emily was talking about the economics professor who she *loved*—no really she was *in love*, guys—he was so brilliant, so knowledgeable, and, "he's got the sexy professor thing going on, and when I went to office hours last week and he took a pencil from me to draw out a problem, he touched my hand."

July didn't take economics, so she wasn't really listening; she was pushing around the stringy London Broil on her plate instead. She was too preoccupied with Toby, the Starbucks guy who had asked her out just after she quit. Was it creepy? Weird?

"Hey July, did you quit your job today?" asked Rachel, anxious to get off the subject of Professor Omigod.

"Oh, yeah."

"Too bad," said Emily. "No more free unsold muffins."

"But afterwards, as I was walking out of the coffee shop, one of the regulars asked me out."

"He just—asked you out? Just like that?" said Emily.

"Yeah."

"And *how* many times have you talked to this guy before?" asked Rachel.

"Three or four maybe? He came in every day."

Rachel rolled her eyes and took a bite of her pasta, "Does he go here?"

July frowned, "No. He's out of school."

"Ooh, an older man," said Emily, leaning forward. "How old is he?"

"At least forty," said July.

Emily's eyebrows went up like pieces of toast springing fresh from the toaster.

"Whoa."

"*Forty?*" said Rachel. "Are you actually going to meet him?"

"Well, I mean, I said I would," said July.

"That doesn't mean you have to *go*," said Rachel.

"Is he cute?" asked Emily. "Is he like, George Clooney forty or like, my dad forty?"

"He's like …" July thought for a moment. Who did he remind her of, this man who had suddenly appeared in her Starbucks, making enjoyable but seemingly innocent conversation? "He was like … Tony Blair."

"*Tony Blair?*" said Emily.

"Well not exactly, just kind of, in the eyes," said July, trying to justify herself. "He's not British, and Tony Blair's not so bad looking."

"For a politician," said Emily. "This guy isn't a politician, is he? What does he do?"

"I don't know," shrugged July.

"July, he could be a drug dealer for all you know," said Rachel.

"He's not a *drug dealer*."

"You don't know that. He probably has a ton of STDs. Or he's a serial killer."

"Oh come on, Rachel," said Emily. "Professor Burke is almost forty and he doesn't have STDs."

"You don't know that, and July, you have to wonder why a forty-year-old guy is single in the first place. Especially if he's asking out college students. There must be something wrong with him."

"Nice, Rachel," said July, rolling her eyes.

"Did he give you a sketchy vibe?" asked Emily.

"He just seemed like a nice guy. He'd come in every day and we'd chat or make jokes or whatever. It's not like I was turning on the charm."

"So then what's the big deal?"

"I just—nothing, I guess. I mean he seems perfectly fine, cute even, but it just seemed a little—random. And maybe weird."

"It is weird," said Emily. "But that doesn't make it dangerous."

"Don't let him drive you anywhere. Don't let him take you to a second location," said Rachel.

"Thank you, Oprah," said Emily.

July had wanted a little reassurance and she wasn't sure if she had gotten it. Rachel had been saying things she had wondered herself.

"What about Chris?" asked Rachel.

"What *about* Chris? We broke up," said July.

"It hasn't been that long."

"It's been two weeks, and you know I wasn't—I was ready for it to be over."

"What time are you meeting him tomorrow?" interrupted Emily.

"Five thirty for drinks. And then dinner at some place in Boston by Eagle Hill, near Logan Airport."

"Okay, look. Tell me exactly where you're going, then text me at eight. If I don't hear from you by eight fifteen, I'll call you. If you don't pick up, I'll call the cops," said Emily.

"That's a little extreme," frowned July.

"Not if you text me at eight telling me you're fine."

July looked at Rachel, who had her eyebrows raised in surprised approval.

"Okay," July shrugged.

II

THEY WERE BOTH EARLY, BUT HE WAS EARLIER. IT WAS ONE OF THE
last warm late summer days, a mention of chill in the breeze. The
door to the bar was propped open with a cement block. Inside, it was
simple—no sports memorabilia, no trendy lights or booths, just a bar
and some neon beer signs. Three men sat in a booth at the very back,
a centerpiece of empty beer bottles on the table glittering beneath
the lamp.

July stopped for just a moment at the open door and saw Toby
sitting at the bar, sliding and spinning his Blackberry on the counter,
his legs reaching down the barstool like perfect denim sculptures. He
turned around as she came in and smiled. She smiled back, they said
hello, and she sat on the stool to his right.

He was better looking than she remembered. Steel colored eyes,
crow's feet reaching from their outer corners like paper fans. She
wanted to trace them with her finger. The rest of his face was a premonition of the kind of wrinkles that make men look better instead of
older. Behind the Tony Blair, she sensed a bit of John Wayne.

She looked again at the legs in perfect jeans, teasing with sex appeal
that looked like he hadn't thought about it. The kind of jeans a wife or
girlfriend or gay friend buys for you.

Toby ordered a margarita for each of them, and they sat facing
each other, legs interlocked. She said something funny, and when he
laughed he put a hand on her thigh, lightly enough to be first-date

appropriate, firmly enough to be acceptably suggestive. She thought he might burn a handprint on her pants, like an iron left too long.

When she asked about him, he started out a little vague—grew up in Colorado (but July guessed it had been quite a while ago), worked in real estate, liked to travel.

"So where's your favorite place you've been?" she asked.

"Florence. It's the most beautiful city I've ever seen."

"I've always wanted to go to Italy. Tuscany and pasta. I've been studying Italian for four years."

"I'll take you there someday," he said and took a sip of his drink.

July frowned inwardly. It must be some throwaway line—was he trying to charm her, or—what? Why would he say that? Toby must have started talking again, because suddenly she heard the words.

"Took my daughters there. They wanted gelato after every meal, even breakfast."

Wait—daughters? He has kids? This should be a deal breaker and I should be totally shocked because I could probably be his daughter and this should be totally weird.

"You have daughters?"

"Actually, I have three."

"What are their names? How old are they?" she asked, thinking, *three?*

"Well there's Chloe, she's ten, and Sophia is eight, and Grace is four."

I'm only twelve years older than his oldest daughter, she thought. *That's a little weird.*

As he talked about them, his faced crinkled with the smitten willingness to do anything for them, a man strong and weak. July felt a wistful pang—*I wish someone looked like that when they thought of me,* she thought. Her heart became a kebab.

Soccer, baseball, gymnastics, rock climbing, clarinet and cello, camping and hiking and swimming and drawing.

"They sound like the coolest girls in the world," she said, while she thought, *I wish my childhood had been like that. I don't hold a candle to those girls.*

"Sure you do," he said.

She had said that out loud? *Oh God.*

"Tell me about all the things that you do. I've been talking too much." He took a sip of his drink, then leaned toward her, a small, enticingly ambiguous smile scrunching the fans around his eyes, "I always ramble about my girls."

"Well." Her life seemed so basic, so laughable next to his extensive travels and a family. What had she ever actually done?

"Well," she started again. "I cook a lot."

He smiled. "What's your favorite thing to make?"

"Cake."

"Why cake?"

"Because cake always feels special. Like you're celebrating."

"What's your major?" he asked, then cracked a smile and chuckled. "I haven't asked that question in years."

"International Relations."

"What made you decide to major in International Relations?"

"Well, it was kind of a compromise with my parents. They wanted me to study economics or business. I wanted to study anthropology. But they pay tuition, so I was able to strike a deal."

"Maybe you should study contract negotiations instead," he said, tilting his head back for the dregs of his margarita. "What are you going to do after you graduate?"

She hated this question, "Well, my parents want me to move back home to Tucson and find a job there."

"What do you really want to do?"

"Honestly?" She paused for a moment, anticipating the puzzled, slightly pitying look that she always got, "I don't have the faintest fucking idea."

And then he laughed, loud and deep. He leaned forward, put his hand back on her thigh and looked into her eyes, "Neither do I."

Her soul poured onto the floor but her eyes stayed connected to his like the ends of invisible barbells.

"Come on," he said. "Let's get some food. It's just up the street."

They left the bar and turned up a steep hill. The breeze was cool, chilling the wet fabric under July's arms. She glanced down and saw dark, damp sweat stains. Why hadn't she worn black? She did her best to keep her arms pinned to her sides as they climbed up the hill. About halfway up the road was a Mexican restaurant, a small place with ochre walls and seven tables. They were in a snow globe, there was no time, no before or after, just the liquid around them to keep them suspended and connected as they shared their dinner selections like people with a history of fluid familiarity.

"What do you want for dessert?" asked Toby after the waiter cleared away their empty plates.

July smiled. He hadn't asked *if*, but *what*, "What's your recommendation?"

"The flan is fantastic."

"Okay then," she said, flipping the menu closed decisively. "If you've got it, flant it."

Toby chuckled and shook his head.

"Well," he replied. "If it's nacho cup of tea, I'd go for the *arroz con leche*."

"In that *queso*, I want both."

"Who tortilla your manners?"

"You can't taco to me like that!" said July, as they both burst out laughing.

"I love a girl who knows how to have a fun time," he said, wiping laughter tears from his eyes.

July's tongue froze, and she could only look at where the lines at the corners of his mouth seemed to meet his pupils, shimmering like two buffed watermelon seeds.

Just before eight o'clock, July slipped into the bathroom and sent a text to Emily.

Making food puns. Unlikely serial killer.

After dinner he walked her back to campus. She walked with her arms crossed, the cool night air prickled on her skin, but she kept thinking of all the articles in those stupid women's magazines about how crossing your arms was hostile, closed body language. But what if you were just cold?

They stopped walking at a corner of academic buildings.

"You're okay to walk from here?" he asked.

"Yeah, I'm just over there." She made a vague motion with one of her hands, then forced both arms down by her sides and into her back pockets.

She heard someone shout from the quad. A car drove by. A few leaves that had fallen early rustled at her feet. July was suddenly very cognizant of her cheeks.

"Give me a hug," Toby said.

His chest wrapped her in dark heat, like she had dived into a pool of warm melted caramel. Then she was released back into the starkly cool world, but he stayed close, and a moment later, her mouth was alive with his. It was the only part of her that existed. Her body had fizzled away into her mouth.

She had never been kissed like that before, when lips seem to move in tandem with practiced pleasure, when every surface touched by him came alive. No teeth knocking, awkward head turning, inappropriate or misused tongues. Her other kisses had been wet or sloppy or lasciviously eager. Chris usually just put his lips against hers and expected a kiss to come of its own accord. This was the first kiss she didn't have to think about.

July was suddenly back in her body, which felt more foreign and strange than she remembered, like she had come back home to find that the furniture had been rearranged.

"You're grinning like an idiot," he said.

"Am I?" she put a hand to her lips and found that she was.

III

THERE WERE STILL MORNINGS WHEN, AS HE CRAWLED UP FROM SLEEP to awake, he forgot that Jenny wasn't sleeping next to him. He expected to wake up with her whispery blonde hair in his face. The first nine months or so, when there were no women at all, he had to put a body pillow next to him, so strange was an empty bed. The first woman, Liza, had been blonde, too. Waking up to her that morning had really fucked with his head, like an encounter with a ghost, the painful twinge of a familiar tragedy.

After that he had consciously avoided blondes. He had dinner with a few brunettes and a woman who said she was a redhead but that was just wishful thinking on her part. Usually, he only let them spend the night if he didn't want to have to deal with how resoundingly empty the house would feel later. In the mornings he would rise early, make noise to wake her up, then pretend to have somewhere to be so that he wouldn't have to make her breakfast.

In his early bachelor days, back when his age started with a two, there had been enough women who stayed over to keep him busy but fairly unattached, yet not enough to seem like a womanizer. When a woman he genuinely liked and who was probably too good for him stayed the night, he would make her pancakes the next morning. He had been a pretty good cook, especially compared to his other bachelor friends, but his pancakes were his crowning achievement. He had figured out the perfect ingredient ratio, the exact number of times to stir the batter around, the perfect amount of time a pancake should sit in the griddle. His pancakes were the second seduction.

The morning after his first date with July, he awoke just as his windows had turned light. This morning the bed seemed bigger and emptier than it had before. He turned on his side to face the mesa of empty bed sheets. July was probably a pancake kind of girl.

The last woman he had re-seduced with his pancakes had been Jenny. He had made them the first time she stayed over, and a few times thereafter until they moved in together, and on the weekends when they were newlyweds, and on Mother's Day and her birthday. But she had stopped eating the pancakes around the same time their marriage had started cracking.

The only women he made pancakes for now were his daughters. When it was their turn to stay with him, he made them pancakes almost every day, even though Jenny had asked him to "feed them eggs or oatmeal or hell even frozen sausage for Christ's sake, just not so many carbs." He ignored her and always made pancakes, except when they were running late, and then it was Froot Loops or Frosted Flakes. Even though he knew the cereals were "essentially boxed cavities and diabetes" thank you Jenny, he decided that his girls only had a few years left when they wouldn't care that they were eating carbs and sugar, and they had the right to enjoy that as long as they could.

Maybe July didn't care that he was old. He hadn't told her exactly how old he was. He was afraid that if he did, she would say, Wow, you and my dad are like the same age. He didn't need to hear that. He also hadn't told her that he wasn't exactly divorced. Yet. He was getting divorced, in the process, had eighteen months worth of papers and lawyer bills to prove it. But since she hadn't asked, he wasn't going to bring it up. Yet.

When he asked her out, he had known she was in college like he knew that a tomato was a fruit; he had learned that it was a fruit, but he still called it a vegetable and only remembered that it wasn't when some stickler (Jenny) corrected him. If July had never mentioned her age, he would have pinned her as at least twenty-four, perhaps twenty-six. He had always been torn about the "age is just a number" trope. He still felt twenty-one inside—sometimes—like when he played soccer with the girls, or when he was alone riding his bicycle or visiting Florida in the winter. But the rest of the time he just felt expired. There were younger real estate go-getters, new music and jargon and texting etiquette, more food that gave him heartburn. Each day he felt a little more unmoored.

Last night with July, he had felt a little more in touch, like perhaps youth wasn't such a foreign land after all. Maybe kids today had it more together than he thought.

He didn't have the girls until tomorrow after school. He and July could see each other again tonight. Two dates in two days—was that a little ... desperate? But is it desperation when you actually like the person instead of just wanting to screw her?

What are you doing you old man? You aren't young any more, grow up, buy a BMW.

For their second date, he planned to take her to an Italian bistro. Her dorm, she said, was a five-minute walk from his house, so she would come to his house and they would take his car. So Toby spent an hour making his house seem lived in but neat, adult but kid-friendly. It was totally different than prepping a house to show a client, when he wanted the house to look more like an exhibit than a habitat. How many jackets should be casually strewn across chairs or the sofa before he looked like a slob or a man with too many jackets?

He remembered Jenny doing this kind of flitting around the house, dusting the tops of ceiling fans and washing the insides of garbage cans before their friends of more than ten years arrived for a casual dinner. She had once accosted him and forced him to clean washed silverware with vinegar, and as he wiped a knife he had briefly questioned whether to use it on himself or her, would vinegar would remove bloodstains, and would bloodstains decrease the market value of the house? After the vinegar knives, Toby had been a very hard man to find in the hours before company was set to arrive.

As he shuffled some newspapers and mail on his coffee table, trying to make them look a spontaneously ordered disorder, the doorbell rang. He paused; he hadn't expected her to be on time—according to a lot of people his age, kids today were always late. He fussed his way to the door, but once he opened it to July, the rest of the world had fallen off a cliff. All that was behind him was space and black, and he pulled her body to him. She fit perfectly between his hipbones.

The world caught up two and a half hours later. When they were supposed to be eating tiramisu and overpriced gelato, they were still on the couch, where they had been furiously kissing. He was sweating, no need for the gym tomorrow, and July, her top rumpled and askew in perfect discordance, had infused the entire room like an incense stick.

Darkness had already permeated the house and swathed them in silken tar. In silence they basked and recuperated. She sighed heavy and long and slow like an ocean wave. His mouth felt full of cotton balls. All of their saliva had passed into a world between their mouths.

"Do you want a glass of water?"

"Yes, please," she said gratefully.

Toby groped his way through the dark, waving his arms in front of him like a swimmer. He reached the fridge and flung it open. The kitchen cracked open with searing light. As he reached for the water jug, hunger punched him in the stomach.

"Are you hungry?" he called to July.

A moment of reflective silence.

"I'm starving!"

He looked in the starkly empty fridge. A few containers of yogurt, some baby carrots, ketchup, beer, orange juice, peanut butter.

He brought the jar of peanut butter and a box of crackers.

"Sorry, I haven't been to the store. I'll have to go in the morning before the girls come over."

"You eat like a college kid," she said.

He shrugged, "I know my audience."

"How long are the girls with you?" she asked, scooping a cracker in the peanut butter.

"Their mom's going out of town for the week, so I'll have them until next Tuesday."

"Oh."

"I don't know how I'll go more than a week without kissing you."

She looked at him, then at the peanut butter.

"I was just thinking the same thing," she said.

He stuck his finger in the peanut butter jar, scooped out a bit, then brought it to her mouth. She put her mouth around his finger, held it there a moment as she looked at him, then wiped the peanut butter off with her tongue. He dipped the same finger back into the jar and had some himself. He'd forgotten how electric romance could be.

"Toby, I ... should've asked this sooner, but am I right in assuming you're divorced?"

Talk about shorting a romantic fuse. He still wasn't sure how to phrase his answer, "Yes."

She nodded.

He could leave it at that. But now he knew firsthand what lies could do to lives.

"Well, I should have the final papers in a month or so."

"Have the papers actually been signed?"

"Well, not yet. We've been at this for a while. It should be done soon. I hope." He exhaled sharply. Thinking about it still made him vaguely nauseous.

After a few moments he looked at July. She was looking at an anonymous patch of sofa. Inside, he fiddled with the tuners around his ears, straining to read her mind. He would have to keep explaining; women needed a little more about specifics. They liked feelings, too, but he wasn't ready to go there.

"I know it's complicated," he ventured. "But we *are* divorcing. We've been separated for two years, and things weren't right for a long time before that. I mean, until last week I didn't think I could even like women anymore."

Her eyes tilted up to his, and he thought he sensed uncertainty. *Please,* he thought, *don't jump to conclusions, don't turn to the arbitrary morals parents teach you that don't account for how complex real life is.*

"Toby. Does it bother you that I'm so young?"

"Honestly, when we're together I don't even notice. I just feel comfortable with you, like I could just take you to Florence this weekend and it wouldn't feel weird or awkward."

Her shoulders relaxed. The outer corners of her mouth and eyes involuntarily moved a millimeter in the start of a smile.

"Does it bother you that I'm an old man?"

She smiled fully, "No. You're not old. You're just … Toby."

Somewhere his body untied itself.

"Toby, how old *are* you?"

"Over forty."

"Well I guessed that."

Ouch. His face told no lies, "How old is your father?"

"Fifty-seven."

"I'm younger than he is."

"By how many years?" she pressed.

"No way. A lady never reveals her age," he said, shaking his head and pursing his lips.

She smiled, amused and coy. A blade of weakness stabbed through his throat down into his chest. Did she know what she did to him? She must. There's no way she could just do that, just reach deep inside him and seep into all those places he had forgotten a woman could burrow.

"Well you, sir, are some lady."

She arched an eyebrow and put a hand on her hip. And then they tumbled together over their lips and off the edge of the world, old and young and no age at all.

IV

JULY AND CHRIS HAD MET LAST DECEMBER AT A HOLIDAY-END-OF-finals party their friend Emmy threw. She had decorated her small room like a Hallmark store, lights and wreaths and vaguely demonic ceramic cherubs that she had taken from her parents' house. Bottles of liquor stored beneath a desk glimmered like stalagmites under the Christmas lights.

By the time July arrived at the party, people were clustered in corners, in doorways, on armchairs, and moving from couch to food table required a tectonic shift of the entire crowd. The room was steamy with breath and sticky with alcohol. July slid through red plastic cups and pretzels looking for a pocket of space. She found the pocket next to the back of a chair, where a group of four huddled in vodka laughs.

In one of the room shifts, Chris ended up next to July. He was two-beers friendly and entertaining to July's sobriety. He was a grad student in physics, dressed in faded, baggy jeans and a white T-shirt July would come to call The Uniform. He seemed nice enough, and she hadn't been on any dates that whole semester, so maybe she would like him more the better she got to know him. But she came to know his inability to assert himself, his fervent and boring interest in cars—not driving them, just looking at them and talking about them—and his unwavering reverence of July. When they broke up, July cried not because she was sad it was over, but because she was relieved to be free of him.

And she cried because, for the first time, it dawned on her that she may never care so deeply for someone again as she had cared for James, her high school boyfriend. They had been friends since elementary school, and by the time she was twelve she had decided she was in love with him, something she didn't tell him until the last day of their junior year of high school.

That day, something in her had decided that she had had enough, and as the last bell rang at three in the afternoon, she walked across the scalding concrete in the schoolyard and shouted his name. He stopped and turned around. An arm punched through her back and out her chest where her heart had been. When she caught up with James she stopped and looked at him in what she could only think now was an utterly ridiculous expression. Her head pecked forward and her lips grabbed his, his lips that stayed limp and shocked until she pulled away and said, "I love you." And then she walked away.

Everyone thought that story was romantic, but her memory of it was drenched in hasty awkwardness. Heartily encouraged by her friends, she had thought it was bold and romantic at the time, but upon endless mental replay, it felt desperate, over-wrought, and, well, just desperate. After she had walked away she didn't hear from him for three agonizing weeks, three weeks in which the only thing in her head was reruns of that kiss, that brief clip that seemed to grow dumber with each viewing, like a joke told a thousand times. When he finally called her and asked her out, she answered the phone in the kitchen pantry, shutting herself in with the cereal and spices, a shuddering wave ricocheting down her body in shivering relief when she realized she wasn't being rejected.

A year later, they decided to break up when they left for different schools and he nestled in the woods of upstate New York. They had completely lost touch; he was now just a whisper on Facebook, where sometimes she would see updates on his sparse profile. Occasionally, there were pictures with the girlfriend he met freshman year, of them sitting happily in a worn out dorm room with crumpled clothes on the floor and empty cans of soda lined along the windowsill. Whenever she saw these pictures, July's heart was dragged into her bowels and it took anywhere from hours to days to find it again.

Sometimes she still dreamt about James. In one dream they were driving down the highway at home. She was in the passenger seat and he drove, and though she could only see where his shoulder met his neck, she knew it was James. An overwhelming feeling of contentment and safety expanded in her chest. Sometimes he just walked in on her dreams unexpectedly, in places he didn't belong, and he would sit beside her, and they would hold hands, completing a puzzle with a missing piece.

Now it seemed that maybe she could care for someone else, as much if not more than she had cared for James. It scared her how after her first two dates with Toby, he was all she could think about. It scared her even more to find that she had been daydreaming about meeting his daughters and the fun things they could do together. When she made dinner in the common kitchen, she would sometimes pretend that she was cooking for his daughters, or making them lunches, or asking them about school. The girls would look up to her, admire her, respect her. In the dorm kitchen, it seemed easy.

She tried to pull her fantasies back to earth, but the appeal of a family that already existed seemed somehow ideal, as though she could just slip in, even though she knew it wasn't that simple. Especially since he was still married. Technically.

Isn't this wrong? But this doesn't seem wrong. This couldn't feel more right.

It would be more wrong if she stood up and walked away forever. It would be the dumbest, wrongest move of her entire life. She had had a week alone to think it over, since his daughters were staying with him for a whole week. He sent her text messages that were so sweet she almost couldn't believe they were meant for her.

Thinking of you ... miss kissing your lips.

The one she got at five in the morning, *Why exactly are you not with me under the covers in this big bed?*

Missing you early in the day.

She sat and stared at the screen for at least twenty minutes, and even though it was five thirty, there was no way she was going back to sleep after that.

One night a few weeks later in early October, as July was wasting time on her computer to avoid doing reading for her seminar, her phone rang. Her heart popped with excitement—Toby? In a quick spurt her arm grabbed the phone, but before her instincts answered the call, she caught a glimpse of the caller ID: Chris.

July froze. She was flashing with heat and sprinkled with chills. What did he want? She didn't want to talk to him. In the weeks after their breakup, he had called almost daily. He fluctuated between hurt, angry, morose, pleading, listlessness, and resolve. His calls were draining, and when July wouldn't pick up, Chris would leave long voicemails, send lengthy, prosaic, pathetic emails. This was the first time he had communicated with July in three days.

July leaned her forehead against the wall. She had already started the call, and she had to speak. There was no accounting for picking up a phone but not answering it. Inhale, exhale sharply, bite the bullet, and speak.

She paused a moment before she said anything, trying to summon patience and neutrality.

"Hi."

"Hi."

A long silence while she waited for him to give the reason for his call. None came.

"What's up?" she asked, not really wanting the answer.

"Who was that guy?"

"What guy?"

"Who is that guy you were with?"

July's jaw jutted out in frustration. He was bringing this on himself.

"You're going to have to give me a little more than that," she said. She could hear the steel in her voice.

"You were with a guy this afternoon in the ice cream shop. I was in town with Emmy, I saw you. He had his arm around you. He was old."

July's first instinct was to go on the indignant defensive—he's not old, what are you doing spying on me, what business is it of yours? But that would only make this conversation longer. He wanted her to get worked up.

"That's Toby."

"Are you dating him?"

"Yes."

Chris was silent.

"How *old* is he?" he finally asked.

July decided not to answer. Just to piss him off a little.

"July?"

"Yes?"

"How *old* is he?"

July remained silent, hoping he would give up.

"July!"

"What?"

"I asked you a question."

"And in case you haven't noticed, I'm not answering. Who do you think you are, my father?"

Stay calm, she thought. *Neutral and even like the horizon. Be the horizon.*

She heard the static, crackly cotton puff exhale on his end of the phone. He always held it too close to his face.

"Chris, what do you want? I'm busy."

"How long have you been seeing him?"

July wished he could hear her roll her eyes; it would bring her much more satisfaction. What are you, a tabloid? Stop tracking me like a PI, get a *life!* she was aching to say.

"Almost a month."

There was dark, stormy silence as he flipped through the mental calendar and aligned the time.

"How could you do this to me?"

This conversation, she decided, had gone on far too long.

"Chris, it's not about you. You aren't my probation officer, I don't have to answer to you. I have things to do. Goodbye."

She hung up the phone. She had never hung up on anyone before, except telemarketers. Inside she felt a pinch, wondering if she was being unfairly cold, but she had had enough.

Though July turned the phone to silent, she could still see the screen illuminate as he called back again and again.

Toby hadn't called July in almost a week. The last time July had seen him was when Chris had seen them getting ice cream. It was Friday night, and while she hadn't necessarily *planned* that she would see Toby, July had kind of counted on the fact that they would spend that night together, as they had for the past three Fridays. But he hadn't called. She called, but he didn't answer, so she texted *Call me.*

What was he doing? He had the kids again this week, she knew they kept him busy. But he could at least return the text messages she had sent him. Was he ignoring her? What had she done wrong? Had he changed his mind about her? After the second text, she had to forcibly stop herself from sending any more.

Don't be needy. You aren't needy. You have your own life.

But the problem was she kind of didn't. Not this weekend, anyway. Most people had midterms next week and were studying or saying that they couldn't go out since they were pretending to study. There was a big frat party, so many of the people studying and not were there, where alcohol clung to the air like a dank mold; where the house was packed so closely with people that you breathed sweat vapors directly off of the person next to you; where the bad techno was so loud the room went silent, except for the bass beat that rattled your ribs like a defibrillator.

So July was in her room, alone, on a Friday night, and at this rate it seemed that her Saturday would look much the same. What was he doing? Did three girls really keep him *that* busy?

He's avoiding me. He finally realized how young I am and decided he doesn't need another daughter. With another woman? No, that doesn't seem right. Unless ... Jenny. His ex-wife. He never talked about the divorce. Not that you asked him, July. What happened? Maybe he cheated on her. I don't want to be with a guy who cheated on his wife. Maybe she cheated on him. Maybe he still loves her.

You're going to drive yourself crazy. Too late.

She pushed the thoughts aside and decided to watch a movie to distract herself. Something not about love. A Western. Something with John Wayne.

She searched for *The Searchers* on her Netflix account.

I wonder if he wants to reconcile with her. Maybe they still love each other but they thought that divorce was the only option and didn't try to work it out. But they've been in the process for two years. They've had time.

Jenny. Jenny, who is Jenny? July saw one of Toby's divorce packets on the coffee table last week. He was writing an email in the other room, and she looked at the top piece of paper, a letter or something. She didn't read it; she didn't want Toby to catch her snooping. But she caught a glimpse of the words Jenny Sivertsen. July remembered this because she wasn't Jenny Alder. Jenny had kept her maiden name.

As the play screen came up for *The Searchers*, July instinctively pulled up Google and typed in "Jenny Sivertsen". There was a Jenny Sivertsen doctor, a lawyer, a ballerina, a writer. Which one was she?

The doctor, probably, thought July. So July Googled "Jenny Sivertsen Toby Alder" and clicked on an article that came up from almost ten years ago. She peered at the small print below the photograph.

> Above: Jenny Sivertsen, trained at the American School of Ballet in New York City and former dancer for the San Francisco Ballet and Boston Ballet, and her husband, Toby Alder, made a dona- tion of $100,000 to support the night's cause.

Oh shit.

Above that caption was a picture of Toby, jarringly young, wearing a tuxedo, standing next to a smiling, pretty, button-nosed blonde, looking refined and regal, as all ballet dancers seem to do naturally. She was nestled in Toby's side, the two of them leaning in together in a glow of happiness.

Shit.

July looked at the date—ten years ago, almost to the month. Right around the time Chloe must have been born. If Jenny was pregnant, or if she had just given birth, she sure didn't look it, even though the photo cut off mid-chest.

He married a ballerina. Oh shit.

What is he doing with someone like me when he had that for more than fifteen years? July had never felt so—soft and plain. This woman was accomplished, noted, philanthropic, cute, rich—and here was July, a *kid* who didn't even know what the hell she was supposed to do with her life, wouldn't know how to start even if she did, and most decidedly would not belong in a leotard.

Shit.

Toby's brain had been put through a trash compactor. Sports games, forgotten shirts or drinks or snacks or shoes or a sock, sunscreen and play dates, lunches for them and all their friends, he had spent almost the entire day imprisoned behind the wheel of his car, shuttling back and forth and all around to the point where he couldn't feel his butt anymore.

Only a few more years until Chloe can drive, was the first coherent thought he had had in the ten minutes he had been lying on the couch.

Saturday night, nine o'clock. Time was, this had been his "bewitching hour," when he would take down a phone number, invite her back to his place, or try to get Jenny in the mood. Now he lay strewn along the couch, empty glass of scotch balancing delicately on his chest, rising and falling with his breath. Tomorrow he was supposed to help the girls pick out Halloween costumes.

Halloween—the calendar's sugar-induced "fuck you" to parents everywhere.

He hadn't talked to July all week. There was no time, and every free moment he had, he wanted to dedicate to anti-being. Sitting, staring, allowing the cotton balls to fill his head until he had to switch back from Toby to Dad again.

What are people like before they're parents? When being is confined only to within your own body, when life is still about what you want, when a meaningful life had a totally different meaning. It was still strange to him that he could be so attracted to a girl, a woman, who should seem like a girl. She hadn't been wrung of her selfishness yet; her life hadn't given way to responsibility. When he was with her, his body remembered what it felt like to be that way; plastic surgery for his soul.

Jenny must have been like that. Sometimes he couldn't remember what she was like back then; he could only conjure the present Jenny, the Jenny with a face lined in bitterness that made the few wrinkles she had seem more profound. He could hardly imagine her without the furrow in her brow that seemed frozen on her face whenever he saw her. But maybe it was there because he too wore a frown.

He thought back to the first time he saw her. She had been eating alone at an Italian bistro on a Saturday night, sitting at a table facing the door. She was the first thing he saw, her observing gaze meeting his blankly as he walked in. Her eyes quickly drifted away from him, barely registering his presence. In the ten seconds before the maitre d' came and seated him, Toby had already memorized the curve at the ends of her straight blonde hair, the slope of her nose, and the black eyeliner painted on to try to mask insecurity and highlight sexuality. Already he pictured what she would look like in bed next to him as the sun rose. He could look at her forever, but it would be even better if she looked back.

Toby was with his older brother Andrew and his new wife Claire. When the maitre d' sat them, Toby vied for the chair facing the beautiful woman drinking a soda all alone on a Saturday night. It briefly occurred to him that she was trying to get picked up, but this was the nineties, so that might not be the case anymore. Plus, when he looked around, he saw that the average patron was sixty and female. She probably wasn't on the prowl for a sugar momma.

If he had been a few years younger, he would have stared the whole night until she walked out of the restaurant and seeped back into the world. But he was twenty-six, in his *late* twenties now, when age starts to tap you on the shoulder, but you look around and no one's there. He was maturing, nearing that time in life when he was supposed to get serious. By then, he had been picking up almost ten years of occasional women and the success of the past year or so had considerably boosted his swagger. So after the waiter had taken their orders, he said, "Could you please send that blonde woman over there a glass of whatever wine complements her entrée?"

The waiter glanced over his shoulder, then back to Toby. His eyebrows raised a millimeter.

"Of course, sir," and he walked away.

Andrew and Claire cocked their heads and raised their eyebrows in near unison.

"Not wasting any time, are we?" remarked Andrew. He swiveled his head to look at the blonde.

"That's your type?" said Claire, turning back from looking at the blonde.

Toby shrugged.

"You can't argue with beauty."

"Shallow, yet somehow charming. How come you never sent me a drink, Andrew?" Claire gave him a good-natured jab in the ribs.

Toby didn't process Andrew's reply; he was too focused on the waiter, who was walking towards the blonde with a glass of white wine in his hand. Toby felt like he was in the audience at a movie theater, on the edge of his seat and wondering what came next. Toby distinctly recalled thinking, *I wonder if this is going to be something.*

The waiter stopped at the blonde's table and set down the wine glass to the side of her fork. His body turned and his arm swept to the side towards Toby. The blonde turned her head and looked straight into Toby's eyes, casting a shimmer all through his shoulders. She turned back to the waiter and said something, probably thank you, and looked down at her plate as the waiter walked away.

"Well?" asked Andrew. He turned in his chair, resting his arms on the back.

She was still looking at her empty plate. Toby was still looking at her, his body and mind suspended as though he were a biology specimen floating in a tube. Time slogged forward as though it weighed a million tons. Suddenly, he felt like he was in high school again, standing at the front of the class with an erection, vulnerable for the whole world to gawk at a private moment.

The blonde was looking at the drink, as though contemplating what she should do. Then she looked up, her hair sliding around in front of her shoulder, and she smiled and lowered her head in acknowledgement. She held Toby's gaze for a moment, then broke it as she took a sip of the wine. Her eyes darted back into his, then back down at her plate. She seemed embarrassed, unsure. Toby guessed that no one had ever sent her a drink before.

Andrew turned around.

"Well, now what?"

Toby shrugged.

"I don't know. I can't tell if she's shy or really creeped out."

"Yeah, for all she knows we're in a threesome," said Claire, and Toby groaned in disgust, not at the thought of Claire, but of Andrew.

He looked back to the blonde and found that her seat was empty. His heart sank; he had scared her off.

"Hi," said a voice, and Toby looked up to see the blonde standing next to his table like a goddess descending.

"I'm sorry to disturb you, but I just wanted to say thank you for the drink."

She stood silent for a minute, unsure if she should say more.

"I'm Toby," he said, standing. She was shorter than he had anticipated, delicate and lithe, like her feet bore no weight.

"I'm Jenny," she said, extending her right hand. He took it, her warm hand lost in his palm.

Andrew and Claire watched behind them, grinning with amusement.

"Would you like to join us?" asked Toby.

"Oh, well, I—wouldn't want to intrude," she replied, sticking her hands awkwardly in her pockets.

"Oh no, please join us," said Claire. "You're not intruding."

"Yes, please," echoed Andrew.

Jenny looked from Claire to Andrew back to Toby.

"Well, I, uh—okay." She smiled, then walked back to her table to gather her purse, jacket, and glass of wine. When she returned and sat next to him, Toby felt that suddenly, he was full where he hadn't known he'd been empty.

The conversation couldn't have been better if it had been scripted, but he couldn't remember what they talked about now. All he remembered was the way Jenny threw her head back when she laughed, exposing her neck, and how when she was listening intently, her pointer finger drew invisible circles on the tablecloth. And how, after they had exchanged numbers outside the restaurant, he found it nearly impossible to wait until the next day to call her. That night he thought he finally understood things and he didn't get any sleep, he thought only of the blonde girl eating alone.

But something had changed in those years between wine and divorce court. She had changed. Sometimes the real Jenny, the one he had married, would haunt him, appear in his dreams and fool him into thinking that ten years ago was now, and his body would settle into that feeling he had had, that sensation he thought his body had forgotten how to feel, that his body suddenly remembered around July.

What would the girls think of July? Truthfully, they'd probably love her, he admitted to himself. Probably. They'd love her for sure if she were their babysitter, but as a … something more? As Daddy's "friend?" It could really fuck them up, a sort of pseudo step-mom half their father's age, barely old enough to have given birth to his youngest, let alone the oldest. They couldn't meet her until after the divorce anyway, not until after things were settled. He didn't need the torrent of ferocity that would surely result when Jenny found out he was seeing someone almost half his age.

I wonder if Jenny has someone, he thought for the millionth time. *I wonder if she's had anyone. Probably. I have, she probably has. What sort of guys does she go for now? Probably a beefcake pretty-boy.* Someone unlike the fit-but-soft Toby who, with graying hair and crow's feet, definitely looked his age. He tried to picture her in bed with someone, which proved almost as impossible and unpleasant as trying to picture his parents in bed together.

Toby always tried to shove away that thought, to not imagine a beefcake pretty-boy moving in, replacing Toby, stepping into his life. He tried not to think of a beefcake pretty-boy playing with his daughters, kissing his almost-ex-wife, eating at his dinner table. He tried not to let his mind run wild with imagining Jenny having an affair for years behind Toby's back. He would almost worry that Grace wasn't his if she wasn't so much like him.

"Daddy?"

Toby opened his eyes, drained his brain of cotton balls.

"What is it, Gracie?"

"Daddy, I can't sleep."

"You want to come sleep in Daddy's bed?"

She nodded.

Crap, he thought. *How am I supposed to get up?* Though his body felt filled with sand, Toby somehow managed to sit up, knocking the glass to the floor.

"Okay, Gracie, up we go."

He stood and picked her up. She would soon be too heavy for him, but now she flopped her head over his shoulder, her blonde curls tickling where his earlobe met his jaw line. He thought for a moment of July.

He carried Grace up the stairs, into his room, and they both flopped onto the bed.

"All right, Gracie, let's get you all tucked in."

They adjusted, tugged, rolled, shifted until Toby was on his back and Grace clung to his side.

He and Grace had always had a special connection, like she had come out of Jenny knowing everything about him. He might as well have been the one to carry her inside him for nine months. But she was a nearly identical physical copy of Jenny; sometimes it was hard for him to look at her, see her looking through Jenny's eyes, the eyes of the woman he had fallen in love with and now despised. *It's not her,* he had to remind himself. *Gracie will be different.*

Gracie's breathing had turned to the rhythmic, nasally sound of sleep. She would hold on to him through the entire night. If he rolled away, she would catch him. Sometimes he awoke on the edge of the bed, Gracie clinging to his arm, and he would have to get up and move back to the other side of the bed. Grace would always find him again.

As long as she always needs me, he thought.

V

HE SAW JULY SITTING IN STARBUCKS ON MONDAY MORNING, AFTER HE had taken the girls to school. He still hadn't called her in, what was it, over a week now? He thought she'd be in class now; he toyed with the idea of turning around without opening the door, but thought better of it.

"Hi," he said, sitting at the table where she sat reading.

She looked up, neutral, guarded.

"Hi."

"I'm sorry I didn't call. Things got really busy with the girls."

"Hm."

"All these sports games and sleepovers and homework and Halloween costumes."

"Wow, sounds busy."

July did not sound convinced. She sighed, and he could practically hear her guard crash to the ground.

"Look," she said. "I know it's busy, and I know I don't understand since I don't have kids, but do you think you could at least text me or something so that I at least know you're not just dropping me without telling me? Or are you dropping me without telling me?"

Wow, he thought. *I don't think a woman has been that honest with me in a long time.* If seventeen years with Jenny had taught him anything, it was to tell a woman she was right.

"You're right, I should have called," he conceded.

35

"Thank you," said July. "So … are you dropping me and telling me now?"

"No, I'm not dropping you."

"Really?" she said, her look clearly skeptical.

"Really."

"Toby," July leaned in. "Are you over Jenny?"

He wanted to shout out, Yes! Oh God, yes! You couldn't *pay* me to stop the divorce! I wish I never had to *see* her again! But that might send the wrong message. So instead he said, "Yes, I am. It's just … the marriage that I'm not over, I guess. It's like, what if, all of a sudden, you found out that your parents didn't want to be your parents anymore, and they just left you? Even if you hated your parents, and you didn't miss them at all, it would still take you a long time to adjust to not having them around. It's kind of like that."

"Oh."

They sat in silence a few moments, the steam rising from their paper cups.

"Toby, what happened with Jenny?"

He looked at her.

"I'll tell you someday."

July nodded, then looked into her steaming cup. "What are the girls going to be for Halloween?"

"Chloe wants to be a fairy princess, Sophia wants to be Dracula, and Gracie wants to be a ballerina."

"A ballerina?" said July.

"Yeah. Jenny's a dancer, so at least that'll be an easy costume."

"Oh. She's a … ballerina?"

"Yeah. Well, was. Now she teaches."

"Oh." July looked slightly uncomfortable. She took a sip of her coffee and made an effort to change the subject. "I was a fairy princess once, for Halloween. Are you going to do Jack o'Lanterns?"

"I don't know. They'll be with Jenny for Halloween."

"I love Jack o'Lanterns. Mostly for the pumpkin seeds that come afterward."

"Look, the girls are with their mother this week. When are you free?"

July shrugged, "No classes today."

Toby smiled, "I'm going to take you somewhere fun. Let's go."

They stood up, and as she moved past him for the door, he slipped his arm around her waist and walked with her, their sides so close that he was sure if they were silhouettes, they would look like one very wide double-headed person.

He took her to a pumpkin stand.

"Omigod, pumpkins!" she gasped in delight. "I haven't carved a pumpkin in years. Once I got past the age of ten, my parents wouldn't let me trick or treat anymore, and they wouldn't do any more pumpkins, either. They'd just buy bags of candy and dump them into a bowl, and then my dad would eat most of it sitting in front of the TV."

"Wow. Don't your parents have fun?"

"No. The only interesting things they've done are to name their children Iago, Ansel, and July."

"Iago?"

"Yeah. The movie *Aladdin* didn't help him much with the kids on the playground."

"They were a bit young for *Othello*, I suppose," he said.

They walked together over to the bales of hay shedding beneath the glowing pumpkins.

"Wait," she stopped.

Toby stopped and turned to her.

"Aren't you going to do this with your girls?"

"They're with their mom this week, so they'll do it at our house. I mean, her house."

"Is she still in your old house?"

"Let's get a pumpkin," said Toby, picking up the one beside him. It happened to weigh more than he thought it would.

"Wow. That doesn't seem …" said July. She trailed off and turned her attention to the pumpkins, fingering them, running her fingers down the orange longitudes and over the white rough patches.

She's on my side, he realized. It seemed most of the friends he and Jenny shared had sided with her, mostly because the wives sided with her and pulled their husbands along with them. One of Jenny's girlfriends, Deborah, herself a divorcee, had verbally berated him when he ran into her at a drugstore, calling him a lousy, good-for-nothing, typical male pig. And, like most of the others who awkwardly averted their gazes when he saw them at the girls' school, she only knew the story that Jenny told them.

Deborah had yelled at him in the paper plate aisle, among red Dixie cups and plastic sporks. With every word she screamed, the store seemed to grow bigger, or he seemed to shrink. The lights grew somehow more fluorescent, buzzing with her voice, and everyone stopped to stare.

"I hope you rot in hell!" snarled Deborah, curling her lip aggressively. She had probably burned a bra or two in her day. "Jenny is such a wonderful person. She doesn't deserve to be treated the way you're treating her."

For a moment there was just the droning buzz of the fluorescents.

Then she looked down at Sophia, just seven then, who had been standing there the whole time. Deborah smiled sweetly, her face changing to the "Mom Mask," and patted her cheek.

"Don't worry honey," she cooed. "It'll all be just fine."

He wanted to hit this woman. He had never hit a woman in his life, but he wanted to right then. He couldn't just let it go, just let her walk away, because now she had involved Sophia.

Deborah stood up and adjusted her purse. She was about to turn away, when Toby covered Sophia's ears and said in a cold, calm stage whisper, "How dare you speak to me that way in front of my daughter you self-righteous shrew. No one was surprised that being married to you turned Tim gay, they're just surprised it took him ten years. Don't go blaming your misery on me."

It took all his will power and a strong bite on the tongue to stop himself from tacking on, "You fucking bitch."

But he said it in his head. Many, many times.

He looked around and saw that the woman in the aisle over, the pharmacist, the cashier, all women—were staring. All the women in town seemed to have agreed to convene right then right there and turn, give reproving, hateful stares in front of his daughter.

"Those men," their faces said, "They just live to fuck us and then fuck us over."

VI

THE TUESDAY BEFORE THANKSGIVING, THEY HAD DINNER AT A SMALL Italian restaurant so dim that the risotto and soup were nearly indistinguishable, a perfect situation for more food puns. Though Toby had long been kissing her in public, July felt a little more affirmed, as though that restaurant was there for the sole purpose of legitimate romance. There had been a moment when July looked at her plate, put food on her fork, and caught Toby looking at her as she put her food into her mouth. His eyes were crinkled and smitten: just like when he talked about his daughters. The look was there only long enough for her to register it; he must have registered it too, for when she caught him looking, he grinned and looked away.

When they arrived back at his house, Toby put on some jazz music and the rest of the night evaporated. July hadn't even realized it had passed until she woke up in Toby's bed as early blocks of sunlight moved in through the windows. Toby's windows didn't have any curtains, and July wasn't very good at sleeping in new places, so she woke up at some unnatural and sadistic hour of the morning, which her internal clock judged to be somewhere between six and half-past. It had been years since she had awoken so prematurely, and when she had it had never been voluntarily. She also wasn't used to sleeping naked. She felt so—frictionless.

She looked at Toby, his back to her like a shadowed mountain. His king sized bed seemed expansive, like what she imagined the Midwest to be, like she could roll and roll and never reach the end.

Her stomach twisted and gurgled. How it could be empty after a meal like last night's was suspicious, but there it was, her hunger. She wanted to go downstairs to see what she could find in his kitchen, but she didn't know the boundaries, or just how familiar she was allowed to be.

So she watched the shapes in the popcorn ceiling change with the light. A lion's head changed into a teddy bear and then an ice cream sundae, and then a bowler hat. She didn't feel Toby wake up and only realized it when he reached his arm around her and pulled her close. They lay like that until the light had lost its gray.

"C'mon," said Toby, his voice cracking the shell of silence. "I'm going to make you breakfast."

As Toby measured the flour for pancakes, July sat at the counter, wrapped in a terrycloth robe he had stolen from a resort in La Jolla, her long fingers grasped tightly around a mug of tea.

"You're not going home for Thanksgiving?" he asked, sifting.

"No. Too far, too expensive. There aren't any direct flights to Tucson. I usually just stay here and cook something. I think this year I'm going to tackle gnocchi."

He separated the yolks from the whites, pouring the yolk back and forth, back and forth between eggshell halves.

"Will you have the girls here?"

"Well," he started, picking up a whisk, an outlet for his frustrations. "Not exactly…" whip clink tick. "Jenny and I agreed to spend it together. As a so-called family."

"That will be good for the girls," said July.

"Well, that's the theory." Whisking harder.

"How will that be for you?"

"Like rubbing sandpaper between my teeth."

July nodded, and Toby was grateful that she didn't push the subject.

"I'm supposed to bring a pie tomorrow," he said, trying to ease the resentment from the sandpaper remark.

"Ooh! What kind?" July perked up.

"I don't know. I guess it'll be whatever kind I find at the store. Any recommendations?" He counted strokes as he stirred the batter—one, two, three …

"You're not going to make one yourself?"

"I can make pancakes, but I can't make a pie."

"I can make a pie!" she said enthusiastically. "It's a piece of cake."

He laughed as he heated up the skillet. This would be a good batch.

"Toby?" She asked tentatively.

"Yeah."

"Can I make your pie?"

"That sounded dirty," he grinned.

She smiled weakly.

For a moment, he felt nothing, but then wondered why she would want to make a pie for his family, for his *ex-wife*, a pie that she wouldn't even get to eat. He felt a bit sorry for her.

"Why?" he asked.

He looked at her, hands clinging to the cooling mug, eyes cast into the well of tea.

"I don't know, never mind," she said quickly.

"No, July ... come on."

She looked up at him and shrugged sheepishly, the robe loosening and falling open across the top of her chest like satin sliding from a marble sculpture.

"I like making pie, and there's no point in making pie for one."

For a moment there was only the sizzle of batter in a pan.

She seized upon the awkwardness and said with false grandeur, "Let me impress you with my baking prowess."

There was probably more truth in that than she tried to let on, he figured. But then, how long had it been since a woman tried to impress him? He tried to think if there was leverage she was trying to gain through pie.

"Just let me do something for you and your family," she said.

He turned to face her, put his thumb on the grape vine, where her earlobe met her jaw. *Leverage? Come on Toby, she's not that devious.*

"Every time I look at Jenny, I'm going to have to think of you to remember that I don't hate all women."

Her laugh sounded almost like a sob.

"Thanks, I'm flattered. I think."

He kissed her, then turned back to the pancakes. It was both sweet and a little pathetic to have July baking for his family, from whom she was still a secret, have her leaving coded, abstract clues. On the other hand, it's just a pie and she likes to bake. It would allow her, in some way, to celebrate the holiday with *someone*. Plus, he could just imagine the smugness he would feel as he watched Jenny eat a pie baked by July. It would be like secretly feeding meat to a vegetarian.

The first pancakes were done. He slid them onto a plate and put them in front of July. She smiled.

"These look amazing."

"Eat up," he said proudly as he spooned more batter into the skillet. A moment later, he looked back at her; she hadn't touched the pancakes, she was just looking at them.

"Don't wait for me, they'll get cold."

She smiled wistfully, "No one's ever cooked me breakfast before."

"Not even your parents?"

"Well, I mean, they have. I mean," she stammered. "I learned how to cook from my dad—he's a fanatic. Sometimes he made really elaborate breakfasts, like brioche or quiche or—"

"Ooh, quiche," said Toby. 'That's for very serious occasions."

She laughed, "But, I mean, he's my dad—he's kind of socially obligated to feed me. But he didn't really make those breakfasts *for* me, they were for him. We were just there to … appreciate them, I guess, to bear witness to his culinary skills. Like an art gallery for food."

She poured syrup over the pancakes, then cut a large, dripping piece and put it in her mouth. She groaned and closed her eyes. "Ohh," she uttered. "I'm going to think of you every time I eat pancakes, because you, sir, have set the standard."

Pancakes worked every time.

She sighed contentedly, "My father would hate you if he knew your pancakes were this good."

"He probably has forty-three other reasons to hate me," he said glibly.

July said nothing.

Maybe he shouldn't have said that.

"Toby?"

"Yeah?"

She hesitated.

"What is it?"

She sighed, "Are you my boyfriend?" she exhaled it out quickly, like she had been holding it in for a while.

So it was time for this conversation. He thought a moment, watching bubbles bloom in the batter. He flipped them, enjoying the sizzle.

"I suppose I am," he said. How strange. He hadn't been a boyfriend in nearly twenty years.

She smiled and ate another bite.

For a moment, he felt innocent again, remembering what having hope felt like. He hadn't felt possibility in a long time. He leaned on the counter across from July, his own plate of pancakes in front of him. Looking at her through the veil of steam, hazy like a dream, he reached across the counter and put a hand on hers.

"After we're done, let's go to the store for pie stuff."

Surprise glowed on her face, and then she smiled, leaned over, and kissed him. The steam from his pancakes dampened the bottom of his chin, and her lips were coated with a slick of syrup.

These were his best pancakes to date, if he did say so himself.

Toby took great care loading the pie into the car the next day. He debated between putting it on the seat or floor, finally choosing the passenger seat so that he could strategically buckle the seatbelt and reach for it should it slide around.

He was glad he let July make the pie. Not only did it save him a surely crowded Thanksgiving Day trip to the store alone, but she had also been so happy as she rolled out the crust, cored the apples, and carefully poked decorative holes in the top crust. She had seemed almost disappointed to put it into the oven. The smell of cinnamon and flour had clung merrily to the house long after July had gone home. He could smell it, even through the tin foil, right then, flooding his mouth with gushes of saliva. For once, he was glad that he had agreed to live so close to Jenny, for the girls, as the pie's aroma could torture him only briefly.

If we ever get married, we're having a wedding pie. As soon as he finished the thought, a chill froze his body. In the two years since his separation from Jenny, he had never had a serious thought about remarriage. Ever. He felt like an amnesiac recovering part of his memory, finding that warmth and ease that come as things finally start to click into place.

Shit. What am I getting myself into?

He stood outside the door of what used to be his home. In an attempt at civility, and in the interest of speeding things along, he had finally agreed to let Jenny have it, so that the girls would still have some semblance of a normal life or, at least the vivid memory of one. But now his throat was consumed with the tension of bitterness, the resentment of having to forfeit his house. He rang the doorbell, realizing how rarely he had used the front door when he lived here. It was a great front door, dark and thick, solid wood, a sleek copper lock, a real selling point. The whole house had been a source of pride for him, giving his wife and daughters such a wonderful home. It really fed his ego when clients said, "Find me a home like yours."

If he could ever have a chance to live here again, he would use the front door every day.

This was the first holiday as a full family since the separation—today had been the girls' doing. There had been begging, "Pleeease Daddy, pleeease Mommy," and pouty faces and tears until he and Jenny finally caved. The only thing they both had in common now was their desire to be around each other as little as possible.

He had expected one of the girls to come bounding to the door, but instead, it was Jenny who answered. Her blonde hair was tied back in a bun, a look he had never particularly liked. Once, years ago, when they were getting ready to go out someplace upscale, she had tied her hair up. "You should wear your hair down," he had said. "I love it when your hair is down."

She wore her hair up every day for the next two months.

"Hi, Toby." Her lips flattened tightly, her attempt at a smile. How was it that she could make him feel like a child?

"Hello, Jenny."

"You remembered the pie."

He was not going to dignify that with an answer. Instead he gave a cold, twisted half-smile. She stared at him, her eyes disinterested marbles.

"Are we having dinner on the front porch?" he asked.

Her jaw jutted out almost imperceptibly, and then she reluctantly moved to the side to let him in. He had come into the house as infrequently as possible since he had moved out, or rather, been forced to move out. After every visit, it was as though his insides had been churned through a meat grinder. Usually, he promptly went back to his place and sat on the couch in the dark.

Now standing in what had been his living room, he felt himself curl away inside. The house looked a little different—new paint, a few new pillows and photographs, but it looked enough the same that spiders of bittersweet nostalgia skittered all over his skin.

"You can set the pie in the kitchen," said Jenny, crossing her arms like she was chilled.

Perhaps the familiarity is strange for her, too, he thought as he walked into the kitchen. He set the pie on the counter, and remembered that early morning before Grace had been born, when he and Jenny hovered by the coffee maker, waiting for two cups worth to brew so they could boot up before waking and dressing the girls. She had looked so real and beautiful in the soft gray morning light, each second like the still frame of a photograph. In the rushed moments before their life as a family was to begin, he untied the drawstring to her pants, then his, and pushed her against the counter, the cold marble on his hands as the coffee dripped and gurgled.

They had all run ten minutes late that day.

Throughout most of dinner, he and Jenny mutually ignored each other. In fact, he hardly looked at her, as if his brain put a movable black patch over wherever Jenny was. He tried hard not to see much of anything, to put a curtain around the rest of the house, a tunnel vision to his daughters.

One thing he didn't miss was Jenny's version of cooking—turkey (store-bought and pre-prepared), mashed potatoes (boxed), cranberry sauce (canned), steamed vegetables (frozen), and dinner rolls (from a tube). He had a clear view of the pie from his seat. He kept glancing at it throughout the meal, grateful that he would eat something that made the holiday seem like it mattered.

It was probably the best pie he had ever eaten. The crust seemed to melt around the apples, which weren't gloppy or gratingly sweet like the ones they usually bought at the store. Crunchy crumbs of crystallized ginger hid in the filling underneath the cinnamon and he tasted, he thought, *was it? In a pie? No ... it is bourbon.* He hadn't seen her put that in.

The girls were eating with a little more enthusiasm than they had during the turkey. Toby removed the conjured eye patch and looked at Jenny, scooping a forkful of July's pie into her mouth, worlds secretly colliding. He was dying to tell her the origin of the pie, but the adult part of him knew better; he didn't need to give her any more leverage to twist against him. So he would hold the warm, smug knowledge inside him, savor it like the pie.

"Can I have seconds?" asked Chloe.

"Sure," said Toby, just as Jenny said, "No, sweetie."

They looked at each other, and Toby moved to cut her another slice. Jenny's jaw jutted forward again.

"This pie is so good!" said Chloe.

"Yeah, Dad, where'd you get it?" asked Sophia.

"Yes, where did you get it?" asked Jenny.

"The store."

"The store sold it in a glass pie dish?" said Jenny, pointing to the pan. *Uh oh. Think fast.*

"Did you make this?" she continued.

"You can cook pie?" asked Grace happily.

"No, Gracie," he said. He then turned to Jenny, "Actually, it's a gift from one of my clients. I made a sale for her, she baked me a pie and brought it over yesterday."

It wasn't the best of lies he had told her. She squinted with mild suspicion.

"She *gave* you a pie dish too?"

"She didn't *give* it to me, I'll give it back. When am I ever going to bake a pie?" he said, as he slid another piece onto his plate. Lie. Obviously. He'd bought it expressly for July to use tonight.

Jenny rolled her eyes. Toby stuck a piece of pie in his mouth, one that was too big so that he wouldn't be able to say anything until the moment of tension had passed. Instead he thought of July and the part of her soul in the pie. *If she were a food, this is how she would taste.*

After dinner, he helped Grace get ready for bed, said goodnight to all of them, and went down to the kitchen to wrap up the leftover pie and get the hell out. Jenny was in the kitchen, putting plates in the dishwasher. It should have felt normal.

Where had his wife gone? For the first time since he moved out all those memories ago, he watched from outside. How was that the same body he had married fifteen years ago? How could the skin-eyes–lips–neck-hips-elbows he had fallen madly in love with then be the same ones he looked at now? In front of him now was the after picture—in his mind was the before picture. The in between had gone so wrong. At this point he didn't want the before back—not now that he knew what came after. He remembered reading that it takes something like seven years for your body to replace every cell. So Jenny was a different person twice over, and so was he.

She shut the dishwasher, and he spurted back into movement to hide his staring. He took a sheaf of tin foil from a drawer and put it over the leftover third of pie. He grabbed his jacket from the kitchen chair and shrugged it on. He didn't even want to talk to her, just wanted out and away to sort it through himself.

He picked the pie up off of the counter.

"Toby," Jenny said.

He looked up at her, raised his eyebrows in expectation.

"Don't forget court on Tuesday."

"It's not *court*."

She rolled her eyes, "You know what I mean."

Toby adjusted his collar and reached into his jacket pocket to check for his car keys.

"Thank your client for the pie," she said, though from the way she said "client," he knew his lie had been unconvincing.

"Will do," he said. Then he turned around and walked through the living room, past the couch where once he had fallen asleep watching

TV, one of the girls lying on his back, also asleep, open-mouthed and drooling on his shirt.

He headed for the door like he was under water swimming to the surface. Closer but farther. In slow motion grabbing the doorknob, twisting, pulling, tumbling. He shut the door behind him and was met with a sharp burst of cold air. He expelled a sigh, heaving a thick white cloud into the black air. He watched as it danced away, fading and scattering, something that had been living inside him, a part of his soul drawn to the sky.

When he got home that night, he sat on the couch, in the dark, with half a gallon of milk and finished the rest of the pie. He didn't want to see, just taste and stay inside himself. He fell asleep on the couch, the milk souring with the steady sunrise.

July spent the afternoon in her dorm's public kitchen, rolling gnocchi and wondering who decided that dating a married man is generally wrong. She and Toby were different. No one stood to get hurt, there was no fault, his marriage was done anyway. Toby was happy now, and Jenny probably was too if she wanted to divorce him. This was a good thing all around.

But still, the fact that her older boyfriend was married was not something she told, well, anyone, and it didn't seem right to feel the need to be so secretive. Toby hadn't told her anything about his divorce or marriage. It was clear he was unhappy to be divorcing. Though he said little, she noticed how his eyes faded in distant stares after a day with the lawyer, and how every wrinkle seemed to deepen like a river eroding a canyon when he talked to Jenny on the phone. July had little to offer in the way of empathy, and her attempts at sympathy seemed weak and infantile. Those were the times she felt the age difference most viscerally.

July's parents had been married for twenty-seven years, and it didn't seem like a divorce was or would ever be an option. Actually, no one in her family was divorced. The only contact she had had with divorce was one of her friends, and his parents had divorced when he was very young. Toby's pain, his situation, was something she could only understand second hand, in the abstract, like he had sent her a picture of the exotic "Land of Divorce," and her perspective of divorce was influenced only by its photograph in the encyclopedia.

I wonder how he's doing, thought July to herself, to the gnocchi she had worked on all afternoon. His dinner was probably almost over by now; it was late. It was dark outside, but July had neglected to turn on a light. There was no one to see here. In Tucson it was two hours ago, but they ate dinner in the afternoon. They would be calling soon.

Thanksgiving with the family, though one of July's favorite holidays in principle (the food part), ran as smoothly as a traffic jam. Every year her mother's sister, her husband and their three kids would come over for dinner, as would her father's parents and whatever girlfriends her brothers were seeing that year. Inevitably, her mother would hate one or both of the girls who came home with Iago or Ansel and spend the evening in passive-aggressive prodding. July's cousins, all younger, would spend as much time as possible hiding with the TV. July's father, the master of the kitchen, would begin preparations a week in advance, drafting timetables of cooking and events in five-minute increments. Nothing from a can, box, mix, or bottle, nothing made in a microwave, mixer, or bread machine. The only concession was vanilla ice cream in the ice cream maker. Pumpkins baked and disemboweled for pumpkin pie, yeast starters years old for the bread. No one else allowed in the kitchen, no one else allowed to help except July, and if you were hungry at noon that was too damn bad. Every year, around midday, there were organized secret trips to the coffee shop for a muffin or bagel disguised as a run out for something unnecessary.

Her phone rang. It was home. She sat at the kitchen table and answered.

"Hello?"

"Hi, honey," said her mom.

"Hi, July," said her dad.

"Hi."

"Happy Thanksgiving, dear," said her mom.

"Thanks. You too, Mom. How was dinner?"

"Oh, delicious as usual. You know your father."

"The turkey was dry, the potatoes were gummy, and the bread didn't rise enough."

"Grayson …" her mom hated criticism of a perfect meal.

"Well they were, Jill. But the cranberry sauce was perfect this year."

"How was your day, dear?"

"Oh, you know. It's just me and my gnocchi."

"Store bought?" asked her dad, as though asking if she were on drugs.

"No, handmade. That's what I did today."

"Are they pillowy or dense? What did you sauce them with?"

"Gray!" snapped her mom. "Honey, why are you alone? Where's Chris?"

"Mom, we broke up like two and a half months ago."

"July!" Her mother let out an exasperated sigh. "July, your eggs don't last forever, you know, and once you pass thirty your body just won't bounce back the same way. Chris was perfect timing."

"Mom, Chris was boring."

"He was *lovely*."

"He's a vegetarian, Jill, how can he be *lovely*?"

"Gray, that has nothing to do with—"

"Would you want to doom your daughter to a life without pork belly? What kind of a mother are you?"

"Mom, I don't love him."

"But he has such a bright future," pressed her mom. "Physics applies to everything. He has plans—you need plans."

"Mom, he's just not interesting. And I have plans."

Her mother sighed heavily, "Oh July, I just want you to be happy."

"I *am* happy."

She perked up, "Oh! Are you seeing someone new?"

July didn't answer. Not sure she should mention Toby, she probably wouldn't react too well to the news that her daughter was dating someone in Mom's age range. *Don't take the bait.* She hesitated too long.

"You are! What's his name? What's he like?"

"Does he eat meat?"

"Yes, he eats meat!" *Oh no*, she winced.

"There *is* someone! Oh July—" cried her mother.

"You heartbreaker you," said Dad, perhaps a bit too proudly.

"Oh, what's he like?"

"He's ... very ... nice."

"Nice? Just nice?"

"Yes. Just nice. And omnivorous."

"Well ... what does he do? What will you two do when graduation comes?"

Graduation ... what *would* they do when July graduated? July didn't have a plan. That had been a lie.

"Mom, that's a bit premature."

"Lay off, Jill, she's not a spinster."

"Not *yet* she's not. I just want to know if she'll stay with him after graduation or if she'll come live back here and get a job."

"It's not either/or, Mom."

"Be realistic, July. You're not being sensible. Where else could you possibly go if you've got no one to follow and no plan?"

"You didn't follow Dad's plan, you made him follow yours."

"Let's not have this conversation today," intervened Dad.

"Yes, we'll save that for when you're home for Christmas," said her mother, her voice a bit harder.

July held the phone away from her ear, aching to hang up, but knew that there would only be a bigger storm waiting if she did.

"I guess we should really do the dishes," said Mom, straightening into her neutrality voice.

"Yes, as usual I made quite a mess," said Dad.

"Bye. Happy Thanksgiving," said July flatly.

She hung up the phone as her parents said goodbye a world away. She sat in silent, seething frustration, engulfed in a darkness of tar. She reached for the large bowl of gnocchi she had set aside for leftovers and ate them one by one with her hands, the sauce staining her fingers red, but she couldn't see it anyway.

Popping the gnocchi one by one into her mouth, a dense richness grew in her stomach until she reached the last one. She mushed it against the roof of her mouth with her tongue and rolled it around until finally it slid down her throat.

A life of no options was not an option. A life with no questions would have no answers.

Sitting at the table, her head slumped over, chin to chest, her eyes closed into a darkness indistinguishable from the first.

VII

"THAT PIE WAS—INCOMPREHENSIBLY DELICIOUS."

"Everyone liked it?"

"It was the star of the night. The leftovers didn't live to see Friday," said Toby, as he held open the door to the bookstore for her.

July smiled, "Good."

"The bourbon was a special touch."

"You could taste that?" she asked in surprise.

"I think you got my daughters buzzed."

"Oh no, I'm sorry," she said, her eyes widening.

"Hey, I'm kidding. The alcohol evaporates during the baking as you well know," he laughed. "Plus, I'm not the one who'd have to deal with their hangovers."

She giggled as they wandered together across the bright patterned carpeting in the children's books section.

"Oh my gosh, I used to love this book!" said July, picking up a copy of *Harold and the Purple Crayon*. She stopped to flip through it as Toby wandered further among the shelves.

"I got the *Nancy Drews*," said Toby, coming back a few moments later. "I'm going to the travel section."

July followed after she read the end of *Harold*, and found Toby looking at books about Italy.

"Ooh, Italy's my dream," she cooed.

"I think I'm going to Florence over Christmas."

"Really?" said July, surprised and a bit disappointed. *He was going to go just like that?*

"Yeah, I promised myself a vacation once the divorce was final."

"So, it's almost done?"

"Yes," he sighed with relief. "The papers should be signed by mid-December."

"That's great!"

"Yeah, so I figured I'd go to Florence for a couple weeks and recharge while Jenny takes the girls to see her parents."

"Oh. Wow, that's great," was all July could say.

I wish I could go with him, she thought. *Not that I could pay for it. Maybe he could pay for it.* The thought crept into her head like a cockroach through a hole in the wall. *No,* she thought as quickly as the thought had come. *Don't wish for that. You aren't like that.* But the thought was there, skittering like a roach across the floor avoiding the shoe trying to smash it.

"When do you go home for Christmas?" he asked.

"Probably around the twentieth."

"Hopefully the papers will be signed by then. We'll go out and celebrate."

Nothing like celebrating the end of a marriage, she thought. It would be a perfect celebration in Italy, but instead she said, "That sounds—nice."

"I guess I don't need a book," he said, putting one back. "I've been to Florence a few times. I know all the good spots. You ready?"

"Yeah, let's go," she replied.

During the drive back to his house, all July could think about was Italy. What it must be like there. How she and Toby would walk arm in arm over the Ponte Vecchio, what their pictures would look like in front of the Duomo, the Uffizi, the sidewalk cafés and pizzas and tomatoes and gelato in the middle of the winter. How it would feel to be somewhere new with someone she might almost love (but he didn't know that and probably didn't love her back), how everything would seem that much better because it was new, it was foreign, it was with him.

There was no sense in daydreaming, so she thought of all the vacations she'd taken with her family, all two of them. Once they went to Ohio to see family she had never met before. The whole trip was a long car drive with her brothers hitting each other and her the whole way, endless conversations with old relatives about things like the weather and *Rin Tin Tin* and casseroles. The other time, they went to Dartmouth when Iago had been accepted to college there.

Her parents weren't travelers. Or rather, her mother was not a traveler. Her father had traveled all over before he met her mother—Morocco, Brazil, Spain, France, Thailand, even China. He convinced July's mother to go to Mexico once before they married, but a bout with Montezuma's revenge topped off her active indifference. Neither of her parents ever left the country again.

"Why would they go all that way just to see a wire tower?" July's mother had mused after some friends returned from Paris. "They don't speak English there. What's the appeal in being ridiculed and confused? It's too much trouble."

Her father had remained pointedly silent.

While her brothers hid *Playboy* in their desks, July collected travel magazines, especially if they had features on Italy. Things just seemed so bright there, a highly concentrated version of beauty and life. But her mother had strangely forbidden July from traveling. Though it was not an express order, it was enforced. July's school had offered a one-year exchange to Europe and July proposed to get a job to pay her way. But her mother would have none of it.

She reminded July over and over, "Why would you want to go to Europe? You're too young. It's not safe. You don't speak any of the languages. There's plenty to see here. I won't have you wandering around some foreign land drinking God knows what with God knows who in God knows where. What does Europe have that we don't? It's still the world. It's all the same."

It was actually a somewhat similar situation with what her friends had said about her relationship with Toby, before she stopped talking about it.

"He's so old. He could be, like, your dad or something."

"He's just using you for sex."

"He probably has STDs."

"He's a creepy cradle-robber."

"He'll cheat on you like he's cheating on his wife."

"You aren't even old enough to be the mother of his daughters."

"He's old."

So she stopped talking to her friends about Toby, and for a while, she stopped talking to her parents about travel. She had studied Italian all four years of college but somehow neglected to mention it to her parents. Instead, she distracted them with information about her International Relations major, of which her parents approved. Though in the end it had been a compromise, they had favored it because of its so-called versatility, which July felt was really a disguise for interdepartmental lack of focus.

With the end of college peeking over the horizon, she had to start making decisions. She couldn't move back home, like her mother wanted, and slowly surrender her soul to a fluorescent light while playing secretary in the front office of the high school with her mother. July had sent up vague trial balloons about graduate school, but she had managed to miss all the application deadlines. Then she floated up jobs at magazines or openings at businesses past her parents, whose approval was inversely proportional to the number of miles the job was from home. The most promising and least soul-flattening job had been a position at an online magazine based in New York that covered global politics.

But secretly, she thought that after graduation she might scrape enough money together for a one-way ticket to Italy and just start a life there. But now with Toby, that seemed somewhat open to reinterpretation.

Not that he wants me to go. Not that he'll ask me to go. But, if he did ... I would.

She shuddered to think that staying with Toby might actually be what her mother would want, too—she would be following a man. His would be a world as different as Europe.

Firenze.

Toby just wanted to get to Florence. He had been five times since he was twenty years old, and it had become more than just a vacation. Florence had become a place to store his memory, where he could check in and compare notes with his younger selves. It was a city that was already so old it never seemed to age. He had traveled to many places around the world, but Toby had always liked that Florence was a narrow city filled with stairways barely wider than his shoulders, two-way roads broad enough for a car and a half. The slenderness of the place always made him feel stronger and more substantial than he did in America. In Florence, his presence made a difference.

He was in Florence when he had decided to ask Jenny to marry him. Perhaps he had been overcome with the romance of Italy, with the sunset over the center of the Arno, been seduced by the aromas of fresh bread and garlic and tomatoes and let the wine go to his head. He and Jenny had been at the Duomo all afternoon. They had toured the inside already, gone up the dome and gazed blissfully out over the red-tiled tops of the city, and then plunged into the cool catacombs that lurked beneath the cathedral floor. Now they were outside with the perpetual mass of sweaty people that clustered outside the white and green and pink façade, and he was taking her picture. It was one of those tourist photos where people would stand, arms awkwardly straight and limp against their sides, smiling against the backdrop of a postcard site.

Jenny struck one of those poses, but then, to Toby's total shock, began dancing in the thick of people milling around her. She propped herself up on the tips of her toes, curved her arms, and bent and swayed and flowed to the score of strangers and foreign languages. At that point in their relationship, Toby had already told her he loved her. But it wasn't until Jenny was arabesque, one foot sticking up where her head should be, that Toby truly felt what he had imagined love would be like. He watched her, half expecting the rest of the world to join in, in a musical song and dance number, but it remained Jenny dancing alone as though she were on top of a music box.

I'm going to marry that girl.

He finally recovered the presence of mind to take the photograph. It was and remained his favorite photograph of her, the only one he hadn't sealed in a shoebox and shoved to the farthest corner of the attic. He kept it now between the pages of the dictionary that sat on the top shelf of his desk. He never looked at it much anymore, but he felt better knowing that he hadn't imagined that Jenny had been the type of girl to pirouette in the streets of Italy. He felt better having proof that, at one time, the decision to marry Jenny had not been unfounded.

They went back to Florence two summers before Grace was born, during the limbo time when their marriage was neither happy nor troubled. He still wasn't sure what had possessed them to travel abroad with a five-year-old and a two-year-old, but surprisingly, the girls had been easier to travel with than Jenny. They could be contented with gelato and pizza. But, as Toby noted for the first time on that trip, Jenny had changed from the pirouette-in-the-*palazzo* girl.

In retrospect, this was probably the time she had first felt the stirrings of discontent. She laughed less, rarely smiled at him, which Toby had attributed to the stress of traveling with the girls. When Toby suggested taking her picture in front of the Duomo again, she rolled her eyes and didn't even bother to tell him "No." When they got back to their hotel room after an early dinner, Jenny promptly informed him she was going out for a walk alone and left without a further word to either him or the girls.

She hadn't come back until late, after the girls had been bathed and tucked in, when the lights in the room were out and Toby lay in bed worrying that something had happened, willing himself to stay awake. But when she finally had returned, his voice seemed frozen. She puttered in the bathroom, then crawled into bed beside him, smelling of limoncello and sweat.

Toby knew it would be strange to return to Florence, having cycled through a lifetime, to travel back in time in the present, to be young and married and divorced all at once. He didn't want the trip to be a droning foreign retrospective of his life, but he wondered if there were anywhere left for new experiences, new memories that might layer over the old ones, cover the old paint with wallpaper, remodel his mind.

He had decided that he wanted to be there during Christmas and through the new year. He wasn't sure when he had the idea to ask July along, but once he had, it didn't seem like such a bad idea. Actually, it made the prospect of spending the holidays without his family seem much less depressing. He envisioned showing her all his favorite spots, especially the restaurants and *gelaterias*. It would be a new city to her, and so to him, too, like all those movies he saw in the eighties that he thought were fantastic but when he watched them again some decades later he realized that they were actually pretty bad. July would give him a new way of seeing, maybe even reformat some of his emotions.

Plus, it didn't hurt that he liked her. A lot. And that she was young and beautiful and exciting and that she liked him too. He pictured a Woody Allen movie with fewer neuroses and better sex scenes.

Jenny had already mandated that she and their daughters would spend the holidays at her parents' house in Virginia, as always. For the two Christmases after they separated, Toby had always spent it alone in his apartment with some scotch, a pre-cooked chicken from the grocery store, and some gingerbread cookies from the bakery. In the misery of last Christmas, he had decided if he had to spend his holidays alone like he had before he got married, he would at least spend them in Florence.

But now he had July. He actually wouldn't mind, theoretically, taking her along to Florence. The only problem was what he would do when they went to the Duomo and she stood where Jenny had sixteen years ago. Toby wanted to avoid all association between Jenny and July, and didn't want to acknowledge that July could change as Jenny had.

It's not like she's the only one that changed. I changed too.

Maybe that change was what he needed to start wallpapering over his insides.

It was getting past the time for him to buy the tickets to Florence. It was already December, and tickets were expensive to begin with. He stood in his living room looking at the phone number for his travel agent, but couldn't make himself dial the number. One person or two?

Why was he being so indecisive? Just call, already. One person or two? How was this call harder to make than the first one he had made to July? If he took her, would that make him a sugar daddy or one of those mid-lifers funding the lavish lifestyles of their pretty-young-things?

He put down the phone. He would just have to ask her.

Do you want to go to Florence with me?

Would you like to go to Florence with me?

I was thinking we could go to Florence together.

It would be nice if we went to Florence together.

I'm taking you to Florence with me.

Come to Florence with me.

You could come with me. If you like.

Shit. This is shaping up to be almost as difficult as proposing.

Toby picked up his phone and called July. It rang and rang and rang, then went to voicemail. This wasn't an appropriate topic for a voicemail. He hung up just before the beep.

Well damn. He needed to know now. The girls were coming over after school today, which benched his phone use for awhile, and it's not like he could have that conversation with his girls around and have them ask, "Daddy, who are you taking to Florence with you?"

If he kept calling every so often, her phone would tell her how many times he had called. *Don't want to look too needy.* But he needed to know, which left only one option, which he really, really didn't want to do, and it was his own damn fault for waiting so long. He hated when he had no one to blame but himself.

The trees along Adams Street were bare and gnarled like barbed wire, brittle with cold. Along the gutter were knee-high piles of putrid, dirty and gasoline-tinted snow, and the sidewalk crunched with the grit of salt and sand. Even with the red car driving by, the world seemed like an old black and white photo.

Even though Toby lived just minutes from the main campus, the grasping December air knifing his ears turned one step into ten. Since he wasn't sure exactly where he was going, he dreaded that he would be outside indefinitely. He had been to July's dorm building once, when he had walked her to the door after their second date. It had been very dark and he had been concentrating on pulling her hips between his instead of where the hips were going. He couldn't pretend it wasn't a middle-aged dream to get naked with a twenty-something.

He could remember the general look of the place, a nondescript dormitory around the corner from the library, or was it the gymnasium? It could have been that big building with the glass and pipes.

When he reached the main campus, he tried calling her again. If she answered he could pretend that he hadn't come all the way over and he could just leave before the students had a chance to wonder whose dad was here to visit.

As he listened to July's phone ring, he looked at all the young people walking by, their pajama pants tucked into funny fur boots, some show-off wearing shorts and flip-flops, endless students cradling books in front of them like shields. Almost everyone who walked by had the same vacant, checked out stare and white ear buds connected to a white cord trickling into a pocket. In seven years, Chloe would be one of them, waltzing around campus to music only she could hear and tempering term papers with keggers. In a few years it could be her with the middle-aged boyfriend. There was a sobering thought.

He hung up the phone at July's voicemail message. Now he would have to try to find the dorm in daylight. Toby continued walking along the frozen sidewalk, hoping he would happen upon the dorm, or better yet, July.

Even though he was forty-three now, undeniably middle-aged, he only really noticed it when he had to hold reading material farther and farther from his eyes. There was no smooth way to break out the reading glasses, and every time he put them on he felt like a pink neon sign started flashing over his head: OVER 40 … OVER 40 … OVER 40 …

Only mirrors reminded him that the days had stacked up against him. He knew what he would see in the mirrors, and he tried to avoid them because they would lure him like sirens and hold him captive as he stared, transfixed at the graying fringes of his hair, like a black shirt washed hundreds of times. He would fixate on the way his skin looked looser and sandier; the deep lines pronging from the outer corners of his eyes as though a fork had carved him like a peanut butter cookie.

A young man with beginner's scruff wearing baggy jeans and a leather jacket walked past, and Toby's creased wrinkles felt deeper, like origami.

But at the same time, his shoulders relaxed and he grinned unconsciously as he felt his wrinkles temporarily disappear. Twenty-one-year-old Toby seeped through middle-aged Toby's skin. He was that skinny college student eating pizza and fries and hot wings for dinner. The fleeting brush with familiar possibility turned quickly back into forty-three. Where was he? He stopped walking. This did not look familiar. Or maybe it did?

Shit. I'm old. Maybe this is what Alzheimer's feels like.

He wandered around for a few more minutes until he recognized the quad with the library. Behind the library across the street was a clump of dormitories. There had been stairs the night he walked her home. He remembered that she was taller than he was when she stood one step above him.

He followed a set of stairs to his left and naturally concluded that the building in front of him was hers. It wasn't until after he had pulled at the door knob a few times that he noticed the electronic card reader to the side of the locked door. Duh.

Which meant he could only wait. Once, when he was fifteen and didn't know better, he had waited outside the music room for an hour waiting for the girl he liked to emerge so he could accidentally run into her.

When she came out, she gave him a puzzled look, "Why are you still here?"

He hadn't had an answer ready, and after a moment of dumb silence, she scoffed and raised her eyebrows in a silent, "What a weirdo."

Now, Toby couldn't feel his nose, and he could swear his jacket was lighter than it had been before. He sat on the short brick wall outside the dorm entryway.

The last time he set foot in a dorm was twenty-two years ago. Oh God, he was living in a dorm when July was born. He tried to picture his old dorm room. Messy. Walls painted white but seeming to pulse with yellow; vibrations from the music next door or from his room; hall parties that drenched the building in beer; amorous carnal grunts and curious squeaks though ambiguous walls. And the communal bathrooms—there's nothing worse than listening to sounds of a stranger's excretion when you're trying to brush your teeth.

A few students walked by him, glancing at him with cursory curiosity but ultimate indifference. What if this was the wrong building? He would sit out here indefinitely and completely miss July. Then what? He ran through the scenarios of trying to call July with the girls around. The papers would be signed in a couple of weeks. He couldn't risk Jenny finding out he had a girlfriend now.

"Toby?"

Toby looked over to see July walking towards him in her puffy down coat. He stood up and walked a few steps in her direction.

"Hi."

She smiled broadly, "What are you doing here?"

Should he kiss her? Would she be embarrassed? She leaned in and kissed him, and his questions ceased. It was good to know she wasn't ashamed.

"I wanted to talk to you about something."

"Oh ... okay."

She paused, her eyes clicking through the possibilities uncertainly, "Do you want to come inside?"

"Sure."

"Good, because it feels like it's fucking winter out here or something," she laughed.

She swiped a card and the door clicked unlocked. It swung open and Toby was met with a rush of warm air. He felt the skin on his face expand and loosen and his extremities tingle with pricks of resuscitation.

"Is everything okay?" asked July, leading him past a desk where a student sat hypnotized by his laptop.

"Oh, yeah, I just—thought this wasn't a phone thing. Were you in class?"

They made small talk as they walked to the back of the building and into a stairwell. After the first flight of stairs, Toby began to steam under his jacket.

He followed July out of the stairwell and into a hallway on the third floor. The dingy, vaguely insulting fluorescent lights hummed a bleak pall over the hallway. The carpet, well worn and smudged with decades of grime, was slippery and thin. This hall turned into another. All the doors exactly the same but decorated with boards plastered in pictures and stickers and slogans meant to assert a modicum of personality in a building of careful anonymity.

July stopped in front of a door whose board was covered with a brightly patterned paper, on top of which were pasted old black and white photographs, one of a man squatting on the ground near a cactus, another of a woman dressed like a fifties mom in front of a fountain.

"Who are they?" he asked, pointing at the pictures.

"I don't know, I just buy the photos from old antique stores and stuff."

She unlocked the door and entered her room.

"Come on in. Sorry, it's a little messy. I would've cleaned it up if I knew you were coming."

"That's okay."

Toby stepped into the room. Though small, it seemed even smaller because it was bursting with stuff. A large rectangle of one wall was covered in postcards bordered by a string of Christmas lights. A stack of food magazines by the bed spilled onto the floor. Bright blue sheets and a green, brown, and pink comforter lay rumpled across the bottom of the unmade bed. A blizzard of papers lay strewn over what Toby presumed to be a desk. All sorts of photos and multicolored knickknacks huddled together on any shelf surface, a few drawers were half open, and several pairs of shoes lay rejected on the floor.

In the organized chaos, Toby noticed a pair of underwear that had fallen just short of the laundry basket. He smiled and looked away, pretending he didn't see it, but every once in awhile, he looked back at the blue striped fabric.

July removed some clothes from a chair and placed them on her bed. "Here, have a seat."

"Thanks."

He sat on the hard wood chair. No wonder it was covered in clothes—it certainly wasn't comfortable.

July took off her jacket and sat down on her bed, "So what did you want to talk about?"

"Uh, well …"

Toby had been so focused on word choice that he had hardly thought about how July would answer. He felt fairly certain that she wanted to go—she had taken more than a passing interest in what he planned to do, see, eat, and over the course of fifteen years of marriage and being grossly outnumbered gender-wise, he had slowly learned to pick up the general pattern of hinting.

"Is everything all right?" she asked again, her brow tilted with an edge of concern.

"Yeah, everything's fine. Actually, we'll be signing the papers next week."

"That's great! We should celebrate!" she said.

Her face, which had perked up in congratulations, promptly fell serious, "Unless, well, maybe divorce isn't something you want to celebrate? Sorry, that was insensitive."

"No, no," he reassured her. "We'll go out. I'll be glad to have it over with."

She smiled and leaned towards him, putting her elbows on her thighs and dangling her hands between her knees, "Is that what you wanted to talk about?"

"No, actually, I've been thinking and, I thought it would be nice if, um, you came to Florence with me."

Her face froze in listening mode. He could almost hear her brain processing, churning like an ice cream maker. She half smiled and drew her neck back.

"Are you serious?"

"Yes."

"You know, I can't really … pay for that."

"I know. I'll … cover the costs."

"That's a lot. I couldn't ask you to do that."

"You didn't. I asked you."

"No I mean ..." July put a hand to her face. "I mean that's ... really ... big."

"I know. But having you with me is worth more than the cost of a plane ticket and some meals. I ... you wouldn't *owe* me anything. You wouldn't have to—*do* anything. I mean, I wasn't going to pay for a second hotel room or anything, because that would be a *lot* extra, but I figured you'd already be okay with that. But July, there's so much to see. You'd love it there, it's your city."

He was rambling. *Shut up, Toby.*

She looked at him for a few moments that would have been a pensive silence if it weren't for some kids who were out in the hallway shouting about something.

"I ... really?" she said disbelievingly.

"Really."

She rubbed her ear up and down a few times.

"Please," he said.

She sighed, and looked at him, her face dissolving into acceptance and joy, her smile spreading wide, "Okay."

"Okay," he smiled, and his shoulders relaxed. "I'll call my travel agent."

"You must be the last person in the world to still have a travel agent," she replied with a smirk.

He stood up to leave.

"Where are you going?" asked July.

"To call my travel agent."

"Can't you do that later?"

"Well, I mean, I should do it as soon as possible, prices are—" he stopped speaking as he recognized the sultry look on her face. "Then again, there's still ..." he looked at his watch, "... an hour before I meet the school bus."

He walked to the bed and leaned over, his lips meeting hers. Still kissing July, he knelt on the bed frame and moved towards her and onto the bed, the springs whimpering with the added weight.

It had been over two decades since he had made love in a dorm room. The worry that every breath and squeak and utterance is audible through the walls wasn't so much difficult now that he had kids and had practice in being quiet. Though even with the pronounced scarcity of silence in a dorm, these sorts of sounds seemed to travel best. Though at the moment, he cared not at all. He was ageing, he was a dad, he was divorcing, but a pretty young thing still wanted him. In his youth he had never felt such power from feeling desired.

They lay for a few minutes in bed, watching out the window as the weak winter afternoon faded. She was so palpably happy, and he hoped he would have a long time of bringing her such naked joy. The first thing July would do this evening, she informed him, was look up places to eat in Florence, and decide what was worth seeing near the restaurants. Then, upon seeing the time, reminded him to call the travel agent, which she giggled at again; apparently all the kids bought tickets online now. Not willing to get up just yet, he called from the bed, confirming dates and the hotel.

July prompted him along in whispers, "What about the layover? What about the hotel?"

She seemed so worried he would forget. She took down two sets of notes and gave him one of them.

When he looked at the clock he realized that the girls were probably already at the bus stop waiting. But after that afternoon, even a brisk jog through the knives of December didn't seem quite as sharp as they had on the way over.

July hadn't moved in the hours since Toby left. She stayed in bed, comforter to chin, watching as the room faded into darkness. She was supposed to be writing a final paper, but trying to focus her mind was as effective as eating soup with chopsticks. Had that really just happened? It seemed somehow criminal that her daydreams had turned real, like she had somehow manipulated the-way-things-are. She was going to Florence. There were dates and times: December 22 to January 5.

She would end a year and begin another in Italy with Toby. Since she was supposed to have gone home the twentieth, she would stay with Toby for the few days before they left. Weeks of uninterrupted Toby. *I hope he doesn't get sick of me. I hope I don't get sick of him.*

July knew this was one of those make-or-break a relationship sort of thing. But at the moment, forefront in her mind was calling her parents to let them know she wouldn't be home for the holidays. This would not go over well, that much was certain. But she had a hard time pinpointing which objection her parents would raise first:

a) Not coming home for Christmas,

b) Going to a foreign country,

c) Going with a man who is oh-by-the-way only four years younger than Mom.

Obviously it would be:

d) All of the above – but she wondered in what order. ABC was probably the best progression, but to her parents, alphabetical order was more of a suggestion.

She did not want to do this. But the holidays were so soon, she couldn't put it off. Or maybe she could just not tell them, and on the twentieth they would be waiting at the airport just outside security, watching as other passengers walked by, dulled and blurred by recycled air, one rolling suitcase clacking by after another, until her parents had waited and waited and waited. But then they would probably call the police, the Transportation Security Administration, the FBI, and then there would be an Amber Alert out for her and Toby would get arrested for kidnapping. Merry Christmas.

Still in bed, she reached for her phone and dialed home. Both her parents should be home by now. It rang a few times, and her mother answered.

"Hello?"

"Hi, Mom."

"July! Hello, sweetie. Gray, it's July!"

After a moment, July's father was on the line.

"Hiya, July."

"Hi Dad."

"What's new, honey?"

"Oh, not much, you know. Class. Study. Test. You know."

"Have you been going out at all?" asked her mother.

Oh, boy. That was fast. Leave it to Mom to jump to answer "C" first. "Um, well ... "

"You have! Is it still this mysterious fellow?"

"Toby? Uh, yeah, actually—"

"Oh he has a name! Well what's Toby like? What's his major?"

"Does he eat meat?"

"Yes, Gray, she already told us he eats meat!" her mother snapped. "What's he like, honey? Is he in the arts or sciences?"

"Well ... actually, he's not in school anymore."

"Oh, an older man!" said her mother, her voice a blend of suspicion and delight. "And what does he do?"

"He's in—real estate."

"I see. So he's already established in life. That's good, that's good. Gives you something concrete for after graduation, none of that drifting around finding yourselves, making your way sort of nonsense."

"How old is this fellow?" asked her dad.

"Uhm ... "

"Oh my, he's not *thirty* is he?" asked her mother. "That would be an awfully big age difference."

"No, he's not thirty."

"I think twenty-eight is the suitable cut off. Is he twenty-eight?"

"No, but he was— fifteen years ago."

There was a moment of crackly pause as her parents processed ... carry the one...

"What?" they said almost simultaneously.

"Um—"

"This Toby is *forty-two*?" her mother cried incredulously.

"Forty-*three*, Jill. Eight plus five is thirteen, not twelve."

"*Forty-three?*"

"Yeah."

"Isn't—That's—That's—That's practically illegal!" she shouted. "This man was older than you are now when you were born! He could be your *father*! What does he want from you?"

"I know what he wants from her," said her father.

"He doesn't want anything, Mom. He just likes me. And I like him."

"He *likes* you? July, men that age don't just *like* girls your age. I can't believe this—it's like an episode of *Jerry Springer*!"

"No it's not, Mom."

"I don't believe this. July, this man is some sort of pedophile."

"He's not a pedophile, Mom. He has three daughters."

"WHAT?"

That was the wrong thing to say.

"He has *three daughters*? I don't believe this. I did not raise you to be a step-mother, July. You're practically dating your father."

"Ugh, Jill!"

"Ew, I am not."

"He isn't *married* is he?"

Why oh why couldn't she just lie? Why did she find it so impossible to just make up something else—something her parents would like to hear? She had never understood the semantics of lying. It just wasn't her language.

"Well ..."

"He's *married*?"

"No! Well, yes. I mean—he's divorcing. The papers are going to be signed next week."

"You are not the cause of this divorce, are you?"

"No ..."

"This is totally inappropriate, July. I forbid you from seeing him."

"Good luck with that, Mom."

"Gray!" intoned her mother with petulant expectation. "Say something!"

July heard him sigh into the phone.

"July …" He sighed again. "July … this sort of age difference doesn't diminish with time, it gets more pronounced, like leftover curry in the fridge. I don't—"

"Look," interrupted July. "The reason I called is because Toby is going to Italy for the holidays, and he's invited me to go with him."

Stone silence at the other end of the line.

"And I'm going. We're leaving the twenty-second and we'll be back the fifth."

"You aren't coming home for *Christmas?*" said her mother, who sounded as though she were speaking through clenched teeth. Actually, every part of her body was probably clenched right about now.

"But who will make dessert?" asked her father. "And the brioche? You know the brioche is finicky."

"Gray, dessert is *not* a priority right now. What makes you think you can skip out on a family holiday? What makes you think we'll pay for this?"

Oh boy. Deploy the airbags.

"Well … he's paying for it."

July's right ear exploded with her mother's shriek and a thundering thwack as one or both of her parents took it out on the telephone. July thought perhaps they had spontaneously combusted, self-destructed, and envisioned a mushroom cloud obliterating her parents' house.

For the next forty minutes, July was aurally assaulted by her mother, and after a while, it did start to sound a bit like *Jerry Springer*. July was abandoning her family for some, some mid-life crisis scumbag who was using her and turning her into nothing better than a prostitute-trophy girlfriend.

"You know how men are!" berated her mother. "They all want the younger, prettier model, and once you show signs of age, whsht! You're out to make way for the next barely-legal bimbo."

"Excuse me?" said her father.

"Oh Gray, obviously not you."

"If all that were true I'd have traded you in long ago."

"Gray, this is not about you, this is about July. She is tarnishing her reputation! What is so special about this man? What is so special about Italy that you would rather be there than at home, a place you know and love?"

July didn't answer. She had given up truly listening and was checking her emails.

"July," said her father, forming a cohesive sentence for the first time all night. "July, I don't like what you're doing. I don't approve of it. I am very disappointed in you; this is not how we raised you. But as I have no jurisdiction and no say, I have only one thing to say to you."

He paused.

"Don't worry, Dad. I'll eat lots of prosciutto."

"And don't skimp on the mortadella. But seriously July—what will come of this? You go with him to Italy, maybe you see him the rest of the semester, and then you graduate and then what? July, you're setting yourself up for disappointment, for him to take advantage of you, and you're setting yourself up to get hurt."

He hung up the phone.

"Oh, July," her mother's tone turned grave. "Who *are* you?"

"Right, well, I'm hanging up now. It's been lovely chatting with you."

July jerked the phone from her ear and vigorously poked the "end" button.

She sat in her bed a while longer. The room was swathed in black, illuminated only by the electronic blue glow of her laptop screen.

Who am I? she thought. *Who are you?*

Even though she had never been out of the country, July had a passport. During her sophomore year, she and her friends had made unrealized plans to go to Mexico over spring break, and July, ignorant of the fact that she wouldn't need a passport for Mexico back then, got one anyway. That was also back when she had thought she could talk her parents into letting her study abroad, so she reasoned she'd need one at some point. But her parents had, unsurprisingly, been wholly unsupportive of her proposal to go to Italy for a semester. They, especially her mother, didn't seem to grasp the "international" aspect of the International Relations major.

"Why would you go half way around the world to go to school when you're already at a perfectly fine college? How does studying in Italy pertain to an International Relations major?"

So her passport languished in her desk drawer for almost two years. Sometimes, when she couldn't fall asleep, she would lie in bed and tell the story of her other life, in which she sold something or found an unmarked, unclaimed wallet stuffed with money or received an inheritance from the millionaire grandmother she never knew. She would buy a plane ticket, pack everything up, and then one day, a day as anonymous as tomorrow, she would fly away in the belly of a metal bird and dissolve into the cobble-stoned history and pasta-curtained mist of Italy. Sometimes she took up with Flavio, the broad, olive-eyed port of passion, who drank cappuccino and wine and smoked cigarettes; other times she lived alone in a small, poorly-lit apartment within a building darkened with the soot of modernity, where she would work at a restaurant as a waitress first, then a kitchen hand, and she would live off the aromas of slow-cooked tomato sauces and garlic and basil until she was a happy old woman who bled marinara and cried olive oil.

Piacere di conoscerti.

VIII

TWO DAYS LATER, ON THURSDAY, TOBY CALLED JULY JUST AFTER DROP-
ping the girls off at school.

"What are you doing for lunch?"

"Um, probably eating an energy bar in the library. I have a paper to
finish by tomorrow. Why?"

"I thought we could get lunch, since I have the girls till next Friday,
and we sign the papers Wednesday morning. I won't be able to see you
until Friday."

"Oh. Well, I could take a break if you're willing to eat in the
Student Union."

"Okay."

"You know where the library is, right? Why don't you just meet me
there and then we can walk over to get food?"

"Sounds good. Noon?"

"Noon."

July kept close track of the time. At eleven fifty-five, she packed
up her books and went through the arduous process of sweater, jacket,
scarf, hat, gloves. At eleven fifty-seven, she went downstairs. At eleven
fifty-eight, she walked out the front doors of the library. Despite her
layers, the cold still lashed at her skin. Her nose started to ache. And as
the world turned at eleven fifty-nine, she heard, "July."

She knew that voice. Her brain clicked through its rolodex, but she couldn't flip to the name. She turned toward the voice and saw Chris walking up the path to the library. *Oh shit.*

"Hi, Chris," she ventured, giving a forced half smile.

"Hi."

He stopped in front of her. His eager, winter-stung face glowed red. Awkward silence hung like an icicle. "So, uh, what are you doing here?" he asked.

"Writing a paper."

"Oh. Cool."

"Not really," said July.

"Yeah, I have to do some studying. You know, research," he said.

"Yeah."

"So ... um, how's everything?"

"Fine."

"Good. Good. Me too."

July raised her eyebrows in acknowledgement. Then, out of the corner of her eye, she saw Toby, huddled against the cold and walking quickly towards her. This was going to be the social equivalent of wearing pants that are two sizes too small. Ten, nine ...

"So, um, you doing anything cool for the holidays?"

Eight, seven. *Oh no, oh no, oh no.* Six.

"Uh, yeah, kinda."

Five. Toby's eyes locked on her and he smiled. Four. Leave Chris, leave Chris, leave, leave, leave.

"Oh yeah? Gonna see your family? Make the big dinner?"

Three, two ...

"Hi there," said Toby.

July's stomach did an excited two-step, jazz hands and all, and her face morphed into a smile of its own accord.

Toby leaned in and kissed her lips. Warm.

"Hi."

He put an arm around her waist, and she reciprocated. Then they simultaneously turned their heads to Chris, as though they had rehearsed the timing perfectly.

"Oh. Hi," said Toby, slightly sheepish.

Chris' face seemed to have been botoxed into an expression of indignant confusion, like his stomach had dropped down his pant leg and he was desperately hoping that no one had noticed it draped over his shoe.

Oh God, oh God, oh God.

"Uh, Toby, this is Chris."

"Oh! Right. Chris. July told me about you."

July looked at Toby. He had had twice her lifetime to perfect his poker face, and it had paid off. But the little lines forking from his eyes like Cleopatra squinted subtly, his only tell.

Chris' expression didn't change, like he was practicing for his debut as a gargoyle, "The ice cream guy?"

"What?" said Toby. "I'm in—real estate …"

"Chris—"

"You're still—I thought you'd—I –"

"Chris—" But July had nothing to say.

It was a triangle of silence. Chris' face slowly defrosted, brows melting, mouth drooping, July had seen this expression twice, and she knew what was coming. Tears. She felt awful.

"We should be going," rushed July, leading Toby down the steps. "See you later, Chris. Have a good break."

As she and Toby scuttled wordlessly across the street to the Student Union, July imagined Chris standing frozen in that spot like a statue, icicle tears tangled in his eyelashes, his face the mask of tragedy.

Looking into Chris' face had been like looking at an old home movie of himself. Toby remembered that feeling of shock and rejection and self-pity. Chris was Toby before he learned to just get on with life and deal with the hurt. Toby estimated he had hit that mark around twenty-three, when a girlfriend he had been crazy about dumped him two days before he was giving a presentation for a business at a huge conference. It's a good thing he had learned that, too, because three days after Jenny kicked him out of the house two years ago, he had a two-day meeting with the heads of the company he worked for. And that's when the stakes had been much higher on both sides of the equation.

From what he could see on Chris' face, Toby guessed that Chris had been harboring the belief, or hope, that the breakup had been more of an intermission than a final curtain. We all have to learn sometime.

Toby and July sat at a white Formica table amidst a checkerboard ocean of identical tables. One of the table legs had lost a foot, and the table wobbled back and forth. They ate sandwiches wrapped in paper off of plastic trays tinted shades of off-color red, blue, and brown.

"So, that was Chris," he started.

"Yeah."

"Hm," he grunted, taking a bite of his sandwich.

"That was really weird," she exhaled quickly.

"Yes it was," Toby paused. "Why did he call me the ice cream guy?"

"He saw us a few months ago getting ice cream. Then he called me about it and—got upset."

They chewed.

"You know," he started, then took a sip of his drink. "About a month after Jenny and I separated, I ran into her in the frozen food section of the grocery store. Her cart was full of those stupid microwave dinners. She can't cook. Anyway, when she looked over and saw me, she had this look on her face, like, I'd rather lick the floor behind the butcher counter than talk to you. I felt like she had reached down my throat and pushed all my organs out my ass. We just stood there, a deer in the other's headlights. I couldn't say anything to her, and she didn't say anything to me. She just turned around and walked away as fast as she could. Later I wondered if I'd had the same look on my face that she'd had on hers."

July looked at her sandwich.

"Did my face look like that?"

"No."

"Did my face look like his?"

"Not quite."

"Oh."

"No, your expression was more like a vase was falling from a table and you were watching it fall, waiting for it to break."

"Ah."

He reached across the table to grab her hand, then pulled it back a little.

"What?" she asked.

"I mean, can I do that here?" he said, looking around.

"Yeah. It's not a prison or a convent."

"It's all right for an old man to eat in here?" he smiled.

"Sure. I mean, for all anyone else knows, you're my professor and this is my last ditch effort to get an A on the final."

He smiled, then took her hand, and she smiled back, a little green wisp of greenery caught between her teeth. Toby reflexively rubbed his tongue over the same spot on his teeth.

"You have a little—" he made a motion to her teeth.

"Oh! God."

She mined out the offending leaf, then showed her teeth to him.

"Gone?"

"Gone."

July took a sip of her drink, "So, you're signing the papers next week."

"Yep. This time next week I'll be officially divorced."

"Hm."

"I hope it's civil. I told her we have to sign it face to face, like we did at our wedding. This is just as binding. Or, unbinding, as it were."

She looked at him, her eyes assessing, her lips twisted into her teeth. "What?"

"What was your wedding like?"

He blinked a few times. His daughters used to ask him that question too, but they had long since learned to avoid that subject.

The wedding was tattooed on his memory. The blurred mass of guests, the fussy flowers, the bridesmaids in matching lavender dresses, Jenny's huge smile, her face framed by the marshmallow shoulder poufs, her blonde hair scraped into an elaborate bun of unnatural curls, a huge bouquet of flowers cascading into her wide princess skirt. But she had been beautiful, and he had loved her; he remembered that.

He supposed it was a fair enough question for July to ask, but he didn't really see what it mattered. If you had told him on his wedding day that fifteen years later after a nasty divorce, he'd be telling his girlfriend, who was in first or second grade on his wedding day, all about that day, well. Who would believe a thing like that? It almost negated the entire thing. But if she wanted to know, he would tell her.

"Well," he began. "There were a lot of people. Jenny wanted it traditional, so it was in a church I'd never attended. Near her parents' house, because they didn't want to travel. It was June. There were a lot of flowers everywhere. It was kind of your basic white wedding like all her friends had. She walked down the aisle to *Pachelbel's Canon*. We had a limo. We had a reception afterward at some hotel, and we had chicken or fish and a big chocolate cake made predominantly of frosting. It was pretty … predictable and the whole production seemed a little routine, like a New Year's Eve party, instead of a day that would never come around again. But of course I say that in retrospect. It was a wonderful day, and I was in love and I felt like the luckiest guy on earth."

Toby fiddled with his napkin, "I try not to think about it too much anymore. It's like watching a movie a second time, when you know something bad is going to happen but you can't go in and stop it. It's hard to look back on happiness that you know will lead to hurt. It kind of makes you wonder about the future price of present happiness."

"Wow," said July heavily.

"I didn't really want to tell you that much. You shouldn't have to think about things like that until your mid-life crisis."

"Toby. What's she like?"

"Jenny?"

"Yeah. I know you probably don't want to talk about it, but ... well, I've kind of been wondering that for a while now and, well, Google doesn't tell me much."

Toby laughed.

"You Googled Jenny?"

July cast her eyes down and to the side sheepishly, and her lips contracted like an accordion, "It's what all the kids do nowadays."

"I guess you'd want to know," he sighed. It was a bit like when his daughters asked him to tell them about how they met, how he proposed, what life was like before they were born. The deeper he got with July, the deeper they would have to wade into the "Before Me" swamp, and his side of the swamp was bigger and much murkier. And apparently it was on Google.

"You don't have to tell me, it's just—I want to stop wondering and making up all these versions of her in my head."

"Well ..." he started.

Jenny ... who is Jenny? Not who she was. "She's a dancer. She was a ballerina, now she's an instructor," he started.

He remembered the first time he saw her dance. Ballet had never been his thing; usually after the first twenty minutes, the story gave way to indecipherable prancing. He saw her dance in *Swan Lake*, and though he was still utterly bored by the whole production, he occupied his thoughts with scrutiny of her body, how it swayed and undulated. And he could see that her face, though covered by the mask of acting, still had that taste of Jenny, and he could see beneath her concentration, a genuine passion and satisfied calm. Like her body fit her best in dance. She used to have that same look when her toe shoes were off, but at some point a veil of increasing opacity obscured it, and by now it had been all but smothered.

After *Swan Lake*, he had waited for her outside the backstage door holding a cone of flowers. She came out, hair slicked into a taut helmet bun. Her lips were coated with such bright red lipstick that it looked like she was wearing wax lips. It was like she had painted an entirely new face over her own. He remembered trying to look underneath the cosmetic drapery, searching for the girl to whom he had sent a drink.

He had done that a lot in the last years of their marriage, too.

"You have to understand," he continued, "that the way Jenny is now is not the way she was. When I loved her she was ..."

Toby closed his eyes, trying to pin a word to a concept, to the way her hair curved against her neck, the way she kicked the dishwasher door closed with her foot as she turned on the ball of her foot.

"She—well, this will sound cheesy. She still enjoyed life and internal satisfaction. But over the years, I guess dissatisfaction outside invaded satisfaction inside, and she became, at least with me, irritated and bitter and jaded. But maybe she's different around other people."

Behind July's intent gaze, he could see her trying to construct a model, a skeleton, something, like a paleontologist piecing together fossilized bones.

"There are some things that never changed, though," he went on. "She still can't cook. Every day since I've known her, her breakfast has always been egg whites and an apple and black coffee. She reads a lot—constantly, actually. She wears a lot of blue, organizes things by lists and tends to get a little nitpicky with the cleaning."

"How did you change?" asked July.

There she went asking intelligent questions.

"Well, I—I guess I got tired. And I worked too much, trying to make her happy by providing when what she wanted, I think, was for me to be home."

Toby was ready to change the subject, "Did you tell your parents about the trip yet?"

"Oh … yeah. That didn't go over so well."

"It'd be tough not to have your kid home for the holidays."

"My parents don't really understand the whole concept of travel. Nor are they thrilled that my honor is being besmirched by a man looking for the newest model of trophy girl."

"Maybe I should talk to them myself," he said.

July's eyes got a little wider and her mouth couldn't decide whether to form a shocked "O" or smile in absurdity.

"That would be—wh—wh—" July rubbed her ear, her thinking mannerism. "I—can't—I can't even *fathom* how that would—no wait, I *can* fathom that conversation but I think it would cause any sane human being to short circuit and spark out the ears."

Toby chuckled.

"*Why* would you want to subject yourself to that?"

Toby thought about how he would feel if any of his daughters told him that she wouldn't be home for Christmas, not that he got to see them on Christmas anyway, because she was going off with a man twice her age. Toby would be pretty pissed, to put it mildly. What kind of a guy, a guy more or less Toby's age, would abscond with one of his little girls and take her away from her family? It must be some lecherous fool who was trying to bribe his way into her pants.

They think I'm "That Guy", he thought. *I am, but I'm not. I am not what I am.* Toby would think this hypothetical guy was That Guy.

Would talking to That Guy make him seem more or less like That Guy? *Shit. This is too confusing.*

"Maybe if I talk to them," he said. "It could ease their minds a bit."

"If one of your daughters came to you in this situation, would talking to you make you feel better?"

Maybe not. But at least he'd know what he was dealing with. "You know how you wanted to know about Jenny because you wanted to stop hypothesizing about all the things she *could* be?"

"Yeah."

"That's what your parents are doing."

"Oh."

"They aren't owed this, but you know, it may help calm their minds just a tad."

"Obviously," she replied. "You have no idea what my family is like."

"Well, we're all parents, so we have that in common."

July rolled her eyes.

"Should we call now?" he asked.

What was he doing? He didn't want to have to talk to her parents! He must be suicidal.

July looked at the clock on her cell phone, "No, they're both at work. It's best to call later at night. It's earlier there."

"Well. Can you come by tonight, after the girls are in bed? We can call then."

July sighed heavily and shook her head, "If they rip you a new one through the phone line and you're in the hospital recovering, I'm going to Italy without you."

"It's a deal," he said.

He must be insane.

Toby must be insane. July stared at her computer screen later that afternoon, trying to concentrate on finishing her final paper. Instead, her eyes focused hypnotically on the blinking cursor, still trying to imagine how the conversation would go.

She remembered back to when her parents first met Chris. They had come to visit her at school, and they had all gone out to dinner one night. Her dad had chosen a well-known steakhouse. When July heard this, she cringed—Chris was vegetarian, and she hadn't told her dad yet.

Chris finally changed out of "The Uniform" of faded, worn baggy jeans and a white T-shirt and wore an impress-the-parents ensemble of khakis, light blue dress shirt, and an inoffensive tie.

Her parents had picked them up on campus. Chris had politely shaken their hands, addressed them as Mr. and Mrs., and turned on the manners necessary to prove he hadn't been raised by a grunting herd of Neolithic nomads, though that may have helped his case, since presumably few Neolithic nomads were vegetarian.

Everything had been tolerably awkward until they were seated and ready to order.

"Chris, what sort of steak tickles your incisors?" her father had ventured, trying to relate. "Of course a porterhouse is tasty, but sometimes I like to splurge on the Kobe."

Chris shot July a look of tentative concern. She had warned him of her dad's carnivorous bias, but Chris had asserted that he wasn't willing to down a dead cow to please her father.

"Actually, sir, I'm not much of a steak man."

July's father wrinkled his brow in confusion, "No? Are you a rib man? That's respectable."

"No, um, actually, I'm a ... vegetarian, sir."

Her father's brow remained frozen. In fact, every part of him remained frozen as he tried to fathom a vegetarian of the male persuasion. He was used to the grass-eating women, but July could bet that her father had never met an herbivore with a Y chromosome.

An uncomfortable silence spread itself over the table. Her father didn't say a thing. In fact, he hardly uttered another word the rest of the night, except to praise the bright pink juicy flesh in front of him, which he had ordered a bit rarer than usual.

July's mother quickly asked Chris about physics to cut the tension, but long after the plates of beef juice and the carcass of Chris' baked potato had been cleared, the tension remained intact.

The next day July met her parents for breakfast at Starbucks. They sat at a table sipping coffee and nibbling bagels.

"Chris seems like a very nice young man," ventured her mother.

"Yeah," said July weakly.

Finally, her father exploded like a shaken soda bottle opened quickly.

"What is that vegetarian crap? I've never met a man who doesn't like meat. A baked potato he ordered. He had the gall to eat a salad. And a baked potato! At one of the finest steakhouses in the country! That's like going to church and praying to Allah!" His face was as red as a rare steak.

"Gray, we've talked about this—"

"No, Jill, a man who cannot appreciate the gustatory pleasures of the flesh is not worthy of July."

"Dad … the girl Ansel brought to Christmas last year was a vegetarian."

"That was different."

"How?"

"No, no! Obviously I have no choice in the matter, but I just wonder what I did to make you spite me like this? Forget this Chris fellow and go find yourself a man who knows his food and knows how to cook. If he cooks you something, you're golden, my girl. I bet Chris couldn't steam you a stalk of broccoli."

July had done just as her father suggested. She had found Toby, who not only enjoyed food *and* made her breakfast, but he made her heart melt and trickle away. Just his presence made her feel more sharply defined, like every part of her body had meaning and a purpose to exist. And he liked her back; she could tell from times like when he would pull his face back from hers in a kissing lull and say, "Do you know what you do to me?"

How the heat from his breath would roll over her skin and down her back until every part of her had washed away in the tide of his breath.

How when she kissed him goodbye, his eyes looked almost forlorn, as thought she would disappear at any moment and leave him only with the mental image that would fuzz gradually over time.

How he would grip the belt loops of her jeans and yank her as close in to his body as he could, stretching them out of shape.

Toby was everything her parents wanted her to find in a man but with a two-decade surplus. You could force-feed a vegetarian a steak, but you couldn't drain a man of age.

July's stomach was a churning sea of worms the rest of the day. She trudged through a fresh coat of snow later that evening, a scarf wrapped around her mouth and nose, only her eyes exposed to the burning freeze. She kept trying to imagine all the different ways this conversation could go, ranging from open hostility and murderous threats to a creepy camaraderie and mutual understanding.

She reached Toby's house and paused on the porch. She usually knocked, but she worried that she would wake up his daughters. To just walk into someone else's living space had always seemed a bit presumptuous to her.

Knocking softly, she hoped that Toby's subconscious would hear the faint rapping outside. She waited. Nothing. She tried again, waited more, but nothing. The cold had fallen all over her body. *Screw this*, she thought, and opened the door.

She took off her wet boots and shed various layers in the dark entryway, listening for any movement. She knew she was still a secret; as much as she wanted to meet Toby's daughters, they didn't need any more family changes at the moment.

But the house was silent. And dark. She groped further inside where the light from a table lamp by the couch cast a small island of glowing yellow. Venturing in further, she could see the back of the couch and the dark television.

"Toby?" she called softly.

"Hm?" came a sleep-coated sigh.

As she walked over to the couch, Toby sat up half way.

She sat by his thighs on the edge of the couch. He sat back, and she leaned over, putting her head on his chest. His breathing turned rhythmic again, and July thought that maybe he had fallen back asleep. *Well, I'm not going to wake him. This whole phone call was his idea.*

But a few minutes later, as if no time had passed at all, he lifted his neck and said to her scalp, "Should we give your folks a call?"

Damn. She sat up, "You really don't have to. It's not like I need their permission or anything."

"No no, I know. But it might be better if they didn't form the impression that I was some swaggering middle-aged playboy."

"Aren't you?"

He sat up and chuckled, "Maybe." He kissed her for a few moments, then reached for his phone.

"Here, I'll do it. I'll set them up for you." She dialed. It rang once, then again an eternity later. Toby leaned his ear close to the receiver. There was a click.

"Hello?"

"Iago?"

"Yeah."

"It's July."

"July," his voice intoned with interest. "I heard you found a new dad to spend the holidays with."

Toby bit his lip and raised his eyebrows, July cringed and sighed.

"Oh, shut up. Why are you at home, anyway? Don't you have your own life?"

"I'm over for dinner. My apartment is close by and I don't want to cook and Dad's making leg of something that's not takeout."

"Put Mom and Dad on the phone."

"You know I was worried about bringing home my tattooed girlfriend, but you really took the heat off."

"Just put them on."

"Ansel could probably bring home a vegan stripper without so much as a raised eyebrow. He should be thanking you, too."

"Iago—"

"Hang on, hang on." Far away he said, "She wants to talk to you guys."

Her father grumbled something garbled in the background. A moment later, there was another click.

"Hello, July," said her mother briskly.

"Yup," said her father.

"Hi," started July. "Listen, I know you're mad, but, well, Toby thought it might be helpful if you heard from him, so here he is."

She didn't allow time to hear their reactions as she shoved the phone at Toby. He put it to his ear, and July leaned close to listen in.

"Hello Mr. and Mrs. Van Buren."

There was a pause. July could imagine her parents exchanging glances of unknowing discomfort.

"Hi," she heard her mother say tentatively.

Toby cleared his throat.

"Mr. and Mrs. Van Buren, I just wanted to, um, to reassure you as best I could." He sounded like a doctor trying to comfort the family of someone in the ER.

"Sir," interrupted her father. "You do know that my daughter is only twenty-two, don't you?"

Toby cleared his throat again, "Uh, yes sir. I do."

"And you are how old?"

"Forty-three," Toby begrudged.

"And you don't think that's a little inappropriate?"

"Well sir, you've raised a wonderful daughter. July is very mature, and, well, I rarely notice the age difference when we're together."

"And you think it's okay to just whisk her around the world during the holidays?" cried her mother. "You are clearly taking advantage of her!"

"No, no I'm not. July is coming of her own accord, on her own terms."

Her mother huffed, "How dare you. I –I—"

"Mrs. Van Buren, I know this is unconventional, but we care for each other. We enjoy each other's company, and I feel quite privileged to be there with her. There's no one I'd rather go with. And this will be good for her. I think your daughter was born for travel."

"Born for travel!" shouted her mother. "What would you know about her birth? I'll tell you about her birth! I know her best, *me!* July should be at home with her family over the holidays. She should be with someone her own age, and she should be content to make her life where she started it! Families stay together! That's how life works!"

"Well, I think July feels very differently."

"How would you feel if I dated *your* daughter?" shot her father.

"Uh, well, sir, my oldest daughter is ten. I would have you arrested."

"You know what I mean. Have you stopped to think about how *you* would feel?"

"Well, yes sir, that's why I called, I thought it might ease your mind a bit."

"Oh it might? It would ease my mind to talk to the virtual pedophile who's taking my daughter to a foreign country? What do you know about Italy? What do you know about Florence? Is this just some lavish whim you're pulling to … to … to influence my daughter?"

"Actually, I've been to Florence five times."

"Five times? Really?" her father's tone turned to curiosity. "You must have a lot of experience with the Florentine steak."

Toby turned and looked at July quizzically. She rolled her eyes in response.

"Well, yes. You can't find a steak like that here."

"Quite right, quite right. Well I've never been to Florence myself, but I've heard, and I've sampled the *Bistecca Fiorentina* at various trattorias stateside."

"Gray! This is not about food!"

"Well at least she's not jetting off with some vegetarian! That would be worse. Those middle-aged vegetarians are a nutty bunch."

"Oh, Gray."

"Well fine then, Jill, if you want me to get serious I will. What exactly are your intentions here, Toby? Where, other than Italy, is this going?"

"Uh, well …"

July looked at Toby. This she was interested in.

"Well, sir, I don't really know. I don't think you can ever really know what's going to happen."

"I see. So you don't know what you want from my daughter, but you're willing to take her halfway around the world."

"I think that what you want from a person changes daily, and you can never *really* know what you'll want for the future. You can get a better and better idea as you spend more time together, and that's what we're doing."

July supposed that was mostly true. She didn't know what she wanted from Toby either, or what her intentions were with him. Toby had once thought he knew what his intentions were with Jenny, but even those had changed. So why did she still feel slightly disappointed?

There was a silence. Toby turned to July and shrugged his eyebrows.

"Toby, you also have children," her mother ventured coldly.

"Yes, three daughters. They're ten, eight, and four."

"And why are you abandoning them at Christmas? Don't you feel that children should be with their families?"

"Well yes I do, but you see my ... ex-wife has requested that she take the children to her parents' house out of state. So it's not by choice that I won't be with them. I'll miss them a lot."

I'm just a second choice, thought July. Of course. She would worry if his daughters *didn't* come first. But part of her still wanted to be at the top of the list. *At least I'm on the list.*

"Oh that's awful," said her mother. "Why would a mother ever deprive her children of their father? Goodness, I can't imagine becoming a single parent after so long."

"It's nearly impossible," Toby replied. "Those girls keep me running. We always need to be three places at once and there's no more tag-teaming anymore."

"I remember when ours were young—July was seven and her brothers were nine and ten. No rest for the weary," said her mom sympathetically.

"Honey, do you remember that time when July had that bathroom issue during school and I had to go get her and bring her home instead of picking up the boys, and then you had to pick up the boys and then we had to stagger going back to work to finish things up?"

Toby looked over at July and mouthed *bathroom issue?*

Oh God. July wanted to hide under the couch.

"Dad! Stop it!" she said loudly into the phone.

"Oh now, July."

"No, this is weird. This conversation is over."

"Good bye, Mr. and Mrs. Van Buren. Happy Holidays."

"Well it won't be so nice with July off jet-setting. I just don't understand why you'd need to go all that way when you can have a perfectly lovely time at home. All that time and money and strangeness—"

"Good bye, Mom."

Toby ceded control of the phone and July hung it up.

She sighed and rubbed her hand over her face.

"Why did you do that?" she asked.

"I think it helped," said Toby.

They sat for a moment in the ochre vibes of the lamp.

"I guess that was a little surreal, huh?" he said.

"Yeah."

"Your dad's a little preoccupied with food."

July snorted, "That's an understatement. I think he uses it as a distraction or something."

He leaned over and hugged her, and she buried her face in the groove where his neck met his shoulders. He was warm and solid.

What if the phone call had changed his perception of her? Of course her parents had deliberately tried to appeal to him as a parent, to make him think of her more like a child than as a girlfriend.

But then Toby readjusted his head and kissed her on the mouth in a way a father wouldn't, eroding a layer of her fears. He gently pushed her so that she reclined along the sofa and shifted on top of her.

"Daddy?" came a small voice from the darkness.

July snapped her eyes open and froze, frantically awaiting Toby's reaction. He stiffened and jerked his head over the top of the sofa.

"Gracie?"

"What are you doing, Daddy? Who's that?"

Toby hesitated for a moment. "It's my friend. What are you doing out of bed, Gracie?"

"I can't go back to sleep."

Toby and July looked at each other in a slice of time, the shared sheepishness of being caught. Toby got up and walked around the couch, and July stayed prone, pressing herself further into the cushions, willing herself not to be noticed.

"You can't sleep? Do you want Daddy to tuck you in?"

"Uh huh."

Toby stooped and picked her up and carried her away, disappearing into the darkness.

"Come on, Daddy's here."

July sat up, alone on the couch marooned in an island of light. Should she go, or wait? She felt like an invader, like she had somehow taken Toby from his daughters, and a wave of foolishness came over her. She fiddled with a throw pillow. *Does he have room for me in his life? Do I belong here? Is he ashamed?*

Toby still hadn't come downstairs. He might never come down, and then July would fall asleep on the couch and be discovered in the morning, either by Toby or by one of his daughters, and then she would feel even more foolish, and then he would feel foolish and have to explain her away. It was time to leave.

July stood and waded off the island of light, groping her way through the sea of black and back into the cold that stung like a thousand bees.

Toby and Grace lay side by side, her bed wide enough so that Toby could lie on his back and just keep from falling off. When he had stirred to go back down to July, Grace had muttered, "No Daddy, don't go."

So he stayed. Only moments later, he heard the front door open and close. He wished he could have gone back down and held her and kissed her goodnight. In his fantasy he wished she could have stayed the night, stayed warm in his bed next to him instead of fighting the vicious late night blades of cold.

There are too many females in my life, he thought, *a blessing and a curse.*

As he drifted into the warm suspension of sleep, he thought of July's parents, and how even though they must resent him, they had still formed the common parent bond. How surreal that the parents of his girlfriend were also his peers, and may understand parts of his life much better than July would. Just before he slipped into the exhale of sleep, he envisioned July trudging away, alone and cold, through the snow of the day-abandoned world.

IX

IT WAS WEDNESDAY. IT WAS HIS DAY OF EMANCIPATION. THE LONG and bloody battle would come to an end. He could feel the sandbags that had encumbered him for so long begin to slide toward the ground.

He had awoken much earlier than usual. It was dark, the girls were still asleep, but anticipation was gnawing at his stomach, and he knew he wouldn't be able to sleep any longer. So he got up and went down to the kitchen to make himself some coffee.

He stood in the dark kitchen. The coffee pot gurgled.

Toby thought about the house, which he had bought for his family with the money he made selling houses to other people. He thought about the master bedroom with a balcony where he could stand and watch the girls play in the back yard; about the entrance hall with the wall perfectly suited for family photographs; about the purple stripe he painted where the ceiling met the wall in Sophia's room, because purple was her favorite color; and about his favorite spot, the brick fireplace, where he had roasted marshmallows with the girls and hosted romantic evenings with Jenny. He thought about Jenny and the girls living there without him. It was almost as though he had died and they had moved on in his absence.

Today he was about to forfeit any claim he had ever had on that house. His house.

He glanced at the sink, or the darkness covering it, and remembered the two-day old pan soaking beneath it. The egg was hard to get off.

After he took the girls to school on Monday he'd had July over for breakfast. Since the conversation with her parents the week prior, July had been a bit cool in texts and on the phone, and he had the suspicion that he had blown it, whatever it was. He decided that making breakfast was the best way to atone and, in so doing, figure out what he was atoning for. Pancakes weren't right for the mood, so he settled for omelets, since they seemed more suited to the serious questions she posed that morning, like, "Where do I fit into your life?"

Though he hadn't forgotten how women over think things, he'd forgotten how much that applied to relationships. This discussion was better suited for quiche. He told her as much, wondering how she'd respond.

"Yes," she said. "Crusts give everything a more serious tone."

"Well, you'll have to do with my crusty old age instead," he replied.

She had laughed like a wind chime.

Now he stood sipping coffee in the dark, the kitchen illuminated only by the green digital clock on the microwave. Today was the day he had feared, dreaded, wished for. Today he would negate seventeen years of his life. That long ago glass of wine had been a mistake.

When he married Jenny and had children, his life had done a one-eighty, but now he was back where he started.

It had snowed overnight, and Toby heard a plow a block or two over. He was glad his marriage was ending when everything was cold and dead. If it had been summer, it would have proven harder to brood in the warmth and sunshine. This way, he could build a new life right along with the world.

It was time to wake the girls, which meant a flurry of shirts and pants and hats and boots and sugary carbs and excuses and backpacks, missing socks and I don't wannas! Before he knew it, he was alone in the car, driving away from the elementary school towards Jenny's lawyer's office. He was twitchy and nervous. He had to turn off the radio because it seemed like it was nagging him for attention. Next to his wedding day, this was probably the most important day of his life, but this time there was no party.

He arrived at the law office ten minutes early, but drove past. It was probably bad form to look too eager on your divorce day. Plus, Jenny's car wasn't there yet. He didn't want to arrive first.

So he drove around the adjacent neighborhood, past the white houses distinguished by the colors of their doors and window shutters. He used to live in a house like that, with a family.

Families stay together! That's how life works! July's mother had said that to him last week. So his life didn't work.

Life works, that's how families stay together. And then your life stops working.

In the years before they separated, Toby had reassured himself he could fix this. He was the broken part. If he could just love her again, the machine would be back in working order. But he couldn't do it. His love had been buried beneath the fights and the yelling, heaped beneath insults and crushed into a thin film of memory.

When Jenny had kicked him out, he realized that maybe he wasn't the only broken part of a machine. At first he thought maybe she was looking for a new machine.

"No, there's no one else," she had said that night. But she didn't look at him, she said it the way someone gives a white lie to get you to shut up and move on already. She wanted him gone.

"Toby."

He had been taking off one of his shoes, ready to change into his pajamas after putting the girls to bed. It had been a long day, he was tired, but something in her voice stopped him. He stood beside the bed, one shoe on, one shoe off, and looked at Jenny, already in her pajamas, her arms crossed.

"Toby," she said again.

"What?" he stood up straight and turned his body towards her.

"I …" she sighed heavily. She was psyching herself up.

His mind ran through the possibilities. Not pregnant, it had been awhile. Was she sick? Apologizing? And then she bit her lower lip, cocked her head, and looked down.

Oh my God, she's leaving me. Oh shit.

Finally.

"I want you to leave."

"Leave?" She wasn't leaving him—she was requesting his resignation.

"I think you should leave. I think we should—I want a divorce." She was still looking at the carpet. She couldn't even look him in the eye.

"Why?"

"I want a divorce, and I want you to leave now."

"Now? Why don't you leave? You want this."

"Don't be ridiculous," she scoffed, then rolled her eyes and looked into his. "You want this too."

He kind of did, but he tried not to acknowledge that he was the kind of man who toyed with the idea of walking out on his family. It wasn't one of those daydreams where he fantasized about some of the fun things he would do, like see a movie without anyone talking to him or eat some exotic meal or watch TV naked. It had gone beyond that, into looking at apartments for rent, reading up on divorce laws, and even Googling "How to Leave Your Wife." If she hadn't done it first, he probably would have gotten the nerve. Eventually.

He tried not to concede that part of him that was relieved, grateful even, that he was getting out. How could any decent human being be happy that something had turned his family into a broken home? He needed to cling to hating Jenny; if he hated himself too, he might not make it out the other end. For some reason, he chose to be obstinate.

"Why? Why now? After all these years, why now?"

They hadn't fought for a week. Actually, they hadn't spoken in a week, since that huge scene. It wasn't a surprise, but it was.

She looked back to the carpet, "I don't want to be married to you anymore."

Then she looked back at him with anticipation, fear. Did she think he was going to yell? Hit her? Cry?

Instead, he went numb. In all the times he had imagined this scenario, he had been the one doing the breaking. She would cry a little, then become belligerent, then cry again, and he would walk out quietly with his suitcase full of guilt and turn into the middle-aged guy who leaves his wife just before she turns forty.

He wanted to prod further, insist that she be the one to leave since she brought it up. But he didn't really want to have to wake the girls in the morning and explain to them why Mommy left. Not that it was much better to have Mommy do the explaining; who knows what she might say.

"What will you tell the girls?"

"I don't know yet."

"Good to see you've considered them."

"Toby. Just leave."

She looked over by the closet. Toby followed her gaze and noticed that she had taken out his suitcase and placed it preemptively on his side of the closet.

"Did you pack it, too?"

She sighed impatiently, percolating with resentment.

He unzipped the suitcase and threw in whatever was in reach. He crouched to zip it back up, then stood and looked back at Jenny. All this because one night, lives ago, she had been alone and beautiful and he had sent her a drink. He had gone to her graduation. He had bought tampons for this woman, watched their children come out of her body, told her his secrets and fears—she had held him as he cried like a baby in the hospital after they and their two daughters had been in a car accident that was his fault.

"Is there someone else?"

"No there's no one else," she said quickly, like she had practiced saying that in front of the mirror all day.

Toby walked in Jenny's general direction back to where he had been standing.

"Toby, please just go," she said, but this time there was a note of fear, alarm, dread. He knew she was thinking about all those episodes of *Law and Order* that she watched, a man enraged, a crime of passion.

"Jenny, I'm just getting my shoe," he said, holding up a socked foot as proof. He sat on the bed and put on his shoe.

But her guard was up now. Her eyes kept shifting behind her into the bathroom. What did she have in there?

Toby stood and walked towards the bathroom.

"Toothbrush," he said.

As he was reaching into the medicine cabinet for his toothpaste and vitamins, he saw it in the corner, resting against the laundry basket. A baseball bat. A shiver ran down his throat.

"A baseball bat?" he said. "Really, Jenny. Who do you think you're married to, OJ Simpson?"

Then she finally lost it, breaking down in tears. Half of him wanted to comfort her, hold her and tell her it was all right. But it wasn't. He moved over so he could see her through the door. For a few minutes, he just watched her cry. She had never been a particularly pretty crier. Her face was red, her nose running, her face slimy from snot and tears. Finally he walked over to her, shifted his toiletries to one hand, and put the other gently on the side of her arm.

"When have I ever given you reason to fear me?"

This just made her cry harder.

"Please just go," she said, heaving between sobs. "Just *go*."

He closed everything into his suitcase, then stood it upright and looked at her. She was a mess, and she knew it. Ironically, she wanted him to comfort her, assure her it was all right that she was telling him to leave his family. He could practically hear her think, *Are you really going to leave me here like this?*

Yes.

He walked out of their room, through the hall, down the stairs, the wheels of his suitcase thudding dully as he descended each carpeted stair. He wanted to kiss his daughters goodbye, but knew he would never be able to leave if he saw them.

It wasn't until he had backed out of the driveway and reached the stop sign at the end of the street that he felt his heart break open. He put his head against the steering wheel and cried, sobbing and idling for almost half an hour in front of the stop sign at Cross Street and Martling Avenue.

He had circled the law office three times now and he was coming up on it again. He looked at the clock. Now he was three minutes late. Probably not a good idea to be really late, either.

He pulled into the parking lot, got out of his car, and walked into the building. His lawyer, Howard Rockman, a short man who looked like his suit had been dripped over him, was waiting in the lobby.

"Toby," he said. "Nice to see you."

"Hi there, Howard. How are you?"

"Fine, thanks. How are you holding up?"

"Oh, you know …" said Toby, though he didn't know himself.

Howard smiled sympathetically.

"Well, now that you're here we can go back to the conference room. I believe they're waiting."

Toby followed Howard back through the corridors of cubicles and windowed offices, and led him into a conference room. There was a long shiny table like a wooden mirror. One entire wall was a bookcase stuffed with law books to provide the official comfort of legality.

Jenny and her lawyer were already sitting at the table, conversing over one of its corners. They looked up as Toby and Howard walked in.

"Hello, gentlemen," said Jenny's lawyer, a woman in her late fifties with graying short curly hair and a thick New York accent. She wore a dowdy black skirt suit that bunched in all the wrong places.

"Hello," replied Howard.

Toby sat across from Jenny. She had pulled her hair back into a bun, revealing her ears, in which sat a pair of silver knot earrings that Toby was pretty sure he had given her as a gift on some holiday. Had she forgotten that he gave those to her? Or was she just trying to stick it to him? Thank God she made almost as much money as he did; otherwise she probably would have sucked him dry and taken his viscera, too. She had all ready done enough, and Lord knows the child support payments weren't insubstantial.

"Hi, Jenny," he said.

"Hello, Toby," she replied. Her tone was cold, but she sounded smug, like her team was about to score the winning point and he just didn't know it yet.

Toby still didn't understand from where her hatred of him had stemmed. It was as though through the sheer act of loving her, he had seized her like Snidely Whiplash and absconded with her into the night, forcing her to be his bride, to bear his children. He done her wrong.

He had tried to ask her many times why. "I understand falling out of love," he had said, "but I don't understand why that love has turned to hate."

She looked at him, her eyes cold, trying to ward him off. But he just kept looking at her, and her eyes would get softer and softer, until the hate had given way to an intense sadness.

"What is it?" he would ask, and she would just look away and slam the door.

One day he had gone back to their house to pick up the girls, but they weren't home yet. It was the time of year just before summer, before the warmth became oppressive and smothered the beauty of green in a fog of heat. She didn't ask him in. So he stood on the front stoop and asked her again, why?

This time, when the anger funneled into sadness, she did not look away. She clung to the half-open door like a scared child. Leaning against the door's edge, she swung back and forth, open and closed.

"You still don't know?" she said, like he was supposed to have guessed, a soul detective piecing it together.

He shook his head.

She sighed, "Do you remember the time, before we had Grace, when my parents came to visit? Just before we took the girls to Florence?"

He remembered.

"The first night they were here, the two of us had a huge fight because I had written out an itinerary and planned our days so that we could be prepared with the girls, and you insisted—you *insisted*—that we did *not* need an itinerary and that travel was about going with the flow even though we were traveling with two small children and some places don't have the right accommodations for them."

Toby, on the doorstep, recalled the fight. It had not been one of his shining moments.

"It got to the point where we weren't even arguing about the trip anymore. Suddenly it was about how you thought that things just happened, that life will always accommodate you and you won't think things through *even though* things had gone wrong because you refused to plan for them. Like when you bought that fucking *couch* before you even *measured* the room *or* the doorway and when it was delivered they couldn't get it in and you thought it was no big deal because you could return it only you didn't think to make sure that the couch could *be* returned and, lo and behold, the store was snotty and artistic and you couldn't return it and the couch cost four thousand *fucking* dollars. Who spends that on a *couch?*"

It was a very comfortable couch, he thought. "That's why you hate me? Because I made a stupid impulse purchase?"

"No. That's not why. But when we were fighting I brought up the couch, and I said, you just don't get that things go wrong when you don't think them through. And you said, yeah, I realized that after I married you."

Toby suddenly felt as though all the neighbors were looking out their windows at him. He remembered. He had tried to forget, but it was one of those moments your brain won't let you forget, when you do something so stupid that the proper punishment is the eternal cycle of self-shame and humiliation.

"I was angry," he said. "I wasn't thinking. I didn't mean it."

He had thought he didn't mean it, that it was just one of those things you say when you're angry and want to hurt the person you're fighting with. But when he looked back on it, knowing what came after, he thought maybe he *had* meant it.

"But you did mean it," she said. "We know *that* wasn't the deadly blow. But I saw things differently after that. I tried to think you didn't mean it. But that sentence was like … like taking a blindfold off my eyes. Suddenly I saw the ways you tried to avoid me, the ways you belittled me and made me feel like nothing."

"Me? That's what *you* were doing to *me!*"

"I could see your regret, Toby. It's like it was tattooed on your eyes."

Toby couldn't recall what happened after that. His mind skipped forward like a scratched DVD.

"Well," said Howard, "this is pretty straightforward, so let's get started. I believe you have the papers, Robin?"

"Yes," replied Jenny's lawyer. The papers were already out, stacked and perfectly aligned. Robin pushed the set of papers over to Howard. "I've highlighted every spot you two need to sign," she continued. "Jenny, once you've signed everything, just pass them to Toby, and then you're done."

Howard took the papers, gave them the once-over and nodded, sliding them to Jenny.

Jenny had a pen ready and got to work on her first signature. Her pen made a low scratching sound against the table, whoosh whoosh. As Toby watched her sign, he remembered all the programs she signed after performances, mostly for little girls who took ballet and watched her dance. Was this like another program for her? Was it just another autograph?

She slid the first paper across the table to Toby. They had played air hockey once with Chloe and Sophia, Toby guiding Sophia's hands, Jenny guiding Chloe's.

Toby looked at the papers. They were peppered with Roman numerals and the word "Party." This was not a party. On the bottom of the paper, below Jenny's swoopy signature, was a highlighted X and a line.

Toby looked back at Jenny, at her earlobe and the earring that twinkled slightly as her arm swooped her name across the paper. That earring. It had been an anniversary gift, right? *That bitch, how dare she.* His esophagus burned. He remembered now—he had given her those a few months after Chloe had been born. He remembered picking them out, pleased with himself and sure that they would get him laid that night. The look on her face when she opened the box, how the corners of her eyes had relaxed and how her thin lips had smiled and suddenly her whole face turned soft, and he could tell that she felt beautiful again after months of an agonizing pregnancy, nearly two days of birthing, and a month of recovery and breast feeding and a crying baby. The earrings had brought back that look of love and appreciation that had disappeared beneath the stress.

"Didn't I give you those earrings?" he found himself saying as she passed him the next paper.

Jenny frowned, annoyed, and touched her earrings with her free hand. "Did you?" She shrugged and looked at her lawyer. She bent her head, trying to hide the furrow that had burrowed between her brows. She twirled a piece of hair towards the back of her neck. It was her guilty tell. Whenever she did that, Toby knew something was up. She had done it the time she put a dent in his car.

Toby looked back at his papers and signed. It didn't feel any different than signing a credit card receipt. He signed the next one. And the next one, and then he was looking at himself in the table. He had signed them all.

He looked up and saw that Jenny was fiddling with one of her earrings.

"Well, then," said Robin, who took the papers and slipped them into her bag.

That was it?

Everyone stood up. Was he supposed to say something? Were they?

"Well then. That's it," said Howard. "We'll take it from here."

Jenny and Robin started walking out of the room.

"Jenny," said Toby.

She looked at him and froze, sitting on the edge of the fear that he would say something that would ruin what they had just done.

"Uh, I … uh, realized this morning that my passport is still at your house. In the safe. Could you … could you uh, bring it on Friday when you come pick up the girls? Please?"

"Sure," she said quickly and noncommittally. "I'll be there right after school, around three."

She turned and walked out.

Toby remained standing where he was, feeling like an actor who had missed his exit cue.

"Toby," said Howard. "It's been a pleasure working with you. Best of luck."

Howard extended his right hand.

"Oh. Right, thanks," he said, and shook Howard's hand.

Yes, he thought. *It's been a pleasure getting divorced with you.*

"Take care now," said Howard, and picked up his briefcase. "You'll get your final bill in the next few days, after I give you the rest of the documents you need."

Howard stood for a moment, as if Toby might respond, then walked out of the conference room with Robin.

Toby looked at the phone on the mirror table. Nine forty-three a.m. Just ten minutes ago, he was married. He looked at his left hand. He hadn't worn his wedding ring for two years, but its absence seemed more pronounced now.

He combed through his insides, trying to figure out exactly how he felt. Sad angry lonely happy liberated relieved? No. He felt like he had just played a long game of high-stakes poker. First he had been up, then down, and now he was walking away down from what he'd started with.

X

I'm not dating a married man anymore. JULY WAS SITTING ON HER BED
eating Honey Nut Cheerios from a box. It was ten twenty-three a.m.,
and if all went according to plan, he was divorced.

Unless, as their pens hovered over the empty lines, Toby and Jenny
suddenly realized they were making a huge mistake. About to sign,
they both simultaneously look up and lock eyes. They hold the gaze for
a moment, and then one of them blurts, "I'm so sorry! I love you!"

They stand up and somehow the table between them disappears
and they're kissing and crying and saying, "I can't believe we almost
did that!"

Toby would never call again, and Jenny would go to Florence
instead of July, who would never see him again.

Shut up, July, she thought, shoving a handful of cereal in her mouth,
trying to drown out her thoughts with crunching. Now that her paper
was done, she had nothing academic to use as a distraction. She had
two days to simmer and nothing to do.

Outside her window, the world had blended behind a mist of fresh
flurries. If the world flipped upside down, it would look no different. It
was like everything had been sealed in a soundproof room, the quiet of
snow seeping through the walls, draped over everything like a blanket.

Well she sure as hell wasn't going outside. July started to check her
email, and then her phone rang. Toby! Her heart leapt. Where was

her phone? She stood quickly and jerked her head trying to find the source of sound.

Come on, come on, come on, where are you?

She fumbled around her desk and found her phone beneath a magazine. Without even looking at the number on the screen, she answered the call.

"Hello?" she said breathlessly.

"Hi ... July?"

July's heart flew up her throat and out her mouth. That familiar smooth voice she thought she heard sometimes, hoped to hear, but always turned out to be someone else's voice.

For a moment, she couldn't push the words out. "...James?"

"Hey. How are you?"

"I'm—good. How are you?"

"Yeah, I'm doin' pretty good. It's been awhile."

"Yeah," she said. "It's been a long time."

"So ... I hope this isn't a bad time. It's just—well, I'm at La Guardia and I have like an hour before my flight and I was like, I should call someone. And I was looking through my contact list and I saw your name and I thought, hey, I haven't talked to July for a while, and then ... I called."

"I'm surprised you still have my number," she said. When he didn't respond, she continued. "The airport? Where are you going?"

"Oh! I'm going home. For Christmas, you know. For the first time in like two years."

"Yeah, I thought you always went with your girlfriend."

"Yeah, yeah. Well, I mean, we, um, we broke up. Like a month ago."

"Oh." Somewhere on the floor, July's heart did a flip, "Oh, that's too bad. What happened?"

"Yeah, well, you know, she ... decided I didn't like, factor in to her life plan and stuff. Which she decided to tell me by sleeping with some frat guy. After two and a half years with me."

"Classy," said July, feeling just a bit smug.

"You have a boyfriend, right? Chris?"

"Oh, yeah. We broke up, too. We broke up in like September."

"Oh! It's an epidemic, I guess."

"Yeah. But he didn't sleep with a frat guy. At least not to my knowledge."

James chuckled uncomfortably.

There was a pause as they waited for the other to say something.

"So!" James started again, "So, um, are you like, going to be home over the holidays? I'd love to catch up, you know, if you ... want."

Why couldn't this have happened last year? thought July. Chris would have been so much easier to disregard than Toby. She had been dying to see James for years. Each time he came into her dreams he was a little more nebulous, more of an idea, a feeling, than a being. But now, well. She couldn't forget Toby as easily as she could Chris.

"Oh, no. I mean, I would like to. But actually I'm not coming home this year."

"Really?" said Chris in genuine surprise. "Where are you going?"

"I'm, um. I'm going to Italy. Florence. For a few weeks."

"Are your parents okay with that?"

"Uh, well, they're not. But it's a little out of their hands."

"Oh," said James, his voice falling a bit. "Well, that's too bad. I haven't seen you in ... so long."

"Yeah."

"So ... um. What's new?"

For half an hour, James and July recapped the last few years of their lives. He had spent a semester in Japan, played varsity tennis, hit a deer with his car one night last year. July's heart remained gasping and flopping on the ground the entire time, and realized she hadn't mentioned Toby at all when James said, "I should probably go now, I think my flight is boarding in a minute."

"Right," said July, but she didn't believe him.

"Look it was really good to talk to you," he said.

"Yeah, you too. Thanks for calling."

"Yeah, sure. Well, I mean, if you're ever in New York give me a call."

"Same with you, if you're ever around here."

"Right. Merry Christmas."

"Merry Christmas."

They sat silent for a moment, and July wondered what it was he'd really wanted to say.

"Bye, July."

"Bye, James."

After a moment the line went dead, and July set down her phone.

Shit. Whoever was in charge of timing seemed to have hit the snooze button on this one.

July stood still, looking vacantly out the window. The last time she had seen James had been in front of his house, in the hazy early morning summer light. His father put James' bags in the car, his mother was in the house closing windows and locking doors. James and July stood off behind a tree. His hands were in his pockets. She stared at his gray tennis team T-shirt. And then she was driving herself home through a blurry curtain of tears.

July snapped back to life and looked at the box of cereal on her bed. She picked it up and started eating, crunching and crunching to distract from the penetrating, earsplitting silence bombarding her from all directions.

Toby sent her a text message just before noon, "Its official i have three showings before fri plus lots of stuff w the girls so will talk to you fri cant wait thinking of you."

For the next two days, July tried to distract herself from counting down until Friday afternoon at four. She tried watching movies with friends, eating meals with them, reading books, cleaning—anything to coax time, but she always found herself searching for the clock, counting backwards from Friday. Forty hours, thirty-two hours, eighteen hours. She tried to sleep as late as possible on Friday, but found herself triple-espresso awake just after six. Though she hadn't allowed herself to pack until Friday, she had thought about packing so many times that she finished packing in under half an hour. Friday seemed to go slower than both Wednesday and Thursday combined.

Finally, quarter to four rolled around. It was the earliest time she allowed herself to leave, though she tried to dawdle as much as possible. She didn't want to arrive early, but she couldn't help herself, and two hour-long minutes later, she was maneuvering her rolling suitcase down the stairway.

Dragging the suitcase to Toby's proved to be more difficult than she thought. The roads had been plowed that morning, but a fresh dusting of snow had slicked the walkways, and the cleared paths were barely wide enough for her suitcase, which was soon bracketed with wet, snowy corners.

Together July and her suitcase clacked off campus, the wheels rhythmic and repetitive as they passed over cracks and crags in the sidewalk. July was probably cold, but she all she could think of was Toby's face at the door, their weekend together, Florence draping over the horizon.

When July at last arrived at Toby's, it was just after four. Perfect timing. She dragged her suitcase, the bottom lined in a rim of snow moustache, up to the porch and knocked on the door.

Moments later, she heard footsteps. Her heart beat faster. This would be the first time she saw Toby as an unmarried man. She was entering into time that was theirs alone, that would remain insulated from school and kids and parents and exes.

The door flew open and there was Toby. July smiled and opened her mouth but Toby spoke first.

"The girls are here," he said quickly. He looked frazzled.

"What?"

"Jenny's running late. The girls are still here."

"Oh. That's okay."

"She was supposed to be here and gone already."

"Toby, it's okay," repeated July. "It's really cold, can I come in?"

Toby hesitated for a moment, but smiled and said, "Of course."

July slid into the entryway, knocking snow off her boots and suitcase. After removing her boots, she moved her suitcase near the bottom of the stairs, careful to leave it on the tiled section of the floor so that melting snow wouldn't get on the carpet.

"You don't have to meet her if you don't want to."

"Relax, Toby. We're all adults, right?"

He ran a hand through his hair and led the way into the house.

The girls, all three varying degrees of blonde, were sitting at the table in the kitchen. The oldest one was reading a book while the younger two were watching TV.

The one July guessed to be Sophia looked up and smiled.

"Hi!" she said.

"Hi," July replied tentatively.

"Are you Daddy's friend?"

"Sophia, this is my friend July," said Toby, taking the lead. "And that's Grace next to Sophia, and Chloe is reading."

"Hi," July repeated.

"Do you want to watch TV with us?" asked Sophia.

"Um, okay," answered July. She walked to the table and sat next to Grace, who had the blondest hair, but her cheeks were fuller than those of the other girls, and her dark eyes had a penetrating twinkle. Grace looked as though she might get up and flutter around the room like a butterfly at any moment. In front of her she had a plate of peanut butter, which she was eating with a popsicle stick. The girls were watching some cartoon that July didn't recognize.

"What are you watching?" July asked Grace.

"*Go Diego Go!*" Grace replied.

"That's Diego, and that's Alicia," said Sophia knowledgeably and pointing at the screen.

"Wow," said July. "I've never even heard of this show before."

"Can I have some more peanut butter?" asked Grace, looking straight at July.

July turned around to look at Toby, who nodded.

"Sure," she said, standing up. "Do you want some milk, too? I always like milk with my peanut butter."

"Okay," said Grace.

July headed to the kitchen to where the peanut butter jar sat open. She scooped some onto the plate and poured her a glass of milk.

"You don't like jelly with peanut butter?" asked July.

"Daddy doesn't have any jelly."

July looked in a cupboard over the stove and saw honey.

"You know what's yummy? Peanut butter and honey."

Grace frowned.

"Do you want to try a little bit? Just a little?"

"Okay."

July put a little dab of honey on top of a part of the peanut butter. Grace scooped it up with the stick.

"Yum!" she said.

"You like it?"

"Yeah."

"Do you want more?"

"Yeah."

Toby stood next to the table and motioned to July to follow him. She did, and followed him around the corner to the staircase.

"I'm going out front to wait for Jenny, let her know that you're here before she comes inside. I don't want her creating a scene in front of the girls."

"Oh, right, okay," said July. "You don't want me to like, hide in the bathroom?"

"No, nothing like that," said Toby, smirking. He kissed her on the cheek, then headed for the front hall. A minute later, she heard the door open and close.

"Where's Daddy going?" asked Chloe.

"He just went out to wait for your mom," said July.

"Why?"

July was about to make something up when she heard the back door open behind her. Confused, she turned around and found herself looking at another blonde. It was Jenny.

July froze.

Oh God oh God oh God. For all the confidence she'd projected about all being adults, this was worse than Chris and Toby. July felt hot all over. Jenny, clearly the genetic baseline for her daughters, was a nice looking woman made more attractive by careful grooming. Her hair fell over her shoulders, curling a bit at the bottom. She wore a tailored collared shirt and expensive looking jeans, but she stood as though she were wearing sweats. July noticed that her fingers were manicured, painted in a chic dark purple. July suddenly felt like the dowdy one in the room, even though Jenny had nearly two decades on her. *Be a grown up*, she reminded herself. *Be mature about this.*

"Hi girls," called Jenny. "Oh! Hi," she said, looking at July. "And you are …?"

"I'm July," she replied a bit weakly.

"Where's Toby?"

"He's—out front. Waiting for you."

Jenny frowned, "Why would he be waiting for me outside?"

July could not reply. All she could think of was to shrug.

"I'm sorry, who are you?"

"July."

"Are you a student at the university?" asked Jenny.

"Yeah."

Jenny raised her eyebrows, clearly waiting for further explanation. When she didn't get it, she said, "I didn't realize Toby had a sitter." Jenny smiled, "Let alone such a pretty sitter."

"Oh, I'm not the –"

"Well, I'm sorry I'm late. One of my classes ran over. Girls! Come on, let's go upstairs and get your things!"

Jenny swept past July, turned off the television, and ushered the girls out of the kitchen.

"Oh!" She popped back into the kitchen, then threw something on the counter.

"Don't want to forget. I brought this for Toby."

And she bounced out of the room again.

July picked up the passport that Jenny had thrown on the counter. She opened it and saw a picture of Toby, darker hair, smoother face. He looked *so* young, though the passport had been issued seven years ago. Date of Birth: July 7, 1967. He had never mentioned his birthday was in July.

July leaned against the counter. *So that's Jenny. She seemed … nice. Friendly. Like a real person.* July knew she shouldn't be surprised about that, but her own imagination, Toby's sparse descriptions, and Google had colored her picture of Jenny. She seemed entirely different in the flesh.

Remembering Toby was still out front, she ran to the door, pulled it open, and shouted, "Toby!"

"What?" he asked, alarmed, as he wasn't three feet from the door.

"Jenny's here," July said, reducing her volume. "She came through the back."

"But she always comes through the front."

July shrugged, and he followed her hastily back inside and they returned to the kitchen.

They heard clamoring as the girls were coming down the stairs with suitcases.

"Do you girls need some help?" Toby asked as Chloe came through with her suitcase.

"I could use a hand!" called Jenny. "Grace and Sophia are just getting their coats."

A moment later Toby came in with a suitcase. Jenny followed him but stopped abruptly halfway through the kitchen door, then turned around and dragged in July's suitcase.

"Chloe, is this yours?"

"No," Chloe shook her head as she shrugged on her jacket.

"That's—mine," said July stupidly.

Jenny furrowed her brow and pursed her lips as if to ask why, but she said nothing, just held her lips like that.

"Jenny ..." started Toby, but he didn't seem to know what to say.

"Are you the ... house ... sitter?" Jenny asked, unconvinced.

"No, July is ... We've been—seeing each other."

July noted that he hadn't explained the suitcase or their impending trip.

Jenny's face expanded from its intense contraction of concentration; her brows sprang up, her mouth widened, and her eyes grew with comprehension.

"How *old* is she? Twenty?"

"Two. Twenty-two," piped July, then instantly regretted speaking.

Toby put a hand on July's shoulder. His hand said, *Don't talk. I'll handle this.*

"She's not the sitter, she's my girlfriend."

"Your girlfriend? How long has this been going on?"

"Chloe, honey, go outside please," said Toby.

Without saying anything, Chloe turned and went out the back door.

"How long has this been going on?" Jenny repeated.

"That doesn't concern you, Jenny."

"Of course it fucking *concerns* me. She's around my *kids*. What do they think of your little girlfriend here? She's young enough to be their *sister*."

"The girls just met her today."

I can't handle this, July thought. *This is too much for me. I don't understand. I don't want to get involved in this. I'm just a kid.* She wished she could curl up and hide in the oven.

"I don't want my kids around your—your little college *plaything*."

July felt like the teacher was reprimanding her in front of the entire class.

"Hey. Don't talk about July like that," said Toby forcefully. Toby would keep her safe.

"I don't believe this!" Jenny shouted. "Divorced for two days and already parading the new piece of ass around."

"Like you're one to talk, Jenny?"

"Mommy?"

Sophia appeared at the entrance to the kitchen.

Jenny turned around and softened immediately.

"Yes, honey?"

"Mom, did you bring my game?"

"Yes, sweetie, it's in the car. Are you and Grace all ready to go?"

"Almost."

Sophia turned around and walked back upstairs.

Jenny looked after Sophia for a moment, then turned back to July and Toby.

"We need to talk about this," she said to Toby sternly.

"No, Jenny, we don't. When you kicked me out and divorced me you lost the right to talk to me about my love life. You cannot weasel your controlling little nose into my life anymore!"

"Do you know what this will do to the girls, Toby?"

"Jenny, I'm their father. They're my priority. I have good judgment. July is a good person. If and when she's around them, she certainly won't do any harm."

July bit her lower lip hard. Now would be the absolute wrong time to smile even though her cheeks were yanking on the corners of her mouth. While she didn't relish the confrontation, she felt proud to be defended. Though she had never found brawling males alluring, perhaps fisticuffs would have more appeal than she'd originally considered.

"Really, Toby? And how are you going to explain to your daughters that your girlfriend could be their sister?"

"Jenny, they don't know she's my girlfriend."

"Well they have to find out sometime!"

"Christ, Jenny! It's not like we're getting married!"

"Yeah, because we know how good you are at being married."

We're not getting married? thought July. *Does he mean soon, or, like, ever?*

"Oh, like you're the marriage pro. The constant nagging, trying to discipline me. You're an insufferable bitch! You try being married to that!"

July's mouth dropped open as she turned to look at Toby. His face was red. Did he really just call Jenny a bitch?

"Look, Jenny," said Toby, forcibly calming his voice. "Please just take the girls and leave."

"Two days," said Jenny. "It's been *two days*."

She turned to July.

"This man was still married when you started dating. That's the kind of man you're with."

"Oh, come on Jenny! Don't give me this self-righteous Virgin Mary bullshit. Tom saw you all over some beefcake at Chloe's soccer game months ago. I bet I know who it was, too."

Jenny stiffened; her head jerked back and her jaw dropped open. She had no comeback—she could only look astonished.

"That—I did—not. It—it wasn't—"

Toby moved away from July's side and over to the kitchen entrance. "Sophia! Grace!" he called out of the kitchen. "It's time to go! Bring your stuff down."

July looked at Jenny. Her jaw jutted out slightly; her eyes were fixated on one spot out in front of her trying to keep from boiling over with tears of anger. Her fists clenched at her sides, her breathing stiff and controlled.

This poor woman, thought July.

Jenny looked up into July's eyes with the hardness of anger and hurt.

"Everything's a party for you, isn't it? You're in college—life isn't serious yet. Some older guy'll pay for your dinner, he's so worldly and mature, makes you feel like something special. You don't know any better."

"Get out of my house," said Toby, trying to contain his rage.

Jenny was about to respond when the girls came clattering down the stairs with their suitcases. They kept their eyes cast down, their faces sober and unsmiling.

"Come on, girls," said Jenny with feigned sweetness. "Say goodbye to Daddy."

"I'll help bring stuff out to the car," said Toby. "I'll kiss them goodbye outside."

They all walked by July, going out through the kitchen door, Toby helping with the suitcases.

"Bye, July," said Grace, waving.

July put on a smile.

"Bye, Grace. Merry Christmas."

The door closed behind them. The house reverberated with silence. July stood in the kitchen trying to collect herself. She felt like she were a large bell; someone had struck her and she was still vibrating.

She leaned against the counter and slid down a cabinet, sitting on the wood floor and staring far away. Though it was not yet five o'clock, it was nearly dark outside.

Wow, thought July. *Reality sucks.*

A few minutes later, Toby came back inside, aged since the last time he came in that door. The lines on his face seemed deeper, and the hollows under his eyes looked as though a spoon had dug into them. July suddenly felt no right to feel as she did—he had it much worse.

Toby sighed and looked at July. He came over and sat beside her on the kitchen floor. They sat, their shoulders touching, the silence crawling all over them. They stayed like that for a while—it could have been five minutes or two hours. Finally, when Jenny's grip on July's stomach had loosened, July turned to Toby.

"Toby," she said. "It's time for you to tell me what happened with you and Jenny."

He could tell it to her cut and dry, the facts as he saw them, like a sworn affidavit for a trial. But he hadn't told anyone the whole story before. His parents and friends only knew parts of it; they didn't need to know everything. July wouldn't buy it if he told only the things that made Jenny look fallible. She would wonder what he was hiding.

Sitting next to July on the kitchen floor, Toby felt the wood wearing down his butt deep into his bones. He closed his eyes and tried to picture everything that had happened, piece together the montage of his erosion of his marriage. He began to translate the memories to words.

Once upon a time ...

Toby is dressing three-year old Chloe for preschool. Jenny is nursing Sophia upstairs and they come down while Chloe is eating her breakfast.

"Toby!" Jenny says. "Chloe's clothes don't match!"

"What?"

"Her clothes! She's wearing a purple shirt with her red pants!"

"So? She wants to!"

"So! The colors clash! She can't go to school like that!"

"Why not?"

"She looks like the child of a color blind clown!"

"Jenny, we're already running late, it doesn't matter."

"You didn't do it *right*, Toby. It *does* matter."

Jenny is dragging Chloe upstairs and changing her pants, Chloe is ten minutes late for school, and Jenny holds Chloe's tardiness against him. From then on, Jenny never lets him choose clothes for any of their daughters.

Toby is loading the dishwasher.

"You aren't doing it *right*," says Jenny. "The glasses have to go on top, the bowls go here, and you haven't washed these plates first."

"If I wash them first, what's the point of having a dishwasher?"

"You have to wash them first."

"Jenny, I'm trying to help. Just let me do it."

"You're doing it *wrong*. Just let me do it."

She moves him out of the way and starts rearranging the dishwasher herself, fuming at the burden he has shouldered on her.

"You're not doing it right."

Toby comes home with a new video camera when he had gone to the store to buy batteries.

"You bought a video camera? Toby, we can't afford it."

"Yes, we can. "

"We don't need a video camera."

"Sure! This way I can take video of the girls and when they're grown, we'll have the memories."

"But Toby, we have bills this month and we need to be saving for college."

"It's six hundred dollars, Jenny, it won't matter in the long run."

"*Six hundred dollars*! Toby, you should have asked me before spending six *hundred* dollars!"

"If I had asked you, you would have said no."

"Well, yeah! The girls grow out of their shoes in weeks! The roof needs to be repaired soon! Christmas is coming up and we have to buy presents! You're being impractical!"

"I'm not being impractical—you're being a controlling dictator! I make a good living—we're not hurting!"

"We need to make sure we have enough for a rainy day! The Toyota is nine years old—what if we need a new car? What if you lose your job? What if one of the girls gets sick? Or one of us?"

"You can't live your life always wondering what if, Jenny."

"Toby, we're parents. We *have* to!"

"It's a *video camera*! It's not going to be the downfall of our family!"

Toby finds a new pair of shoes on Jenny's side of the closet soon after.

"What the fuck, Jenny? You read me the riot act with the video camera!"

"They were on sale!"

"They look like every other fucking pair of shoes you have. What happened to buying Christmas presents?"

Toby wakes up and wonders if they're going to fight today.

Toby reaches across the bed for Jenny, Jenny turns away saying, "Not tonight."

"I'm too tired."

"I don't feel well."

"No, Toby."

Toby drives below the speed limit so it takes longer to get home.

Toby takes the long way home.

Toby stays up later than usual doing work and falling asleep on the couch. And again. And again.

A pretty young woman starts working at his firm. He finds out they went to the same college, though she graduated eight years after he did. Toby sneaks out for a coffee break one day and asks if she wants anything. He remembers her drink and brings it to her once a week or so. Sometimes he takes his lunch with her. He doesn't mention her to Jenny.

"I'm pregnant," says Jenny.

They look at each other like maybe they can make this work again. Maybe this will save them.

Toby gives Jenny foot rubs. Toby cooks dinner and comes home earlier. Toby takes the girls out to putt putt golf on a Saturday so that Jenny can rest.

Toby comes home with a stuffed animal.

"We already have plenty of stuffed animals," says Jenny, her hand on her round stomach.

"I just thought—"

"We have so much left from the first two. All we need are diapers."

"But—"

"Be practical, Toby."

"It's one stuffed animal. The kid deserves its own stuffed animal."

Jenny rolls her eyes and sighs impatiently.

"Don't you know anything?"

Toby tells her he returned it, but he hides it in the trunk of his car.

A few weeks later Jenny finds it.

"What the hell, Toby?" she yells, waving the stuffed dog around, its ears flopping up and down. "I told you we don't *need* any more stuffed animals!"

"Jenny, it's a stuffed dog. Let the kid have its own toy."

"I don't understand! Why don't you ever listen to me?"

"It's a *dog*! It's not like I brought home a live pet."

Jenny throws the stuffed animal at him.

"Man, those pregnancy hormones make you a bitch."

Jenny's jaw drops open.

"What?" she roars. "The problem isn't me or my pregnancy hormones! The problem is that *you* never *listen*! You never plan! You never stop to think whether we need something. You just go out and do whatever it is you want and you never think about your family."

"That is not true!" Toby yells. He forgets the girls are upstairs. He has never yelled this loud before.

"I *always* think about my family! Those girls are the most important things to me! Everything—*everything* I do is for them! For you! The stuffed animal isn't about *you* Jenny—it's about her! Or him! Or whatever it's going to be!" he says, pointing at her stomach.

"Not everything is about *you*! I don't go through my day thinking about how to piss you off! I think about what my family needs. Do you see me out golfing every weekend? Or staying late at work? Or blowing my paycheck on cars or booze? Or fucking other women? Do I go out shopping every weekend buying shoes and clothes I don't need and hiding them in the back of the closet? NO! Don't you ever, EVER tell me I don't think about my family!"

He walks past her and up the stairs. He wants to punch or slam or break something. But he stops when he sees the closet door open. Chloe, only six, and Sophia almost four, huddle together beneath the long coats and next to the vacuum cleaner, their eyes as wide as their heads. Toby wants to cry.

Grace is born. A few weeks of tentative happiness.

Then more fights.

Toby rolls out of bed wondering not if they'll fight, but what they'll fight about.

Jenny reprises a role for one night at a benefit ballet event. Toby sees a glimpse of the girl he married, but she doesn't wait for him backstage and he doesn't see her until the reception afterwards. She doesn't talk to him much, so he spends the evening at the bar and then talking to one of her former students who is now a member of the company. Toby remembers when the girl was ten—Jenny became good friends with the girl's mother, and had them over to dinner once or twice. They have a fight off in a corner when Jenny accuses him of flirting with the young girl, who is hardly legal.

One of the male dancers comes to find Jenny for a photo, and as they walk away, Toby yells after her, "The only reason you would say that is because you're probably screwing around yourself!"

People turn to stare and she looks like she will castrate him that night in his sleep. He immediately wishes he could burrow so far into the earth that time would reverse. Something is wrong with him. He leaves early and vomits on the way to his car. He doesn't know where to go. He wants to shatter his body, destroy it, pummel his way out. He is lost in a prison cell. He wants to curl up in the smallest darkest place possible and wind so tightly around himself that he becomes a bowling ball and rolls away. He and Jenny don't speak for a week.

Toby and his pretty coworker go to Subway for lunch. As she is eating her turkey sandwich, a gob of mustard attaches itself to the corner of her mouth. She quickly puts her hand over her mouth and giggles. Toby giggles too, because he thinks it's the most beautiful thing he's seen in a long time.

That night he has a very vivid sex dream about her and thinks about her too much in the ensuing days. The only thing that happens is that their lunches get longer, and once after work, they go out for drinks. Toby lies to Jenny about whom he was with.

Jenny goes away for a weekend and Toby feels more like himself than he has in years. One night, after the girls are in bed and he is doing the dishes his way, he suddenly realizes that he doesn't love her anymore. He had fought against it as hard as he could. But with the simple, "I don't love her anymore," the door to his cell has been opened and a map put in his hands. All he needs is a compass.

And then, The Big One.

Toby and Jenny are dressed up and driving to her younger sister's wedding. Jenny is angry because Toby couldn't find his wallet and they're running late, Toby is annoyed because Jenny gave the seventeen-year-old sitter a what-to-do-if-when list more detailed than the *Magna Carta*. Jenny is the matron of honor and wears a strapless red dress. She looks nice, but Toby doesn't really care.

They get to the church with plenty of time. Toby sits in the pews and looks at the bride, Sarah, and thinks about his own wedding. He looks at Jenny, who seems wholly disengaged from the ritual. When she smiles with her mouth, her eyes double with distress.

At the reception, Toby ends up dancing with Sarah, with whom he's always been friendly. He looks at her in her white dress and veil and sees the Sivertsen glow that Jenny had the day he married her. Jenny and Sarah look similar, but today their differences couldn't be more pronounced. He looks over at Jenny, who is dancing with the groom. Now she is just another woman in a room full of strangers. He feels like an unrelated acquaintance watching from one of the dinner tables, wondering who that woman dancing with Ryan is.

Sarah and Ryan are cutting the cake. Toby and Jenny stand next to each other, looking on. Sarah smashes cake into Ryan's face, he reciprocates. Toby giggles.

"Remember when we did that?" he hears himself say to Jenny.

Jenny looks at him and rolls her eyes.

"You ruined my makeup. And my dress. That chocolate stain never came out."

"It's not like you were going to wear it again anyway."

"That's not the point, Toby," she says, her voice getting harder. "The point is that that was my wedding dress. Now our girls will never be able to wear it. It's worthless."

"I can't imagine the girls would want to wear it—those poofy things were bigger than your head."

He grins to convince her he is joking.

"What is your problem?" she says, her voice rising a little. "You never take anything seriously. You can't even take our wedding seriously!"

"What are you talking about? A dress is not a wedding."

"Even back then you had no respect for the institution of marriage."

"I'd say managing to stay married to *you* for thirteen years demonstrates *considerable* respect."

Their voices are louder than appropriate. People are turning to look at them, but Toby and Jenny don't even notice. They can't stop themselves. The cannon ball of happiness in the room displaced enough water to overflow their brimming tubs of anger.

"Oh, that's what our marriage is to you? Something to manage, to suffer through?" she yells shrilly.

"Well you certainly don't make it easy!"

"It's not my job to make your life easy!"

"And you've done your 'not my job' remarkably well!"

"Like being married to you has been a picnic! Thinking everything just happens, disregarding logic and planning! Life is one big whim for you! This marriage was a whim to you!"

Everyone in the room is frozen, silent, gaping.

"Oh it was? Well you would know! Always telling me what I do, what I think, what I feel. Well if this marriage was such a whim then ending it should be too!"

This time it is his turn to walk away from her. He bolts through the crowd; everyone moves aside like they knew where he was going when he himself does not. He can't see anymore; his eyes had receded into the mass of anger and frustration that had begun to burrow into the base of his skull four years ago.

Jenny probably yells something after him, but his ears too have dissolved away. He is throwing his drink glass at the wall in the hallway, and then he is screaming *fucking bitch, fucking bitch* in his car, and then he is home and sleeping in their bed because she can fucking sleep someplace else the fucking bitch.

After an icy week of silence and secret lawyer calling, Jenny has his suitcase out of the closet and a baseball bat in the bathroom and he is crying in his car, crying because he is relieved and devastated and where was the Jenny he married and how could he do this to his kids, to his family and how did his life turn into this?

Toby had planned to make July dinner, a pasta with shrimp that was simple but romantic. Now he had no desire to stand up and make dinner. So instead he and July sat on the kitchen floor for a while longer. She held him, leaning her body against him, reaching her arms around and cradling his head, giving him small kisses and just letting him be. He had forgotten how a woman could make him feel better, soothe the raw sunburns inside, take the sting away. He hadn't had that in a long time. It was just what he needed, and she stayed like that until he shifted position.

What did she think of him now? He had called his ex-wife a bitch in front of her; he had told her some of the horrible ways he had acted. She had looked behind the curtain.

He hadn't looked at her the entire time he had spoken—he didn't want to see her gape or cringe, but mostly, he didn't want to see her eyes change from the soft, caring intent to the hardness of angry shock or disbelief. It was like one of those Rubin's vase illusions, where you look first and see two faces, but once you notice the vase, you'll never go back to just seeing two faces. He would be almost glad if he were suddenly stricken blind.

He pulled his head up and looked in her eyes. Her face was a juxtaposition of emotion. Her eyes were still soft, intent, caring; her brow was furrowed in concentration, like she was trying to figure out the answer to a difficult calculus equation; her mouth tugged out to the side and slightly up sympathetically.

"I know that was hard," she said after a moment. "But thank you for telling me."

"Do you hate me?" He knew it was a foolish question, but he had to ask.

"No. Nobody's perfect. We all do things we shouldn't, say things we shouldn't, do things we wish we could take back. I don't like some of the things you said, but—you're not perfect."

She shrugged.

"So, you still want to go to Italy with your highly imperfect old man?"

She threw back her head and laughed. His lungs, which seemed to have been pressed underneath a stack of books, expanded again. He smiled involuntarily.

"Of course!" she said. "There's nothing I want more."

He shifted his position so that his shoulder pressed against the cabinet and he was facing her. In one movement, her grabbed around her waist and drew her close so that their noses were touching.

"Good," he said, his voice low. "Because now I have you all to myself."

He kissed her, his lips firmly against hers like they were an oasis and he had been wandering the desert for days. There wasn't enough of her—his hands were too small—he wanted to feel all of her at once.

Her hands, her lips in all the right places—they were starving, they were free. Everything was more than it was—his skin felt every point of contact; his clothes as thick as dictionaries. It was dark but he could see; she was close but never enough, a horizon of flesh and heat and wet; they were there and gone.

The kitchen air poured shivers down his chest. The wood floor was cold against his bare legs but her body coated him in warmth. Clattering cupboards and breaths and intonations but no one else around to hear them so did they still make a sound?

XI

JULY HAD ONE OF THOSE DREAMLESS SLEEPS, THE ONES SO DEEP YOU just float and don't realize you are alive until a large hand reaches down and pulls you from the molasses of sleep that coats you long after your eyes have opened.

Toby was still asleep beside her, the white down comforter moving up and down. After a few minutes, the coating of sleep had slid off her body and the memory set in.

You're an insufferable bitch.

That's the kind of man you're with.

You're not perfect.

It's not like we're getting married.

July looked at the rising falling mass of flesh beside her. This man had had two lifetimes before her. If he could hate the woman who gave him his daughters, what could he think of July?

She tried to think of when her love for Chris had turned to ambivalence and then mild revulsion. It was hard to think of many defining moments in their relationship, but Chris was a man with few distinct attributes.

Perhaps it was that day in the park when he said, "The girls I knew before you were so shallow, all the girls but you are so trite. They hate guys like me who would treat them better than any stupid jock or frat boy."

If they had managed to stay together for more than ten years, though, she thought they would have slid into passive disrespect and silent disgust instead of verbally bare-knuckled brawls. She tried to imagine herself with Toby in ten years. It seemed fair to assume that her thirties would look far different than her twenties, and Toby could become anything in his fifties—reborn with mid-life crisis energy, resigned to the end of youth, doddering and hermetic in his golden years.

She would cook the family Thanksgiving dinner one year, planning her week down to the five-minute increments like her father. Toby would despise her for her meticulous control, or find it endearing, or be resolved to her ways but removed from all emotion. How long did it take to change apart like they had?

July didn't want to think about it. She wanted to enjoy this weekend, this insulation from anything and anyone else except for Toby. She wanted to enjoy Florence, to have the quintessential romantic vacation in Italy. She wanted Audrey Hepburn and Gregory Peck in the snow.

July's stomach churned vacantly. She was famished—they had forgotten to eat anything last night. July never forgot to eat—this was a first.

July slid out from the comforter, trying to disturb it as little as possible. It was cold off the island of the bed, but she didn't feel like putting on clothes. So instead, she stole Toby's robe and tiptoed downstairs and into the kitchen. Their clothes were still on the floor, and July decided not to move them. They looked so urgently still.

Toby didn't have much food left; he didn't want to leave anything around to fester while they were gone.

Shit. She was *hungry*. Her options were peanut butter, an overripe avocado, frozen shrimp or dry pasta and a few random remnants. She wanted something hot, something real. Like eggs, or oatmeal or pancakes or lox and bagels or—

Food. She was consumed by thoughts of food. It may be more than an hour before Toby awoke. If she woke him up, would she be an insufferable bitch? The store was out; there was no way she was going outside. That would be cold and require clothes.

She looked at the clock. For a moment she thought it must be wrong, there must have been a power outage because she never slept until eleven thirty. Then she realized the numbers weren't flashing and the clock on her phone corroborated the one on the coffee maker. The morning was gone.

At least it was late enough to order in. She had the numbers of a few places stored in her phone, for those dining hall emergencies when dinner looked like food only because it came on a plate. She decided on her old standby, China Jade.

July waited by the door; she didn't want the delivery person to ring the bell. About half an hour later a car pulled up and a man carrying two full paper bags got out and approached the door.

July recognized him—it was Ping, the deliveryman who almost always delivered to July's dorm. July had made friends with him and he frequently gave her free egg rolls. His brother owned China Jade.

This would be strange. She was still in the bathrobe.

She opened the door as he approached.

"Hi," she said.

"Hello, I have order here."

He looked at a piece of paper in his hand, and then up at July.

"July? What you doing here?"

"Hi, Ping. How are you?"

"Fine, fine, very cold. Why you here?"

"Oh! Um, well, I, um, know the guy who lives here."

Ping furrowed his brow.

"Nn," he said, connecting the dots.

They were silent for a moment. July hugged the robe closer; she wanted to close the door and eat already.

She handed Ping money from the pocket of her robe.

"Here you go, this should cover it," she said.

"Oh," said Ping. He transferred the bags over to July, "Thank you, thank you."

He counted the money, then looked back at July.

"Okay … well, you have good Christmas, okay? I see you back at school?"

"Yes, I'll see you when I'm back at school. Thanks, Ping. Happy holidays."

Ping gave a tight-lipped smile, nodded his head, and walked back to his car. July shut the door and hurried into the kitchen.

Toby came down as July started on the box of chicken in black bean sauce.

"Morning," he said, cocking his head and looking at the boxes on the counter.

"Afternoon," said July mid chew.

"What is this?"

"Brunch. You have no food in this house."

Toby laughed.

"You ordered Chinese?"

"I got enough for you."

"Yeah. A morning dose of MSG will perk me right up."

"Beats peanut butter and pasta."

Toby pulled up a chair and opened up a box. July handed him chopsticks.

"I was wondering where my robe was," he said, after swallowing a bite of noodles.

"Oh, sorry. All my clothes were down here."

They ate in silence; quiet was enough.

They spent the rest of the day inside and largely unclothed, catching their breath or second wind. Toby had told her he would take her out to dinner, but by dinner time neither of them felt like getting dressed or going out, so they ordered in again. When July suggested Thai, Toby happily agreed.

Toby hadn't had Thai but once or twice when he was married. Once, before he knew better, he brought Jenny to a Thai restaurant, convinced that if she just tried it, she would like it. That night Jenny, whose diet was almost exclusively beige, had seethed and stared frozen steel rods at him from across the table. He had placed small samples of each very mild dish on a plate in front of her. She stuck one fork tine into a pool of green coconut milk and dabbed it on the end of her tongue. Her nose scrunched into her eyebrows. The rest of her meal consisted of grains of white steamed rice that she picked from the red plastic tub. She had held it against him for all of their marriage, so he had ceded control of picking restaurants. They ate a lot of dinners at The Olive Garden.

But the first night after she had kicked him out, when he realized that he needed to eat something, he went to a Thai restaurant across the street from his hotel.

"As spicy as humanly possible," he had requested.

The Thai waiter looked at him with the skepticism special to the non-Asian patrons.

"No, I really mean it. I don't want to feel my tongue."

The waiter raised his eyebrows. You're asking for it, said his eyes, and then he marked something on his notepad and walked back to the kitchen. Toby could swear he heard laughter drift from the hisses and sizzles of the kitchen.

Soon he had a red curry steaming beneath his chin. His nasal passage seized with spice as it wound through his head and tickled the bottom of his throat. Toby coughed, then looked up to see his waiter and a few other staff members watching him from beside the kitchen door.

By the time Toby finished the whole bowl, he had gone through nine large glasses of water, half of the napkins in the dispenser, and the entire plastic container of rice. His nose ran uncontrollably, every mucus membrane in his entire body stampeding out his nostrils. With every exhale, his tongue grew a garden of fire. From his eyes sprang an endless trickle of tears, dribbles of chili and divorce. It was the only way he could allow himself to cry again.

Eating it now with July on the floor over the coffee table, the curry stoked his happiness instead of charring his pain.

"So," he began.

July looked at him.

"So," he continued. "I have to go pick up a few things tomorrow that I need for Florence."

"Okay."

"Is there anything you need? Anywhere you need to go?"

"No. I don't think so. Thanks."

"Sure."

They fell into another eating silence.

Is it bad that I have nothing to say to her? Toby thought. *Are we supposed to be talking? Should I ask her about school or something?* They'd have eight hours on a plane together, not to mention all that time in Florence—they'd better have something to say.

The next afternoon, July lay on Toby's bed as he packed his suitcase. She hadn't worn clothes since Friday night, and Toby preferred it that way. She spanned the length of his bed, her olive skin silhouetted against the white sheets, looking like she belonged in a Godard film or Degas painting.

"What time is our cab coming tonight?" she asked lazily.

"Quarter of five."

She flopped over on her back.

Toby looked over from the shirt he was rolling, "Hey. Hey! You're distracting me."

She giggled and flipped back over.

"If I don't finish packing I'll be walking around Florence naked."

"That wouldn't be so bad," she said. "You'd be the living *David*."

"Ha! I'd be the living *David* twenty years after Michelangelo sculpted him."

"Or maybe not. Maybe the *David* was airbrushed sixteenth century style."

Toby laughed. A year before he met Jenny, he had been snowed in at the Denver Airport. All flights had been canceled for two or three days and Toby had to spend a night on the airport floor underneath some payphones.

Most of the people around him had been despondent over missing their holidays. They were angry and frustrated and crying and yelling at the airline employees who were at the mercy of meteorology.

Toby had taken up position against a wall—there wasn't anything he could do, so he might as well try to have a good time. After a while, a pretty young woman sat on the floor across from him. Toby sat up straighter—things were starting to look up.

"Where are you supposed to be right now?" he asked.

She sighed.

"San Diego."

"Ouch."

"So much for a sunny Christmas. I'm Leslie."

After that they teamed up, watching the other's things to go to the bathroom, sharing food, keeping each other laughing. They sat shoulder to shoulder against the wall, touching each other flirtatiously, those electric zaps when someone new brushes a hand or touches an arm or leg. It had been one of the best traveling experiences of Toby's life. They exchanged contact info, but twenty years ago there was no email, no cell phones. If there had been, he always thought he might have married her instead of Jenny.

By now his mental picture of her had smeared; he could only remember her luscious brown hair and the way the bottom of her red turtleneck rode up, exposing a halo of golden skin around her waist. He had started to think about her again after he stopped loving Jenny. He had even tried Googling her with the information about her he could remember, but it was too vague. She had probably married and maybe changed her last name. She was just a cameo in his life.

Jenny had always been a stressed traveler, worrying and fretting, getting to the airport earlier than necessary, wondering about the weather. She got cranky over delays, fidgeting like there was something that she could be doing, some way that she could fix circumstance.

He was glad to have July with him. It wouldn't matter if they were snowed in at the airport. He had a gorgeous twenty-two-year-old woman with him—he was the envy of pretty much every man. People would see him with July and wonder how much money he had, how powerful he was, why he was so damn special that *she* would give him a drink from her fountain. He could be anything from a business tycoon to a successful writer to—hell, he could be royalty for all anyone knew. With her, he could pretend he was anyone. She made him special. She gave him lives.

Unless they thought he was her father.

He would make it apparent that it wasn't that sort of relationship.

Somewhere far below—or was it above?—something was sounding. A tone, repeating rhythmically, disturbing all the nothing that was not there. Suddenly it was pulling; the world of nothing was falling, being taken—she was being vacuumed from the comfort of being unaware. For a moment she was awake behind her closed eyes.

What is that sound? It sounds like an alarm clock. But I wasn't asleep ... July opened her eyes. *Oh. Yes I was.*

Her body was drenched with the weight of sleep. Perhaps an afternoon nap hadn't been such a great idea. *That noise! Make it stop! The incessant beeping. Why is it beeping in the dark? It must be four thirty.* The thought slammed into her head unexpectedly. Florence. Toby. Right. She tried to summon her arm to reach for the alarm, but found that the mind-body connection had been severed.

The beeping stopped. She felt the bed beside her move as Toby shifted. He groaned. July pulled the covers tighter around her. Sleep was dragging her back down, tugging at her eyelids.

No, she thought forcing her eyes open like they had rusted shut. *No. Wake up. Florence. Sit up on three. One, two, three. Okay, try that again: one, two, three.*

Summoning all her will, she sat up. Oh. Four thirty in the afternoon and it was *dark.*

Toby's breathing was rhythmic again.

"Toby," she slurred. She flung an arm at his body, "Toby. It's time to go to Italy."

He groaned again.

"Come on. The nap was your idea. Time to get up and feel refreshed."

She rolled over him and stood up. Still sleep was trying to pull her back. She turned on a light. That was a mistake. The yellow brightness seared her eyeballs; it was like a fire had ignited behind them.

"Agh!" gurgled Toby. "Unhhhhh."

But he sat up. Thank God. July did not want to have to force him out of bed like a child.

One weekend when she and Chris were still together, they were supposed to meet some of his friends for dim sum in the morning. Chris usually stayed up well into the night to play *World of Warcraft*, and it was up to July to cajole him awake if he were to wake up remotely close to the timeframe generally considered lunchtime.

First she would hover close to his ear, stroke his hair or back, and coo that it was time to get up. A few minutes later, she would say the same thing a little more firmly and give him a gentle shake. Then a firmer voice and a good shake. Blinds were opened, pillows and covers confiscated as necessary. A good poke or pinch and then eventually, after much goading and nagging, he would be awake.

Except this day, he wouldn't budge. July had recalled waking up at five thirty that morning and Chris had still been awake, the computer's blue emanations illuminating the room in a gray pallor and buzzing into Chris' eyeballs, which were less than a foot from the screen.

They were going to be late, and July was not going to let his stupid digital antics deprive her of pork buns and dumplings. She had given threats and ultimatums, but five minutes after they were supposed to have left, she left him to his bed.

To her surprise, Chris was furious and hurt that she would just leave him though she spent fifty minutes of her Saturday morning trying to drag his dead weight from the bed. A huge fight ensued, which spurred July to realize that dim sum was not for night owls and he'd had enough mothering.

The air seized her all at once as she stepped from the house into the dark early evening air, cutting inside her down jacket and scraping her skin with its sharp nails. Paralyzed with frost, July footed gingerly to the cab, her boots crunching like cereal against the ice and snow and salt.

"Hi," she said to the cab driver, an older, graying heavy man eating an egg sandwich. He got out of the cab and took July's suitcase.

"Evenin', darlin'. Where're you goin' at rush hour?"

"Uh, Italy," said July, her breath undulating from her mouth.

"It'ly, huh? My family's Italian! Whereabouts?"

"Uh, Florence," said July.

She didn't want to stand out here, congealing in the time between night and day, chatting with the cab driver.

Toby came out of the house, stopped on the porch, and locked the door. He crackled across the lawn over to the cab.

"Evenin'," said the cab driver.

"Evening," replied Toby, handing over his suitcase. "Let's get in," he said to July.

He opened the door. She crawled in and Toby followed. Simultaneously, they exhaled in relief. Anywhere was warmer than outside. July moved to the center seat next to Toby.

The driver came back around the car and got in.

"All right, airport, right?"

"Yep," said Toby.

"Ha! Or should I drive you to Florence?"

The driver put the car in gear and drove off down the street.

"I got a daughter too. She's thirteen. My family's Italian, and I've always thought I should take her back there with me on a trip. I guess I should. But I wouldn't do it *this* time-a year."

Toby and July looked at each other.

"He's not—my dad," said July.

The driver looked at her in the rearview mirror and kept glancing back at them a few times in confusion.

Toby put his arm on the top of the seat behind July.

"Oh," the driver said. "Oh. Right."

July slid down the seat and put her head on Toby's shoulder as the cab sped through the darkness before light, the ungodly hours when the world has only plans and hope and exists only in possibility and imagination.

The driver did not speak the rest of the trip, except to say, "Here we are."

He maneuvered through the Tetris of cabs and buses and cars and pulled alongside the curb. Toby half sat up and dug his wallet from the back of his pants as July slid out on the curbside. Jarred from the cozy cocoon of the cab, July seized in shock for a moment, then forced herself to inch over to her suitcase.

Toby paid the cabbie, then took his own suitcase and joined July at the curb.

She wondered how much Toby had tipped the driver. That father daughter comment was kind of a tip killer.

Toby put a hand on her back as they passed through the automatic doors.

"Ahh," sighed July. "At least we'll be warm for a while now."

She looked left and right, up and down the row of plastic counters and various red and blue insignias. The fluorescent lights pulsed against the defiant evening darkness, swallowing the room in a blindingly dull shade of gray.

"This way," said Toby, motioning to the left. "We're on Delta."

July followed him past the other airlines, each one differing only in logo, like the repeating scenery in an old cartoon.

When they reached the Delta counter, July took her place in the back of the long line behind a white-haired older couple, the woman in pale pink sweatpants and a Christmas sweater and gold jewelry that looked as though it came from a low-end antique shop.

"No, July, over here," said Toby.

July looked around; she hadn't realized Toby wasn't standing with her.

"Oh," she said, seeing that he was standing in the much shorter line for people with some special membership. She ducked under one of the seatbelt line indicators and joined Toby in the shorter line.

"You have one of those memberships?"

"Yeah, I joined the gold level when Jenny and I first went to Florence. She's kind of a high strung traveler."

"You mean when you took the girls?"

"Yeah. Well, no, I bought it the first time, when it was just me and Jenny. Before we were married."

"Oh."

Wait, so—how many other women had he taken to Florence? Toby and Jenny, young and in love in Florence, it must have been a pretty romantic trip.

"What?" asked Toby. "What's wrong?"

"Nothing," said July, smiling with weak reassurance.

For a moment, July didn't want to go—she'd seen what could happen after the trip, and she could only wonder if in a few years Toby would be bringing someone else to Florence in her stead, and whether July would factor into his feelings about that at all.

Usually when he was stuck in lines, Toby would examine the women around him to determine which of them he would sleep with if they were all stuck in the room forever. It was an easy way to pass the time, and now he hardly realized he did it anymore. Tonight it seemed a little strange since July was in line with him, and he would probably choose her, so game over.

Instead, he had the taxi driver's comment stuck in his brain like a piece of food stuck between his back teeth. He supposed he didn't mind the scorn, really. The problem was really when he thought about his daughters doing things like what he and July did in her dorm room a few weeks ago, and the other night on the kitchen floor. He didn't like thinking about them doing that at all, but it seemed a little more palatable when their counterpart wasn't a man who was his age, which would mean a man who was in his thirties now. While he managed to look past that, he wondered for a moment why it didn't disturb July the same way. Didn't she realize?

Years ago, Toby's uncle Ken left his wife for a younger woman. The news spread quickly through the family grapevine—it was the most salacious and eyebrow-raising occurrence since Toby's cousin had been charged with a DUI two years prior. Toby told Jenny about Ken after he heard it from his mother. Jenny had taken the news hard. She had just given birth to Chloe and felt insecure and sensitive about everything. Jenny had been breastfeeding, and when she heard that the "other woman" was twenty-four to his uncle's fifty-three, she started weeping.

"What's wrong?" he had implored. It took him a few minutes to coax it out of her.

"Promise me," she said, her voice dripping with anguish. "Promise me you'll never do that to me."

"Jenny—I'll never do that to you." He meant it.

"I mean it, Toby. It's—it's just so *unfair* that a man can just throw away his wife of decades because he found someone younger and smoother. It's not *fair*. It's not FAIR."

She continued sobbing for a few more minutes and Toby held her as best he could with Chloe attached to Jenny's chest, and assured her that he would never do that to her.

He hadn't told any of his family about July. He wondered what they would say if he did. Probably the same things they said about his uncle and the woman they deemed "His Little Plaything."

"That little whore."

"What a home wrecker. A gold digger."

"What kind of a woman would date a married man?"

"He could be her father!"

"Typical mid-life crisis. I thought he was better than that."

The woman left nearly two years later, just after his divorce to Toby's aunt had been finalized. She took off in a car Ken had bought for her, after shopping at Nordstrom a day before with Ken's money.

Toby wondered what Jenny's family would say about him and July. She had surely told them about July. He envisioned her anger, her sympathetic parents, her enraged righteous ultra-feminist sister, all shaking their heads and cursing his name and his gender. He hoped they weren't doing it around the girls.

"It's going to be noon when we get there," he said to July later as they stood in the security area. "We're going to have to fight to stay awake."

"Well, we'll just have to go out and eat a big Italian meal then, won't we?" she replied, grinning happily.

"That we will."

Toby loved that grin—it seemed to appear a lot when he was with July. He often wondered if she smiled that much in real life, when she wasn't around him. He hoped that she didn't; he would like to think that that smile was specific to him.

"What do you want to eat first?" he asked. "Pasta? Pizza? Lasagna?"

She thought a moment,

"Yes," she said definitively. "And gelato. I think gelato, then lunch, and then if the stars align, gelato again."

"My dear, you can eat gelato for breakfast."

She smiled, "I think I will."

So perfectly straddling the line between girl and woman. He wished all women could stay like that.

He and July reached the front of the line. The man at the counter checking tickets and IDs directed them to a security gate, and he and July fumbled through pulling out keys and removing shoes and jackets and belts.

Toby walked through first. On the other side, he looked back as July walked through. The alarm went off. She tried stepping through again, and again the alarm sounded. She looked at Toby and gave a shrug.

"Did you put a metal plate in my head while I was sleeping?" she asked.

"No. It was a rod in your spine."

"That's why my back is sore today."

One of the security agents went through July's bag; another moved her off to the side and began stroking the wand up and down over July's body. Toby watched as she stood like the Vitruvian Man. Was that in Florence? he wondered.

When July failed to set off the wand, the agents released her and her bag.

"Well," she said after she had put her shoes back on. "That was exciting."

He ran two fingers up her spine and she squirmed a bit.

They walked in the direction of their gate, and the clinging aroma of grease, potatoes, coffee and pastries smashed into Toby's face, spurring his stomach to undulate in hunger.

"I'm hungry. Should we get some dinner?"

"Sure," she replied.

They turned into a little food court area, where they were surrounded on three sides by a McDonald's, a Dunkin Donuts, a salad snack bar, and a closed Pizza Hut.

"The options are overwhelming," she mocked.

"Here. Why don't we get a table and I'll get us some food?"

"Okay."

They rolled over to a table and July sat down.

"What do you want?"

"Uh ..." she sighed. "I guess a bagel and cream cheese?"

"You got it."

Toby set his things down and turned to wade through the tables to join yet another line.

He looked at July, sitting still on a checkerboard of tables. Toby could look and see her face, but if he concentrated on one part of it, his perception of it totally changed. She was like a piece of pointillism—from afar you see a woman holding an umbrella, but up close she's just dots of color that mean something entirely different.

She looked into Toby's gaze; her expression didn't change, but her eyes did. Even from afar, Toby saw in them a cupped softness, the devoted sluggishness in the lines of the eyes of someone who cares about you.

She just might love me, thought Toby.

He finally got back to the table with the food. He sat and returned to July's eyes. He felt like, after hours of shallow wheezing, he had just filled his body with a breath that reached into the very bottom of everything.

They slowly ate their bagels, their eyes hardly unclasping from each other.

You could cut my tongue out right now, he thought, *and I wouldn't mind a bit.*

He had never thought that he could actually look forward to more than eight hours on a plane.

"Do you mind if I take the aisle seat?" Toby asked. "That way I can stretch my legs out into the aisle a little."

"Oh. Sure," said July.

"Are you sure? I know the middle is uncomfortable, but your legs are shorter and—"

"Toby, it's fine," July reassured him. "As long as I can fall asleep on you."

Toby smiled, then leaned in and kissed her lips quickly.

"Thank you."

Toby stood aside to let July on the plane first and put his hand on her lower back as she walked past him and stepped onto the plane. July liked it when he did that; the appropriate intimacy of it made her feel like he was passing secrets through his hand.

Though it was less than a foot between the ramp and the airplane door, to July it seemed like a four-wall gorge that fell through to the core of the earth. *What if my foot got stuck in it? What if I dropped something down there?* If she fell through, would Toby catch her, and hold on to her as their fingers slipped apart like in the movies?

The winter swooped through the chasm of interiors. July stood huddled and waited for the glacial line to move forward.

As soon as she stepped further into the plane, she almost wished she were back at the gorge—the air inside instantly clung to her. It was like being sealed into a brand new Tupperware container, trapped with the fumes of newly manufactured plastic. Like artificial sweeteners never tasted quite like sugar, the atmosphere similarly failed to entirely mimic the sensation of air. It made July feel like she had started to swallow a plastic bouncy ball that had gotten stuck before in her throat.

"Good evening, welcome aboard," said a flight attendant in distractingly unnatural berry-colored lipstick.

"Hi," smiled July as the line staggered forward. She turned down the aisle and inched through first class. The people on either side of her had settled in rather comfortably; they were sipping water, relaxing underneath blankets, and swimming in personal space.

Jerks, thought July. *Aren't they just so special.*

Earlier that morning she had been pleasantly surprised by Toby's airline membership. She wished he would surprise her with first class tickets. But with "Row 48" stamped on her ticket, that didn't seem so likely.

July moved past the partition into economy. The aisles seemed narrower now, and July involuntarily hunched her shoulders in. Her bag and legs kept hitting armrests and the sides of the seats.

"Excuse me. I'm sorry. Sorry."

Past the newspapers and shrunken pillows she trudged, until she finally arrived at row forty-eight. Sitting in the window seat was a puffy-faced middle-aged man in a suit. His hair was thinning a bit on the sides, as though his hair were starting to recede into a natural Mohawk. The area beneath his eyes drooped and shaded as though the bottoms of his eye sockets were exact reflections of the tops. Nonetheless, the rest of his face was an assembly of ferocity, like a man always looking for the deal or the quick solution, his face sanded away through years of late nights in a fluorescent office and shady deals. He looked like his name was Cal, something that fell from the tongue in a viscous sneer.

Cal was reading the *Wall Street Journal*. He looked up when July stopped at his row, smiled blandly, looked back down at the paper, then immediately looked back up at July. He smiled with a bit more this time, so that his eyes creased up a little. His pupils moved up and down quickly with a false sense of subtlety.

Oh great, thought July as she picked up her bag to put it in the overhead bin.

"Here," said Toby as he helped her lift and push it in.

"Thanks."

July hunched over and sidestepped into the middle seat as Toby put his own bag in the overhead. July shuffled around, trying to shove her backpack beneath the seat, sit on her jacket and buckle her seatbelt. Her backpack would be impossible to reach without putting her head in either of her seatmates' laps.

Once she finally buckled her seatbelt, July sat back and exhaled with relief. There was nothing she had to do until they landed in Paris for their layover.

Toby sat down to her right in the aisle seat.

"Ugh," he exhaled. "Why is just getting on the plane such an endeavor?"

"Because everything is about thirty percent too narrow," said July.

Cal chuckled, "So true—you're quite right there."

July turned to Cal with an unconvincing polite smile.

"That's the problem with the world," Cal continued. "People think small, too small like that makes it more efficient and economical but really it's like coupons."

"Coupons?" said July, realizing she had just been hooked into conversation by illogic.

"Yes, yes coupons. You see a coupon for something you don't need; you go buy it because it's a good deal when in fact you just lost money because you didn't need that thing to begin with. Or sales! You see something on sale and you think you just can't pass up a steal like that because look how much it's marked down and you buy it even though you wouldn't have bought it anyway so you just threw away that money."

July was silent for a moment, "So planes are like coupons."

"Exactly!"

July turned back to the seat in front of her, tilting her head slightly away from Cal. She looked at Toby, trying to send him an SOS message through her eyes and eyebrows.

Toby looked at her and gave her a sucks-to-be-you grin. He pursed his mouth to keep from laughing. He was just waiting to make fun of this guy once they got to Paris.

"Yes sir, people don't think *big* anymore," continued Cal. "Just look at cell phones! Computers! You can practically crush them with your pinkie. And today's celebrities they're brittle as dried chicken bones like that's beauty like you want a woman who'll snap once she's under you. No sir, ladies should have a little *curve* to 'em just a little something you can *pinch* and yank."

July wasn't even looking at him, but he kept talking to her. Cal, the wretch who spoke in run-ons. "But that's more *second* date material," he said in feigned jest.

"I'm seeing someone," said July curtly.

"Vision fades," Cal gave an exaggerated shrug.

Toby leaned forward and looked past July. *Now he's listening,* she thought.

Toby was about to say something when a woman, who had stopped to sit in the aisle seat across from him, knocked his shoulder with her bag.

"Oh, excuse me, I'm so sorry!" she said.

Toby turned toward her.

"Oh, no problem, it's fine."

Cal took the interruption as a chance to keep talking.

"Now I just don't understand why anyone would want less of something especially if it's a good thing; less is never more, more is more. Would you want less steak or less money or less cell phone? At some point things are going to start disappearing and suddenly nothing will exist and then you'll be paying more for nothing and soon it'll just be the *idea* of something the *shadow* of something and then we'll have to squint just to see our computers and then things start disappearing and you wonder if things are actually disappearing or if you're going blind."

Please make him stop, please make him shut up! thought July, who ducked down to her backpack and started fishing for her magazines.

"Getting older is the same way, you know; as you age people think you're less and less important, less vital, less beautiful, and even though you're more you're less and suddenly you disappear too; you become invisible and you wonder if you've really disintegrated or if everyone around you is just blind. Vision fades."

"Ladies and gentlemen, on behalf of the pilots and crew I would like to welcome you aboard Delta flight 8399 with non-stop service to Paris Charles de Gaulle," came a woman's voice over the intercom.

Thank God, thought July, as she pretended to concentrate on what the woman was saying. Cal seemed to take the cue and after moment, he looked back at his newspaper.

As the flight attendant launched into the emergency procedures, July looked over at Toby, who turned and smiled at her. July wished she could section them off from the rest of the plane. All she wanted was to rest her head on his shoulder, to look at him and be with him for the duration.

The plane pushed back from the gate. July looked out the window and watched everything move backwards. This was it—they were going— it was actually happening. July felt as though she had been staring at an extreme close up photo of some unidentifiable item, and she was just about to be told what it was. *What is this future I see?*

Soon they were hurtling down the runway, the roar of speed pressing against her ears like headphones. Force pushed her harder into her chair, the plane leaned back and just before the forces of physics yanked her back and into the air, Toby's hand found hers and they looked at each other, reclining together into a world growing and shrinking.

By the time the first beverage cart had come around, July had already finished one of her magazines. *Crap. Eight hours feels longer than it sounds.* She looked over at Toby, who had already managed to fall asleep. His neck crooked toward July, his head straining painfully for the floor.

A deficit of sleep pooled behind July's eyes, pressing out and enticing her eyelids down. But whenever she closed her eyes and tried to push back from the dock of consciousness, she was anchored in wakefulness.

July crunched carefully down to her backpack and fished around for the snacks she had bought at the newsstand in the airport. Eating would help pass the time.

She decided on her Butterfinger bar. Chocolate—aloe vera for the soul. She nibbled, trying to stretch out the entertainment for as long as possible.

"I'm a Snickers man myself," said Cal.

July closed her eyes. *Oh no*, she thought. Instead of answering, she took another bite.

"You been to Paris before?" he asked.

Shit. July didn't like to just ignore people, but this guy was irritating, the seatmate telemarketer. She could just not answer, but whenever she acted rudely, she immediately felt a pressing sense of guilt.

"No," she answered, hoping she hadn't just walked into a trap that would require her to gnaw her leg off later.

"Beautiful city. Gorgeous. Of course they don't call it the city of love for nothing."

"Hm," nodded July.

"You should make sure to see the *l'Opéra*. My favorite building by far."

"Hm."

"Yep, this is my fourth trip to Paris. Decided I didn't have anyone to spend Christmas with so I might as well spend it somewhere beautiful even if it is colder'n a stuffy nose but unless you want to go below the equator that's how everywhere'll be this time of year but I couldn't imagine spending Christmas in a bathing suit in the warm sun it wouldn't be Christmas if it weren't cold now would it?"

Cal kept talking and July stopped listening. How unfortunate that a chocolate bar could hold a better conversation than Cal. July turned and looked back at Toby. *Wake up*, she willed.

After a moment, she gave up, laid her head back against the headrest and closed her eyes, Cal's voice melting the cement as she pushed off into the black pond behind her eyes.

When Toby woke up, he was staring at his clavicle. A little puddle of drool had formed on his lower lip. He straightened up and quickly wiped it away, hoping no one had noticed. Then he noticed that his neck felt like it had been belted to a two-by-four and jammed into the space between the seats in front of him. Gingerly, he tried to move his neck the other way. It cracked and cranked, yanking pain up into his skull and down his back.

He looked at July; she was sleeping. She had managed to somehow keep her head against the back of the chair instead of allowing gravity to contort it. In her hand was a half finished Butterfinger. God, she was pretty. He thought that maybe, out of everything he had seen in his entire life, the girl with grape drop lobes and switchback hair and breath like a lake shore and pencil fingers holding an open candy bar was the most beautiful thing he'd ever seen, and he had seen the pyramids, the Mediterranean coastline, Machu Picchu, and a handful of naked women.

He reached below the seat in front of him and rummaged around for his camera. He turned it on and quickly took a picture. Like that picture of Jenny pirouetting before the Duomo, this would be the mental picture of July that would stay with him.

The man next to July looked up from his paper as Toby took the picture.

"Hey, she could sue you for that you know," said the man.

"What?"

"She could sue you for that; that could be construed as sexual harassment."

"Why? Why would—Huh?"

"I mean she's a piece I'll give you that but it's a little creepy to take a picture of a strange woman while she's sleeping don't you think?"

"What are you talking about? She's my girlfriend."

The man's brow froze in a furrow. They were passing confusion between them, like monkey in the middle over July.

"She's your *girlfriend?*"

"Yeah."

The man's jaw dropped open a little. Toby couldn't tell if this guy was indignant or envious.

"Man you are my hero. I'm Rob," said the man, as he reached his right arm awkwardly over July and offered a handshake.

Toby was not going to have this conversation.

"Excuse me," said Toby as he unbuckled his seatbelt and stood into the aisle. He would rather spend the flight trapped in the toilet closet than chatting with Rob.

What if July was only half asleep and had heard that? Toby replayed the exchange to make sure he hadn't unwittingly said anything incriminating. No, he hadn't. At least he didn't think so, but sometimes women had a way of pulling rabbits out of hats like that.

It felt good to stretch his legs. Maybe he would just stand at the back of the plane for a few minutes.

At the back there was a little alcove by an emergency door where he stood looking out the window. Not that there was anything to see—it was nighttime over the ocean.

The woman sitting in the aisle across from him, who had bumped him with her bag, was coming up the aisle. She acknowledged him with one of those demure smiles women give when they pretend they're shy and want you to say something first.

She was pretty, maybe eight or ten years younger than he was. She was also a blonde, so even if he *had* been interested he would have kept his distance anyway. But Toby didn't really have anything to say to her, so he just smiled back, that hi-you-hit-me-with-your-bag-but-no-hard-feelings smile. She went in the bathroom and he resumed watching the back of people's heads. Lots of bald and gray. He rubbed his hair. He probably wasn't doing anything to help skew the color to gray ratio towards the color side. His hair was like the time just before autumn when some of the leaves start to yellow and turn red with fire and then suddenly the next day everything is a dying brown. One step closer to falling off the tree.

The woman came out of the bathroom and stopped in the space next to Toby.

"Sorry again about the bag thing earlier."

"Don't worry about it. It's fine," he said.

"Thanks," she said. She crossed her arms and looked around, contemplating whether she should leave or try again.

"So!" she started. "What brings you to Paris?"

"A layover."

"Oh! Right, of course ... Where's your—final destination?"

"Italy. Florence."

"Oh wow!" she said. "How wonderful. Gorgeous city."

"Oh, you've been there?"

"No, no, I would love to, though."

Right, he thought. *Why is she talking to me?*

"Look, I know this seems really strange but you look really familiar. Did you go to Tulane?"

"No," he said as gently as he could. Was she using the do-we-know-each-other line? He'd tried that one before.

"Oh God, sorry. It's just I—I could swear we've met."

Toby looked closer at her face. She had freckles so thick her eyebrows nearly faded away. Toby remembered the time, years and years ago, when he would have welcomed this sort of opportunity. He would have jumped at the chance to have a European fling like in the movies. Back when he probably would have pretended he *had* gone to Tulane just to see if it would lead to anything. He couldn't believe he didn't want to now. It was like telling a five-year-old that in ten years he wouldn't *want* toys for Christmas anymore. No one believes that sort of thing.

"Have you been to Paris before?" she ventured.

"Yes. But that was about twenty years ago."

"Well you should consider going back for a few days. It's marvelous. I could show you around. I know all the best cafés and museums."

"I think my girlfriend has her heart set on Florence," said Toby. "But thanks."

"Right," she said. There was a pause. "Well, sorry to bother you. I'm gonna—go back. To my seat."

Toby loitered for a few more minutes then made his way back to his seat, too. The freckled woman was watching the in-flight movie, and if she noticed him she didn't let him know it. July was awake now and finishing her candy bar.

"Hi," she said as he sat down.

"Hi."

He put his hand on her thigh and squeezed.

"So ... are we there yet?" she asked.

"No," he grinned, and tucked some of her hair behind her ear.

She put her hand on top of his. They sat like that for a few minutes.

"What should we do?" she asked. "Look for license plates?"

"Well, we could hijack a beverage cart."

"That would kill a good five minutes before they placed us under citizen's arrest and called the TSA."

"I guess we'll just have to read, then."

"I guess. I didn't bring enough snacks to keep me chewing for all eight hours."

"That's why we hijack the beverage cart. Endless pretzels and peanuts."

"I love the way your mind works," she said, looking right into his eyes.

Her eyes, where he could get lost forever. Her eyes were like the stars that are so faint you have to look just to the side to see them—every time he looked in her eyes, he couldn't see them because they were all he could see.

As the plane began to sink a few hours later, July leaned forward and looked past Rob out the window, straining to see her first glimpse of Europe. The plane descended through the clouds, like mashed potatoes, Toby always thought. Then the world faded in through the mist revealing the steely Seine and the patches of land sewn on and everything brown or gray.

"Look at that," said July reverently. "Even from here it looks different."

Toby leaned over to look out the window. He had been to or flown through Paris quite a few times, and he supposed the excitement of it had worn off. But to July it was new, and he saw the spin of excitement in her eyes that he remembered he felt the first time he had been abroad, as a teenager when he had gone with his parents to Scotland. Chloe and Sophia had been too young when he and Jenny had taken them to Florence, too young to get that shrinking feeling when you realize that there really is a lot of world outside your own, and your world is not your own.

XII

AS THE PLANE ROLLED UP TO THE GATE, JULY HEARD SEATBELTS clicking open like a metronome in need of winding. She felt prodded and sore, and wondered if her bones had frozen.

She leaned forward and looked out the window; the sky was an icy gray, like the clouds were made of stone. It looked like the same sky in America. The airport looked like the airport they had left over eight hours ago. She was in Paris—surely she should feel different than she did in America? She was disappointed to realize that she felt the same, albeit atrophied. It was like feeling the same on her birthday as she did the day before.

The seatbelt sign chimed off. All the passengers stood up almost simultaneously, jockeying for a place to stand in the immediately crowded aisle. July stood up and felt warm crackly relief as the blood that had pooled in her butt rushed back down into her legs. She couldn't hold the position for long; the control panel above her was so low that she had to stoop over like a hag. She sat back down.

Toby hadn't stood up—he didn't seem to be in a rush. July wished he had stood, so that she could slide over and stand herself, but there was no point because he was walled in by a blonde freckly woman now. Great. She would have to sit here for at least five more minutes, which might as well have been another eight hours.

"We're lucky," said Toby, turning to her. "Our next flight is in the same terminal, just in a different hall, so we won't have to take a terminal bus and run through the airport."

"That's good," said July, trying to sound happy.

"This airport," he continued, "is one of the most confusing, frustrating airports in the world. And everything is always late."

"How long is our layover?"

"Not long, only an hour and a half."

"Good," she said.

She wanted to be off this plane and in Florence *now*. And she was hungry. The plane food had been miserable, and since the bulk of her snacks, long since consumed, had been candy, her stomach had turned into a ravenous, hollow sugar brick with a nasty temper. If she were a toddler, a tantrum would be coming.

July started jiggling her leg up and down. She had to get off this plane

Toby put a hand on her neck and started massaging.

"Hey, you okay?"

"I'm just—really stiff. And *really* hungry. I get crabby when I get this hungry."

"I'm hungry, too," he said, still rubbing. "We'll get something to eat as soon as we get off, I promise."

July tried to smile at him but all she wanted was to stand up and shove a baguette in her mouth.

"City of love, last chance," murmured Cal, with a look so unctuous and oily July was sure he repelled even water. "Vision fades, remember that."

When she and Toby stepped off the plane at last, July just wanted to spread herself as wide as possible, stretch out her arms and legs and back and leap around, to broaden from floor to ceiling, window to window. How did people ever fly to China, or Australia, or somewhere dozens of hours away? She had never been so grateful for the use of her legs.

Be nice, she reminded herself. *You will eat.*

"What time is it here?" she asked.

"I think it's about eight," replied Toby. "My watch is still on Eastern time."

"It's like we're chasing the sun."

Toby smiled. "Let's get to our gate so we can eat."

"*Yes.*"

They walked through the terminal, suitcases clacking like trains. *It doesn't feel like Paris. It doesn't feel like Europe,* thought July. *Shouldn't the people look different? Shouldn't they be … more … chic?*

As they walked out the security gates, Toby stopped.

"What?" asked July.

"I forgot about immigration."

"What?"

"Immigration, a passport check. We have to get our passports stamped."

"I thought we'd get our passports stamped in Italy," mused July.

"No, they stamp your passport at the first port of arrival."

"Oh. How long does that take?"

"I don't know, but everything takes longer than it should. We have about an hour before we board; we'd better hurry."

July's body deflated as she had the sudden premonition that they weren't going to eat anything before getting on the plane.

The coming holiday made the line-up even more constipated than normal. July felt like there was a clock ticking over their heads, reminding her of each second that the line was not moving. What if they missed their flight? They would have to try to rebook, they would be stranded in Charles de Gaulle for hours, maybe a few days! The whole trip would be ruined. July's eyes burned with frustration and anger. Of course it would all go wrong—everything had been right. Karma needed a big fuck up to restore balance.

Toby seemed fairly calm, so July tried to mask her anxiety, but she still found herself biting her nails, twiddling her fingers, shifting positions. Her brow was permanently trussed inward. The line was going nowhere; the men checking passports were so slow, lazy, like it didn't matter that people had somewhere to be.

July had been so frantic figuring and refiguring time and distance that she didn't notice that she had handed her passport to the slothful man behind the counter.

"Here it is, the first stamp in your passport," said Toby, jarring her from her mathematical fog.

He put his arm around her back and gave her side a little squeeze. Her mind quieted and she looked at Toby, smiling for the first time in over an hour.

And then she turned to the man, tall and lean, who was inspecting her passport. Reaching languidly for the stamp, he rocked it gently back and forth on an inkpad, and with a hollow thunk, stamped her passport, then Toby's.

The pages that had been blank for so long were finally inked. Her passport had a purpose—it was no longer a dream for the future, but a function of the present and past. Her passport worked.

The man handed back their passports. July immediately flipped to the page he had stamped. It looked so official. July remembered when she was perhaps seven or eight, her family had gone to Disneyland, a fairly short trip from home. July had an autograph book so that she could collect the signatures of every Disney character, from Belle to Mickey. Collecting those autographs had been an assignment, a duty, a mission; instead of going on rides like the Matterhorn and Splash Mountain, she dragged her father around scouring the premises for every person in a Disney costume.

She couldn't remember now how many autographs she had obtained, but now she felt like a seven-year-old in Disneyland. She wanted to collect them all. She was hooked.

"Hey," said Toby, who had already begun walking and was by now ten feet away. "Let's go! We don't want to miss the flight!"

July looked up, grabbed her bag and walked briskly to catch up, but kept her passport out in her hand. This stamp would always belong to Toby. Every time she looked at this stamp, every time her passport would be stamped in the future, she would hear him say, "Here it is, the first stamp in your passport."

She would feel his arm across her back and a pinch on her left side and see his crinkly metallic eyes and his shoulder and she would see him stopped ten feet ahead of her, a bag across his shoulder and another in his left hand, the jeans and the light blue shirt and him looking back, standing like a perfect candid photograph, calling her forward into a new world like a ghost. She wondered if this might be what she would see before she died.

Toby looked at his watch and walked a little faster. July stretched her legs as far apart as she could to gain on his stride, doing the splits with every pace forward, like a leaping ballerina.

They reached the gate as the last ten or so passengers stood waiting to board.

"This has got to be the only flight that's ever boarded on time in the entire history of this airport," said Toby breathing heavily.

They scurried into the back of the line, huffing and grinning at each other in relief. It wasn't until they had boarded the plane and sat down and July had buckled her seatbelt when she remembered that she was famished. They hadn't had time to get any food.

Toby was leaning back against his seat, eyes closed, and like a yawn, his fatigue spread to her. July leaned over and placed her head on his shoulder. This time she was in the window seat, Toby in the middle. No pestering stranger this time, just a portal to a foreign world. Though she tried to tell herself to stay awake for snacks with the beverage cart, her eyelids wouldn't listen and she fell under the heavy curtain of sleep before the plane had left the ground.

When she awoke, they were still on the ground and out the window she could see the airport. Had there been a delay? How long would it be? And more importantly, could they de-plane for food? She lifted her head off of Toby's shoulder.

"Welcome to Italy," he said.

"Huh?"

"We're here."

"I slept the whole two hours?"

"Lucky you. I woke up just after snack service."

July's stomach roared as she remembered that she was hungry.

"Oh God, I'm starving."

"Me too. Don't you have any food left?"

"No, I ate the candy bar and I think you ate all the nuts. Is there anything to eat here?" she asked hopefully.

"Peretola Airport has a couple of basic sandwich places. We can find you one after we get our bags. Or, there's a nice little café a few minutes from the hotel, they have a variety of breads and sandwiches, if you can stand to wait a bit longer."

Burning despair crept up July's throat. She wanted her first meal in Italy, in Europe, to be a good one, though part of her—namely her stomach—demanded food now, she resolved to hold out for the café near the hotel. *The hungrier you are, the better the food will taste,* she told herself.

They repeated the seatbelt standing waiting ritual again, but when July stood, she noticed that they hadn't pulled up to the terminal. Instead, there was a staircase that led from the plane door to the tarmac, and then some awnings set up that covered the path into the airport.

Wow, just like in old movies, thought July. *Cool.*

Cold. Frigid, actually. July had failed to take into account that it was still December. It was too late to put on her coat without holding up the whole line. As she stepped out of the plane, she felt as though a careening wall of ice had slammed into her body.

She placed a hand on the railing and descended gingerly down the first step, then promptly removed her hand with a jolt. Her bare hand stung white-hot and the words freezer burn passed through her mind. She saw that most of the people in front of her had on gloves and coats.

Duh, she thought. *Idiot.* Though she wanted to scurry down the steps and run inside as fast as she could, July descended glacially down the steps. The last thing she needed now that she was here was an injury. No dying allowed yet.

As soon as she scampered inside and away from the doors, she threw down her bags and put on her coat. Toby came in after she did, in his coat, of course, grinned, wrapped July in a bear hug and ran his hands up and down her body. He stopped after a moment and they looked at each other, then kissed a few times. His face, shaded in stubble, was still cool, especially his nose, but his mouth was a steamy jungle. July wanted to burrow inside and never leave.

About an hour later, they were in the taxi driving into Florence. July kept her head to the window, straining to overcome the impediment of the roof, which limited her vision like the bill of a baseball cap. The roads were narrower, the cars were smaller, there were confusing roundabouts instead of traffic lights. There were no high rises or ugly office buildings or shopping malls. Everything looked aged, stylish, *Italian.* It *looked* like Italy—it *felt* like Italy.

Everything was something to look at. Everything had a character, a history, a culture, an identity that existed beyond July. There was a reality behind the photographs, the travel guides, and the textbooks. It existed; it was true. People lived here whom July had never heard of, whom she had never met, never would meet, would never know existed.

So this is what it's like.

Her eyes would never be big enough, two weeks would never be long enough. This was travel—to never be or have enough, the inability to recover. It was like she had been abducted by aliens—how could she ever live her life again knowing that there were other worlds out there?

How could she ever go home?

Italia. Come una malattia.

Toby spent most of the cab ride watching July instead of looking out the window. His smile broadened every time she said, "Wow!" or "Oh my gosh!" or "Look at that!" and her neck craned around trying to follow the vanishing landmark. Like she had been blind and just obtained sight.

All I know, he thought, *is once I was blind and now I can see.*

He remembered this cab ride the first time he came with Jenny. It had been summer, just after she graduated. She had been happy but rather passive, staring blankly out the window, trying, Toby guessed, to seem a seasoned woman of the world. But the first thing she wanted to do when they got to the hotel was call her parents.

Jenny had been willing to go along with nearly anything he suggested. She wanted to see things but hadn't planned or scheduled anything; she was content just to be with him. Where had that woman gone? Why had she changed so much?

Though he tried to steer himself back to the present, he couldn't help wondering: *What will life do to July? What will a husband and children and being a grown-up change her into? Do people really change?*

He recognized where they were now. They pulled up to a pale yellow building, anonymous except for the white awning that said Hotel Ariele. He had stayed here every time he came to Florence. Small and tucked away from all the tourist bustle of the Ponte Vecchio, it was cozy and family run. Toby couldn't imagine what else four or five-star hotels could possibly have; this three-star hotel had character that hadn't been smothered by the ambivalence of opulence.

The lobby was simple, with a wooden desk, red tiled floors, and a few framed pictures on the white walls. Past the desk was an extension of the lobby, where a dark, serious, wooden table sat atop a worn woven red rug. To the left was a sitting room with a fireplace, pink swirly wallpaper, more rugs and chairs upholstered in luxurious looking fabric. Adjacent was a dining area, and outside was a courtyard with a garden, which in friendlier weather had a green lawn and blooming potted flowers. It was the perfect setting for taking breakfast or reading or letting kids run around or sneaking in a little kissing session.

Behind the front desk stood a spectacled, completely bald man in a suit. As Toby and July walked in he looked up; the light reflected off his skull moving as his head lifted.

"Hello, welcome to the Hotel Ariele," he said in English.

Toby never quite figured out how all Italians could pinpoint Americans like that. What gave them away?

"Hi," he said, stopping at the counter. "I have a reservation under Toby Alder."

The man consulted a large book and scanned through with his finger.

"Ah yes, I see you'll be with us until the fifth," he said. His accent almost made it sound like he was speaking in iambic pentameter.

"That's right."

"*Bene.* I will need your passports, please."

Toby fished his passport out of his pocket and handed it over. July looked a bit confused but obeyed.

"You will be in room eight. Here is your key."

With a turn of his wrist, he handed them a brass key attached to a diamond plastic key ring with the number eight on it.

"The elevator is down the hall to the right, and the stairs are behind you."

"Thank you," said Toby.

"*Grazie,*" said July.

Toby turned to July, "The elevator is the size of an airplane bathroom. It should just barely fit one of us and our suitcases. Do you want to take the stairs or the elevator?"

"Um, stairs," she replied.

"Okay. I'll take the bags up the elevator and you take the stairs and meet me on the second floor."

"Okay."

They walked over to the elevator. When the door opened, Toby thought it must have expanded in his memory; it was much smaller than he remembered.

"Here we go," he said, rolling his suitcase behind him and swiveling it against one wall. He leaned over and wheeled July's suitcase in front of him. He was cornered, trapped behind a fort of luggage.

"Wow, it's like a broom closet," said July.

"Yep, see you upstairs," he said to July as the door closed. She waved and turned toward the stairs.

The elevator moved slowly, as though not moving at all. Perhaps it was the building that was moving. He tried to remember which room he and Jenny and stayed in; he hoped it wasn't number eight. That would be like having two women in bed with him and not in the fun way.

Did Jenny know that July was here with him? He hadn't told her, and he assumed July hadn't either. He should call the girls. What time was it there? He subtracted eight from two o'clock. Six in the morning. He would call Jenny's family tonight.

Jenny's family. Hers. They were no longer his family. But what about his daughters? Her taking them away at Christmas made it seem as though they were a family and Toby was the expendable, and expended, exception. *They* were still a family; he was not. *They* still lived in *their* house; *he* lived in *his*. And now he was away with someone new doing things for him, things he wanted. Part of him could not help being pleased with the chance to be a little selfish again. With his exclusion came the freedom of possibility.

Being so completely removed from everything he had, Toby now realized that he could marry again. He could even have more kids. He could have a whole new family, an entirely different life. There were so many "coulds." He could, but could he?

Until the papers had been signed last week, a small section of Toby had believed that Jenny didn't really mean it, that she would call off the divorce, realize that what they had created was worth salvaging, that someone would jump out and yell, "You're on candid camera!"

How illusory reality became, now that he was forced into the freedom of youth in mid-life.

This time around, he resolved, *youth will not be wasted on the young.*

Finally, the elevator heaved to a stop and the door clanged open. July was standing there patiently, the whisper of a smile pulling her lips. She looked worn out, a bit pale and rumpled, her hair rubbed with the muss of wear. But, Toby thought, he had never been happier to see her—his companion in facing future and possibility.

July came forward and rolled out her suitcase.

"I looked around—we're this way," she said, and walked into a hallway on the left.

They stopped a few feet later outside room eight.

Good, thought Toby. *I don't think we stayed in this room.*

He took out the key and tried to unlock the door, but he couldn't figure out which way he was supposed to turn the key—neither way seemed to work. Perhaps the jet lag had eroded his motor skills. He tried again, but the door remained locked.

July stood by quietly as he tried a few more times, shaking the key and knob more vigorously with each attempt.

"Can I try?" she asked gently.

"Sure," said Toby, lifting his hands like he was under arrest. "I don't know what the deal is with—"

The lock clicked satisfactorily and the door popped open.

"How did you do that?"

"I pulled the knob up and in and then turned the key."

"I loosened it for you," said Toby. He held out his arm and motioned her to enter the room first.

"I know, it's why I keep you around," she replied as she walked past him into the room.

He followed her and looked around. Just to the right of the door was the bathroom.

"Wow, it's a tub instead of a shower!" said July. "I haven't had a bath in years."

She moved further into the room past a large stained wardrobe opposite the bathroom. The zig zag wooden floor resonated below the suitcase wheels. On the right, outfitted in deep red quilted blankets, were two twin size beds. Though they were pushed together as closely as possible, a gap of an inch or two remained between them.

Was that how the beds had always been? Toby couldn't remember.

July turned her head and looked at him, one eyebrow raised.

"Are we in a fifties TV show?"

"So it would seem."

Adjacent the bed was a dark wooden desk, upon which sat a small television set. On the far wall, a windowed set of doors looked out into the courtyard. July walked over to the window and moved the sheer curtains aside.

Toby walked over to her and put his arms around her, holding her close. Beneath the lingering aroma of airplane he could smell July, something behind her skin that was sweet and deep, like cookies baking in the rain. He put his nose to that spot behind her earlobe and inhaled slowly. Her head tilted away from his, opening her neck; his hands found her waist, her hips, her ribs.

"Why don't we try out those beds?" he whispered.

He felt her smile against his ear.

"But I'm so hungry …"

"Me too," he said, pulling her in closer.

She groaned, the agonizing choice of what to sate.

As she hesitated, he pivoted her around and walked her backwards to the beds like a waltz. He wouldn't give her a chance to answer.

Nine hours. July hadn't had a single thing to eat in nine hours. It had been even longer since she had had a real meal; airplane food and convenience snacks did not count. Now, lying here on the beds, July was so hungry she didn't even feel hungry anymore—she just felt nauseous, like a bag of marbles had been poured down her throat and had fused together inside her stomach.

There was no way she could enjoy her first meal in Florence now. Glancing out the window, she saw the light was weakening. The winter's early sunset couldn't be long in arriving. Restaurants wouldn't start serving dinner for a few hours yet, but if she waited a few hours without anything, she would be so hungry that by the time the food came she wouldn't enjoy it anyway.

This didn't seem to bother Toby at all, as he had fallen asleep beside her. He lay perpendicular to the gap between the beds, and against the red bedspread his bare skin seemed faintly blue. July wouldn't mind falling asleep, either, but she knew that then neither of them would wake up until two the next morning and then there would be no food for even longer.

July decided instead that she would take a hot bath, then go downstairs and beg for food, no matter its form or quality. Maybe they had leftovers from breakfast. Or maybe the concierge had brought a bagged meal that she could charm from him.

July opened her suitcase, gathered her toiletries, and walked to the bathroom to run the water. Soon, she slid into the full, steaming bath and felt the stench of tension and airplane rinse away.

You're in Italy, she thought, resting her head against the edge of the tub. This is something she had wanted for at least fifteen years; it should feel more like a landmark moment. So why did it feel so … normal? Why is it that the anticipation of achieving a goal feels more fulfilling than actually achieving it? Is this how it would feel when she graduated, or got married, or … divorced?

No, thought July. *No, I will never get divorced.*

She had seen what divorce had done to Toby, how even enjoyment was accompanied by an underlying sense of loss. Or was it regret? Disillusionment? Tragedy? July couldn't tell, but she didn't want to experience that firsthand. Perhaps he had once told himself that he would never divorce.

Until she met Toby, she had never really experienced how painful divorce made everything. It always seemed like one of those disasters that happen to other people. But now the man she loved was other people.

Wait—love? She jerked her head up from the back of the tub.

July hadn't even been thinking about her thoughts, and suddenly the word love popped in. *Oh no.* She had been trying to avoid this, as he would almost certainly never love her back. It wasn't realistic.

Was it?

What horrible timing. This would just make things even more complicated, now *and* later. It was too difficult to be the first—possibly only—one in the relationship to love first. She remembered Chris, how she had known he loved her, and the pity with which she tried to love him back.

She imagined telling Toby she loved him. They would be standing somewhere out in Florence, with cobblestones and ochre buildings that had stood through centuries of love. And she would say, "I love you."

And he would look at her, that tender look of dread that people get when someone doesn't want to hurt your feelings. He would just look at her for a few moments, and maybe his eyes would crinkle, and maybe he would put a hand on her shoulder or brush her cheek with his thumb, but then he would look away, like this whole thing had gone too far now that some kid thought she was in love with him, and maybe he would say something like, "July, you know I care about you, but I just got through a nasty divorce …" and maybe he would enumerate the reasons why he couldn't, didn't love her, like his daughters and her age and practicalities and realities and logistics.

Or maybe he wouldn't say anything at all, and then the rest of the trip would be blown. *That cannot happen*, she thought. *I cannot tell him that I love him. Love will only ruin it.*

A roaring growl of hunger interrupted July's mental suspension. She promptly lifted herself from the tub and dried off, trying to drain her thoughts with the water in the bathtub. She dressed and got herself together as quickly as she could, then grabbed the room key and headed downstairs.

The man was not behind the desk, so July rang the little bell on the counter. A moment later, he came out from an office behind the desk.

"Hello. How can I help you?"

"Um, do you have any food? I haven't eaten in at least ten hours."

"Ah, I'm sorry, but we serve only breakfast. Breakfast ends at ten."

The man glanced back toward the office.

"You don't have any leftovers or anything? Please. I'm willing to pay for it. I'm so hungry."

"Ah, I am sorry, but the kitchen staff, they have gone home."

July could hear a television from the back office. This was a hotel—they had to have food somewhere. Was he really trying to avoid her to get back to some sports game?

"I saw a bar over there," said July, gesturing to a small room next to the elevator. "Is there any food there? Anything?"

"I am sorry, but the bar does not open until eight o'clock this evening."

"You can't spare me like a candy bar or a piece of bread or something?"

He glanced behind him again.

"I am sorry, but—"

The phone in the office rang.

"Excuse me," he said hurriedly, and turned so abruptly on his heel that he was already back in the office before the phone rang a second time.

July had a feeling that he wouldn't be back out.

Great. Just fucking great. I'm starving and in love and there's no food. Aside from the sex she'd just had, this trip was off to a lousy start.

She trudged back up to the room and unlocked the door as noisily as possible, hoping the rattle would accidentally wake Toby so they could go get something to eat.

Wait, why do I have to wait for him? she thought. *I'll just walk a few blocks, find a store or something, and then come back just in time to wake him and get dinner.*

She rustled up the Euros she had exchanged in the airport, put on her winter clothes, and promptly left again. Why not go out by herself? She was a big girl, she had studied Italian in school; she could find her way around.

When she exited the hotel, she took a moment to look around. Hotel Ariele, Via Magenta. She walked up to the corner and looked up and down the street for anything: a store, a restaurant. But the street was completely desolate save one or two other hotels.

The street was practically deserted; there was a gravel path, some gray naked trees, some dumpsters. Most of the buildings were a light yellow or sandy old color. When she had been to New York City, July felt claustrophobic because the buildings were so tall they seemed to join in an A-frame over her head. Here, they were only two, maybe three stories high, but the streets were so narrow that her claustrophobia came from the side instead of above.

She stopped at a corner, where there were some shops, but it was just a hardware store and a greeting card store, closed. Where was the city?

She moved out to a busier street to stoke her sense of direction, but this larger street showed only marginally more signs of life. She felt a bit like Lawrence of Arabia crossing the desert.

She looked for a supermarket or a café, but all she saw was more of the same sandy gray walls and gated doors for at least a block in either direction. Arbitrarily, she turned right. There weren't many people out; they were all probably on some break in the day. Or maybe it was just too damn cold. It was probably both.

July's hair was still damp, so her head felt as though it were covered in frozen spaghetti. She hunched her shoulders closer to her ears and flipped her hood over her head. Winter felt the same in Italy—cold.

After a few minutes, she saw a sign for a café.

Thank God, she thought, speeding up.

When she reached it, she pushed the door and went in, relieved to be back under the blanket of heating. It was a very small café, scattered with a few two-person round tables. Mostly a place to get coffee, it seemed, but tucked away on the short corner of the counter was a glass case containing a few stale-looking pieces of focaccia and some filmed-over, wilting panini.

Her stomach greedily launched itself towards the counter.

A couple, perhaps in their fifties, lingered behind the counter, their attention directed at a television in the corner.

"*Per favore, vorrei una focaccia,*" said July, enjoying the chance to finally use her Italian outside the classroom.

The woman behind the counter looked up at her with a slightly puzzled expression.

She can probably tell I'm American, thought July, *and wondering what the hell I'm doing here asking for her old bread.*

But instead the woman replied, in Italian, "How many?"

"One," replied July.

"One Euro fifty."

That much for a piece of bread? thought July as she handed over five Euro.

The woman handed her change, then fetched the bread with a piece of waxed paper.

"*Grazie*," said July, putting it in her mouth as soon as the bread was in her hand. It was room temperature, and the drizzle of olive oil on top hand long since been absorbed and softened the surface of the bread, but she still thought this salty, yeasty, aged and soggy focaccia was the best piece of bread she had ever tasted.

July walked over to a table and sat in a chair. Half the bread was already gone, and she pushed in a new mouthful before she had swallowed the previous one. When she finished, she sighed as relief and carbohydrates flooded through her body. Unfortunately, she felt hungrier than before she had eaten the focaccia.

The woman stood behind the counter, her head tilted up, eyes fixed on the television in the corner. *I could do this*, thought July. *Maybe they need a waitress. I could become like their daughter, running the café with them, learn the ropes, open my own café.*

That would be making stellar use of your International Relations degree, she thought as she stood from the table and walked towards the door. *Bar-side diplomacy.*

She exited the café and turned left. She knew she needed to make another left turn in a few blocks, but she couldn't remember where. Was it this corner, or the next one? A gust of wind slashed her cheeks as she turned left at the next corner. She walked a few blocks but couldn't figure out if the hotel was now on her left or her right. How far over had she come? There were so few landmarks on this street. Why had Toby chosen a hotel so removed from anything?

She wandered left, then right, crossed a few more blocks, and ended up at the Arno, an unmoving snake with steel, leafy scales. July walked toward the river and looked left and right. Across the river was a massive cluster of buildings painted pale yellow, pale pink, and sandy old, like a gingerbread model of an ancient city. Bridges stretched at intervals over the river, and a few bridges to the left July could see a larger, built up bridge—the Ponte Vecchio. To the right, the buildings petered out, and there were trees and fewer buildings lining the banks.

July turned back to the neighborhood where her hotel was hiding. After a few more minutes of walking up and down, she found Via Magenta. Her shoulders eased and she exhaled audibly—she had envisioned wandering around the neighborhood, still and hushed like a graveyard, until the day was gone. Her ears stung from numbness, so she pressed them to her head to thaw them as she walked beneath the awning and up the stairs.

July unlocked room eight and slid in. The room had darkened considerably, the sun fading into the west and pulling its light through the curtains and out the window into the west. Toby was still asleep, lying naked on his back. Had he moved at all in July's absence?

July sat on the end of the bed next to Toby's shoulder. A fair portion of the hairs on his chest had turned gray, as had the hair by his temples. July examined him closely, remembering a photograph he hung on his wall of him kneeling in a field beside a dog. The photo was dated 1987, when he must have been July's age. The wind had blown his jacket open and his hair afluff; he looked so young, so much smoother than the boys her age looked. She tried to imagine how his wrinkles may deepen, how his hair might turn or thin, how his skin may sag with translucence. By the time that happened, she would look at pictures taken now and be struck at his youth.

He had twice her years, more than four decades of life without her, three lives that had come from his. Could there be any room left for her? A hand inside July's chest wrung her heart of all twenty-two years of emotion; two walls pressed against her chest and back and squeezed it all out her eyes. *Why do I have to love you?*

She wished she could put her head close to his and eavesdrop on his dreams and thoughts and feelings. What was she—just for now? What did he want?

"It's not like we're getting married!" he had yelled at Jenny.

They weren't. But—well—couldn't they? Hypothetically? But July couldn't even preface her fantasies with "In a Perfect World." Her mind set up barriers with flashing lights and orange and white stripes. There were always the girls, there was always Jenny. A life with Toby would come with a lot of labels she had never thought would fit her, like being impoverished but wearing expensive designer labels.

Rebound.

Mid-life crisis.

Trophy Wife.

Second Wife.

Step Mom.

July Alder.

Oh God, that sounded horrible.

What if Toby didn't want more kids? July might be okay with that; she would have his girls. But what if they didn't like her? What if Jenny turned them against her? Toby was generally healthy now, but he had high blood pressure and took a pill for it. She would almost certainly be a relatively young widow, single in her middle age, and if the girls didn't like her and Toby didn't want more kids, she would be alone. She would have to gamble her future on the present.

Shut up, shut up! Fantasies are not supposed to work like this, she thought. Yet in spite of the reflective roadblocks set up every ten feet in her head, her heart drove up on the shoulder. She didn't know what she wanted to do after college anyway. Perhaps if she fit into his life, that would give her more direction. Ugh, she sounded like her mother. Could she bring herself to shape her life according to one that was already set up? His life could be like a long running Broadway show and she was the ill-prepared understudy who didn't know the lines or stage directions.

And that might pretty much fuck her life.

Running over all these practicalities washed through her head and eroded her brain into a small, smooth pebble. *Is this what it's like to be an adult—to always worry about everything?* she wondered.

If only their lives together could be eternally Florence. July curled up beside Toby and rested her head on his chest. His chest hairs crimped under her cheek, and his skin was warm like a rock sitting in the sun. She could hear his heart beat like the wheels of a train chugging in common time beneath the hiss of his breath. It was like listening to an important conversation through a closed door.

The pressure on his chest brought Toby's head up groggily, "July?"

She lifted up her head and smiled, "Hi."

"What time is it?"

July sat up, "Um, almost five."

"Oh," He put his head back down.

Please don't go back to sleep, thought July. "Let's go out," she said gently.

"Mm."

"You won't be able to sleep tonight if you stay there."

"Enhh."

"You owe me dinner."

"I know, I know."

With great effort, as though gravity had doubled in strength, Toby sat up. He sat for a minute, recalibrating, then he looked over at July, "Why are you in your coat?"

"I went out. There was no food here and I needed something to eat."

"Oh."

"I didn't want to wake you. I figured you needed the rest."

"Mm. Yeah. I guess I did."

Toby didn't sound like he meant it.

"Don't worry. All I had was a piece of semi-stale focaccia."

He smiled a little and rocked himself up to standing.

"I'll be ready in a few minutes," he said as he padded to the bathroom.

July turned on a light and took a few minutes to make herself look a little better, figuring they were on a romantic getaway so she should at least make an effort. She sat at the desk with her travel mirror and dabbed some makeup on her winter-flushed cheeks. Toby came out of the bathroom and rifled around in his suitcase. When July finished, she turned to watch a shirtless Toby, who was looping a belt through the pair of jeans he had worn on their first date.

"I love those jeans," said July.

Toby, shirt in his hand, looked over at her with a playful smile, then put the shirt over his head, followed by a sweater. Then he walked over to July, took her hand and pulled her from her chair right into his body. When they kissed, July could tell he had just brushed his teeth.

"Oh, no. You have to feed me first," she said against his lips.

"Tease."

He pinched her hip and picked his coat up.

"All right," he said. "Come on. We'll be the city's first diners of the night."

XIII

Toby knew exactly where he would take July for their first meal: a restaurant across the river with views of the Arno, the Ponte Vecchio, and the Uffizi. It wasn't the best restaurant in Florence by far, but it was decent and romantic and picturesque.

To get there, they took the longer route through the streets instead of along the Arno. July could see the neighborhoods, and Toby could let the stream of memory trickle back into the dry riverbed Florence had worn into his mind. When he had been married, he harbored the golden retirement fantasy that once the girls had moved out, he and Jenny would buy an apartment here, one with a balcony overlooking the river.

He and July had started out holding hands, but even though they were wearing gloves, the cold sunk through and they had to tuck their hands away into pockets. The light was gray and soft and their breaths bloomed into the air like swirling veils. The buildings along the narrow streets curved around them like a Dali painting. Past small groceries, closed trattorias, drug stores, antique stores, book stores, each of them small and personal, like the city was a sprawling mansion with thousands of rooms.

As they neared the Ponte Vecchio the stores became chicer and pricier. July's head constantly swiveled one way or another as she gawked through the window of every shop. They reached the Ferragamo store on Via Dei Tournabuoni, which Toby had used as a landmark since Jenny had taken a picture of an outfit glowing in the window. Every time they had passed the window, she lingered just to get another look.

"You're taking a picture of a mannequin?"

"That outfit is gorgeous. And those shoes!" she had said, staring up at the window.

They didn't look special to Toby; they were just another pair of high-heeled shoes that she would complain hurt her feet. That from the woman who spun her toes on wood.

"They're just shoes," he said.

"They are *not* just shoes," Jenny replied, turning to him and raising her eyebrows. "Ferragamo shoes are like works of art; they're finely crafted and they ..."

Jenny had continued talking about shoes for three more blocks while Toby tuned her out.

Toby and July continued past the store, down a slim, darker street.

"All the roads here are diagonal," said July. "It's confusing; I'm totally disoriented."

"You'll get used to it," said Toby. "Just remember where the river is and where things are in relation to the Ponte Vecchio. That's how I remember."

A few minutes later, a slim shadowy way emerged onto Via Por Santa Maria, the street that connected to the north side of the Ponte Vecchio. People swirled about taking pictures, eating gelato off of neon plastic spoons, shopping. There were Christmas lights strung up above the surrounding streets like extra stars that twinkled with seasonally required cheer.

Souvenir carts scattered the street, and Toby had seen vendors here selling knockoffs of bags or sunglasses laid out on blankets; when the police came, the vendors quickly bundled up the blankets and made themselves scarce, trickling back ten or fifteen minutes later. This was the center of tourism, the meaning of Florence for sightseers and travel guides, so all the prices at the shops and cafés on this road were exorbitant, but prices fell the further one walked from the Ponte Vecchio.

"Just up there is the Duomo," said Toby, pointing to the left. "Straight ahead is the Uffizi, to the right is the Ponte Vecchio."

They stood for a minute on the street as July looked around. The sweet smell of gelato and waffles mingled with the doughy, savory aroma of pizza.

"Oh, it smells so good," she groaned. "Let's get some gelato."

"No no, not only is the gelato here overpriced, it's not as good. The best place is across the river. We can go there after dinner."

"How will I know it's the best if I don't have a point of reference?"

"Touché," Toby conceded.

He followed her as she veered for the closest *gelateria*. Inside it was narrow but cheerily decorated, seeping with yellow. Beneath the dome of glass sat rows of square metal basins filled with carved mounds of gelato of all colors, illuminated like precious gems and edible prisms.

July closely scanned the tags of each flavor, bent over the case hm-ing softly to herself. Finally she stood straight and looked at the quiet woman behind the counter.

She ordered in Italian, pistachio and coffee—Toby knew enough Italian to catch that. The woman handed her a small pointed waffle cone with brown on top of green and a neon pink spoon stuck in the brown like a wayward antenna. July fumbled for some money in her pocket, but Toby moved to the counter and handed the woman five Euro.

"No, no, it's okay," said July. "I can get it."

"Nope. How could I not buy you your first Italian gelato?"

July smiled, "Thank you."

She reached up to the counter and took another plastic paddle—a green one. She carved it against the coffee flavor and held it in front of Toby.

"Here. Taste."

"But you haven't had a bite y—"

She stuck the spoon in his mouth.

As his mouth came alive with smooth and cold and sweet bitterness, his stomach violently unrolled itself, reminding his brain that he hadn't eaten in at least twelve hours.

"Good?" asked July, as she carved a bite for herself and put it in her mouth.

"Oh, good," she said, the gelato still in her mouth. "Oh, *good*."

"Not bad," agreed Toby.

He took a few more bites as the brown and green disappeared quickly. After July popped the last of the cone into her mouth, she stood and said, "Now let's go eat!"

Toby laughed and stood up. July smiled at him, and he leaned in and kissed her quickly. Beneath the cone and coffee and sugar, she tasted like the tinge of blood, mellow and alive.

"Yes, let's."

They walked back into the street and turned toward the Ponte Vecchio.

"Ooh, now I'm cold inside *and* out," said July.

They walked past shops with glittering clothes and bags and jewelry, pizzerias with yards of pizza beneath every color topping, sidewalk cafés with outdoor heaters and lasagna twice as expensive as it should be.

They stepped onto the Ponte Vecchio, navigating through a thicker cloud of people. Toby recalled what it was like in the summer, the air shimmering and sticky with heat, the streets thick with tourists taking photos of themselves and the hundreds of strangers around them. People stuffed themselves onto the Ponte Vecchio, clutching their purses and wallets, sweaty skin sticking to the people they elbowed past. The bridge was populated tonight, but not like it was in July.

To the right and left, jewelry stores displayed gleaming gold and gems. Stores were closing, and employees were pulling jewelry from the windows. July slowed to look in the windows of necklaces and rings and earrings, which all just blurred together to Toby.

In a moment of irresponsible fiscal romanticism, he had contemplated buying Jenny's engagement ring at one of these shops, mostly for the story she could tell about a ring from the Ponte Vecchio and an Italian proposal. The price tag had quickly cured him, and he instead waited until they returned to the States.

Now, after two decades of real estate, he had his picture on bus benches and before movie previews and the signs of many houses for sale, so his threshold for purchasing pain had increased accordingly. But for some reason, Jenny's threshold had, if anything, gone down, even after she returned to work and made good money teaching private classes. But she wasn't here now to chide him if he bought something.

July stopped in the middle section where the bridge opened to the river on both sides. The whole city was lit up like a sprawling museum. Toby stopped beside July, who leaned against him and put her head against his shoulder. They stood like that for a moment, Toby's nose staying warm in her hair, inhaling the fragrance of scalp and bottled flowers.

Standing on the bridge, where he had been so many times before, was like time traveling through his memories. All his lives converged here; he stood here at twenty, twenty-two, twenty-five, twenty-seven, thirty-five, forty-three, moving backward and forward.

It had been a roasting day when occasional gusts of wind swept the pounding rays of sun from the skin. He and Jenny were walking with two pizzas. Jenny was wearing a blue tank top and a ruffled blue and white skirt. Her blonde hair spun like electric currents with the wind, and her sunglasses were pushed on top of her head to keep the hair out of her face, her bare eyes squinting against the day's oppressive brightness. The entire world was whited out with light except for Jenny, who was perfectly vivid and exposed. She walked with a dancer's bounce in her step, like her toes might spring her free from the claws of gravity at any moment and she would float away into the sky.

They had spent the entire morning in the hotel room, probably disrupting their neighbors with clumping furniture and the insensitive audibility of passionate youth. While Toby would have been content to keep that up the entire day, Jenny had insisted that they leave the hotel and do *some*thing with the day. So they walked along the Arno, pizzas in one hand and the other's hand in the other, leaning over occasionally to kiss and walk.

From the white beyond, a man on a Vespa rode past and shouted "*Ciao, bella!*" as he passed Jenny. She giggled and looked at Toby. Instead of feeling threatened, he felt proud that this *bella* was with him. But if that had happened in the States, Jenny would have been offended and Toby might have been socially obligated to confront the guy. Life was easier on the Arno—everything was *bella*.

The crowds became denser as they turned onto the Ponte Vecchio. Without releasing their hands, Toby moved in front of Jenny and led her through the crowd, past the street artists selling prints and between the group of tourists from Germany. They stopped in front of the bust of Benvenuto Cellini and looked around for a place they could sit and be alone in the crowd.

People took turns standing against the ledge, which was the perfect width to serve as a bench, and taking their picture in front of the river. That's where Toby wanted to sit—right in the middle of their photos.

They shifted over to a corner where the ledge met a wall. An American family was there taking pictures, switching themselves in and out. After the woman in a fanny pack and ill-fitting khaki shorts had smiled vacantly for her Hawaiian-shirted husband for the last time, Toby moved into the open space and sat on the ledge, resting his back against the wall. He put his left leg up on the ledge, Jenny sat beside him and they became part of the scenery.

They fed each other pizza and kissed and laughed, and Toby thought that all those people searching for the meaning of life just needed to have lunch with Jenny on the Ponte Vecchio and they would never have to wonder again. This was the answer, the ease and happiness that passes between two people who understand each other. This moment was all he ever needed. He wished that they were invisible so that they could go at it right there, strip everything away and make Florence their hotel room.

They lay like that for a while, Toby lined up with the ledge, his back against the wall, Jenny leaning back onto him. Her shoulders started to turn pink, his arms darkened. He was thirsty, but he would rather blister and burn and shrivel into a parched corpse than move.

At one point he left her for a few minutes to buy them some water. He worried that leaving would be like waking from a wonderful dream in the middle of the night and then trying to fall back asleep and continue the same dream. He tried to hold onto the feeling of peace as he staggered through the crowd, stopping short to avoid running into people or ruining their pictures. He worried that he would get back and she would be gone, disappeared without a trace or explanation, like a mirage, like she had been nothing but a drug-induced hallucination.

But when he returned she was still there, and now she sat with her back against the wall. He handed her water and they chugged, and then Toby sat back down, leaning against her, his head and shoulders moving up and down with her breathing. She twirled her fingers gently through his dull dark brown hair, her fingers sending every conscious part of him into his head, into those few points beneath her fingertips.

This body, he realized, *holds my children*. He closed his eyes and tried to envision his family. They would become extensions of each other. He had never thought of a woman's body as serving a greater purpose, but with Jenny, he felt she held the answers as if she had all the things inside her that a person would need. She could take the place of stuff and boxes. He could feel the future.

Toby hadn't thought of that moment in years. *We had a moment of such perfection. How did we fuck it up so bad?* This was not the right future.

"Toby?" asked July. "Want to go eat?"

"Yeah," said Toby unintelligibly. It could have been a whimper, an ambiguous plea, a cry of anguish.

He looked at the place where he and Jenny had idled beyond time. He could see them lying there, feel the stone beneath him and the heat of the sun intensifying between their bodies. He had crawled inside her and understood how they would be. How had he been so wrong? This was not how his life should have been.

Taglierini all'alfredo con funghi porcini e prosciutto cotto. La bistecca alla fiorentina.

It just didn't sound as good in English, and it probably wouldn't taste as good in English either. Earthy mushrooms and the thin delicate salt of prosciutto in a cream that coated her mouth; a steak so thick and juicy and rare that she wondered what she had been eating all these years, because it surely could not have been beef.

Basking in the glow of good food and a sated appetite, July looked across the white tablecloth at Toby, who silently sipped the last of his red wine. He had been quiet and reserved for the entire meal and spent most of it looking out the window at the Arno.

What did I say? wondered July. *Is he angry that I went out alone this afternoon? Did I do something wrong? He's finally seen I'm not smart or knowing or worldly or pretty enough, and he realized that I'm an awful travel companion and he doesn't really like me so much and now he's stuck with me for two weeks and he's trying to figure out how to ditch me and get an early flight home. Or maybe he's sick or jet lagged or misses his daughters.*

She hadn't really noticed anything strange until their first courses came and Toby barely noticed the taste of his ravioli and hardly seemed to care that it was July's first meal in Florence. He had cared about her first gelato—what had changed in less than an hour?

He absently swirled his wine glass and finished the last crimson swig. A moment later he took a sip again, not realizing that the glass was empty. What was he thinking about?

Because he didn't look back at her, looking at Toby had become uncomfortable. July looked at the table on their right, where an elderly couple was sipping wine and speaking rapidly in French. The waiters moved about in black pants, white dress shirts and bow ties and plates of food passed by, all the aromas of tomatoes and meat and garlic and olive oil.

July looked back at Toby, who was again sipping at his phantom wine, "Toby?"

Silence.

"Toby?" July reached across the table and put a hand on his, "Toby."

He looked at her.

"What's wrong?"

"Nothing," he said flatly.

"You haven't said anything the entire meal."

He shrugged.

July jutted her jaw, "You've been someplace else all night. What's up?"

He sighed, "Nothing. I'm sorry."

July sat back in her chair and folded her arms. Something was pushing out of her chest, the hot claws of anger trying to escape through her rib cage. Was he just going to sulk the rest of the night? The rest of the trip? She had to share a room and a table with a man steeped in his own thoughts, who had practically flown home already. There was nothing worse than being with someone who no longer wanted to be with you, because then you didn't want to be with you either.

They sat a few minutes longer until July summoned the waiter for the check. She wondered if Toby would take her to his favorite *gelateria*. She still wanted gelato, and she would go by herself if she knew where it was. She wondered if he would move at all to pay the bill, to stand and put on his coat and walk out of the restaurant and all the way back to the hotel. He was frozen and he didn't have a restart button.

The waiter placed the check on the table and left again. Was Toby going to pay? She had been under the impression that he would. This place was expensive—the bill was surely at least a hundred Euro—and July couldn't really afford that, especially on her first day on an unfavorable exchange rate.

Tendrils of tense heat spread through her shoulders and up her neck into her jaw. This wasn't fair.

"Toby," she said sharply.

He looked up blankly, like he didn't realize they had been in a restaurant for the last two hours.

"*What* is going *on?*"

Recognition finally clicked into his eyes.

"I don't know if you noticed but we just ate dinner."

He took a deep breath and blinked a few times.

"You haven't said a word the whole meal."

She was trying to keep her tone neutral, but she was sure he could hear the sharpness underneath, like the lip of an envelope ready to give his tongue a paper cut.

"So, are you going to tell me what's wrong or are you just going to let me figure out what it is that I did wrong?"

"You didn't do anything wrong."

"Then why are you acting like this?"

"I'm sorry, I was just—remembering."

July's body stiffened, as though all of her had turned into steel rods. Remembering. He was remembering being here with Jenny. *Oh God, he was remembering how great it was, how I'm not Jenny. I should have known. How could I ever succeed a thin beautiful blonde ballerina? He wasn't remembering—he was wishing. Wishing it were Jenny instead of me.*

"Oh," she said quietly, her eyes smarting with a film of tears.

She looked into her lap, her white napkin smudged with the juices of steak. She felt like there was a spotlight on her shoulders beaming down shame and humiliation, showcasing that she was a poor substitute. She thought of the scene in *Vertigo* where Jimmy Stewart tries to make Kim Novak into the woman he loved before. But unlike her, July was not the same person in a different hair color.

A warm tear fell involuntarily into her lap. She wanted to crawl under the table.

"Oh July, no," said Toby, reaching across the table. "No, it's got nothing to do with you."

"Of course it does."

"No, no. July, I know it's hard to understand, but—" he exhaled sharply. "It's just hard to remember being happy with someone who made me so miserable."

July stared hard into her lap. *Stop crying. Stop it.*

"So now you're just going to be miserable to me? I thought I made you happy."

"You do, I—I'm sorry."

I thought he was over her, she thought. *I thought he hated her, hated women, hadn't loved her for years.*

Toby reached for the bill and pulled out his wallet, "I'm sorry, July."

She shrugged and looked out the window at the black river, its surface scattered with blurry deposits of leftover light. Now she didn't know how *she* was going to move. She just wanted to dissolve and slither away into the river.

"Please don't cry, July."

"I'm not," she said, but found that there was a wet slide down her cheek.

Stupid. Stupid, *stupid*, falling in love with a haunted man. Didn't she know she was just setting herself up to get hurt? Just like her mother predicted. But she deserved it, didn't she? For not loving Chris the way he loved her, for not feeling bad about their breakup, for being with a married man. She had it coming—it was her turn to be heartbroken. *Fuck. Why are you so stupid?*

"July," said Toby.

She couldn't look at him. She felt too ashamed.

"What?" she asked, pointing her nose at her napkin.

"I mean it when I say you're the only person I want to be with right now. It's just—it's just that it's really hard to—to remember happiness after it's brought you pain. That's the best I can explain it. Does that make sense?"

July nodded.

I wonder if that's how I'll feel about you? she wondered.

"July, look at me."

Don't be a baby, she thought. *Just look at him.*

She looked at him. His face had changed back into the Toby she came over with.

"Do you wish you were here with Jenny instead?" she asked.

"No," he replied without blinking.

He either meant it or had learned to lie really well.

"No I don't, not at all. It's just that my past caught up with me. Or maybe I caught up with my past."

It wasn't until July's shoulders slackened that she realized they had been hunched toward her ears.

When they were outside the restaurant, Toby hugged her tightly, stroked her face, kissed her nose, her lips, her forehead, and held her close to his chest. Her ire, her anger, reluctantly melted away into the night freeze. She shouldn't still love him. *Would loving me make him feel better or worse?*

He did take her for gelato. The *gelateria* was one bridge west on the same side of the river, a larger shop with even more flavors to choose from. This time July ordered a larger size and tried yogurt and crème caramel. Toby got a large cone with yogurt and strawberry.

July's combination was so creamy, so sweet and soothing, that soon the warm relief of sugar loosened the rest of her body, lifting her mind from the churning well of doubt. It was wonderful, gelato. She would eat it everyday.

"Every day?" said Toby.

"Yep. At least once. Ideally twice. And you're right—this gelato is much better than the other one we had today."

There were no tables in the *gelateria*, so rather than eat in the cold, they sat close to the floor on the window ledge.

"I could bathe in a pool of this," she said, licking drippings from around her cone.

Toby seemed more relaxed, too, as his eyes slowly refocused on the world, as though he had been in a dark movie theater and had just stepped into the bright sunlight.

"We should get back to the hotel," he said as they finished. "I want to give my girls a call, and you should probably call your parents and let them know you're safe."

My parents, thought July. *I haven't thought of them in ages.*

"I guess I *should* call them," said July. But she didn't want to. She didn't want to remember that there was a world waiting for her return, that this was only temporary. Let her family wonder. Let them wonder if she had made it, so they may wonder whether she would return.

When they arrived back at the hotel, much of the frost in both of their demeanors had thawed. *Tomorrow morning it might be all right again*, thought July.

"Want to use the phone first?" asked Toby.

"No. You want to talk to your daughters more than I want to talk to my parents."

Maybe once he got off the phone she could say she was too tired and put it off until Christmas. She would have to call on Christmas.

Instead, July decided to unpack her suitcase and put her clothes in the bureau. She wanted to seem more organized on this trip—she had been embarrassed when Toby had seen her dorm room a few weeks ago.

"Hello—Miriam?" said Toby.

July looked at him as she put a stack of shirts on a shelf. Who was Miriam?

"Miriam, hi it's Toby."

He sounded uncomfortable. Who was Miriam?

"Fine, and yourself?"

July tried to hang her clothes as quietly as possible.

"Um, are my daughters there by chance? I wanted to say—Oh! Lunch. Right. Well, when will they—? Okay, yes, I'll be up another hour or so, so could you have them call me when—? Thank you. Let me give you my number and the country code ..."

Miriam. Miriam? Had she heard that name before?

"Thank you Miriam, Merry Christmas. Thank you. Good—"

He paused a moment then hung up the phone.

"Who's Miriam?" asked July reflexively. It then occurred to her that she should have acted like she wasn't listening.

"Miriam is Jenny's mother. They're at her house for Christmas."

"Oh."

"She didn't sound too pleased to talk to me."

"Oh," said July, for lack of anything else to say.

"The girls are out at lunch, they should be back soon, so I'm going to take a quick shower."

"Okay."

"Oh, and maybe we should call the front desk for a wake up call tomorrow? Otherwise we might sleep till noon."

"Right. I'll do that while you're in the shower."

"Thanks."

Toby gathered some of his things and went into the bathroom. After a moment the wall rumbled as he turned on the water.

July went to the phone and called the front desk. She hung up and went back to unpacking the rest of her things. A few moments later the phone rang. It must be the front desk. *Should I answer in English or Italian?* she wondered as she picked up the phone.

"Hello?"

"Hello?" said a confused American woman on the other end. "Is—I'm sorry I thought I was calling—Hotel Ariele."

July frowned. "Uh, yeah."

"Is—this—Toby Alder's room?"

July froze. Jenny.

"Hello?"

"Uh, yes. Yes this is Toby Alder's room."

"Who is this?"

July's body turned into quivering jelly. It didn't matter that Jenny was an ocean away; July felt like she had five seconds to choose between the red or blue wire. Should she address her with any familiarity at all?

"Um, Toby's in the ... shower."

"I wanna talk to Daddy!" July heard one of the girls yell from the background.

"In a minute sweetie, go play in the other room," said Jenny away from the phone.

There was another crackled pause.

"You're the girl from the other day," she said accusatorily. There was a pause. "It's July, right?"

"Uh. Yeah."

"He took you to Florence. Which of course he neglected to mention when we met the other day. And you're staying at the Ariele?" she asked, her voice like dry ice.

"Uh, yeah."

"Hm. Yes, we stayed there, too. Twice."

July said nothing. *The same hotel? What if they were in the same room?*

"I'm sure he'll take you to the Duomo, the Uffizi, long walks along the Arno, take you to his favorite restaurant tucked away on a dark corner. An old dog can't learn new tricks, you know. At least this way he doesn't have to think about it."

"You know, why don't I go get Toby for you? I think he's out of the shower," said July, and put the phone down before Jenny could say any more.

She knocked on the bathroom door.

"Come in," said Toby.

July opened the door and a waft of steam covered her face, causing her eyelashes to stick together.

He smiled at her when she opened the door.

"Hey," he said.

"Hey, um … Jenny's on the phone."

The smile faded from his face. "That was quick."

He stood up and reached for a towel, "She didn't give you a hard time, did she?"

July shrugged and looked at the grout in the floor tiles.

"Jesus Christ, that—" he muttered as he stepped out of the tub and slid past July.

July wasn't really sure if she should listen, but in a room this size it was hard not to. Instead she stayed by the bathroom door where she couldn't see Toby. She remembered once when she was young, no more than eight. During class that day, another girl had taken July's calculator, a shiny gold plastic calculator with buttons made of cheap, brightly colored fake gemstones. July had tried to take it back, lunging after the girl, who refused to return it and held it teasingly in the air. July grabbed the girl's yellow shirt and the girl lost her balance, falling sideways. The girl fell at a strange angle and hit the desk nose first. July had watched in horror as the girl started gushing blood from the middle of her face. As she remembered it, the blood spilled everywhere, down the yellow shirt, onto the blue-pilled carpet, all over the teacher and the desk and worst of all, July's beloved calculator.

July was sent to the principal's office. The principal called her mother as July sat in his office, crying uncontrollably. July felt sick the rest of the day, knowing that an awful reprimand and punishment awaited her that evening. She took the bus home and arrived before her mother did, so July hid in her closet, behind her bright purple rain boots, as though staying out of sight would make her disappear, and the girl's broken nose with her.

She heard Toby in the other room, his voice strained and emphatic. They were arguing again, and July felt as she imagined his daughters felt when their parents fought.

"Jenny," Toby was saying. "Who I see is *my* business. It doesn't concern you. Just put the girls on."

They'll fight about this until they die, thought July.

"Florence has nothing to do with it!" he said. "Florence is not exclusive to you and me—I came here three times before I knew you! This is not *our* place. It's just the world! It's not gall or nerve—it's just *life.*"

There wasn't enough gelato in Florence to make this better.

July was overcome with fatigue. She hadn't had a decent night's sleep in days. Leaning her head against the doorframe of the bathroom, she slid down its groove until she was tucked on the floor. She closed her eyes, wanting to be in one of the twin beds with Toby beside her. She wanted it to be tomorrow, when new light would give them another chance. She wanted her calculator back, and she wanted someone to acknowledge that the other girl had started it in the first place.

XIV

"*Buon giorno, signor.* IT IS NINEAYEM," A VOICE SPOKE INTO HIS EAR.
When had he picked up the phone?

"Um, *grazie*," said Toby.

He hung the phone up and rolled onto his back, ready to slip back
into sleep, but he looked to his left first to look at July. But she wasn't
there. Where—?

"Hi," she said.

He lifted his chin and looked around the darkened room. She had
moved the desk chair next to the bathroom doorway and was reading
by the blue light of the bathroom.

"How long have you been awake?"

"A few hours," she said. "This jet lag is screwing with me."

Toby remembered finding her in nearly the same spot the night
before, sleeping with her head against the doorframe while he had
talked to the girls and argued with Jenny.

He had stroked July's face and she half woke. He helped her up
and she leaned into his body. They moved together across the room to
the bed, onto which she flopped and immediately gave herself to sleep
again. As he put the covers over her, Toby promised that tomorrow
would be better. Tomorrow he would show her the day she deserved,
the day they both had hoped for.

He forced himself to sit up higher, trying to wriggle from the
bed's gravity.

July came over and sat on her side of the bed, her thumb wedged between the pages of her book.

"Merry Christmas Eve," she said.

"Huh? Oh God, I forgot."

He rubbed the sandpaper on his cheek. Once he had the girls he had grown to dread Christmas Eve. They were so antsy the entire day, asking if it was Christmas yet, would Santa bring them this or that toy, and then they couldn't fall asleep at bedtime. After the separation, he missed the excitement of shiny wrapping paper and stockings. He would have to remember to call the girls again tomorrow night when it was Christmas morning their time.

He looked at July. She was already dressed and ready to go.

"Have you been out already?"

"No. Well I went downstairs to get some coffee, but that's all."

"Did you eat anything?"

"No, I was waiting for you."

"When does it close?

"Ten."

"Well let's get down there before they take your food away," he said.

There were still a few people at breakfast when Toby and July arrived. In the corner were two couples, their plates nearly empty. Along the wall was another couple, in their thirties Toby guessed, who looked American, or maybe British.

July moved immediately for the breakfast table, which had croissants and pastries, toast, butter and jams, yogurt, fruit, cheese, and cold cereal. Toby headed first to the coffee machine and drank half a cup and refilled it before considering the food.

July sat at a table closest to the food spread. She was pulling apart a croissant, and on her plate were two buttered and jammed pieces of toast and at least one of everything else on the table.

Toby picked a few things and joined her at the table.

"Jet lag makes me hungry," said July.

Toby chuckled.

"You must be perpetually jet lagged."

"Maybe," she smiled, popping a golden croissant knob into her mouth.

"What do you want to do today?" he asked.

"Mm ... eat gelato. Walk around a little bit. Maybe see the Duomo if it's open, or at least the outside. Or a museum. Eat a pizza in a piazza, get gelato, walk around, see everything, get dinner somewhere good, eat more gelato. You know," she shrugged. "You know this city better than I do, so I'll have to defer to you."

"All right. There's a Christmas tree in the Piazza della Repubblica. We should see that."

"We can eat pizza there," chirped July.

"But it would be beautiful at night with all the lights."

"We could see it twice."

"If we just start walking we'll see more than if we plan it."

"Sounds good," July said. "As long as there's gelato."

Toby smiled and reached across the table. She smiled and put her hand in his. He liked the flowing forgiveness of a relationship that hadn't worn canyons bickering over the same things, that didn't have the long memories of every perceived slight and flaw. Was every relationship like that, or just the one he had with Jenny? If he stayed with July for fifteen years, would they grind the same grooves of tension and resentment, or would she be different? Were women *really* different from each other?

He tried to think back to his relationships before Jenny. Most of them had broken before they could erode. There was Elena, his college girlfriend, whom he met his sophomore year on the crew team; she was also a rower, and she was tall and toned like a sculpture. They had been together from that year until a year after they graduated. They had broken up because she wanted to get married and go to grad school in Michigan. Toby told her he didn't want to move to Ann Arbor and leave his emerging real estate career, but the real reason had been that he hadn't wanted to marry yet, so he hadn't seen if the friction grew between them.

When he and Jenny had started dating it had been much more stomach butterflies and infatuation, like sending the drink had been arranged by a fate from the restaurant's ceiling. Now with July, he couldn't see himself ending it, but he wasn't sure he could see where they were headed. Like voyagers, they were sailing together through an ocean without knowing if they would hit land, and what land it would be, or if they would just fall off the edge of the earth. He had long since stopped looking for the future—he always ended up on an entirely new continent.

They left the hotel soon after breakfast. It was chilly and bright, though the sky was fogged over by a tulle layer of clouds. Together Toby and July walked, away from the Arno toward the train station. They passed laundromats, kebab stores and residences, soon entering a more touristy area with cafés, restaurants, and clothing stores.

"You lead the way," he told July. "Let's explore."

"I have a terrible sense of direction—we'll get lost."

"I know where we are. Just go."

She went, and Toby followed. Into the dingy train station, where July stood watching the numbers and locations on the timetable click and shuffle; out past a McDonald's, along a street so busy it was nearly impossible to cross; past stores decorated for Christmas; endless bars and bookstores; burrowed away from the Arno there was a Greek restaurant, and soon a Chinese restaurant; they walked by small groceries, art stores, and Internet cafés and into smaller streets that wound around dark buildings with dumpster stench. They walked further east, into a district with small local shops and antique stores. A few times, when July lost her bearings, they circled the same place more than once, and July stopped on a corner, looking at a familiar sign and frowning.

"Wait … were we just here?"

"This is the third time we've passed this place," Toby laughed.

"Oh, whoops!" she shrugged sheepishly.

They walked in periods of silence until one of them, usually July, had something to say.

"What do you think Italian Chinese food tastes like?"

"Has Florence changed at all?"

"Do you think it *will* change?"

"Why would you travel all the way to Italy just to buy Louis Vuitton?"

"Why is Florence your favorite city?" July asked as they emerged at the Arno on the other side of the Ponte Vecchio.

"Well," he started. "I guess because it's old, and it's probably looked the same for a long time. It's comforting to know that there's someplace in the world that doesn't change much. But I guess you could say that for most places in Italy."

They stopped at the Arno and leaned against a wall.

"But why Florence?" she persisted.

"Well. Rome is really big, and more modern. I don't know, it's not that I don't like Milan or Venice, it's just that … I've always felt like Florence has this calm buzz, like things are happening but slower. More relaxed. It's easy to know; it's open; and it's smaller but there's always something to discover. I guess a lot of places are like that but …"

He turned and looked at July, "What do you think? First impressions?"

"I think I could live here," she said. "And I don't think it would ever get old."

"I've always wanted to live here. To just sell everything and move here once the girls grew up, get one of those apartments there and just be here every day. Just live out life and never know it. Burrow in and never come out."

"That sounds intriguing."

"I always wanted to be an expat, but I never had the guts."

They stood in silence. Toby watched the breeze ruffle the Arno. Even though he had the guts now, he also had responsibility. He couldn't leave the girls behind; see them less than he already did. Even if he moved after they had grown, it would be easier to just visit Mom. If Mom and Dad had stayed together, the girls wouldn't have a choice. But now they did, and they would choose Mom. He would be an island here, the abstract dad who lives in Italy and sends checks for gifts. But maybe that was just another way of not having the guts. Not having the guts to hope that his girls would go out of their way to see him because he was their dad and not forget him. How much could they forget?

"I think we need pizza," said July.

Toby looked at his watch. She was right—they had been walking for almost three hours, and his breakfast had worn off. An espresso would be perfect, too, just to warm his insides a little.

"Let's head towards the Ponte Vecchio a bit," he said. "There aren't many places to eat over here."

"You lead," said July.

At the next bridge they turned back into corridors of the city. They rolled over the cobblestone streets, past a few cafés and stores. Two blocks in from the river the right side of the street gaped open like a window onto a broad piazza. Flat and paved in stone the same color as the clouded sky, the piazza was surrounded by buildings of varying shades of yellow, souvenir carts and restaurants. Lording over the titan gray field was a cathedral, its exterior large and imposing, white and intricate as though it had been carved out of sugar.

The center section of the church stood almost twice as tall as the two sections flanking it. Each section had a door, and the three doors in a row made Toby think of a game show—what's behind door number one? Green grids divided the façade into rows of rectangles liked stacked dominoes. A blue six-pointed star pressed into the top of the center section like an Indian *bindi* and shrouded renovation scaffolds clung to the left side of the church like moss.

"Wow," said July, stopping at the edge of the piazza.

"The Santa Croce," said Toby. "Let's get some pizza, and we can eat here. Pizza in the piazza."

July smiled and leaned against him, folding her head onto his shoulder. He was being thoughtful, he realized, and not because he was trying to get credit at the wife bank. For a long while it had been only his girls who warranted such treatment. His heart had built a moat around itself and sequestered his daughters; July had swum across and stood knocking at the door.

A few minutes later they sat on the steps in front of the Santa Croce with pizzas in their laps warming their thighs through cardboard boxes. There were only a few other people loitering about; the world always seemed lonelier in winter.

"It must be perfect here when it's warmer," said July before taking a bite of her pizza.

"It is," Toby said, thinking of the sun's intensity, the vibrations from endless pools of visitors, the women everywhere showing legs and shoulders.

"In the summer," he said, "the sun feels like it's ten feet away, always basting you with your own sweat. The crowds are bigger and noisier. There's always someone shouting. There's an electricity when the whole piazza is filled with people brushing each other, taking pictures for strangers, smoking and eating and lazing. Everyone's in sunglasses, or their hands are always above their eyes to shield the sun. And if we were sitting still right here, like this, the energy of lifting the pizza to your mouth would be a heavy exertion, but the faint breeze on your arm would tickle like a paintbrush."

July looked at him but beyond him, remembering what it was like to be warm.

"And a little trickle of sweat would trail down past your ear," he said as he traced his finger along her hairline and past her ear. "Your lips would be coated in a layer of salt," as he traced his finger along her lips. "And your nose would turn pink like a slice of prosciutto," as his finger ran the slope of her nose and she laughed out loud.

"Let's stay until summer comes," she said, looking at him, her essence creeping under his eyeballs, pooling into the bags beneath his eyes and trickling down his throat.

He put his hand on the side of her face and leaned in, resting his forehead against hers. They sat with their heads together like conjoined twins, leaning into each other as though they might fuse. When they finally separated, they each had large red spots on their foreheads like the star atop the Santa Croce.

July in Florence was a beautiful thing.

"July," would come a hoarse whisper from the darkness.
"July."

A hand on her shoulder.

"Up and at 'em July. Yeast waits for no slumber."

Her father would be sitting on the edge of her bed, an apron already tied over his flannel pajamas. Her light would be on, a grating orange laser cutting open her skull. It was still dark outside, and would be for at least an hour yet.

"Dad, make the brioche yourself," she would say, hoping that maybe this year she would convince him.

"No. Up up, up. Brioche is best when kneaded by four hands."

She would sigh and roll her eyes but sit up, "Dad, how come Ansel and Iago never have to help?"

Every year he gave a new excuse, "Everyone knows you can't make brioche with more than one Y chromosome."

"Your brothers have hands like chicken feet and because you're my favorite kid, now get up."

And always, "You'll thank me tomorrow when we're eating sticky buns from heaven."

Eventually she would put on a sweatshirt and some heavy socks and trudge down to the kitchen, lit by the fluorescent overhead but negated by the dark matter flooding through the windows.

Her father would be waiting behind the counter, holding her apron. He would tie it around her waist, clap his hands and pronounce, "Let's get to work!"

They would measure the yeast, take the temperature of the milk to make sure it was warm but not so hot that it would kill the yeast. They would cut perfect dice of frozen butter and mix it with the flour and sugar and salt by hand—no machines allowed in the kitchen of Gray Van Buren—handing off the spoon like a relay baton when their arms got tired. They would mix it with all the eggs, cream, yeast and flour, stirring and fighting against the thickening dough.

Then they would knead, leaning in, the heels of their hands thrusting all their weight into the floured counter. As she got older and his hands grew a bit arthritic, her father ceded more of the kneading responsibilities to her. When the dough was finally smooth, long past the time July's muscles had surrendered, they would let the dough rest. Usually the windows would be turning ashen as the plastic wrap covered the dough, and while the dough rose inside the balmy oven, July and her father would eat two or three bowls of don't-tell-your-mother Golden Grahams, drinking the yellowish milk from the bottom of the bowl with each serving.

Then they would go to the spare freezer in the garage and take out the whole goose that Dad had bought weeks before and set it on the counter to thaw, then sit at the table with a stack of Dad's cookbooks, and Dad would say, "Okay July, what are we having for dessert this year?"

Each year July would choose—sour cream apple pie, chocolate peanut butter cake, pear gingerbread, caramel nut tart—but he mandated that it be different every year. By the time she decided, the dough would be ready to be sealed into a plastic bag and refrigerated until the next morning. Then each had a hot shower until the water ran cold, got dressed, and took a daybreak trip to the grocery store to get dessert ingredients and last minute provisions.

Last year on the way to the store, her father had been talking about the intricacies of some Indian dish he wanted to make, when July finally asked, "Dad, why do you care about food so much?"

"I've told you, July, what you eat matters. It says something about who you are, how you live your life."

"What does this curry say about your life?"

"It says, I'm open, I'm interested, I want to see your world."

"Right. And what does Golden Grahams say about your life?"

"Ah well," he turned to her with a sly grin, "even the most discerning of palates is allowed his vices. But your life will improve with the quality of the food you eat."

"I know that, you've practically brainwashed me my whole life. But *why*? Why do you spend virtually all your time cooking or recipe hunting? Mom says you didn't know how to cook when you met her, you only knew how to eat."

"You've eaten your mother's food, July. Learning to cook was a matter of survival."

"It's not *that* bad, Dad, it's just nothing special."

"It's ignorant and blindingly unimaginative," he responded, a bit of sharpness jutting through his words.

"Whoa, geez, Dad," July frowned. "But Mom likes different kinds of food. She'll eat anything."

"Your mother would eat rocks if someone told her they were rice. She doesn't appreciate the subtle and defining characteristics of foods or cuisines. She doesn't even know there's a difference between basmati rice and arborio. She once tried to make *paella* with jasmine rice! Oh when I was in Valencia, the *paella* was cosmic, July."

"You went to Valencia?"

"Yes, a long time ago," he sighed. "Just after I met your mother. She heard me rave about that *paella* and thought she'd make it for me herself. Back when she was still trying to impress me. By then I had mastered the basics of cooking, but when I tried to teach her after the *paella* fiasco, she just shrugged. So I took her to a Spanish restaurant instead, and she seemed to enjoy the *paella*. A month or two later I took her to a Mexican restaurant, since they were sending me to Mexico next. She seemed to enjoy that restaurant, too, and since she was still trying to impress me, I managed to convince her to come along to Mexico."

He gazed out the windshield.

"What happened?" asked July. She had never heard so much of the story before.

He scratched his head vigorously.

"Some people are just not cut out for travel."

"But—why? What happened? Why did *you* have to stop?"

"Your mother has a very concrete idea of how life should work, July. The best I could do was travel in the kitchen."

"But I don't understand."

"Trust me. It was the preferable choice. I figured if I couldn't take you around the world, I might as well raise you to cook and eat well. That's why we get up at dawn to make brioche. I won't get a chance to take you to France on a bakery tour, but that doesn't mean you should never experience it as best you can."

July thought of this now, sitting next to Toby on the numbing steps of the Santa Croce and watching him finish his pizza. He had said that Jenny was not a cook. Could that have had anything to do with their relationship? She scoffed. Her father had brainwashed her to think like him. It was ridiculous—no one would divorce because of irreconcilable culinary differences.

Her father would be starting the brioche dough in only a few hours. July imagined him this year, alone under the fluorescent kitchen spotlight, switching the spoon from his right arm to his left and back again, his prematurely arthritic hands cramping around the wooden spoon, sharing the crunch of Golden Grahams with only himself and the morning light, choosing the dessert on his own, eating two-handed brioche sticky buns on Christmas morning. Or maybe he would enlist another helper. Maybe she was easier to replace than her father let on.

"What's the matter?" asked Toby.

"Oh nothing," sighed July. "I was just thinking about my dad. I always help him cook for the holidays."

"You haven't called home yet."

July shrugged.

"So what should we do now?" she asked, changing the subject.

"I don't know," sighed Toby. "Let's find someplace warm."

About ten minutes later they found an open bookstore a bit north of the Duomo where they could relax. Toby wandered off to the children's section while July meandered past the bookstore café and over to the section with books about food. She brought a book about Indian food written in Italian over to the café and sat at the only available place, on a stool at the coffee bar.

"The best Indian food in the city is across the river," said the bartender in Italian-accented English.

July looked up. Slightly taller than July, the man had a buzz cut and a dark Italian brow. His nose was boxy, like two wider Legos lined end to end. Actually his physique seemed to be made of rectangles of all sizes and scales. A simple gray sweater stretched across his chest beneath a black apron. He was young—younger than Toby, at least—but no more than thirty.

"Florence has Indian food?" she replied in Italian.

"American?" he asked in English.

"*Sì.*"

"*Parla Italiano.*"

"*Sì.*"

"*Va bene.*"

They continued to converse in Italian. *Finally*, thought July, *four years of studying pays off.*

"There's Indian food in Florence?" July asked again.

"Yes, across the river and a bit west. It's very good. Most restaurants are closed on Christmas, but this one is open."

"Good, I'll need somewhere to eat tomorrow."

"Are you with your family?"

"No, they're back in America."

"Not with your family on Christmas? That's sad."

July shrugged, "It's okay."

"I'm not with my family either; they are in Torino."

"Is that where you're from?

"Yes. I've been in Florence for a long time, studying architecture. I'm practically Florentine."

"Was it hard to move away from your family?"

He shrugged, swirling his wrist as though he were scattering confetti.

"I did not want to stay in Torino. I don't know if I want to stay in Italy. The world is more than Italy. I hope to design buildings for all of it."

"It would be like you lived everywhere."

"Would you like some coffee? On the house."

"Oh. Yes, thank you," said July.

"What's your name?" he asked as he was making her coffee.

"July."

"*Luglio.*"

"Yes."

"That's a pretty name, for a pretty girl. I'm Massimo," he leaned forward and reached his hand over the counter.

"Nice to meet you," said July, shaking his hand.

"You have beautiful hair," he said. "Like the color of the rooftops."

As he said this he swooped his wrist with a flourish.

July smiled and laughed in embarrassment, "Thanks."

He put a cup of coffee on the counter for her, then leaned on the counter, his arms crossed so that his hands cupped his opposite elbow. Sometimes he would lean closer, to her, like he was trying to pull her in; then he would lean back and stretch his arms straight in front of him and make a broad generalization.

"Have you seen the *David* yet?"

"No," said July, sipping her coffee.

"You must see it; it's beautiful. Even though most places are closed during Christmas there are still many things to see. It's good to be here now. There are fewer tourists. I can take you to the Indian restaurant tomorrow for Christmas dinner."

"Oh, uh …"

July looked at Massimo, the straightness to him, sharply chiseled. Though he must be older than she was, to July he looked very young. There were no crinkles around his eyes, or rivers across his forehead. The way he stood and moved his hands and wrists, how he smiled and how his dark eyes could still seem bright, all this made it seem as though his life were nimbler. How was he so forward, so at ease with making plans with a total stranger?

"I would like that, but I'm not here alone. I'm here with my boyfriend."

Massimo's face didn't register a change, "Which one is your boyfriend? Where is he?"

He turned and surveyed the bookstore, "Is he that one?" He pointed to a young man in a navy sweater with glasses and gelled hair.

"No," she laughed. "No, he's—" She scanned the store and found Toby perusing the English language section.

"He's that one," she said, pointing to Toby.

"He's that one? The old man? He's not your father?"

"Uh, no," smiled July.

"He is rich?"

"Uh—" she frowned. She really didn't know.

"It's okay. I will take you both to the Indian restaurant. You both have to eat, yes?"

"Well, I'll have to—ask and, see if he's okay with that. He may have something else in mind."

"Let's bring him over here. We'll ask."

"Uh—"

"What's his name?"

"Um, Toby?" said July, confused.

"Toby!" shouted Massimo. "Toby!"

Toby looked up, his face contorted in perplexity. He looked lost, like he had heard a phantom voice calling his name, until the movement of Massimo's arm wave registered and he saw July at the counter.

July's mouth dropped open a bit. Did he really just do that? Was it July's imagination that Massimo had been hitting on her, or seemed interested in her to some degree? Nothing in his demeanor had changed when she mentioned Toby. Maybe he was just one of those really friendly, flirty people who don't like you that way, he treats everybody *that way*. Or he just had total disregard for her relationship with Toby.

July wasn't supposed to be agonizing about this. Having a boyfriend was supposed to free her from that one burden.

Toby walked over to the counter, a book still in his hand. His eyes went from July to Massimo and back again, squinting a little tighter the closer he got.

"Hey," he said to July, putting a hand on her back. "Is everything okay?"

"Yeah, uh. Toby, this is Massimo."

"*Piacere*," said Massimo in an operatic Italian accent. "I was telling your July about a wonderful Indian restaurant that will be open tomorrow night, Christmas. I would like to invite you both to have dinner with me there tomorrow."

"Oh! Well, uh, let me have a moment with July so we can discuss this."

"Of course," said Massimo, bending a little at the waist and moving to another part of the counter.

Toby turned to July. His brow furrowed, his eyes squeezed more confusion, and his mouth opened as if he were going to say something, but instead he just cocked his head.

July shrugged. "He just started talking to me."

"Was he hitting on you?"

"I don't know!"

"Of course he was, it's Italy. He's a man, he's Italian, you're pretty."

"Well—maybe he's just friendly," July shrugged again.

"Do you want to go?"

"I don't know. I mean, Florentine Indian food sounds intriguing, but ... I'm here to spend time with you."

July wanted to go, but she didn't want to hurt Toby's feelings. Going out for dinner, them and another guy who was probably hitting on July? Weird ... but still—dinner with an Italian, a local, was an enticing prospect.

Toby took a long breath and shifted his weight, putting his free hand in his pocket.

Was he angry? Or suspicious? July looked around his face for signs of disturbance, but he had on the same poker face as when he had met Chris.

"Where did you have in mind for our Christmas dinner?" asked July.

"I didn't really. A lot of places are going to be closed though, he's right about that. I hadn't really planned it out, to be honest. Do you want to?"

"Oh. Well I —I don't know. It might be ... interesting."

"Well, what's going to happen? I'll be there and maybe it'll make for a good travel story. We can always say we'll go and change our minds."

"True," said July, trying to sound impartial. "I guess let's do it then."

Toby played with a section of her hair.

"It'll be an adventure," he said. "You and me. And—Massimo."

July leaned over the counter, "Massimo," she called.

He slid back over to them.

"Dinner tomorrow sounds great," she said.

"*Molto bene,*" he said. "I will bring a friend, so that we are not the odd number."

"Where should we meet you?" asked Toby.

"Where are you staying?"

"The Hotel Ariele," said Toby. "It's on Via Magenta, a few bridges west of here."

"Ah, *bene*. Let's meet at the Westin Excelsior, just past the Ponte Amerigo Vespucci. You know it?"

"Yes, I know it," said Toby.

"Eight o'clock?" said Massimo.

"Eight o'clock."

"*Bene, bene, bel Natale. Arrivederci.*"

"*Arrivederci,*" said July and Toby.

July stood up and Toby put an arm around her, "Where to?" he asked.

"Can we go back to the hotel? I need a nap."

"Sure thing."

Toby, arm still around July, held the door open for her, and as she passed him, she thought she felt his body twist as his neck craned around back towards Massimo. Did he see him, watching them go? Did their eyes meet? What, if they had connected, could two men who had never met say to each other across the arena of a flurried bookstore?

As soon as she stood from the café stool, a leaden weariness had burrowed into the hollows of July's cheeks. *So this is jet lag,* she thought, *where your soul feels light but your body feels heavy, when your body wants to sleep but your mind wants to see, and the only remedy is a frenzied dreamless sleep.*

They walked through the stiffened air, the street frosty with anticipation, with the promise that tomorrow the Christmas cold would feel more sensual and eloquent than it did on normal days.

Florence stretched out before her, longer and more elastic than it had seemed that morning. The hotel expanded away from her like they were at two ends of a rubber band, the hotel lengthening away. The buildings passed by, meaningless in their indication of how close the hotel was. When at last they passed beneath the hotel's awning, July felt as though she were no longer awake, like she was dreaming and what she was seeing now she was remembering from a dream from which she already awoke.

Each stair steeper than the last, her body heavier, her legs weaker, the hall longer, Toby struggled with the lock for years, until it finally gave way and July pushed in, falling through the room to the bed, an insect towards sugar she tumbled in, engulfed by the mattress like she had been swimming beneath a roof of ice and had finally found a hole to break the surface.

July was sprawled stomach down into the bed. One arm draped off the side and grazed the floor, and her feet, still in black boots, splayed heels apart at the bottom of the bed.

Toby removed his coat and shoes and sat on his side of the bed. He should sleep, too. At his age he sometimes had problems seeing nine o'clock without the inebriation of jet lag. He drank a large glass of water to insure that he would wake up in a few hours, then kicked his legs along the bed and lay down, staring at the ceiling.

So there it was. The younger man had to come some time. But a younger *Italian* man—that was like telling someone who lived in a house with fading paint and weakening plumbing that they could just switch to a new, state-of-the-art, two-story house with an ocean view—no charge.

July hadn't seemed overly charmed by Massimo. Toby could tell she wanted to go to dinner, but she had asked him, and she hadn't kept it secret, so maybe she wasn't lusting after this guy. Yet. And Massimo was bringing a wingman to dinner tomorrow night. Toby had pulled that trick once or twice before with moderate success, but never on an attached woman. But with Italian men, the line was a fine fishing wire. Italian men could flirt and touch you or put their arm around you and disguise it as their culture. Toby could work around a wingman easily enough, but to get around Massimo's inherent Italian-ness would require some cunning.

This is where four decades of life and fifteen years of marriage had gotten him—strategizing and dueling like July had no agency. All those years and he still hadn't shaken the jealousy and competitiveness.

While Toby and Jenny were still dating, Jenny became very close with a fellow dancer, Kevin. Kevin was, like a fierce majority of male dancers, very good looking. A chiseled, anatomical model with an underwear model's face. Toby had been under the impression that an identical majority of male dancers were gay, and that they made up the most good looking ones. But Toby hadn't been so sure about Kevin. Jenny talked about him a lot.

"Oh my God, last week in New York Kevin and I went out after rehearsal to this little French place and he ordered in French!"

"Kevin told me the funniest thing!"

"Kevin and I are going out for a drink after the show. You can come if you want."

"I was in Kevin's dressing room before the show last night, and—"

Of course, Jenny had denied anything romantic, pulling out the "friends" excuse. But she had never said anything about Kevin's sexuality, or whether she found him attractive or not. Her words slid around, unwinding like twine but never reaching the center cone. Toby decided not to worry too much; if there were really something going on, Jenny would have let on some time.

Eventually Kevin moved to another company and Toby and Jenny married. But a couple years into the marriage, Kevin resurfaced at Jenny's new company. There were post rehearsal drinks and dinners and more dressing room banter. Kevin reemerged as the new catchphrase in the Jenny lexicon.

Toby and Kevin had met a few times, exchanging brief good-to-see-yous backstage or at some company function, when Toby always had an arm around Jenny and always watched the two of them closely. But mostly he kept his suspicions, his fears, his frustrations to himself.

Then Toby and Jenny threw a New Year's party, to which Jenny suggested inviting Kevin. Toby agreed; he didn't want to play the jealous husband. On the night of the party, Kevin kissed Jenny on the cheek and put a hand on her lower back to say hello, then shook Toby's hand. The two of them wandered off to the kitchen, leaving Toby among the festive chatter.

A bit later, Kevin went to the restroom, the first time he had un-Velcro-ed himself from Jenny all night. So Toby waited outside the door until Kevin came out.

"Oh, excuse me," said Kevin, exiting the bathroom and swishing out of Toby's way.

"Look, Kevin," said Toby, stopping him in the dark hallway.

Kevin turned to Toby, eyebrows raised.

"You and my wife seem awfully friendly."

"Well, we get along. Most ballerinas are chain-smoking prima donnas. They're hard to take."

"Look. I don't know what you're trying to pull here, but I don't like it."

"Excuse me?"

"She's *my* wife. Take a few steps back."

Kevin stepped backwards.

"No, I mean figuratively," spat Toby. *What a moron.*

"There's … nothing *inappropriate* going on here. Maybe you should try trusting you wife a little."

Toby couldn't really remember what he had said after that, or how the conversation had ended. He only remembered that Kevin had run off to tell Jenny everything, because she was cold to Toby the rest of the night, begrudged him a midnight kiss like a concubine held against her will, and exploded at him later after everyone had gone home. What Toby saw as a simple Kevin issue, Jenny quilted into an expansive constitution on trust and marriage without uttering Kevin's name but once or twice. But they were young, it was early on. Things patched up.

Soon after, Jenny got pregnant and went on leave. She never mentioned Kevin again, so Toby thought of him only when he wasn't sure where Jenny was; why she wasn't home yet, who that was on the phone.

The divorce had evicted his life of Kevin. He thought he would never have to deal with another Kevin, and he hadn't counted on an Italian Kevin. *I'm too old for this.*

He decided that he didn't lack trust in July but instead lacked trust in her age. He sighed and tried to rid himself of worry, giving himself over to the fatigue brimming inside him.

When Toby awoke, the room had been fogged with black haze and the window had seeped into the night. Toby turned on a light and looked at his watch. Six seventeen. Good. Not too late.

He rose and shuffled to the bathroom. As he brushed his teeth he decided to wake July, and then shave for dinner while she called her parents. He went back to the bed, where July lay, unmoved and dripping from the bed in her coat and boots. He lay down alongside her and traced her earlobe and jaw line gently, and then along her hairline, down her nose and to her mouth, open slightly and a wet spot on the bed beneath it.

"Hey," he said quietly.

Stillness.

"Hey," he tried again.

Not even an eyelash flutter.

"It's dinner time," he coaxed.

Her eyes opened slowly and Toby laughed. Of course that would wake her.

"Huh?"

"Up you get. Sleep any more and you won't sleep tonight."

"Ugh."

She turned her face into the pillow, then sat up, head bobbing up on her neck well after her body.

"Come on. Call your family and then we'll get some dinner."

"Do I have to?"

"Yes."

She flopped back onto the bed, "I need a hot bath."

"Call your family first."

"Yes, Daddy," she said, sliding to the other side of the bed and picking up the phone.

Oh God, I sounded like her father, he thought, his stomach sinking. *Oh God.*

"Hey, how do you dial America?" she asked, sounding totally befuddled.

"Oh, country code—

"What's the country code?"

"Zero zero one."

"Okay …"

"Area code, then number."

"Thanks."

He stayed on the bed to make sure she connected.

"Hi, Dad."

Toby stood up and walked over to the bathroom to shave.

"Good," he heard her say.

He listened in over the gristly friction of blade to stubble.

"Uh, we walked around and had lunch, and—oh, pizza ... Uh, prosciutto, mozzarella, and mushroom ... I had one last night. It was good. Rare, juicy, thick. The way you like it ... No Mom, all the stores here are too expensive ... Mom, I don't *need* a leather purse ... Yeah, well."

Toby peeked out of the bathroom. July was holding the phone about a foot from her ear. "That's good ... How's your brioche, Dad? ... Oh. That sucks. Maybe your yeast is off? ... Well I don't know! ... Dad I don't really think it has anything to do with fewer hands ..."

She was probably holding the phone away from her head again. Hands and brioche?

"Right, well, I'm going to go because it's almost dinner time and— Dad I had one last night, I'm going to get something different ... I don't know ... Dad, I don't know if they'll *have* that ...Yes! Fine, I'll get it, I'll get it ... Okay ... Yeah, Merry Christmas Eve. Say hi to Iago and Ansel for me ... Okay—yeah, I'll call tomorrow. Okay ... Okay ... Yes, Mom ... Okay ... Bye."

Toby wiped his face and came out of the bathroom. July was standing beside the bed. She had taken off her coat and was pulling off a boot.

"Everything okay?" he asked.

"Oh, yeah, just fine," she said, pulling her shirt over her head. "Though I'm apparently bound by culinary accords to order lasagna tonight."

She rolled her eyes as she took off her pants.

"I think we could arrange that."

He didn't hear her response; the sound of her undergarments coming off had deafened him. *No matter how many times you see a beautiful woman naked, watching her undress never gets old,* Toby thought. *The only good that came of women wearing clothes was watching the clothes come off.* She walked past him in a blur of flesh.

"I'm taking a bath," she said as she entered the bathroom. A moment later she leaned out the door, "Feel free to join me."

Had Toby's clothes ever come off so fast?

The narrow rectangular tub could sit one person, knees bent, with moderate comfort. Fitting two people was like a game of Tetris, but Toby and July managed to fit, facing each other, by interlocking their knees.

"This looks a whole lot more glamorous in the movies," said July.

"In movies there are always bubbles blocking your view. It's much better like this," he replied.

July laughed, then leaned her head back, the tips of her hair darkening like calligraphy brushes as they swept the surface of water, her neck open and vulnerable and inviting, her clavicles protruding like shallow incense holders. The insides of his legs clasped and skated around the smooth outsides of hers. He liked that he had her securely, like he could clamp his legs around hers in case she turned into a mermaid and tried to swim away.

They stayed like that until the heat of the water had dissipated. July leaned forward and added a shaft of hot water.

"Come over here," said Toby.

July took half a stroke forward and brushed his chest. They kissed, and then July corkscrewed around so that she was leaning her back against his chest. Toby's mouth was perfectly positioned next to her earlobe grapevine, and he scraped his teeth gently against the spot and she shuddered and jolted and giggled.

This was all he wanted. At this moment, the divorce seemed like something positive. No divorce, no July, no July in a tub in Florence. In this one selfish moment, the divorce had had no emotional, financial, or familial tolls. Instead it was part of a journey that led here, to the back of July's neck, to her body floating against his.

"July," he said.

She turned her head over her shoulder.

Before he had time to think first, it slipped out, "You aren't going to go off with Massimo are you?"

Oh shit. Did I really just say that? Did I just bring up Massimo while we're in the bath together? Holy fuck, Toby, just put your head under the water and end it now.

July's head cocked backward and she let out a monosyllabic laugh, "What?"

Toby opened his mouth but he was pretty sure that anything he said would make it worse. Instead he jutted his lower jaw and swiveled it from side to side.

July swiveled her body around to face him, "Are you kidding?"

"I didn't ... mean to say that ..."

"Toby, are you *kidding*? I—"

She stopped abruptly, just short of forming whatever came after that. Her eyes pulled back slightly and her brow slackened up a centimeter.

What had she meant to say? What was the sentence that had begun out loud but continued only in her thoughts?

"What?" he asked.

"I … would … never … I couldn't—*leave* you like that. For a *stranger*. For—anyone," she whispered that last word.

July was shaking her head, her eyes clinging to his. The inner corners of her eyes looked as though they may tilt skyward and slide down her face, trickling and dripping hollowly into the water like two dulcet plops on a marimba.

"July, hey," he framed her face in his hands. "Hey, I'm sorry, I just—I don't know. He's young. And … Italian. And, you know, a *hunk*."

July laughed, her shoulders rolling forward and neck falling open.

"Toby, *you're* a hunk."

She leaned in and kissed him as he laughed, as though he had never heard a sentence more absurd. *Minds change, vision fades,* he thought. *I hope hers doesn't.*

He pushed the thought from his mind, because he was kissing a gorgeous woman in a bathtub, and she was kissing him and her hands had slipped below the water.

If my life were a movie, the screen would fade to black, he thought. *How wonderful that life doesn't do that.*

They walked east along the Arno in search of an open restaurant. The air felt minty against his newly-shaved face. They passed the Excelsior on their left, and though they both looked at it as they walked by, neither he nor July said anything.

July had on a long forest green coat and a white scarf nested around her neck, and while Toby always preferred women's summer attire, July looked like the present any man would hope to find under his Christmas tree.

They turned away from the river as they reached the Ponte Vecchio. The streets were hushed and quiet like the backstage at a play. Soon they came upon the brightly lit display window of a Louis Vuitton store, the headless white mannequins contorted to showcase various LV branded pieces of clothing.

Ahead Toby recognized the Piazza della Repubblica, the archway and columns. Just through the archway was a carousel and beyond it, a Christmas tree.

"Oh, look," sighed July as she sped up toward the tree. She stopped a few feet away and gazed at it, reflections of the red lights sprinkling her pupils.

"On Christmas Eve we always make sugar cookies and eat them by the tree after dinner," she said.

"That sounds special," said Toby.

"What do you guys do for Christmas?" she asked.

"Well, it's different now."

"Oh."

"When I was a kid, we used to go to have a big dinner with my paternal grandparents. My mom would usually make a ham with potatoes and a pie or two. And then we would open a present each, and we would play games and nap until we all went to midnight mass. In the morning we would get up early and look in our stockings until our parents woke up. Mom would fix sweet rolls from a Pillsbury tube and we would open presents and go to church again. We would go to my maternal grandparents' house for dinner and eat my grandmother's dry turkey and fruit cake."

July stood looking at him long after he finished.

"What?" he asked.

"It's just—you've never told me about your family before. I mean, your childhood family."

"Oh. Yeah. Well, it was a long time ago."

"Are your parents still alive?"

He sighed. "Yeah. Yeah, they are. We ... haven't been on the best of terms, especially since the divorce. They really loved Jenny, and the kids of course. They're pretty against divorce in general. They think it's a sign of failure to accept God. They go to church too much."

"Oh. I'm sorry," said July.

Toby shrugged.

"I didn't know you grew up with religion," she said.

He had grown up with too much religion—spending every Sunday in church wishing he were climbing trees, always saying family prayers and graces, doing forced missionary work the summer he was sixteen, attending church socials and enduring endless lectures from his parents about God's plan for him.

"I never bought it. I hated church. But," he said, sticking his hands in his pockets. "I still pray. I don't even know why I do it, or whom I'm praying to. But sometimes it's comforting to think that by hoping enough, you can will something to happen."

Toby looked back at the Christmas tree, red and white lights peeping through the branches. Prayer, he knew, was futile. How many times had he begged.

Please let me love my wife again.

Please help me save my marriage.

Please help me fix my life.

It hadn't worked. Solutions lay only in the past, locked away and displayed in a memory zoo like animals strutting circles of regret behind bars. Prayer just made way for more cages and new species.

After a few minutes of silence, July threaded her arm through Toby's. "Let's find an open restaurant," she said, gently.

He nodded and they walked slowly beneath two sets of stars, one strung in a canopy over the street, the other laced into the ebony sky.

Is there a God? Toby wondered. *Does he have a plan? And is this part of it?*

If there is a God, thought July, *then this is it.*

A lump in a bowl, covered by white and red and a helmet of baked cheese and bathing in a swirl of red and white. She sat, staring dumbly at her lasagna, her throat numbed by the first forkful of béchamel and tomato.

"Good?" asked Toby, looking up from his pasta.

"It's—I—"

Toby raised his eyebrows, waiting for the sentence.

July had nothing.

"That good, huh?" he said, his eyebrows raising higher. He reached his fork across the table for a bite.

"Hey!" shouted July, moving her fork defensively in front of his.

"Who's paying for this?"

"Fine. One bite. A *small* one," she begrudged.

Toby scooped in his fork, which emerged with a bite bigger than July would like. He lifted it to his mouth, dripping a blob of precious cheese onto the white tablecloth. July reached over, picked it up with her fingers and placed it in her mouth.

"Wow," swallowed Toby. "Did you just eat that from the table?"

"You wasted it," shrugged July, and returned her attention to the steaming bowl in front of her. Somewhere in there, between the crystal ball of noodles and endless cheese and tomato, lay the answer to any question she may have. Soft and smooth and rich, the way the world should be, not the way it was.

After dinner, July made Toby take her back to the *gelateria*, since she reminded him that they hadn't had any gelato all day. They sat on the window ledge again, scooping and licking. July finished hers first and watched Toby slowly and deliberately nibble down his cone.

"Toby," she said.

He looked over at her mid nibble.

"Thank you."

"Sure."

"No, I mean … thank you. For the whole trip."

He lowered his cone, "You're welcome."

They kissed briefly and Toby turned back to his diminishing cone.

"Toby," she said again.

He looked back at her, popping the pointy end of the cone into his mouth.

"Why did you bring me here?"

"Because you get nasty without your gelato fix."

"You know what I mean."

Toby rubbed a napkin over his lips, chewed, swallowed and cleared his throat.

"Well," he started, then cleared his throat again. "I wanted to. I knew we would have fun together."

"That was it?"

"No, well, I mean ... I knew that if I came alone, I would just spend the whole time thinking about you anyway."

July wanted to ask him about the future. Where were they going? But they had had such a good day together, and during dinner he had been present and his eyes had crinkled affectionately. Today should remain as it was, unspoiled and pure.

So she smiled and propped her chin on his shoulder, so that her mouth was right at his ear.

"I'm so glad you did," she said. "Because otherwise I'd be at home right now wishing I was with you."

"And what would you be imagining us doing?" he asked in a low voice.

She giggled. "Eating gelato," she said, raising an eyebrow.

Toby smiled and turned his face towards hers, rubbing his nose against hers, kissing the tip of it, and moving his lips up to her forehead, down to each of her cheeks, and then to her mouth.

"What do you say we take this back to the hotel?" he asked.

"I'd say that sounds like a fine idea."

He stood up and held out his hand, "Follow me, my lady."

July took his hand and stood. Toby smiled and led her out of the shop.

In following him, I follow but myself. I am not what I am, she thought.

Toby was on the phone with his daughters again. From what July could discern, they had spent the day making snowmen, baking cookies with their grandma, playing games. July could tell when Jenny got on the line; Toby's voice shifted abruptly from doting fascination to guarded aloofness.

July lay on the bed reading. She had been half listening as Toby talked to his daughters, but when his voice turned steely, she listened more closely, like she was a detective trying to solve a mystery. She just didn't know yet what the crime was.

"What did you get the girls for the holidays? ... hm. Mm-hm ... An iPod? What does a four-year old need with an iPod? ... Jenny, she's *four*... I thought we agreed that—Well I'm their *father*, I'm just as much a parent as you are—What'd you get Chloe ... a cell phone? I mean come on Jenny, they're still kids."

He sighed heavily and stuck his forehead into the space between his thumb and forefinger, "Fine. Great. Whatever. Just—"

He sighed again, "What are you all going to do tomorrow? ... Okay, so what's a good time for me to call? ... That's about eleven my time. Okay, I'll try to call sometime after that ... Yeah. Okay. Give the girls kisses for me ... Yeah. Bye."

He hung up and turned to July.

"She bought Grace an iPod."

"That seems a little ..." July wasn't sure whether she was allowed to give an opinion on child rearing strategies given her significant lack of parenting experience.

"Inappropriate?" he finished for her. "Yeah. It is."

He lay back against the pillows.

"So what are we going to do tomorrow?" asked July. "It's Christmas, after all."

"Well, pretty much everything's going to be closed. Most of the shops and restaurants and stuff. We could see what's open, relax, walk around."

"But we should do something to celebrate," she said. "We could wrap our books in newspaper and open them like presents."

Toby laughed. "Or," he ventured, rolling over and pulling his body against July's. "We could stay in all day. Open each other like presents."

July laughed. "That's one of the worst lines I've ever heard," she said, smiling and shaking her head.

"I thought it was pretty good," he said, grinning.

They wrapped themselves around each other, July's head facing into his neck, the warmth of his body and her breath thickening the air like summer in the South. A few minutes later, his breath turned rhythmic, sucking in and out faintly like a sea diving air hose.

XV

SINCE HE HAD MET JENNY, TOBY HAD ALWAYS SPENT CHRISTMAS AT her parents' house in Charlottesville, Virginia. Toby didn't really mind, since Christmas with his family was weighted with church and a lot of things he didn't believe. He first met Miriam and Alan after he and Jenny had been together nearly a year, a few months before their first trip to Florence. They lived in a large Tudor house with blue siding and white shutters.

He could remember standing on the stoop outside beneath the looming gold knocker in the ebony door, wondering what sort of people had raised a girl like Jenny. Strings of icicle lights hung dark on the roof gutters. He held Jenny's bag and she opened the door. Upon entering, Toby saw Christmas garlands all along the walls.

"Mom?" called Jenny. "Dad?"

Toby expected a motherly looking woman to emerge from the kitchen wiping her hands on a towel, but instead a slim woman with graying blonde hair like golden ashes poked her head from the living room. Her hair was expertly combed into a side part bun and she wore a flowing black turtleneck long sleeve dress, and around her neck hung a gold globe on a gold chain.

"Jenny!" she cried joyously.

"Hi, Mom."

They hugged, then Jenny stepped aside and motioned Toby forward.

"Mom, this is Toby."

"Toby," smiled her mother. "We've heard a lot about you; it's so good to finally meet you."

"Mrs. Sivertsen, I've heard a lot about you as well. It's a pleasure to meet you."

"Please, please, my name is Miriam," she waved. "Alan!"

"What?" came a voice burrowed upstairs.

"Alan! Jenny's home!"

"Wha—?"

"Jenny's home!"

A few moments later he appeared on the staircase, tall and not at all gray, wearing a flannel shirt tucked into his jeans. He padded down the stairs in his brown socks.

"Hiya Blondie!"

"Hi, Dad!" said Jenny, smiling.

They hugged, and then Alan turned to Toby, cocking his head expectantly.

"Daddy, this is Toby."

"Toby. Nice to meet you," Alan extended his had.

Toby took it and shook firmly, "Mr. Sivertsen. It's a pleasure."

"Please, please, come in."

In the living room stood a large, fragrant pine tree, blinking and glittering and twinkling, draped in so much tinsel that it seemed almost alive. Beneath the tree, a wall of presents wrapped in iridescent wrapping papers sat stacked and beckoning.

"That's quite a tree," said Toby.

"Well, we like our Christmas around here," smiled Miriam.

"Do you go to midnight mass?" he asked.

"Oh, no," she waved. "Family is spiritual enough."

It was the first Christmas that Toby had ever enjoyed. He remembered it in a mesh of turkey and wreaths and lights, wrapping paper and lots of laughter around a table. There had even been a present for him under the tree.

They continued going there for every Christmas after that. Though Alan had a way of droning on about his model plane hobby and Miriam always over cooked something, Christmas with the Sivertsens had always been a pleasant experience.

Three years ago, the last Christmas he spent with them, their welcoming smiles became a bit tighter, a bit more wary. Jenny had been telling them about her unhappiness, Toby's shortcomings, his total disregard for organization and logic. In retrospect, Toby thought that perhaps Jenny had informed her parents of her desire for a divorce before she had alerted Toby. Perhaps they had known that he would never celebrate with them again.

After the separation, Toby had been dismayed that Miriam and Alan became very aloof towards him. He had been under the impression that they had actually liked him, maybe even considered him part of the family, but their responses in their infrequent exchanges became monosyllabic, their tones noncommittal and begrudging. Toby took a two-year hiatus from celebrating Christmas.

Now he had July, who was reason to resume the celebration, at least minimally. Though the trip had been a gift to her, her companionship seemed more like a gift for him. He found himself awake with the start of the morning light, much too early for vacation, but July's presence had awakened him with some fraction of his former childish excitement for presents.

For a while he stared at the ceiling, thinking about his girls opening presents, and how their grandparents would be there to celebrate, more than adequately filling the "Dad Void." Maybe next year he would insist that the girls stay with him. But Jenny would never allow that. He didn't want to have to make a legal request, but maybe he would. Just to stick it to Alan and Miriam.

Toby turned his head to look at July, who, to his surprise, was also staring up at the ceiling.

"What are you doing awake?" he asked.

"I could ask the same of you."

He raised his eyebrows. Somehow, "I was plotting revenge on my former in-laws" didn't seem like a merry reply.

"It's Christmas," she smiled. "I still wake up early. It still makes me excited."

"Even without presents?"

"I have a present that I get to open for two weeks."

After a bit of unwrapping, they showered and dressed to go down to breakfast. But just before Toby could open the door, he looked at July and felt a beam of urgency explode from his chest out his sides and leaned in and kissed her hard, pushing her against the wall. Half clothed and frantic, they were constricted and uninhibited, the wall pushing and thudding back.

With the insistence expelled, Toby felt a burning in his thighs, and July rubbed her back and twisted it around. They grinned at each other, kissed, and opened the door, stepping together into the hallway. As they closed the door behind them, the door to room nine opened and a couple in their early fifties entered the hallway.

The man was almost completely bald, his head reflecting a stripe of the lights overhead. His overly round glasses flanked his long, skinny nose that ended in a rounded tip. The woman was petite and slim, her hair cropped in what Toby recognized as the "mom over forty" bob. They stopped outside their door and looked at July and Toby, acknowledging what they had heard through the wall by fighting to keep their expressions completely blank.

"Merry Christmas," said the man after a moment.

His eyes glanced between July and Toby, no doubt, Toby thought, trying not to raise his eyebrows as he reconciled their ages.

"Merry Christmas," replied Toby.

Mr. and Mrs. Room Nine ended up walking down the stairs behind July and Toby, probably passing glances at each other with raised eyebrows. July and Toby looked at each other from the sides of their eyes, sheepish but amused.

The Room Nines quickly selected an austere breakfast of coffee and a plain croissant. They sat themselves at a table in the middle of the room, sipping their coffee and hardly looking at each other.

July and Toby took ample breakfast, and while they were both filling their cups at the coffee machine, Toby found that he felt oddly jovial.

"Let's mess with them a bit," he muttered low under his breath.

July looked at him and raised her eyebrows in question.

Toby turned around and headed to Room Nine's table.

"Good morning, Merry Christmas," he said. "Do you mind if we eat with you? Get to know our neighbors."

The Room Nines exchanged a glance.

"Of—of course," motioned Mr. Room Nine.

Toby sat down next to Mrs. Room Nine, and July took a seat across from him.

"I'm July," she said.

She kept her eyes focused mainly at the table; Toby could sense her discomfort.

"We're the Rothmans," said Mr. Rothman.

"Toby Alder. First time in Florence?" he asked, biting the tip of his croissant.

"No," replied Mr. Rothman. "Our second. We came twenty-five years ago on our honeymoon."

"Oh, happy anniversary," said July.

Mrs. Rothman smiled blandly.

"Thank you," she said in a robotic monotone, "and what brings you to Florence?"

"Oh, a nice Christmas trip," replied Toby.

"What's your business, Mr. Alder?" asked Mr. Rothman.

"Real estate. And yourself?"

"Law."

Toby had dealt with enough lawyers in the past two years. Figures he picked one out now.

"And how about you, Mrs ... Alder, is it? What's your profession?"

"Oh," said July, her lips forming an uncertain ring. She flashed her eyes at Toby. "I'm ... ah ... in ... education," her cheeks bloomed pink.

Toby could see that Mr. Rothman had a better understanding of the situation than he let on with the Mrs. Alder remark. Damn lawyers cross-examined even when there wasn't a witness on the stand.

There never had been a Mrs. Alder before; Jenny had kept her maiden name, since that's how the dance world knew her. Before their problems started, Toby had secretly wished that she would change her name. He had always wanted to see an envelope addressed correctly to "The Alders" instead of the "Alder-Sivertsen Family." The hyphen was prescient.

"Mrs. Rothman?" said Toby, quickly changing the subject. "How about you?"

"I'm a nutritionist," she replied, her mouth tight.

"Ah," said Toby, looking at the pastries on his plate.

That's why she's so thin, he thought as he noticed that July set down her Danish.

The conversation remained as comfortable as a pair of wet jeans. Toby tried to steer the conversation towards the Rothmans, hoping to avoid any more remarks of the Mrs. Alder nature. Luckily, Mr. Rothman seemed to enjoy talking about himself.

When everyone had stopped eating, a damp silence covered the table.

"Well!" said Mr. Rothman a bit too abruptly, "we'd best return to our room, prepare to meet the day."

He stood up and Mrs. Rothman followed suit.

"Right, well, pleasure meeting you," said Toby, not bothering to stand up with them. "See you around the neighborhood."

The Rothmans smiled and walked quietly away. When they were out of sight, July took a large bite of her Danish.

"Well that was fun," she said, her cheek bulging with pastry. "I swear, one more conversation with that guy and I'll know more about him than I know about myself."

As Toby and July walked down the hall to their room, the Rothmans were walking out of theirs in heavy coats, hats and gloves.

Toby gave a tentative smile and Mr. Rothman saluted. As soon as they turned down the stairs, July broke out into giggles.

"Is that how people get when they're old?" she said between giggles.

"They aren't old," said Toby.

July laughed harder.

"They aren't *old*," he persisted with a smile. "Everyone seems old to a twenty-two year old."

"I'm surprised you can remember back that far," she said, smiling and tilting her chin. "You haven't been twenty-two in over twenty years."

Toby laughed and swatted her playfully across her backside. She laughed and walked into the bathroom, leaving Toby with a moment to himself. In that exchange, the chasm between them had become transparent. For just a moment, he was old like the Rothmans. Or he soon would be.

July soon came out of the bathroom and bounced onto the bed, "So! What are we doing today?"

"I don't know. Did you have anything in mind?"

"How about the Duomo? I haven't seen it yet."

"Okay," he nodded.

He was wary of the Duomo, where Jenny was still posed like a ballerina in a music box.

"And I guess whatever is open for lunch. Or anything, really. And if there's nothing else we just come back here and hunker down."

"Sounds like a plan."

So they tunneled back out into the silent city, muted by a quilt of holiday. Though there was still the occasional car or Vespa, it was almost like visiting the ruins of an abandoned city struck by the plague. Stores closed and gated and dark, the whole place in hiding.

As they neared the Ponte Vecchio there was more movement. They walked through the Piazza della Repubblica and turned left up to the Duomo, around which comparatively many people had clustered.

From above, the Duomo looked totally different than it did at ground level. Standing on the top of the hill across the river, Toby had seen it—fiery red, round and supple. But at street level it was entirely another structure—ornate, white and detailed with pink and green, a solid elaborate block. It was thick and imposing yet delicate as a carefully iced gingerbread house. Its proximity to the octagonal baptistery made the Duomo seem even more imposing, as though it were invading the baptistery's personal space, pushing it out of the square.

"Wow," said July, her neck craned back so the base of her skull rested at the top of her spine.

"Yeah," echoed Toby. "Wait till you see the rest of it. We'll walk around the outside and make sure to get inside and go to the top, and also see it from on top of a hill across the river."

But his words were drowned out by the complexity of the façade. July was already looking through the viewfinder of her camera, stepping forward and backward in the futile attempt to capture the detail and the façade from side to side.

"Will you take my picture in front of it?" asked July.

"Of course," he said, taking the camera in his mitten covered hands.

It was impossible to prepare for the moment when your girlfriend would stand in the place your future ex-wife and mother of your children had stood, looking beautiful and being unbearably lovable even after she had been just unbearable.

July paced backward and stood in front of the Duomo.

"I don't have a good pose," she shrugged. "I guess I'll just stand here like an idiot."

As he raised the camera to his eye, he could see Jenny dancing in front of him in the middle of the summer as people, unaware of the pure beauty of the moment beside them, milled around in their own lives. And then Chloe and Sophia where Jenny had been, grinning goofily and unaware of their surroundings, perfect just by virtue of being. *This will be painfully disappointing*, he thought.

But then he looked through the viewfinder and saw July standing simply, left leg crossed in front of the right, right hand in the pocket of her forest green jacket, her white scarf beneath her auburn hair, smiling gaily, her cheeks pink with frost. In that moment, she seemed to blend almost seamlessly into the Duomo, into Florence like she had been born in Italy camouflage. She was no ballerina, but she looked perfectly like herself. This would probably be one of the pictures she kept in a frame on a prominent table every place she would live.

The shutter clicked a few times, and then Toby moved the camera out in front of him and looked at the preview of the pictures he had just taken. There she was, white and green and red like the Duomo inside the camera.

"Did they come out okay?" asked July, coming beside him and looking over his arm at the previews.

"Perfectly," he said.

"We should ask someone to take one of us together," she said looking around.

"*Scusi*," she said to a passerby, and just a moment later he and July were standing close, arms around waists and July's other hand resting on Toby's chest. Toby, thinking the woman taking their picture had finished, leaned over and kissed July's lips. A few moments later the woman returned the camera and they clicked through the pictures. The final picture was one of them kissing, looking like a commercial for romance. Toby stared, fascinated. He hadn't seen himself kiss a woman perhaps since his wedding photos, and it unnerved him a bit how together they looked. Were real people supposed to look that ... *cute?*

They walked around the Duomo, the whole façade aged with time and wrinkled with sooty pollution. The shops around the Duomo pushed in as the Duomo pushed them away like two north sides of a magnetic pole, backing everyone around it against a wall.

As he and July rounded the corner back by the baptistery where they had begun, July stopped and pointed.

"Look," she said. "It's the Rothmans."

"So it is," he replied.

The Rothmans stood next to the baptistery looking at a guide-book. Mr. Rothman held it low for Mrs. Rothman, so he stooped and twisted awkwardly for a better angle. They seemed to be quibbling about directions or where to go next.

"No, we should see this first," he insisted. "We should go that way, it will be faster and better."

"No, I want to see that first, and this way would be so much prettier, it will go right past that shop with the pretty jewelry."

"I remember where we're going; it's this way."

"Well I've been here, too, and it's *that* way."

"You have no sense of direction. You always get us lost. Remember that time in Boston? We ended up on the wrong side of the river."

So that's what twenty-five years looks like, thought Toby. Back and forth with a person you'd grown so used to that you forget that the whole reason you were together in the first place was because you were in love. Maybe, if you were lucky. If you were like Toby and Jenny though, twenty-five years would have worn them into wholly bitter, spiteful people, the antonym of marriage.

He and July observed the Rothmans from a distance, like they were on safari gawking at the lions.

"They called me Mrs. Alder."

Toby looked at her. She didn't seem to be awaiting a response; she was still looking at the Rothmans. Instead, it seemed as though her words had been more of a trial balloon, acknowledging some greater goal and seeing how it went over. Toby remembered the first time Jenny mentioned marriage, about five months into their relationship, when *(Love Is) The Tender Trap* came on the radio.

"If we get married," she said, "we should have our first dance to Frank Sinatra." Toby hadn't said anything, but his mind leaped with the joy and fear of real possibility—this might really happen. And at their wedding they had danced to Frank Sinatra—*How Little It Matters, How Little We Know.* It had felt a bit glamorous, like a black and white movie. As they danced, he could only remember that moment with Jenny and the radio and remark on how literary life could seem sometimes, how it worked in a circle and things took on meaning, like someone had placed them there on purpose. But meaning changed the further into the story he read.

And now, almost four months in, July's first abstract mention came out. Would it mean anything later?

He decided not to say anything. There wasn't really anything *to* say.

"So what should we do now?" she asked.

"We could have lunch with the Rothmans."

July rolled her eyes and stuck out her tongue. "Please tell me you're joking."

"I am."

July shuddered, "Yuck."

"Well," he said, navigating through his mental map of Florence, but knowing that most places were closed made it difficult.

"Excuse me," said a voice.

Toby and July looked up to see the Rothmans standing next to them.

"We were wondering if you could take our picture," asked Mr. Rothman.

"Yes," continued Mrs. Rothman. "We figured we could trust you not to steal our camera, since we know where you live."

July made a funny face, frowning like she was trying not to.

"Uh, sure," said Toby. "Where do you want to stand?"

Toby took a few pictures of the Rothmans standing stiffly in front of the Duomo, arms at their sides, wan smiles patted on their faces.

When he took the last picture they came and retrieved their camera.

"That should make a nice holiday card," said Mrs. Rothman.

They all stood in a circle, waiting until one of them came up with something socially acceptable to say.

"Well!" said Mr. Rothman. "What do you say we go get some lunch, Susan?"

"All right, dear," she replied with a tight smile. "I could use a nice salad. I never get enough fiber when I travel."

"*Insalata mista* here we come," Mr. Rothman laughed uncomfortably. "Would you two care to join us?"

July looked at Toby, her eyes wider, mouth frozen half-open.

"Oh, well," Toby hesitated.

"Unless you have other Christmas plans, of course," interjected Mrs. Rothman.

"Oh, no, well," stammered July.

"Come with us then!" gestured Mr. Rothman a bit too theatrically. "Our treat."

Toby had forgotten how to politely refuse an invitation; he had always left that up to Jenny. "Well, thank you. Lead the way then, I guess."

Mr. Rothman smiled, then he and his wife turned their backs to Toby and July and began walking, wandering down the street like two parallel lines.

July looked at Toby, her mouth puckered like acid, her eyebrows in pretzels, her eyes grunting, *Thanks a lot.*

"I went to see my personal banker and he said that I may be eligible for this new loan payment plan, where they'll refinance my mortgage and eliminate some of my debt, so that my mortgage would be like a first time buyer's rates. Which I think is great, because then I can put more money towards my retirement. And if I land that airline case I was telling you about, the settlement would be in the tens, if not hundreds of millions, and in that case we'd be almost set for life."

Mr. Rothman paused for a drink of water. His fork had hovered over his plate, frozen en route to his mouth, for the better part of the meal.

July had no idea what he was talking about, nor did she really care, so she just nodded and said, "Wow" at all the parts that seemed appropriate, throwing in the occasional, "Really?" just to keep things unpredictable.

"Are you sure about that?" said Toby. "I've had some home buyers who think that refinancing will be the key to getting a good mortgage on a bigger house, but then it turns out that they can't afford it and they end up losing a lot of money in the process."

July couldn't tell if Toby was really interested in the conversation or if he was just a good faker. But he looked interested. It had to do with houses and realty, and July couldn't provide Toby with this kind of stimulation. Her eyes rather glazed over when he started talking about housing prices or the bubble or the lack thereof.

Mrs. Rothman seemed likewise disengaged. Having finished her salad, she slowly spooned her way through a bowl of minestrone soup. She scooped the spoon away from her body, slowly and deliberately, then put the spoon in her mouth, drew it out clean, and swallowed silently. The silent, methodical eating made July's bones itch, like when someone in a movie theater opened something in plastic wrap, drawing out the crinkling over minutes instead of just tearing it open.

July tried to amuse herself with her *penne*, mushing it with her tongue, chewing in nibbles like it was corn on the cob; she tried drawing designs in the sweat pulsing from her water glass; she tried observing other patrons. Eventually her mind drifted out to May, to graduation. She tried to think beyond it, but it was like trying to see past infinity. Technically, she could do anything. But what *was* anything?

"Well the thing about real estate in Las Vegas," Toby was in the middle of saying, "is that to live on the strip, like you're talking about, you have your monthly rent and then your dues to the building, which are adjusted with formulas depending on your floor and unit. You can end up paying at least six thousand dollars extra a month, maybe more."

"But it's such a good investment right now," said Mr. Rothman. "With prices like they are. It's just a matter of finding the right tenant."

"Well right now, everyone's looking for that same tenant, Mr. Rothman. And in the meantime, it could lose you money. Especially due to costs for refurnishing and repairing."

"I think we have enough to spare. I mean I did do that big deal for Greyhound, and we're sitting rather pretty right now," Mr. Rothman said, looking at his wife.

Why was this man always talking about money? He didn't dress like a man who wanted to flaunt his wealth. He wore a simple black shirt, a gray fleece, and light jeans that looked as though they'd been worn a few years. Mrs. Rothman was well-dressed and well-groomed, but the only hint at exceeding financial comfort was the large diamond on her ring finger, which seemed to be rather too big for comfort. She kept fiddling with it as it fell into the webbing between her fingers, twirling and twisting and demanding constant attention like a mosquito bite.

July hoped that dinner with Massimo and his friend wouldn't be such a dud. Not that July had had high hopes for this meal. Once Toby had accepted Mr. Rothman's invitation, she knew that the entire afternoon was going the way of the Holy Roman Empire.

July cocked her head and looked at Toby's watch. It was nearly two; her family was still asleep, except for her father, who was probably just waking to finish final preparations for the brioche and the glaze. Unless he wasn't this year, since something had gone wrong with the dough. July pictured the Christmas tree in their living room, crouched and cramped into the corner between the piano and the stopped grandfather clock and blocking half of the bookshelf. The pine needles spiking the white carpeting; the rainbow halos peppered throughout the tree; the scary porcelain-faced, ringlet-haired satiny angel her mother put on top of the tree every year that looked like it belonged in a horror movie; the way the tree seemed so much bigger in her memories, when the ornaments hanging off the bottom branches had been at eye level; her favorite ornament, a silver snowflake with a crystal dangling in the middle, and how she hung it in the center of the front of the tree every year; sneaking out of bed in the middle of the night to go count the presents under the tree; the heaviness in her stomach after eating four large, puffy brioche cinnamon rolls, the pride in her father's eyes as he served her every one.

"July?"

"Huh? What?"

Everyone at the table was looking at her.

"Sorry, what?"

"Did you want some dessert?" asked Toby.

"*Absolute*ly! Is that even a question?"

Mr. Rothman laughed.

"I told you," shrugged Toby.

"How about you, darling? Dessert for you?" said Mr. Rothman.

"I don't think so," said Mrs. Rothman. "I'll just have a cappuccino."

"Oh, come on, Susan, it's vacation, it's Christmas. Let loose today."

"If I did that every time you said that I would be a blimp," she replied, eyebrows raised like a mother calling her child by his full name—middle name included.

But when the waiter came by, Mr. Rothman ordered her a chocolate cake anyway. She crossed her arms and pursed her tongue in front of her top teeth.

"It's rare to see a woman who enjoys her dessert," said Mr. Rothman when the chocolate cake and July's *pandoro* had arrived and July had already taken a few bites. "Refreshing to see you aren't caught up in all that body image, diet, skinny thing."

"Refreshing to see you aren't caught up in all that not being an asshole thing," muttered July as she took another bite of *pandoro*. From the corner of her eye, she saw Toby giving her a stern, trying-not-to-be-amused look.

But Mr. Rothman, oblivious, cut a bite of cake onto his fork, then glided it forward towards Mrs. Rothman's mouth, making airplane noises with his lips.

"Oh for heaven's sake, Martin!" she cried rather loudly, reflexively knocking the fork away from her mouth and onto the table

A moment of tension pulsated through the table. July stopped chewing, Toby's coffee cup paused at his lips, and Mr. and Mrs. Rothman looked at each other, eyes locked, until Mr. Rothman broke the gaze and turned to July and Toby, his eyes suddenly brighter.

"Ah well, that's why I have such a gorgeous wife! She can still fit into her wedding dress!"

Mrs. Rothman's face morphed instantly from irritation into pride. "It's even a little loose!" she effused.

July and Toby looked at each other for a brief moment and Toby put his hand on July's thigh, which somehow felt much bigger to her than it had this morning.

"You know that Vegas deal I was telling you about, Toby—if I get that airline deal ..." said Mr. Rothman for the sixth or seventh time at the meal.

July tuned out again, wondering how her father's two-handed brioche was coming out, and imagining how the house would soon smell. Where would she be next Christmas? Would she be back at her house, back in the past after a taste of the future? Would she spend the rest of her life having Christmas at her house without having to fight with anyone about whose family they would see that year? Or would she be with Toby again and maybe his daughters? Would she be the one under the tree opening gifts, or the one watching from the side, remembering the wavy shocks that ran through her body at the arrival of Santa, remembering how special it was to be young? Who would she be next Christmas?

Her head remained floating and wondering for the remainder of the meal and the whole walk back to the hotel, which they also shared with the Rothmans. When finally their hotel door closed behind them, July let out a heaving sigh and flopped herself onto the bed.

"That ... was ... *painful*," she said, her cheek pressed into the red quilted spread.

Toby said nothing and sat on the bed beside July's torso.

"Ugh. I just wanted to shove the chocolate cake in that woman's face."

Toby laughed, "I used to be married to someone like that. But she had the excuse of being a dancer."

July had no reply. That was one area in which she clearly surpassed Jenny—her weight.

"What time is it?" she finally asked.

Toby looked at his watch, "Three."

Toby looked at the ceiling, "My girls are probably opening their presents now."

"At seven o'clock?" asked July, raising her head. "They have restraint."

"Yeah," he replied vaguely, lost in a fog of deferred fatherhood.

She could practically see him drifting away, like they were both tethered to the outside of the space station and his hose had come unattached, and he was floating away, away, away, helpless and surrendering back into the funk he had been in their first night.

Other women are always stealing his thoughts. I wonder if he'll ever think about me like that.

July marked the passing of the rest of the afternoon in page numbers. Sometimes she looked at the same page number three or four times, forgetting that she had not turned the page and wasn't going anywhere. Toby took a nap, or at least lay down and closed his eyes.

She decided to call her family before dinner, when they were still in Christmas morning, wearing pajamas and rifling through stockings. She sat on the floor, her back against the side of the bed, as if the change in elevation would keep Toby undisturbed.

"Hello?"

"Hi, Mom, Merry Christmas."

"Oh, Merry Christmas, dear. Everyone! It's July!" she shouted into the room behind her.

Momentarily her father was on the line, too. "How's the food over there in Florence? You're being fed well?"

"Yes, Dad."

"You know what your mother got me this year? A smoker!" he said with childish relish. "I'm gonna smoke us a brisket for the New Year!"

"That's great, Dad."

"I got your mother that coat rack she wanted."

"It's wonderful," said her mother.

"Wow, that's pretty exciting, Mom."

"It's about time we get a coat rack in this house. I've only been asking for twenty-seven years."

"Mom, it's Tucson. It's only cold like three weeks out of the whole year."

"People wear coats, July."

"Okay, Mom."

"Iago brought along that Catherine girl again, the plump blonde girl from last year. The teacher who likes the ocean? I bought her a picture frame with dolphins. I think she likes it."

July gave her parents a vague overview of her day, but when she tried to describe the Duomo, her parents seemed unimpressed.

"That sounds nice," said her mother, who was probably doing a crossword puzzle on the other end of the line.

"Mm," her father vibrated, his mouth probably occupied by a coffee cup. She had thought he'd be interested.

Suddenly, July saw her parents as Jill and Gray instead of Mom and Dad, people who had led entire lives, who had likes and dislikes wholly separate from their children. Mom and Dad cared about daughter, but Gray and Jill were disengaged by July.

Even if I go back for Christmas next year, she thought, *it will never be the same. There will always be the Christmas that I left them, the Christmas I did what I wanted instead of what they taught me to do. The rest of our Christmases will be obligation instead of celebration.*

"July," said her mother, her tone of voice indicating a change of subject, "have you given any more thought to what you'll do after graduation?"

July rolled her eyes. *Not this again. Of course I've thought about it,* she thought.

"Well, actually Mom, I was just thinking about it today."

"Really?" said her mom, her voice turning with interest.

"Well, I decided that you know what's best for me. So after I graduate, I'll return home, and then I would like you and Dad to arrange my marriage to a reliable businessman whom I've never met so that I can have three or four children and never worry again that I haven't lived up to my potential as a woman."

Her father coughed at the other end, but she was pretty sure he was hiding a laugh.

"July, joke all you want, but you can't keep putting this off, the real world will come at you whether you like it or not," said her mother harshly.

"Mom, come on."

"She's right, July," interjected her father.

July was surprised; he usually distanced himself from this topic. Maybe he hadn't been stifling a laugh after all.

"July, dear," he continued. "You don't have to pop out babies right away, but you've got to do something once you graduate. You know just the other day I had a talk with Dave Gold, and he said that he'll probably have an opening this summer—"

"Dad, I don't want to work at a bank."

"I'm not saying it has to be your career, but you need something until you get ... settled."

July could practically see her mother coaxing him along, mouthing the words, twisting her wrist in circles, pushing him on.

"What about a restaurant?" he continued. "You could get into the food business, or a bakery or something. Anyone would be lucky to have you, and you could open your own eventually."

"What does that have to do with International Relations?"

"Well come on, July," shot her mother. "Haven't you thought at all about what you want your life to be like? Life doesn't just end after graduation."

"I know, Mom!"

"But what do you *want?*"

"I don't *know!*"

I just want to stay here, she thought. *I want to stay here like this forever, and I don't want anything to change. I never want to come home, I never want to be the July I was before. I want to jam a stick in the cogs of time, and I want everything to squeak to a halt, and I don't want it to ever be fixed.*

"You need direction, July."

She had direction—away.

"Do we have to talk about this now?" she pleaded. "It's Christmas. I don't want to think about this today."

"You have to think about it sometime. Once you get back home, we're going to have a serious discussion about this. We're going to map out your life," said her mother.

How could you draw a map of something that you hadn't seen in its entirety? Look at all the maps that showed the world as flat. What good were they to anyone now?

After July hung up, she stayed on the floor, her knees folded into her chest like a wall. She put her head on her knees and stayed like that for what felt a long time, drifting through the black wells in her eyes, as though she could travel through their blackness and emerge on the other end, somehow knowing which direction to keep moving.

Were life maps ever right? Who knew the shape of the world when they were graduating college?

"Hey," came Toby's voice seconds and hours later, pulling her back to the beginning of the tunnel. "Are you okay?"

She sighed.

"We should go soon," he said.

"Yeah."

"I just want to make sure I'm back by eleven so I can call my girls."

"Right."

She watched as Toby changed out of his jeans into some slacks. Had he only recently discovered the shape of the world? Could she start off knowing its shape?

"You about ready? Don't want to keep MASsimo awaiting," he said with a hyperbolic Italian accent.

"Yeah," she said.

How did she stand up? How did she put on her jacket and walk down the stairs? She couldn't remember doing anything, and yet here she was walking toward the Excelsior in Italian black. The world might as well have been a triangle.

XVI

"ARE YOU SURE HE SAID EIGHT?" TOBY ASKED AGAIN.

"Yep, he said eight," confirmed July.

Toby looked at his watch again. It was already eight fifteen and there was no sign of Massimo or his wingman. Toby had sharpened up a bit with his nap, but most of him was fighting the urge to say "Fuck it" and drag July away before Massimo could arrive.

After a few more minutes of cross-armed one-man huddles and weight shifting to keep warm, Toby saw two figures approaching the hotel. They could have been anyone, but something told Toby that this was Massimo and his companion.

"Hello!" called Massimo in his Italian lilt before he had stepped into the light, "I am—so sorry to be late."

He stopped in front of Toby and July, wearing only a light camouflage green jacket over a black T-shirt.

Idiot twenty-something, thought Toby.

"It is so good to see you again," Massimo continued. "This is my good friend, Astrid."

Behind him, a woman stepped into the light of the hotel sign. Shapely and curvy like the Italians Toby had seen in the movies, Astrid stood like she had been born to look beautiful. She was a woman made of hips—even if Toby were to look only at her face, all he would see were her hips, and he wondered if she could balance a glass of water on each hip without spilling.

"*Buona sera,*" she intoned like a ripple of silk.

Oh, damn. Toby's hard drive was wiped clean.

"We are—old friends," said Massimo. "She is—ah, how you say—my *angelo custode.*"

Astrid laughed, throwing her head back and putting her hand on Massimo's shoulder. Her English was more heavily accented than Massimo's but was more melodic drawl than fiery emphasis.

"He is like my brother. My *older* brother!"

Massimo laughed, and somewhere Toby heard July give a polite chuckle.

"Well, *andiamo!* Should we go to the restaurant? Follow me."

They set off in an amorphous blob of four, but soon they were walking two abreast along the Arno, Massimo and July in front babbling in Italian, and Toby and Astrid following.

For a few minutes Toby and Astrid said nothing. Toby was still trying to reclaim his wits from Astrid's hips.

"Your name is Tony, is that right?" asked Astrid from the darkness.

"Uh, no, Toby."

"Ah, To-by. I have a cousin named Tony. He is very stupid."

"Ah."

"It is good that you are not named this."

She paused. "Do you know what Astrid means?"

"Uh—no."

"It means beautiful goddess. What does Toby mean?"

"Uh—it's—something—Biblical, I think."

"I see. And what is your business?"

"I'm in real estate."

"*Molto bene,* people always need someplace to live. This is a good business, I think."

"What do you do?"

"Me? Oh, I am, how you say, in the law."

"A lawyer."

"*Sì.* This also is a good profession. People will always want to sue each other."

Astrid laughed like the sunrise as they turned and crossed a bridge over the river.

Did the whole world have a law degree now? How could a woman like Astrid be a lawyer? She seemed too … alive for such an arid profession of books and desks and confusing words and loopholes. Toby was afraid to find out what her specialty was, so instead he tried to listen to what Massimo and July were talking about, but even if he could have heard them, he couldn't have understood.

"You are her boyfriend?" asked Astrid.

"Uh, yeah."

"But she is so young. It is not serious."

"It's not?"

"I remember when I was that age, I was very ..."

Astrid made large circular motions with her wrist and forearms and wiggled her hips a bit. "I was very ... not sure."

"Not sure of what?"

"*Esattamente.*"

Toby looked ahead of him again, and saw that the distance between him and July and Massimo had lengthened by several paces. Massimo leaned towards July, then put a hand on her back to steer her in the right direction as they stepped off the bridge. *That little*—

"How do you like Firenze? You have been here before."

"Uh, yeah, I've been here many times."

"*Parla italiano?*"

"Oh, uh, no, I just like it here."

"I like Firenze as well, but I am also from Torino, as Massimo. But that was a long time ago. I am a Florentine now."

"I see."

"I have been to America once, to New York City. You have been there, yes?"

"Uh, yes, many times."

"It is so big, the buildings are so tall, I feel like they are going to fall on me, and push me through the earth into Asia."

Ahead, July and Massimo turned a corner.

"Do you know where we're going?" asked Toby.

"*Si si*, it is just up this street," Astrid motioned with her arm as she and Toby turned the corner. "But why would you want to live in the city that never sleeps? What is so wrong with sleep? Is my favorite thing to do! The bed is the most magical place!"

Don't think about it, thought Toby. *Don't, or you won't be able to see for the rest of the night.* So he focused on his surroundings. Most of the windows on street level were dark, gates pulled down over front doors. He searched the darkness for light and life to distract his mind from Astrid's bed.

"Everyone is with their families," said Astrid. "On Christmas there is no city, only *famiglia.*"

"Where is your family?" asked Toby.

"Ah, *mia famiglia,* they are some in Torino—Ah! Here we are."

Toby would have walked right past it if she hadn't stopped him, but when he looked up he saw the white fluorescent sign that said *Ashoka.*

Even though it was open for business, the restaurant cast little light through the windows, and the menu that clung to the glass was nearly indecipherable in the surrounding dimness.

Astrid opened the door and sashayed inside as Toby followed. The restaurant was long and thin, like a pencil box. Tables lined the long walls with just enough space for a cart to wobble its way between the tables. On the walls hung sparkling, opulent Indian pictures of elephants, gods and goddesses feeding each other or entwined in each other's arms. The lighting was dim but dramatic, pockets of light casting *noir*-ish shadows of color around the space. One wall was mirrored, the swirls of color and sequins and candlelight bouncing around in an endless whirlpool.

Massimo was speaking with one of the waiters, and it seemed that they knew each other. They laughed and Massimo clapped the waiter on the back. The waiter led them to a table along the mirrored wall. Massimo ushered July into the chair furthest in, then sat down beside her.

Irked, Toby took the chair opposite July, a seat which also happened to be up against a pillar, so that Toby's shoulder was always jutted against it, no matter how he shifted around.

Astrid sat beside Toby, and for a moment, all four of them exchanged silent, warming glances across the white tablecloth.

"So!" said Massimo eventually. "You do not worry about a thing—I will order all the specialties. They know me, they will treat us right."

"Great," said Toby flatly.

"Toby," said Massimo, leaning forward and crossing his arms on the table, "what is your business?"

"Real estate."

"Yes, it is a good job, no?" chimed in Astrid. "Everyone needs places to live."

"*Bene, bene*," replied Massimo, leaning back, jutting his pelvis and resting his arm along the top of July's chair.

Oh come on, thought Toby. He looked at July, who seemed oblivious. *Come on July, you're not stupid. Don't you see what this guy wants from you?*

"You two," said Massimo, motioning between July and Toby with his pointer finger, "you have been together how long?"

"Three and a half months," said July.

Massimo raised his eyebrows, pouted his lower lip, and nodded knowingly, as though he had just come up with the formula to solve a complex math problem.

"Uh, how old are you, Massimo?" asked Toby, leaning forward himself.

"I am twenty-seven," he replied, leaning forward again. "I study the architecture, and someday I will design the buildings all over the world."

"Toby, maybe you can sell them!" crooned Astrid.

"Mm," nodded Toby noncommittally, raising his eyebrows.

Toby looked at July, who was looking back at him. She was smiling slightly, and seemed to be enjoying herself more than she had at lunch. Toby tried to figure out what her eyes were saying. Were they reassessing his aging face, wondering how much longer it would stand up to the storm of time? Was she thinking of a way to let him down nicely, maybe after the trip was over, because flying home after breaking up would be more than uncomfortable? He couldn't tell in this light, with this man, with these mirrors playing tricks on his over-forty eyes.

The waiter came over and Massimo ordered some wine and rattled off a bunch of Italian as the waiter scribbled furiously.

"It will be a *Natale* feast!" Massimo proclaimed after the waiter had walked away.

July sat up straight and smiled giddily.

"*Luglio,*" said Massimo to July, and then he launched into the smooth turbulence of Italian, leaving Toby behind and lost.

July responded in Italian, and after a few more sentences, they seemed deep in conversation. She laughed at something he said, and he laughed after she did. He gestured wildly around the room. He could be saying, "Someday I will design something like this." Or, "Look around you, there is so much to do and see. What are you doing with this old man?" Or, "I will show you the world; we can discover it together."

On a magic fucking carpet, Toby added to his own thoughts.

"Toby," Astrid's voice sparkled like crystal.

Toby turned to look at her, her eyes lined in perfect, deliberate black, winging at the outer corners like someone was tugging at them with a string. Her face was smooth and youthful, misted with the fine whispers of a past thirtieth birthday.

"Tell me, To-by. What are the passions of a man alike you?"

"My passions?" repeated Toby. He hadn't been asked that question since, well, probably since he was July's age, trying to figure where his life was going.

"Well, I guess, my daughters."

"You have daughters?" said Astrid, perking up. "How wonderful! How old are they?"

"Ten, eight and four."

"How wonderful! I love little girls!"

"Do you have kids?"

"*Io?* No, no, not me. No children, not yet. So then you have a wife, ayes?"

"Had. Had a wife."

"Oh, I see. But why are you not with them on *Natale?*"

Toby launched into the lengthy explanation, wishing he didn't have to, but there was no brief way around it. Astrid nodded along, sometimes cooing in sympathy, touching his hand occasionally when she was particularly moved, or maybe when she thought he was. He was lost in a jungle of words.

"This is the hard thing about *amore*," waved Astrid. "It is here today, but tomorrow maybe it has gone. It is too hard to come and too easy to leave."

Toby looked at his glass and realized that he had already finished a glass of wine and the food had not come yet. Astrid reached over and refilled his glass and hers as well.

Too hard to come and too easy to leave. Toby looked at July. She was listening intently to Massimo, nodding her head and looking hard at him. Maybe she could leave Toby easily, now that she had met someone like Massimo. Was she enraptured, or just trying to grasp his meaning? Massimo leaned forward, drawing invisible shapes out on the white tablecloth.

"What are they talking about?" Toby asked Astrid.

"He is telling her about building, how buildings tell the story, how they can tell you how to feel."

This building was telling Toby that he was cornered, surrounded, blocked on this side by sequins and walls and on this side a wingman who was a wingwoman with winged eye makeup and hips like wings and on this side of the table age and time and on that side youth and passion, and then everywhere the mirrors bouncing everything back, so that everything was multiplied by infinity, a never ending corridor of entrapment.

Could a building tell him how to feel? *How do I feel? Do I feel by remembering or forgetting?*

He looked across the table at July, her profile as she turned toward Massimo, listening, nodding, her face seeming so delicate that he wanted to wrap it in bubble wrap and surround it with packing peanuts and newspaper and foam so that she would never break. Did she really buy his crap?

Toby turned back to Astrid, who sat with her hips turned towards him, full and sharp like a cliff. She seemed one of those women who seemed to completely know and understand herself and what she wanted, like she could and did make full use of those hips. She was at no one's mercy but her own. It was as though she had managed to free her mind from her head and release it throughout her body, so that even her fingernails grew in accordance to Astrid.

The waiter arrived with a plate of appetizers, samosas and fritters and chutneys.

"Ah, *bene!*" said Massimo. "*Salute! Cin cin!*"

He raised his glass and clinked it with July, and then Astrid. He held out his glass towards Toby.

"*Salute!*" he repeated.

Did he really have to toast this guy? Toby glared at him for a moment, just long enough to say *Fuck you* in his head, and then he raised his glass, already half empty, and bounced it off of Massimo's.

July clinked her glass with Astrid, and then turned to Toby.

"*Salute,*" she smiled.

"*Salute,*" he said.

She looked at him as their glasses touched. Toby's gaze stayed on her, but when the glass touched her lips, July looked at Massimo, raising the glass and looking out of the tops of her eyes, her eyelashes nearly touching her brow bone.

Hey, thought Toby. *That's mine.*

At that moment, he probably could have stood up and knocked the glass from Massimo's hand and thrown it against the wall so that it shattered satisfactorily. And then maybe he could have punched Massimo, even though it seemed like some clichéd scene from a movie. He could have, but Astrid said, "*Salute,* To-by."

And he was obligated to turn, restrain himself, and civilly touch his glass to hers. Astrid, he noticed, looked at him over her glass as she drank. As she finished her sip and replaced her glass on the table, she subtly moved her shoulders back, sticking out her chest, emphasizing her already noticeable breasts.

This woman knows too much about men, thought Toby, but that didn't stop that stirring tickle deep inside.

"Eat! Eat!" cried Massimo.

"Please, Toby, try," waved Massimo.

Another bottle of wine appeared and it was being poured into Toby's glass.

Astrid reached forward and delicately put some chutney on something fried. She took a bite, delicately raising her lips around the fritter and taking half a bite without spilling a crumb or a droplet of chutney.

"*Molto bene,*" she purred around her food.

Massimo reached forward and took a samosa, which seemed to fly of its own accord from plate to mouth, like only a young man with no heartburn could eat.

Just wait till he hits thirty, thought Toby vindictively. *I hope his indigestion is so bad that he can only eat rice cakes for the rest of his life.*

But now Massimo was caught mouth full, mid chew. Toby should seize this opportunity and dominate the conversation. No more of this Italian July hogging.

"Say, Massimo," said Toby, not exactly sure what he was going to say next.

Massimo, chewing a large wad of samosa, leaned his elbows forward on the table.

Think, thought Toby. *Ask him something. Anything.*

Massimo raised his eyebrows.

He was almost done chewing. He was about to swallow. *Think, think, shit, shit, shit, don't let him talk.*

"How long have you been working at the coffee bar?"

Oh well, he thought to himself. *It was better than what's your major?*

Massimo swallowed, ducking his head as the food went down his esophagus. "Eight months."

"That must be an interesting job."

"*Si,*" started Massimo.

"I used to work at a coffee shop," said July, turning to Massimo.

Oh, fuck, thought Toby. *That wasn't the point.*

"*Davvero?*" Really?

"Yeah, it's how I met Toby!"

"Aha, you must meet all your men in the cafés!" said Massimo, laughing.

July laughed too, but Toby couldn't tell if she really meant it or if it was a laugh of politeness.

"Not quite," she responded at the tail end of her laughter.

And then Massimo said something to her in Italian, and she laughed again.

"What was that?" asked Toby. He was just going to have to be aggressive against ignorance.

"Oh, is nothing," said Massimo. "Please, have another," he motioned to the plate of fried goodies.

"I'll have another," said July, reaching forward.

"Ah yes, enjoy it awhile you are young," said Astrid. "I cannot have more than one or else pfft! My clothes tomorrow no longer fit—I am as big as the Duomo!" She put a hand on Toby's shoulder in commiseration and laughed.

"That is how it is when you pass thirty, no?"

Toby smiled weakly.

"Tell me, Toby," said Massimo, leaning forward. "What is it that this young woman is with you?"

"Excuse me?" asked Toby.

"Massimo!" tutted Astrid.

"*Che?* I just want to know. I would ask this of anybody, no matter his age."

"Maybe you should ask *July* that," said Toby.

Toby could hardly believe that had come out of his mouth, but he thought better of retracting it, so he stayed staring steel at Massimo. Through the corner of his eye, Toby could see July turn beet red.

"I—" July let out a helpless half-laugh half-sigh.

Toby wanted to hear her answer.

"Well, I mean, because—" she exhaled heavily again. "He—understands me. He humors me and seems to enjoy it. He treats me like a person, like I matter." She cast her eyes down at the table, "It doesn't matter how old I am, or how old he is."

"How old are you, Toby?" asked Massimo.

Toby's eyes racked over to Massimo. If Toby could box with his eyes, Massimo would be face down and bleeding on the floor with a ref counting to ten.

"How old do I look?" he retorted, trying as hard as he could to make his words sound like a razor edge.

Massimo leaned back with arrogant ease, putting his arm behind July and jutting his pelvis.

"My father, he is fifty."

That pompous little fucker.

"*Ma per favore!*" cried Astrid. "To-by is not this old! No no, he is no more than, what, *quaranta?*"

"What's *quaranta?*" asked Toby.

"Forty," said July, covering her mouth with her hand as she chewed.

"*Ma guardagli gli occhi, ha così tante rughe,*" said Massimo rapidly, making some spirit fingers gesture around his eyes.

Toby squinted, confused, and looked to July, who looked confused as well.

Astrid turned and examined Toby's face closely.

"*Ma no, non e' così vecchio.*"

"*Potrebbe essere suo padre.*"

Padre. Father. Toby knew that. He wasn't stupid.

"What was that?" he challenged.

July looked at him tentatively.

"He said you could be my father," she said quietly.

That was it. He had heard that comment enough.

"Well I'm *not* her father!" said Toby defensively, and perhaps a little louder than he had intended. He thrust his pointer finger into the table like a dagger.

His words lingered above the table in a cartoon dialogue balloon, and as they bounced off the mirrors and echoed through his ears, they sounded more and more like one of his daughters on the verge of a tantrum.

July looked down at her plate, Massimo's eyebrows raised in a what's-his-problem arch, and Astrid sipped her wine.

Fuck, thought Toby, draining the last of his wine. He didn't care that it was his third glass, that he hadn't eaten dinner, and that tomorrow his head would punish him for this, unlike Massimo, who could probably drink a whole bottle of wine without the slightest hangover and then down an entire pizza with everything on it and still sleep well and fit loosely into his jeans the next morning, that twenty-something fucker.

Toby wished the food would just come already, so their mouths could do something besides talking. He felt like he was back in high school, when he was trying to talk to the girl with hair so long that when she wore that backless halter, her hair covered the ties and she looked naked from the back. Vivian. They sat across from each other in English class, and he was working up the nerve to ask her to prom. Or was it homecoming?

He had been telling her about something or other when one of those good looking guys who hit puberty early and looked well out of his teens and happened to be one of the super jocks came in and took his seat behind Vivian. She turned and smiled at him and said hi, and then a few sentences later the post adolescent super jock was taking Vivian-naked-from-the-back to prom or homecoming and Toby was stuck going stag with his friends and watching Vivian in that low cut red dress as she danced with the super jock who had the perfect view right down into her cleavage and probably got to at least third base in his sports car later that night. And a few months later, super jock cheated on Vivian with a cheerleader, and she didn't give anyone a second glance for the rest of the year.

That fucker.

Toby's face was turning a bit red, like it was filling with wine, but July couldn't tell whether it was the alcohol or anger or both. Why was he getting so upset about that father remark? Sure it was annoying, but he'd heard it before. He said the age difference didn't bother him. Maybe it did. But other than the father remark, the night seemed to be going well. Massimo was a lot of fun, and July liked that she could practice her Italian, even if she didn't understand everything he said. Sometimes she just nodded along, not wanting to stop his fast talking pace, but for the most part she could hold her own.

July was surprised that Massimo brought Astrid along. Massimo said he and Astrid were friends, but July doubted that a man could just be friends with a woman that gorgeous. When Astrid showed up, July felt superfluous. A woman like Astrid had enough beauty for scores of men to admire; hell, July could hardly concentrate with Astrid around and she wasn't even a man. She couldn't imagine how males could form a coherent thought around her. July had never felt so dowdy, and this woman had at least ten years on her. July could only hope to age that well.

"Tell me, July", started Astrid, the first person to speak in the moments after Toby's outburst. "What do you do?"

"Oh, uh, I'm still in school."

"Ah, you are in university, no?"

"I graduate next May."

"*Che bello*, and what will you do after that? You will be with Toby and his daughters?"

"I, uh, well—"

"You should come back to *Italia!*" Astrid exclaimed gaily. "The life here is so much more ... *bella! La dolce vita!* They do not understand this in America."

"Yes, yes, it is so much better here," chimed in Massimo.

July looked at Toby, but his mouth was in wine. He should slow down; they hadn't eaten yet.

"You come to Firenze, I will help you, I can find you place to live, find job, *è facile!* You have friends, here!" Massimo glistened.

July's insides melted and trickled to her toes. It sounded like a movie, like the dreams people have when they're young that they never fulfill, or don't fulfill until they're old and retired. Wouldn't it be exciting just to skip all that? To pick up and move to Italy, do what no one expected and take life for what she could?

But there was Toby. He would, could never leave his daughters, that was the way it should be—she could never matter more than they, no matter how hard she wished she could, or how much she gave him. It was an either-or situation. Either Toby or Italy. This would be the only time she could have both.

"I don't know," she shrugged, trying to sound indifferent.

She looked right into Toby's eyes and said, "Who knows where I'll be in May?"

But in her head, she thought, *where do you want me to be in May?*

He looked away, tilted his head down and scratched his neck.

She tried to hold her gaze at him until he looked up at her again, but instead he looked over his shoulder and back down at his hands.

With me, thought July. *You're supposed to say, with me.*

But something had frozen his previously lava tongue.

She didn't like being at his mercy, planning her life around his desires. But she couldn't help it. She was on her back, vulnerable; she had to be malleable where he could not be.

"*Chi lascia la via vecchia per la nuova, sa quel che lascia, ma non quel che trova* ," said Massimo.

"What the hell is that supposed to mean?" asked Toby dully.

"It means, he who leaves the old street for the new street knows what he left, but not what he will find," said Astrid. "Is very true."

"Astrid," said July, wanting to shift the focus away from herself. "Are you married?"

"*Io?* No, no, I am not married. Not really."

"You used to be?"

"*Si, si,* but it was a long time ago, I was very young."

"You are still young!" protested Massimo.

Astrid giggled, "Not so young anymore."

"Did you get divorced?" asked Toby, his voice regaining the tone of interest.

"*No. No,* he is still alive in Torino. But has been many years since we are together. I have not seen him since I left Torino."

"What happened?" asked Toby.

"I was young. Very young. It is alike I said earlier—love is too hard to come and too easy to go. One day there was a love, the next day there was a no, and so I go with the love."

Toby nodded his head silently.

"You know this?" asked Astrid. "You have felt this, *no?* This one day yes, the next day no?"

He nodded again, pausing before he said quietly, "Yes."

July frowned. Was it really that simple, to fall out of love in a day with someone you had loved for years?

"One day he realized he didn't love me anymore," said Astrid slowly. "I was crushed. I thought, my life is over. I was young, maybe not even your age," she motioned to July with that perfectly formed, smooth hand.

"How? Why?" asked July. If a man could stop loving a woman like that, then women everywhere were doomed.

"There is never this one why. It is alike the silent letter in a word. You never know it is there until it is spelled out for you."

"I've never heard it put that way," said Toby. "But you're absolutely right."

Astrid turned and smiled, and he smiled back, two people bonding over pain. July felt as if Toby and Astrid had entered their own room and shut the door before July could follow them.

"We are still *bambini*," said Massimo to July. "We have so much to look forward to, *no*?"

"Mm," muttered July.

She wanted to skip all that, to skip all that growing up and way making. Toby had done that, and she was with him. He could be her crib sheet.

The waiter arrived alongside the table pushing a metal cart, on which sat dishes of yellow, red, and green steaming gloppy foods, at least double the number of diners. And baskets of bubbled *naan*. Suddenly, July's stomach was roaring with hunger.

There wasn't enough room on the table for all the food that Massimo ordered, so he and Astrid put baskets of *naan* in their laps.

"Just grab," he said to July as he set the basket on his thighs.

"Yes, just grab," echoed Astrid to Toby.

July and Toby looked at each other, each simultaneously aware of the forced intimacy of such a suggestion.

"All right, then," said Toby after a minute, reaching into Astrid's lap.

July felt something fall within her, as though her heart had been cut from a string. She reached towards Massimo's lap and plucked a piece of *naan* with the tips of her thumb and pointer finger like it was a dirty tissue.

Massimo was already plopping some yellow cauliflower and potato onto her plate, and then rice and soon her plate was a painter's palette, filled with shades of everything.

For a few moments she could be lost in the spices. Split peas laced with turmeric stained her fingers yellow; whole seeds of cumin and fenugreek burst in her mouth or caught in her teeth; creamy spinach wrapped her stomach in a heavy blanket; chili peppers stung craters into her tongue; and *naan* and rice filled all the corners that Toby had emptied.

Was Toby starting another glass of wine, or was it her imagination?

She finished her piece of *naan* and glanced sideways at the basket in Massimo's lap. Great. She slid her arm over and tried to pluck another piece, but Massimo chose that moment to shift his weight and her hand ended up on one of his thighs.

"Oh, sorry," said July, recoiling her hand like it had touched a hot burner.

"*È bene*," he said. "Here, you can hold it," and he placed the basket in July's lap.

This temporarily eased her anxiety, but a few minutes later as she was amid some *baingan bartha*, Massimo's hand was in her lap digging for *naan*. July looked up and caught Toby's eye. She tried to send him "help me" signals, but his eyes were filtered with wine. Or something. What was his problem?

"Is good?" asked Massimo.

"Brilliant," nodded July, returning her head to the table. "Much better than the Indian food I've had in the States."

"You see? America, is not so special."

Soon the plates were empty or nearly so, reddish oil pooling on the bottoms of the metal dishes.

"What's for dessert?" asked July.

Astrid laughed like glittering snowflakes, "This *ragazza!*" she said, putting her hand on Toby's arm. "She has no end to the stomach!"

"Don't I know it."

"Ah, *bene*, Massimo, you have not satisfied her!"

"*Mio Dio*. I think I want dessert too. It's *Natale*, you cannot have a *Natale* without something sweet!"

"You're right, it's *Natale*, I will have dessert too and regret it all tomorrow!" Astrid tinkled.

"Toby?" said Massimo. "You will join us in the dessert?"

Toby sighed heavily, then looked at his watch.

"You know, it's just after ten. By the time we get out of here, I won't have enough time if I'm going to call my daughters."

"That's okay," said July. "We don't have to eat dessert. It's okay."

"No no," said Massimo. "Here dessert will take a long time. Let's get gelato, you can eat as you walk."

"Perfect," said July, looking at Toby.

Toby shrugged and sighed.

"You are a good father," said Massimo. "Not all men would rush home from dinner with two beautiful women to talk to his *bambini*."

"Toby is a wonderful father," said July, looking at Toby. "He loves his daughters more than any father I've ever seen."

Toby looked back at her, and July thought his eye lines lessened slightly.

There was a small pause all around, and then Massimo slapped his hand lightly on the table. "*Va bene, gelato!*" He motioned for the check.

"I am sorry we could not stay together longer," he said. "Perhaps we can meet again? When do you return to America?"

"The fifth," said July.

"*Molto bene*, we have plenty of time!" clapped Astrid. "It has been so wonderful! *Che bel Natale!*"

"Yes," smiled July politely, but inside she wished that this Christmas had not been shared with the Rothmans or Massimo and Astrid. Something was churning in Toby, but she didn't know what.

The waiter brought over the check and Massimo and Toby simultaneously shifted their weight and withdrew their wallets from their pants.

"*Non, non*, it is my treat."

"No, it's too much," said Toby.

"*Non non*, I invited you, you shared your *Natale* with me, I must to share something with you," said Massimo, pulling the check towards him.

"No, really," said Toby firmly, grabbing the check away from Massimo.

"I'm afraid I must protest," said Massimo, and he stood up, reached across the table, and plucked the check from Toby's hands. "It is my pleasure to treat you and these two beautiful women to dinner on Christmas."

With that, he walked over to the counter and handed the waiter his credit card and the check.

Toby looked like he had sprouted cactus spines. July didn't see what the big deal was. Toby had saved at least two hundred Euro; they could have an extra special dinner tomorrow.

Massimo returned to the table, tucking his wallet into his back pocket. July noticed for the first time that evening that his jeans, dark and tailored and light in just the right spots, looked as though they had been painted on his leg. Those were good jeans.

"And now gelato," said Massimo grandly.

He gestured his arm towards July.

"Come come, we must satisfy you!"

July slid out of her chair and put on her coat as Astrid, and finally Toby, rose and did the same. They filed out the door, Massimo shouting, "*Grazie!*" to the waiter, and was it July's imagination, or was it colder than any previous night in Florence?

"Come come!" said Massimo. "This man who makes the gelato, he is from Torino, like me *e* Astrid, so you know it must be good—only good things come from Torino."

Astrid walked forward and took July's arm, leaving Toby and Massimo to drift together.

"This man, his gelato is made of blood," said Astrid to July.

"What?"

"No no! I am sorry!" cried Astrid, her hands fluttering to her mouth. "I mean, his blood is made of gelato!"

"That's far preferable," laughed July.

Astrid, holding July's arm, took the lead from Massimo. July glanced back at Massimo and Toby. Toby had placed his hands in his jacket pockets, and Massimo strode down the sidewalk, swinging his arms and looking out in the street away from Toby.

Astrid led them through the streets, black and narrow like an intestine. They weren't going to the *gelateria* that Toby had taken July to; they had moved across the river and wound down alleyways lit only with the reflections of far off lights.

"Will he be open this late? On Christmas?" asked July.

"*Naturalmente*" she chimed. "He is like us, *senza famiglia*. His *gelati* are his *bambini*."

Astrid's thick, ankle-length black coat bristled softly against July's green one, her black heels clacking against the cobblestone alongside July's silent sneakers.

"Almost there!" cried Massimo, taking the lead as they turned a corner.

They turned the corner after him and stood in front of a well lit *gelateria*, whose sign hung above the lights, obscured in the night. Where were they? July had long since lost the river, or anything at all, as a reference point. She would probably never be able to find this place without Massimo.

"Come come!" said Massimo, opening the door and ushering them in. "Is the best gelato in Firenze."

The store was smaller than the *gelateria* Toby and July had been frequenting. The display case was pushing out on the front wall, making it nearly impossible for two people to stand comfortably abreast. Beneath the glass case sat only ten flavors of gelato, shades of brown and white and a pink or yellow to lighten things up.

"Gianni!" bellowed Massimo. *"Dove sei?"*

"Ehh?" came a bellied voice from the back of the shop. "Massimo? *Cazzo, sto arrivando!"*

From his voice, July imagined Gianni to be hefty and imposing, with a round nose and belly, not unlike Pop from the soda shop in the old Archie comics. But instead, a graying but lithe man came out of the back, short and slim, his skin smooth but tough like leather.

"Ahh, *che cazzo fai!*" bellowed Gianni. "*Bel Natale!*"

Then Gianni turned to Astrid and said, "*Ah, o'bella, come la va?*"

"*Gianni, sto bene. Bel Natale!*" she rang, leaning forward and kissing him on each cheek.

"Gianni, these are my American friends, July and Toby," said Massimo in Italian.

"*Ciao, bella,*" said Gianni to July, and leaned in to kiss both her cheeks.

July, in flattered surprise, leaned in and reciprocated.

Gianni tried to get them to sit and drink some coffee, but Toby kept checking his watch, the time creeping closer and closer to eleven. July felt the time hanging lower and lower over their heads, and felt bad that Massimo would have to leave Gianni to show July and Toby how to get back.

"Please, Gianni, we cannot stay, this *cazzo* here has to leave to make a phone call to his daughters in America," Massimo was explaining in Italian. "But I told them they must sample Florence's finest gelato—it would not be Christmas without it."

"I see, I see," said Gianni, nodding his head in disappointment. "You should bring them back, or maybe just the girl if that one is such a *cazzo*."

"*Si, si,*" Massimo assured him, and then July was holding a heaping cup of three flavors of gelato.

"*Grazie mille,*" said July repeatedly as they shuffled out the door.

Astrid stayed behind with Gianni, and July was glad, not only so that Gianni would not be left alone on Christmas, but also so that she would be clear of Toby.

"*Andiamo,*" said Massimo, waving his arm and starting off down the street. Toby followed quickly, paying no attention to the cup of gelato in his hand. July's legs were no match for Toby's or Massimo's, and eating gelato seemed to make them shorter. Soon she was half a block behind Toby, who paid as much attention to her as he did to his gelato.

If he's going to be like that, I'd prefer to be half a block behind, she thought.

Up ahead, Massimo turned a corner, and Toby followed, nearly stepping on Massimo's heels. July reached the corner and turned, but saw no one. It was like they had been shadows, illusions, like the silver heat ribbons that vibrated above the road ahead and dissipated when you reached them. July stopped, her feet stuck in place, the hand holding the gelato paddle suspended in the air, as though staying as still as possible would make Toby and Massimo visible again.

"Toby?" she called into the frosty darkness.

She willed her ears to extend throughout the world, but she heard nothing but the silent crackle of ice. *Fuck.*

"Toby!" she called again. But there was nothing. He might as well be back in America. *What a jerk, just ignoring me like that, taking off as if I don't exist. His girls are important, but isn't there enough space for me, too?*

"Well, shit," she said to the frost beyond.

XVII

SOMETHING HAD BURROWED ITS WAY INTO TOBY'S BODY, SPIRALING down his spine with tightly coiled fingers and encasing his intestines in burning, bubbling bile. As he walked briskly behind Massimo, the only things that stopped him from stopping and sliding down an adjacent wall and disappearing between the cracks of the cobblestones were his daughters. Their voices could be his antacid and free his tailbone from whatever cast iron vise had gripped it.

They had already been walking for nearly twenty minutes—the Arno was rarely farther than that from most places in the city. *Where the hell are we? Where does this punk think he's going?* Toby didn't recognize this place at all. On his right there was an open plaza, where there seemed to be some sort of celebration. Ahead, the road sloped down and went beneath an underpass. They must be way west of the train station. *What the fuck?*

Toby burped strong and acidic, and he had the sensation that his insides had been worn as thin as tissue paper, like he might collapse into himself at any moment.

Don't give out on me now, Toby told his body.

They walked beneath the underpass, slats of orange light from above slotting through invisible cracks. Toby felt like he was in New York, and not in one of the nice parts. Somehow, a few minutes later, there was a line of trees on the right. In front of him hid the silent black snake of the river. Where had that come from?

"Your hotel, it is to the left."

"Right."

"No, left."

"No, I—"

"I'm kidding, I'm kidding," laughed Massimo.

Toby tried for a polite half-smile, but all he could manage was a sneer. But Massimo didn't notice—he was looking past Toby. Toby, confused, turned around. "What?"

"Where is July?"

Toby had almost completely forgotten that July was behind them. He knew, somewhere beneath the grasp around his spine, that she was there, the knowledge like a shadow. But he hadn't thought of her.

"She's probably coming," said Toby. "She has shorter legs."

"No, but I do not see her."

"Look, it's already eleven—"

"Can you find your own way back to the hotel?" asked Massimo in a cold, brusque tone, a remarkable departure from his usual joviality.

"Uh, yeah, I think so."

"It's just that away," said Massimo, gesturing to Toby's left.

"But—"

"I'm going to find July. I do not see her anywhere; she does not know where she is."

Jackass, thought Toby, *July's a smart girl. I just need to talk to my daughters.* But beneath his paternal urge, a fish of worry nibbled the lower edges of his stomach. Where *was* she? What if something happened to her?

"Go to your daughters," said Massimo. "I will find July and bring her back to the hotel."

Before Toby could respond, Massimo was walking away. Toby refocused on the telephone on the desk at the hotel, and stretched his legs as far as they could go. His body clenched as a band of tension wrung his spine tighter.

Toby turned left away from the Arno and saw the hotel's white awning. By his watch, eleven had already passed, and he broke into a half-run. He stormed into the hotel and took the steps up two at a time, even though each stride upward intensified the burning pressure at the base of his spine.

He took out the key as he walked down the hall, holding it ready so as not to lose a second when he reached the door. He stuck the key in the lock and tried for one, swift movement of simultaneously unlocking and opening the door, but the door would not budge. July had opened the door for him nearly every time they had gone out and come back.

"Fuck, come on," grunted Toby, turning the key this way then that, jangling the knob, taking out the key and putting it back in, leaning against the door, pausing, huffing, centering, bargaining with the door. *If you just open I won't fight with Jenny anymore, just please open.*

Finally, it did. Toby didn't stop to think about how it opened, he just barged in and leapt for the phone. His fingers fumbled over the numbers. Why was dialing America from overseas such a bitch?

On the fourth try, the phone rang, and after a few moments, someone picked up.

"Hello?"

It was Jenny; he could tell.

"Hi, Jenny."

"Oh, Toby. I was wondering if you were going to get around to calling."

He was about to go on the defensive, but he remembered the promise he made to the door. So he swallowed and took a deep breath.

"Merry Christmas," he said, summoning what cheer he could.

"Merry ... Christmas," said Jenny, sounding confused.

"Can I talk to the girls?"

"Yeah, hang on."

Toby held while she got the girls. Sophia answered first. Toby forgot about the iron fire within his body, as though it existed only in his head, in his ears to listen, his mouth to talk. He was suspended from the confines of his body until she said, "... but Kevin didn't like the movie at all. He said he did, but I could tell the way he kept moving around and yawning."

"What?"

"He was yawning."

"Who?"

"Kevin, Dad."

"Kevin? Mommy's ... dancer friend?"

"Yeah."

"Why were you with Kevin?"

"He was at Christmas," said Sophia simply.

What the *fuck* was Kevin doing at the Sivertsen house on fucking Christmas?

"He's been there the whole day?"

"I think he came last night on the red nose flight."

What the *fuck.* Burbling heartburn mixed with acidic rage, squeezing through the hand like Play-Doh.

"Can I talk to Mommy?" he managed, teeth clenched.

"Mo-om!" called Sophia offstage. "Mo-om! Dad wants to talk to you!"

There was some plastic rustling as the phone changed hands.

"Hello?" said Jenny.

"Why the fuck is Kevin there?"

Jenny didn't answer.

"Jenny, I said, why. The fuck. Is Kevin. At Christmas?"

Jenny sighed. "Toby, I don't have to talk to you about my love life anymore. Isn't that what you told me?"

That little—Toby wanted to heave the phone across the room and hurl whatever obscenities he could muster with it.

"Jenny, it matters if he's with the girls!"

"Your little thing was with the girls."

"That was like five *minutes*! They don't know her!"

"Toby, it's not your business."

"It's my business who the girls celebrate Christmas with!"

Jenny sighed with exasperation, "Grace wants to talk to you," she said, then promptly handed off the phone.

Toby's body went cold in anger, as though everything within him and around him had stopped completely. His face and ears tingled and prickled like a cactus had been pressed into them, and he thought he felt his soul fly out his armpits as his tissue paper insides deflated on themselves. He hardly heard what he and Grace talked about until he asked about Kevin.

"So Gracie, is Kevin nice?"

"Yeah, he said I could be the flower girl."

"The flower girl?"

"Yeah, at the wedding!" she said brightly.

What?

"Okay, say goodbye to Daddy," he heard Jenny say far off on the other end of the tunnel.

"Bye, Daddy!"

"Bye, Gracie. I love you."

"I love you too."

The phone crackled again.

"Now you're pumping your daughters for information?" said Jenny accusatorily.

"What the fuck, Jenny? You're seriously marrying Kevin?" he spat.

"That doesn't concern you."

"It absolutely concerns me who my daughters are living with."

Jenny was silent.

"How long has this been going on?" he asked.

"It doesn't really concern you, Toby."

"Actually, yes it does. Was this going on while we were married?"

"It doesn't really matter, does it? We aren't married anymore."

"I don't believe this. You make accusations about me and July and then you turn around and go get fucking engaged? You're such a fucking hypocrite!"

"Does this really have a point here, Toby? I'd prefer to spend Christmas with my daughters instead of listening to you spew from your Italian getaway."

"Talking to you is like getting drawn and quartered!" he shouted.

"Goodbye, Toby."

And the tunnel closed.

Toby slammed the phone down.

"FUCK!" he yelled as hard as he could, straining his vocal cords as thin as they would go in hopes they would snap and dissipate his rage.

His hands were on his head, clawing at his scalp, dragging at the skin on his cheeks and he wanted to peel his skin off in one thick layer and throw it as far as he could and paw furiously into his brain, into his past and his memory and rip away anything of Jenny, shred it and burn it and pound it and launch it into space and annihilate it like it never existed in the first place. And then he realized that his body could no longer contain himself, the heat of Indian spice and betrayal and rage, and he spent the next hour on the toilet, his head between his knees, wailing and willing his body to expel his thoughts and being out with the rest of him.

How long had it been? wondered July. It felt like half the night, but it couldn't be more than an hour or so since she had lost Massimo and Toby. *Where were they?* Hadn't they noticed that she wasn't with them?

She had stood totally still for a good ten minutes, waiting to see if someone would come back for her. Then she sat on the curb, waiting because surely one of them would come searching for her. But it had been a long time, and no one had come back. So she stood up and started to walk. Florence wasn't that big, if she walked, eventually she would find something she recognized, the Arno if she was lucky. And once it got light, it would be easier. There would be people with the light. But that was at least eight hours away.

The gelato chilled the rest of July's body, so she was cold from stomach to skin, and no matter how much she huddled into herself, she could find no warmth. Her nose ached numbly, and she tried holding a hand over it to warm it, but then her hand got so cold she had to put it back in her pocket.

She wandered up and down random streets, all dark, all shop gates pulled down apocalyptically, like the rest of the world had hunkered in a bomb shelter and she was left to meet the fate of the imminent meteor.

Soon, her feet had worn to bones, her back ached. So she sat down again, leaning against a stony wall and tucking her knees to her chest. There would be someone eventually. At least she wasn't hungry.

She sighed. Why had Toby done that? He probably didn't even realize how he had acted, which was almost worse. He had forgotten her. But maybe he was searching for her now? Calling her name, scuttling frantically from street to street. She strained to hear his voice. But she doubted this was the case. He was talking to his daughters. That's all he wanted. Why had he come to Italy in the first place, if all he wanted to do was talk to his girls?

She sighed again. What about Massimo? Hadn't he at least noticed she was no longer following them? He wouldn't just leave her out here. He wouldn't do that. Would he? What if someone came and robbed her, or accosted her or hurt her—or even killed her? There was no one around. She would be forgotten, disappear into the gutters of Florence, a mystery unsolved and undiscovered.

Her father was probably prepping Christmas dinner right now. Probably pork belly stewed all day until it was soft and silky, in no need of chewing, it would just dissolve once it hit the tongue. Her mother had probably made sugar cookies in her biannual pilgrimage to the kitchen. Cut into shapes and decorated with sprinkles and icing, warming the whole kitchen, painting the air with sugar.

So this is where a trip with Toby had gotten her? Alone on Christmas at midnight in the street lost and cold? *Thanks. Thanks a lot.* She closed her eyes.

"July?" came a voice in the distance.

She perked her head up sharply. Had she really heard that? Or was she going crazy with cold?

She held perfectly still, as though any movement could drown out another shout. Just as her shoulders fell in the realization that she had imagined the voice, it came again.

"July!"

It was, there was really someone there.

"Toby?" she called. So he had come for her after all.

"July?" The voice was closer.

"Toby!"

The call and answer routine made her remember summers in the backyard pool playing Marco Polo with her brothers, searching for them with her eyes closed and hands out, calling out "Marco!" and springing at them as soon as they shouted back, "Polo!"

"Toby!" she called again.

He turned the corner. She was about to cry his name once more in relief, but stopped when she realized how rectangular this person was.

"No no, is Massimo," he said, approaching July.

"Oh, God, thank God you're here."

"What happened?"

"I don't know! I turned a corner and you were gone."

"Yes, Toby was going very fast. He nearly ran me over."

"Where is he?"

"Ah, he is at the hotel. He must ah, to call his girls."

"Right," said July shortly.

They were silent for a moment.

"You must be very cold," he said. "Come, we will go back to the hotel."

He reached his arm behind her and wrapped it around her shoulders. The right side of her body pressed into his, and she felt just a bit warmer. It was different than Toby's body, she noticed, into which she fit so perfectly. In Massimo's embrace, she felt more protected, like he was her shield.

"I have no idea where I am," she said helplessly.

"Is okay, I know," he replied. "I will show you the way."

"I'm so cold," she said. "How far is the hotel from here?"

"Ah, at least twenty minutes, perhaps more if we do not walk so fast as Toby."

July though she might shatter right there. She was so cold.

"Are you okay?" asked Massimo.

"I'm just so cold."

Massimo stopped, moved in front of her, and enveloped the front of her body in an embrace, the front of his body against hers. He pressed her close and rubbed his arms vigorously up and down her back.

Over Massimo's shoulder, July frowned, tensing her shoulders at the sudden burst of intimacy. What was he doing?

Massimo stopped moving his arms and held her, still. It seemed as though an electricity passed between them, warming July more than the friction Massimo had provided. Suddenly her face was against the bare spot of his neck, warm and rough and smooth, spreading spindles of warmth over the side of her face.

They stayed like that for a moment. July wondered what facial expression Massimo was casting over her right shoulder. Were his eyes closed, or was it just … his face? What was he thinking? She could feel the heat of his breath on her neck—was he breathing louder, or was she just close enough to hear more clearly?

July's heart fluttered like a live chicken held by its feet. The rest of her body melted and loosened internally with warmth and she felt that, despite the cold, she might melt. What was going on? *No, Toby. Toby,* she tried to center thoughts, but they seemed to slip through the net of her mind like minnows in a net meant for bass. *Toby, Toby, Toby* they swam away leaving a net full of tingling, sparkling Massimo.

When she slackened inside, she stiffened outside. Massimo must have noticed, because he released her a moment after.

"Better?" he asked.

"*Si,*" managed July weakly.

"*Andiamo.* We must get you warm."

July and Massimo walked back to the hotel in silence, July's mind buzzed with the embrace that seemed to still hold her entwined. Clinging to her like cigarette smoke, Massimo's arms were still around her, imprinted on her body as if in memory foam. She was not supposed to feel this way. What was happening?

"We are very close to my home," said Massimo.

"Oh.

"It is just over there," he pointed off to the left.

Okay, she thought. *Why is he telling me this?*

"If you are still cold, we can stop at my home and I can get you one of my sweaters."

"Oh," said July.

She had been so enwrapped in her thought that she had separated from her chilling body. Of course now that he mentioned it, she felt as though she were naked she was so cold. But she shouldn't go to his apartment. She should get back to the hotel with Toby and heat and relegate Massimo to a person she met once when she was in Italy with the man she loved.

Wait! You're freezing! cried her body. *You can blow into your hands and rub them together until they wear away—you will never make them warmer. You can pull your jacket tighter around you, but you have no body heat left to keep in.*

"Look at you," said Massimo. "No, we must get you some more clothes. And perhaps a hot drink to warm you inside." He paused for a moment, then added, "Aha, this must be the first time I try to put more clothes on a beautiful woman."

With a light chuckle, he steered her down a side street without giving her time to say anything.

How did this happen? wondered July. She had gone from holiday with Toby to Massimo's apartment. Massimo's arm was around her, her side was pushed into his, holding her safe. Smelts of guilt slid hotly down her throat. She shouldn't be with him like this, enjoying it, liking that he cared about how warm she was or was not. He had come back for her.

It wouldn't be long, anyway. How long could it take to get a jacket and maybe a hot drink?

"This way," clipped Massimo in Italian, turning her around a corner and then stopping outside the gate to a dark building, quiet like its eyes were closed. As he unlocked the gate, she looked up and down the street—they were the only ones there, small and pressed in the narrow space between the walls that held in the lives of Florentines. She heard a jangle and a pop.

"Ah! Please," said Massimo, swinging open the front door to the building and holding it open for her. She walked in but stopped in the hallway, turning back to him for an indication of where to go. Though it was still cold in the hallway, it was less harsh, more bearable, like running cold water over frostbitten extremities.

"I'm that one, right there," he said. "I am right on the *strada*."

His was the first door inside the building, just off to July's left. He moved over and unlocked the door swiftly, "Please, enter, warm yourself."

July stepped into the apartment, warm velvet fingers slowly trickling the cold away from her body. Massimo stepped in after her and closed the door. For a moment, they were in the still, unfocused smothering dark, and July had the passing thought of someone grabbing her from behind and dragging her away from the world.

A light came on, a harsh yellow cringed into her eyes. Decorated simply and sparsely, the apartment somehow had a stylish flair. Behind her, to the right of the door and next to the window sat a blue futon, folded into a couch and covered with a jacket or two, some papers and books. On the dining room table were a few more books, two or three days worth of newspapers, a used coffee mug. She wanted to look inside the refrigerator in the corner—the innards of an icebox could tell you a lot about someone. On the wall above the futon hung an Andy Warhol print of Marilyn Monroe, and on the opposite wall, a poster with the architectural specs of the Notre Dame Cathedral in Paris. A plant, wilted but not dead, sat on the ledge of the window facing the street. A light hung from the ceiling over the kitchen table like an interrogation lamp in a film noir. There were only a few dishes in his sink, and above his stove hung a set of bright red pots and pans.

"Those are great pots and pans," she said without thinking, and moved involuntarily over to them.

"Yes, I get much use out of them," he replied, throwing his jacket onto the futon. "They were a gift from my parents when I moved here. My mother, she does not want me to starve, and she says that the real man, the real person, must cook for himself, so she teach me to cook, give me pots."

"What can you cook?"

"Oh, the ... basic red marinara, some beef, and bruschetta, and many different kinds of chicken, the beef, I say the beef? And the soup, and the pizza *et cetera*. Is not hard, the cooking. You cook, yes?"

She nodded.

"There is nothing cannot be cooked, is just how much time you have, like you can walk anywhere if you have the time. Please, sit down, I will make you some hot drink. Sit ..." he gestured to the futon.

She walked over and collapsed into it, realizing only after she sat that her feet throbbed, her lower back was cramped, her shoulders sloped with passing time.

"I used to work in a restaurant before I work at the *café*," continued Massimo. "But I find it too interesting, too distracting from my studies."

"Then why didn't you just become a chef?"

"No, no, I do not want this. Cooking should be something you do to live, not to make the living."

Massimo moved around the kitchen and July turned to the stack of books beside her. There were a few architecture textbooks, but among them sat a book. She picked it up.

"What's this?" asked July, holding it up.

Massimo turned around from the kitchen counter and squinted, "*Il Sogno Lucido.*"

He turned back to the counter and July caught a moment of his perfectly fitted dark jeans.

"What is that?"

"You have not heard of this ah, lucid dream?" he spoke to the kitchen wall, talking just a little louder.

"I don't think so."

"Is when you are dreaming, and in this dream you realize that you are dreaming. When you realize you are in the dream, you can control what you're dreaming."

"Oh. I've realized I was dreaming before. But I didn't make anything happen."

"There are some people who practice it for many years so that they can control their dreams all the time."

"Have you done it?"

"I'm trying. I first hear about it from Astrid; she's very good at this. At night she likes to take a vacation to the tropics. She give me this book and I have been reading it. There are many techniques and things that can help you prepare your brain for this *sogno lucido*."

"Like what?"

Massimo turned around with a steaming mug in each hand. He walked over to the futon, handed a mug to July, then moved some papers and sat down beside her, rather closer than she had anticipated he would, so that the fabrics of their jeans brushed lightly when one of them moved or breathed. But she found she didn't much mind, and that she wouldn't have minded if his legs were even just a little closer to hers.

"*Come*, in your dreams, you can look at your hands, because they say your hands, they are not steady in dreams, or you have the too many or too little fingers. Or you can try to read something, because the words will jump off the page. Or you can try to turn on and off the light switch, because we cannot change the lights in our dreams."

"Huh?"

"And then when you're awake, you can stop yourself a few times during the day and look at your hands or ask yourself, 'Am I dreaming?' But this can be hard, because sometimes you live an entire day without realizing it until the next one comes."

She looked at her hands. They were still. *Am I dreaming?* "So why do you want to control your dreams, then?" she asked.

"I tell Astrid it was so that I could make my dream of becoming an architect come true."

"That's not the reason?"

"Really?" he paused, and looked out into the apartment as though it were a hundred miles across, "Is to fly."

"To fly?"

"These are the best kinds of dreams, but I stop having them once I was seven or eight, and I always miss them, the freedom and the light that comes when you are just standing there and then suddenly you're levitating above the earth, just hovering there, like the peaceful star."

He gazed across the field of his living room, as though he would break free from the confines of gravity at any moment.

Toby never talked about things like this. He never talked about dreams, the sleeping kind or the future kind. Maybe he had outlived all his dreams, but hers were all July had. *Am I dreaming?*

"So you could go pretty much anywhere and see anyone you wanted in your dreams," she said.

"*Esattamente*," he sighed, placing his hand on her thigh for punctuation and held it there like his finger was stuck on the period key, lines of ellipses.

She looked at Massimo's face, smooth and carved, square but somehow more rounded than it had seemed before. He sat still, waiting to rise up like the steam from his mug. She looked back down at her hands. The world seemed draped in a buzzing, curtain of honey, like everything was a bit less defined than usual. Except Massimo. He was in front of the curtain. *Am I dreaming?*

He turned to her and looked right into her eyes, "What would you do if you could control your dreams?" he asked.

Jenny would never exist, she thought instantly. But she couldn't say that to Massimo. She would make Jenny disappear and then it would be her and Toby, and maybe the girls on the fringes.

"I would—I would make my ideal future, I guess."

"And what is that?"

"Well—I—I don't know, I guess. I guess it would change every night. I would be somewhere new every night."

"Yes. I each time fly somewhere different. Astrid, she goes to the same place every night. But she is the master. I cannot fly every night. But some nights it is better to go with your dreams instead of dream with your go."

They were silent for a moment.

"I'm sorry, this sentence is not correct. Is late."

His hand was on her thigh again … … … … the endless ellipses.

"You don't seem like the kind of guy to try lucid dreaming," she said.

"Yes. I don't look like many things I am. But you maybe don't look like what you are, either."

"What do you mean?"

"I mean, maybe you look like American tourist, *ma*, you are, I think, one of those who like to see and to change with the seeing. We have not spoken for long, but I get the feeling that you are not one content to see every day what you have seen every day already."

"How can you tell?"

"I think we are the same like that. Now I am done with my school here, I will leave Firenze. I will probably leave Italia. I don't know where I will go, but I think I will know when the time comes. It will come soon. I think, maybe, my dreams tell me New York."

July looked into her mug.

"You do not look like who you are, perhaps. I think we are also the same alike this. But I still wonder why you are with this Toby. He is not one who likes to look. He has been to Firenze how many times? *Cinque?* He can afford to go someplace new. He—no. He is trapped in something else. He does not want to see outside. All night he is only thinking his *figlie,* his *figlie.* Of course, he love his *figlie,* but he left them to be with you, and he wants only to see them. They are like Firenze to him, and you are Paris, and he is taking the train back from Paris each night. He sees Paris only in the light, he miss half the Paris."

She wanted to fall into the bottom of the mug, have it swallow her and cover her ears.

"Where will you go?" he asked. "You are almost the time to leave the school."

She shrugged her shoulders so that they brushed against Massimo's.

"I don't know," she sighed. "I don't know where I want to go. Because I would go anywhere." Then she heard that her thoughts and words had been the same, and that Toby had not passed through them. Her stomach clutched and fluttered. What was happening?

"You are young."

"I don't feel young."

"Is not bad, this young."

His shoulder pressed more firmly into hers. Or was it the other way around?

"People think you don't know what you want when you're young," she said.

"You know what you want?"

She paused. "Sometimes I think I want something, but then I want something else at the same time. No, I don't know what I want."

But she wished she did. Her eyes drooped involuntarily and she sighed.

"Here, you lie down," said Massimo, taking her mug and coaxing her head to the end of the futon. The top half of her lay on the futon, the bottom of her still folded as though she were sitting and now she was in half. But then Massimo lifted her legs and stretched them out over his, scooted a bit closer to her head, and placed his arms on either side of her knees.

"People think is too important, this staying in one place. Why must we choose one place to live? The world is infinite."

"So why don't you just pack up and go?" she said from below.

"It's like *il sogno lucido.* I have to prepare my mind first. I'm getting there."

One of his hands wrapped around the side of her thigh just above her kneecap and a vein of gunpowder from her knee to her shoulder ignited. *I should shift my weight,* she thought. *Shake him off.*

But she didn't. She stayed still, transfixed as his hand moved up her leg. How high would he go? She wondered through the jungle of fuse vines ignite catching fire through her body. Her eyes were closed, she realized. Hiding or savoring or tired.

Halfway up her thigh, his hand moved back down again.

So suggestively appropriate, she grinned into herself.

His weight shifted beneath her legs. What was he going to do now? He was leaning more towards her, from perpendicular to parallel. His hand moved up her leg again, but the fuse extended further now, all the way to the back of her throat like a cotton swab. *Am I dreaming?*

His hand brushed through her hair.

"You have such wonderful hair."

The moment was so beautiful her heart wrung out like a sponge.

"I think I am infatuated with your hair," he said, his voice lower.

I should move, she thought.

Her eyes still closed, she imagined what they looked like from outside, as she lay on his couch across him, the two of them the x-and y-axes, the y-axis bending like a Dali painting towards the x-axis.

He's going to kiss me. The thought flashed in her mind like Las Vegas. Her lips seemed to swell with sparkles of anticipation. *Oh God. He's going to kiss me.*

How far away was his face? He could be an inch or a foot away—it all felt the same. *What if he kisses me? Kiss me. That's cheating. Is it? It doesn't feel like it. Cheating shouldn't feel like what you want, like what feels right.*

Toby, she thought, as a pit in her throat grew swiftly into a knot in her stomach, deadening the fuses in her body.

An inch or a mile? I have to. So she turned onto her side, her shoulder to Massimo, "I'm sorry," she whispered so softly, she wasn't sure she had said it at all.

She felt the air around them freeze.

"Is late," he said huskily.

He slid from beneath her legs. A moment later something draped over her, and then footsteps away down the hall, and then silence. She imagined that he was still watching her, that he had crept quietly back in socks to watch her. She didn't open her eyes. She didn't want to see if he was actually there.

She was exhausted. But her body was awake with the jittery reminder of anticipation. She wouldn't come down for a long time.

Her eyes were closed but she had never felt so aware. Her consciousness walked her down the hall into Massimo's room, back into their electric embrace, but she stayed as still as stone on the couch, making the walk with her mind but not with her feet. *Well, shit.*

Toby stared at the white grids on the bathroom floor. Had he fallen asleep on the toilet? God, how pathetic. *How old are you, old man?*

The room outside the bathroom rang with still silence. Wait, where was July?

He stood up, washed his hands, and walked into the room. Why was the phone on the floor—? Toby froze, the shuddering recollection dripping over him. Jenny. Kevin. He must have stood like that for five or ten minutes, listening to his heart thud in his chest, until he managed to sit down on the bed.

She replaced me. It was that easy? Like a rib splitter without amnesia. No, not amnesia, anesthesia. He could use a little of both right now. *Why? How could she do this? But this is divorce, you're supposed to move on, she's supposed to move on, be out of your life. But she's not—I talk to her almost every day still, I was supposed to be free of her, she was supposed to leave my dreams, my thoughts, I wasn't supposed to feel like this anymore, like someone was reaching into my chest and removing me scoop by curling, rolling scoop until there's nothing left and I flatten and roll into myself.*

I gave her the best part of my life. She carried my children, this woman. She knew all those places on my body where if you bit me or pinched me or licked me just so my cells would burst like popcorn. And she could replace me that easy? It was Kevin all along wasn't it? Would she just forget me so easily? Doesn't she care? Doesn't she hurt, too? Was this why she asked for the divorce? For Kevin? How long had they been together? How long had they been in love? What if they had been in love for years, for most of their marriage?

Then not only was his marriage a lie, his divorce was too, and so was his hurt, then it was all fake, a lie. *That bitch. Did she ever love me, and when did she stop? Why did she stop? Had Kevin told her to have the baseball bat ready? Remember what Astrid said about not loving someone anymore, that it was like a silent letter and you don't know it's there until it's spelled out for you. Maybe Kevin taught Jenny how to spell. Maybe Toby was a spelling error.*

Part of him had believed that she wouldn't be able to love anyone else, or that he had been the only man who knew how to love her, that she would spend the rest of her life as a single middle-aged woman, rotting in her own request for "singledom" as he moved on with his life.

She really had wanted to divorce him. How long had she and Kevin—
had they been going at it for their entire marriage? *That little—*

Stop it. Stop it. It doesn't matter. He was free now, wasn't he? There
was no more Jenny in the background, no more possibility. How
long she had been fucking Kevin didn't change the fact that they
were divorced, that he didn't have her anymore. He didn't have all of
anyone anymore, not even his daughters. He had to share half of them.
All he had now was July. She was the only way he could have all of
someone again.

Where was July? He looked at the clock, nearly one o'clock. She
should have come back with him—Massimo. Going back to look
for her because Toby couldn't wait. Where was she? Was she okay?
She must have gotten lost. Had Massimo found her? Had something
happened to her? What if someone robbed her, or kidnapped her or
dragged her into a shadowy park and—?

No no, he tried to push the thought from his mind. He had become
too adept at worrying since he had his girls.

But where were they? What if Massimo ... what if he kidnapped
her? No. But—maybe he made a move? Maybe they were at his
apartment right now, doing God knows what. Doing what Jenny and
Kevin had—

Shut up, shut up, shut up. Toby clasped his hands around his head, as
though that would dampen his rogue thoughts, push them down and
out and away.

He lay down on the bed. He could go out, go look for her, so that at
least he would be moving, doing something, instead of crawling inside
himself like that scene in *Star Wars* when that guy climbs into that
animal's stomach. But what could he really do? He didn't know where
they had been, where Massimo had gone or if he had found her or
where he had taken her if he had. What if he had found her and called
the hotel? He would certainly call just after Toby walked out the door
and was out of earshot of the phone. And then July would have no
choice but to stay with Massimo.

So he would stay. What could he do, outside or in? He was useless
now to all the women around him. To his ex-wife, who would have a
new husband, a new parenting partner; to his daughters, who would
have a new father figure; to his girlfriend who could be his daughter
and what was she doing with me anyway and who had a handsome
Italian man to save her now.

What *was* she doing with him anyway? He seemed to be a perfect
fit for women in their twenties. She would grow out of him. She would
grow away from him. *She's just a kid. No, she's different; she's not like any*

other twenty-two year olds. How many other twenty-two year olds do you know?

Yeah, I thought so.

You just want to think so because you like fucking her.

Well, yeah, but I couldn't do that if she didn't interest me in other ways, too.

What are you going to do once she graduates? Get her her first apartment? Help her find her first job? Help her navigate all those little firsts of life so that she doesn't have to do it herself, so she doesn't have to learn?

And then, just when you get used to having her around, just when you need her, she'll realize how much you're holding her back, how much of the real world, of youth she's missing out on, tying herself to a man pushing fifty who's going to want to retire around the time she's thinking about babies, who will be getting yearly colonoscopies and an AARP membership and maybe a hearing aid and sporting the start of a comb-over and not able to eat that Indian food anymore, who will be about to sprout liver spots and develop arthritis, cataracts, erectile dysfunction, Alzheimer's, heart disease, and she's looking at all the Kevins who can still move and hear and see and who aren't old enough to be her father or act like it either.

At least, if she's smart, she'll realize that.

If she doesn't, then she's stupid, and then you're stuck with an idiot for the second half of your life because you're not getting a second divorce because then no one would want to marry you again and that would just say that you're one of the major screw-ups in life who can't share his life with anyone, especially a woman and then you'll never be able to retire because you'll be paying alimony to two women and you'll work until you die, 94 years old and gray and shriveled and blind and senile and in debt and forgotten by your kids because they love their step-daddy more because they'll always remember the Christmas that real Daddy wasn't there and Kevin Daddy was.

And next year they'll want to carry on the Kevin traditions they started this year, and every year after that because real Daddy will always go to Italy so we'll talk to him on the phone, and then by the time they're graduating from high school and college and getting married they'll accidentally introduce Kevin as their dad, and then when Toby ambles on over they'll correct themselves and say that Kevin is their step-dad but they live with him and their mother and they see their birth dad, not just Dad anymore, on weekends and a few select holidays and you'll be effectively pushed out of the family that you helped create.

And then when the girls have children I'll be the other grandpa, like a sixth finger or a third nipple, always there, but awkward and unnatural and the rest of your life you'll have to wonder why, why, WHY couldn't we just love each other like we said we would? And why didn't it work, and how does anyone else make it work? And am I really that easy to forget and what did I do wrong? What do I lack? Why don't you want to be around me anymore? What did I do WRONG? Why, WHY, WHY AM I SO AWFUL? Why can't I just have the life that I want and why can't you just want that too and why can't you want to do it the same way I do?

Toby leapt off the bed. No. No, he could not stay here, he needed to be outside himself, he needed to run away, far, far away, which was the point of coming to this damned country in the first place.

He grabbed his jacket and stormed out of the room, resisting the urge to slam the door behind him. He clomped rapidly down the stairs, propelled by gravity and remaining upright by muscular memory, because his conscious memory had forgotten how to do anything except run torturous laps on his little hamster wheel brain.

He burst outside and stopped at the curb to catch his breath. It was cold. His exhales puffed into little horizontal mushroom clouds. He looked around, up and down the barren street. The city was silent. What the hell was he doing out in the freezing weather at two o'clock in the morning? Where would he go?

He turned right to walk along the river. Once he reached the path along the Arno, he turned left toward the Ponte Vecchio. *How appropriate,* he thought, *the Old Point.* The point was not that he would go there when he was young, it was that he would return there when he was old and remember being young, rue how stupid he had been, people in their twenties are so stupid, and try to shout back at the Toby lying there on the wall that scorching day, that he was making the biggest, dumbest mistake he could ever make, and when you stand up and go buy water, walk away and never come back, just walk away, because the hurt you would feel then would be infinitely less that what you'll feel in almost twenty years.

You people in your twenties are so stupid, what are you doing? You're the reason people in the world are suffering. Sure, the people who make some of the world's biggest mistakes are well out of their twenties, but why do you think they make those mistakes in the first place? Because they did something stupid in their twenties and it fucked up the rest of their lives. That's why the whole world is fucked: people in their twenties. They're so damn distracted with sex and finding themselves and finding someone else and procreating and starting out that they do it all wrong and then you end up like me.

He listened back to his thoughts. *July is in her twenties. Is she stupid? Maybe she's different? But can you really be different? Can you really understand the world without having lived it? She should do her twenties the right way—don't get attached to anybody, don't start to build your life like people say, because you will do it wrong and you will change your mind and fuck yourself and others and the world completely over. Leave me. Leave me because you will hurt me and you will hurt yourself.*

Don't leave me. I like having you around; you make me feel young again. But young is stupid, right? But maybe because I am not, I can show her. I can show her how to do it right so that she won't make those mistakes, and she will be different.

You sound like a father.

That's what you have daughters for.

But July is not my daughter.

But do you love her?

Well, I don't know. Am I really in a position to love anyone right now?

You are always in a position to love someone—it's just a matter of whether you're willing or not.

You can always love someone.

Can you always love someone? You can love someone always. Can someone always love you? Someone can always love you.

Toby the grammatical error.

Families stay together, that's the way life works. Life works, that's how families stay together. Families work, that's the way life stays together.

Stop repeating everything you think. Stop thinking everything you repeat. Repeat everything you stop thinking.

It's just a matter of whether you're willing to or not.

Toby reached the Ponte Vecchio and turned onto the bridge. It was silent, like he had never seen it before. There was always someone there, but at this time of the night—morning—well, only crazy lonely people like himself would be awake, much less out in this weather and on the damned bridge.

It suddenly occurred to Toby that, if he wanted, he could jump off. He could jump off the side of the bridge and float away like an iceberg and just end it now. Who would find him? Maybe the hotel would notice that he hadn't been in. Or that he failed to check out. Unless someone found his body first, floating and blue and white. What would Jenny think when she found out? Would she think he did it because of her? Wouldn't he have? Would she be wracked with guilt, or think that was a pathetic cop out? What sort of a selfish, emotionally crippled man had she been living with for so long? What about July, how would she find out? What would she do? Would she go to his funeral, and see Jenny and his daughters?

His daughters. While the existence of the option of suicide came through, he never actually considered it. Ending your life was kind of that other option that sat in the back of your brain, so that when you felt like you were out of options, you knew that wasn't really true yet.

He felt a bit like Jimmy Stewart in *It's a Wonderful Life* just before the angel came to show him what others' lives would be like without him. Was Toby really that desperate right now that he needed to create a hallucination to talk him down?

No.

What if he didn't kill himself, he just walked away, packed his things before July came back and took a train to the middle of some place he had never heard of before and just—started over? Or, ended, really. No one would know him, there would be no ex-wife, no Kevin to follow him there. But they would. They would follow. If you have an A, you must have a B.

He walked back toward the spot where he and Jenny had sunned like lizards. His heart, which had been shriveled and blackened, tore itself to shreds and regrew the memory of what it had been that day. Warm and happy, like he had solved the pages of philosophical, emotional turmoil that filled the libraries. Those idiots—they just needed a woman like this.

The black briquette of his heart shook its head bitterly at his youthful disillusionment. *This is why old men like me fuck up the world,* he thought. *We have no more hope. We've seen what hope does to you, and since we've lost it, we'll take it from you and justify it.*

He remembered the words to that Cat Stevens song, *You're still young, that's your fault. Something something something look at me, I am old but I'm happy.*

I'm old. But I'm not happy. Am I supposed to be happy? Or am I not old enough for that? Or did I just do it wrong?

He arrived at the spot where he and Jenny had sat, joining himself seventeen years ago, leaning his back against the wall, moving his leg for room for Jenny to sit against him. He closed his eyes and imagined her body against his, leaning on his thighs so that they fell asleep and lost all feeling. He remembered the sun on his face, the sweat from Jenny's back falling onto his arms, his legs, the way the colors danced in front of his eyes when he closed them to the sun, the leaping flames of red and yellow and orange, or blue if he opened his eyes just a crack.

He started humming Cat Stevens out loud, and then he started singing.

"Meet a girl, if you want, you can marry something mmhmm look at me, I am old but I'm happy."

He imagined what someone might see if they walked by right now. A middle-aged guy lying on the edge of the Ponte Vecchio singing half the words to a Cat Stevens song. He was crazy. But there was no one there.

He imagined Jenny as she was now, sitting next to him, looking at him. He wanted to talk to her, like they used to, before all the fighting and name calling.

What happened to us, Jenny?

She shrugged, the way he remembered her doing, where her shoulders rise to her ears and stay there as she turns her head to the side, touches her chin to her shoulder, and raises her eyebrows.

I don't know.

We were so good together.

"Were we?" She was looking out over the river, shoulders still raised like her eyebrows.

Was it me?

"It must have been both of us."

They were silent again, Jenny's face lit dully by the scraps of light reflected from the river.

He wanted to hear her say she was sorry. He wanted to hear her say that maybe it could have worked out, that they hadn't failed, that they could find their love somewhere deep in the Arno.

Why?

But she wasn't there anymore. He couldn't figure out what she would say. He had lost her. He had lost any idea of what she was really like anymore, the person he had thought he knew better than anyone else. Seeing her nearly every day for seventeen years, sleeping in the same bed she did, sharing the space where she dreamed. He was so close to those dreams, and yet he never knew what they were. For a while, long enough for them to form a life, her dreams had been his and his hers. But they never tell you what to do after your dreams come true. What happens when you run out of dreams?

Toby felt the stone numb his butt through his jeans. He had always thought of life as a progression, as a straight line that moved perceptibly through time. But now, here, his life was the opposite of everything it was sixteen years ago, he felt that maybe life was a tunnel and we moved from one end to the other our entire lives, bouncing back and forth from one extreme to the other. So we were all trapped in our little tubes, intersecting with other tubes along the way. How impossible it was to share movements. Straight lines can only intersect at one point.

Now what? He was at the end of his tube. He could stay there, or he could move back again. But what if he didn't want this tube anymore? Was there a way out?

No. The tube will extend deep into either direction, indefinitely finite. You get one tube, two infinite ends, and he was on the wrong end.

He could use a drink. Was there anything open now? Like trying to find intelligent life in the universe—probably out there, but hard to find if you don't know where to look.

He should go back to the hotel in case July came back or called. He stood up and reflexively put his hand in his pocket for the key. July didn't have a key.

And neither, apparently, did he.

Well shit.

XVIII

IT WAS MORNING. JULY WAS WANDERING THE CROWDED STREETS OF
Florence, pushing her way past her elementary school classmates,
looking for the classroom for Italian 301. She stopped her friend
Ashley, a short girl in a sundress with pigtails.

"Ashley, do you know where Building Ten is?"

"*Non capisco,*" she said, revealing a space where she had lost both her
front teeth, and she moved past July, clutching her Lisa Frank Trapper
Keeper with a picture of a burning orange leopard.

July was lost. There was the Arno a few feet away, but why was the
Duomo on top of the hill by the Boboli Gardens? Wasn't it on this
side of the river? Her gelato was melting and class was going to start
soon—she was going to be late! And Signor Della Ragione did not
like it when you were late; he would send you to the principal's office.

July looked at her schedule to see where she was supposed to be,
but she couldn't see the words clearly. She squinted, but that didn't
help; did she need new glasses? She moved the paper back and forth
away from her eyes like she had seen Toby do many times before.

"Excuse me, what does this say?" she asked Robert, the boy whose
hat she regularly stole because she liked him.

"It says, 'Take once daily with food.'"

"No, that's the directions for his blood pressure medicine."

"Who?"

"Toby."

"Toby's with Jenny. Here," Robert handed the paper back to her. "Toby and Jenny, sitting in a tree. K-I-S-S-I-N-G." He flowed back into the river of ten-year olds.

It was like trying to read her schedule through a lava lamp.

She looked across the Arno to the playground on the other side. There were Toby and Jenny, making out against a picnic table. Those stupid high schoolers. But even though Toby was across the river, July had to crane her neck way up at Toby. The bell rang, and suddenly Toby was next to her.

"Come on, July, it's time for class."

He steered her into a room. She sat at a desk that had an empty desk next to it so that Toby could sit beside her, but Toby moved to the front of the room instead.

"Good morning, class."

"Good morning, Mr. Alder."

Wait, when did he become the teacher? July looked next to her and saw that Grace had taken the empty desk next to hers.

"I hope he goes over the subjunctive," she said to July. "I just don't understand that tense at all."

"Please open your books to page eighty-three," said Mr. Alder.

July opened her book but couldn't read the page numbers.

"What lesson is this?" she asked Grace.

"*Go Diego Go!* Duh," she replied, flipping July's book open for her.

Mr. Alder started speaking in rapid Italian. Where was Signor Della Ragione? July couldn't read this book at all.

Am I dreaming?

Suddenly the world around her stopped. *Am I dreaming?*

She couldn't be dreaming; when had she gone to sleep?

She looked at her hands. Her fingers were blurry and webbed together. *I must be dreaming.*

She stood up and walked over to the light switch by the door and flicked it up and down. Nothing happened.

"July! What are you doing? Sit down and stop playing with the lights!" yelled Mr. Alder.

"No. I'm dreaming. I'm not your student, I'm a big girl. I'm your wife."

Suddenly she felt the cold metal of a large diamond ring on her webby left hand.

"Hi honey," Toby said, walking over and kissing her hello. "What are you doing here? I'm in the middle of class."

"It's okay, school's over. Let's go."

The bell rang.

"Okay," he said, and they walked out of the classroom together and down the halls.

"Wait," she said. "I want to stop at Ferragamo and get my coat."

She went inside, where there were racks of clothes and shoes, and picked out a luscious forest green coat.

"Let's go," she said to Toby.

"Where are we going?" he asked.

"Let's go to Costa Rica, to our house on the beach."

"I can't, I have to call my girls."

"No you don't. I'm dreaming."

"Oh. Okay."

Then, holding hands, they leapt into the air and stayed there. July leaned forward and over the Ponte Vecchio they flew, over the clouds until she saw the sand beneath them. July took off her shoes and landed lightly. The palm trees hung like water droplets over the sand, and everything was bright and green and swirled around them like a Van Gogh comforter. They turned into the forest, and straddling the sand and lush jungle was a large house like the one in *Architectural Digest* that one time. They walked in and sat on the couch, July curled into Toby, safe and warm, and he was thinking only about her, and they were married and would be for a long time.

"We'll stay like this forever," she said.

"Yes."

"I'm pregnant," she said.

He put his hand on her basketball belly, "What should we name her?"

"Sophia."

"I can't wait to be a father for the first time."

And the warmth of happiness spread through her like butter melting into an English muffin. Outside the window, the ocean gurgled like an espresso machine. Louder and louder until a hook grabbed her from Toby's arms and pulled her through her eyelids.

July opened her eyes.

What? Where am I? July tried to move but found her whole body paralyzed with sleep. This wasn't Costa Rica. Where was Toby?

Through the haze came the words *per che.* Signor Della Ragione? Wait, she was still in Italy? Where was Toby? Then she saw a poster of Notre Dame and a lamp dangling over a kitchen table. And then she remembered. X and Y.

"*Buon giorno!*" called Massimo.

"What time is it?"

Massimo craned his head toward a clock, "Is nine twenty."

She sat up quickly and rubbed her face. She could feel last night's makeup flaking off her eyes.

"The bathroom, it is down the hall, that way," he said, pointing.

"Thanks," she said. She must look as bad as she felt.

But when she got to the bathroom and saw herself in the mirror, she saw that she in fact looked much worse. Pale, makeup smudged, frizzy haired, fuzzy mouthed. Not the Brigitte Bardot look she had been hoping for.

She rinsed her face in cold water and stared in the mirror. Costa Rica. Toby. The happiness that came with the dream was like a warm piece of clothing from the dryer—snuggly and comforting, but quick to diffuse.

When she came back to the kitchen, Massimo pushed a little cup her way.

"Espresso!"

She drank.

"You have slept okay?"

"Yeah," she said.

She decided not to tell him about the lucid dream, because then she would have to tell him just what she had dreamt. He probably wouldn't believe her anyway. He had practiced for so long, and she just—did it? That seemed unlikely.

"I called your hotel last night, but no one answered."

"I thought they always had someone at the front desk."

"No, I mean Toby did not answer."

"Oh." *He didn't answer? Where was he? Didn't he care that I didn't come back?*

"I will take you back after espresso. We can get breakfast on the way. *Andiamo.*"

He stood up, drained his espresso, and walked to the door.

"Here, I pick you out one of my coats. Is still very cold outside, you can wear it over your green one."

July stayed at the table. Her brain, still in Costa Rica, had not processed what was happening yet.

"*Andiamo.* We must get you back to Toby, he is probably worried."

July was sure that Massimo said that to be nice, because she looked so awful, and not because he thought it was actually true. She stood up and walked over to where Massimo stood holding out a black trench coat.

"This is a lovely coat," she said, putting it on. "I feel like I should be black and white and have a fedora on my head."

"That is the point of the coat. *Andiamo*," he said, pointing to the door.

He opened the door and moved aside for her to go first. July found that, even in the daylight, she had no idea where she was. Nothing looked familiar, not even from the night before. The streets were still fairly empty, but there were noticeably more people out today than there were yesterday.

"Most people are still on *Natale*," said Massimo, his head covered by a gray wool hat. He looked a bit like a "Most Wanted" sketch. "It will be like this until *nuovo anno*."

"Are there any celebrations in the city on New Year's?"

"*Naturalmente*. There is also a large concert at Piazza Santa Croce, the orchestra plays so many beautiful music. I went last year, *che bella*, I hope to go again this year. Ah!"

He grabbed July's arm and steered her into a café on the corner.

"Is here. I come here most mornings. They have the best coffee and the breakfast pastries. Clara!" he shouted to the woman behind the counter. "Clara! *Come stai, bel Natale!*"

"*Massimo! Bel Natale!*"

"This is my friend, July. She is American, but she speaks Italian," he said in Italian.

"Any friend of Massimo's is a friend of mine," said Clara to July warmly.

"*Piacere*," said July.

"We'll have two of the usual," said Massimo to Clara.

"How do you know she'll like what you like?"

"Ah, she likes everything! She is not like other Americans, she understands how to eat!"

"That's all the Americans understand! All they do is eat, eat, eat."

"No no, but she knows *how* to eat, not just *to* eat."

"*Ah, bene, bene*, sit, sit, warm up, here is your coffee."

Clara sloshed two ceramic mugs of coffee over the counter as Massimo slid her some money.

"No, no," said July. "You should let me get breakfast, you've been so good to me."

"No, no! I will not have this! Sit! Sit!" he waved her over to a small table.

July shuffled over to the table and sat. A few moments later Massimo came over with a white plate in each hand. On each plate was a flaky, golden brioche roll dusted with powdered sugar.

"You eat this every day?" cried July in amazed envy.

"*Sì*," said Massimo simply, biting into the pillow of butter.

July picked hers up and followed suit. It was perfect—everything her father would have wanted from a brioche. She wished she could send some home to him. A slick of butter lined the inside of her mouth. Each bite was soft and flaky, suggestively sweet.

Am I dreaming?

"Is perfect followed by a sip of the coffee," said Massimo as he trailed his food with coffee.

"It's things like this that would make daily life manageable," she said. "You know there's always another pastry tomorrow."

Massimo laughed, "Yes, I live pastry to pastry."

They finished breakfast in silence and lingered a few minutes over crumbs and final coffee swigs.

"*Bene,*" said Massimo. "We should take you back to Toby."

He stood up. July looked up but did not move. She should be more excited to go back, but it had been such a lovely morning. This is what she had wanted with Toby, but it seemed there was always something wrong. Would he even be glad to see her? It was hard to look forward to seeing him when it didn't seem that he cared about her absence in the first place. Nor did she want to leave Massimo. It would be so easy to lie.

She stood up in delayed response.

"He will be glad to see you," said Massimo soothingly.

July put her hands into the coat pockets and said nothing. A lot could change overnight, right? Like Astrid said. "One day is yes, the next day is no." If he could do it with someone he had been with for seventeen years, he could do it with July. *And he probably hasn't loved me like he loved Jenny.*

They walked wordlessly along the street, as though neither one knew how to end the time they had spent together. *Will I ever see him again?* July wondered.

"Here we are," said Massimo suddenly.

July looked up in surprise. She hadn't been paying attention to where they had been walking, and now she found herself staring at the words Hotel Ariele.

"Oh," she said awkwardly.

They stood a moment in silence. Were they supposed to say lifelong farewells, or delude themselves with see you laters?

"Ah! I give you my phone number!" he exclaimed, his words jumping out like an animal in front of a moving car. He pulled a pencil from a pocket somewhere, "Do you have the paper?"

"Uh," July rummaged through her purse. She had no paper, except her passport, which her father had told her to always have on hand, "No, all I have is my passport."

"That's fine," said Massimo, holding his hand out.

"No, I'll find something else," July replied, tucking the passport between two fingers as she rummaged in her bag again.

Massimo reached further and plucked the passport from her fingers.

"Hey! I don't think you're supposed to write in that," she protested as he opened it to a page and wrote something, but it took him longer to write than a phone number should. She dearly hoped that wouldn't invalidate the passport, though she soothed her worry a bit knowing there were worse places to be stuck without a valid passport than Florence, and that he wrote his unapproved information in pencil, which she could erase after transferring the notes to a separate sheet of paper.

"Here," he said, closing her passport and handing it back to her. "You have a problem ... you tell me."

"*Grazie,*" she replied, relieved to have the passport back in her control.

"*Prego, prego,*" he waved, as though clearing the air. "You go to Toby. He is missing you, I'm sure."

"Thanks, Massimo."

He pursed his lips and waved her away with his wrist, then turned away abruptly, as though her entering the hotel was a surgery program on TV and he was squeamish. He walked away, his hands in his pockets, shoulders hunched but still square against the world. A square peg in a round hole.

July turned and walked beneath the awning. The concierge looked up at her as she walked in. Was that a look of recognition? Suspicion?

What have you done? I know what you wanted.

She looked like she had done something—no makeup, messy hair, wearing clothes that weren't hers and had obviously been made for a man.

July looked down and remembered that this was Massimo's coat. The shoulders fell nearly to her elbows. She caught a glimpse of herself in the mirror by the base of the stairs. She looked like the Wicked Witch of the West—her shoulders melting, melting.

Though she had tried to tame it with water, her hair was wild, obviously a deflated, day old style. Her face was pale and undefined like an over-exposed photograph.

I can't go upstairs like this, she thought. *Look at me.*

She felt the concierge looking at her. She could turn around and walk out, or she could go up those stairs.

She trudged up the stairs. With each step up, she was twenty pounds heavier, and when she reached the top she felt like a knight in leaden armor approaching the dragon's cave without a sword.

She turned down the hallway, the walls hanging in with dread. She could still feel Massimo's hand on her leg, in her hair, his whispers.

Her heart thumped in her chest, her face flamed hot as she stopped outside their door. She looked next door, hoping that the Rothmans weren't there to hear her knock, to hear Toby yell if he was going to yell. Those sounds seemed somehow more private than the ones they had already heard.

She lifted her hand to the door. Okay, on three. One, two ... *You have to. Just do it. Don't think about it. Oh God, oh God* ... three.

She knocked five times, and hovered uncertainly. Part of her hoped that the door would open immediately, that Toby had been anticipating her return, and that he would fling the door open and hug her in relief. "There you are, I was so worried about you" and they would hug and it would be okay.

She listened for footsteps, or shuffling, or any sign that Toby was coming. But there was only silence. She put her ear to the door, certain that once she did, the door would open and she would look like a fool. But at least the door would be open.

Nothing. She leaned back and knocked again, uncertainly. Was he messing with her? Trying to prove a point? But she hadn't done anything wrong. At least, he didn't know she had, maybe. *He* had left *her*. Still he didn't come. Why didn't he answer? Was he still asleep? But it was ten thirty. Had he gone out? Maybe he had gone to look for her? But he wouldn't have known where to find her. Was he at breakfast? But breakfast was closed.

She turned and looked down the hall, as though he were hiding in wait. She knocked again. "Toby?" she called into the door.

She pressed her ear against it again. Nothing. She imagined the room inside, the empty bed, the empty room, her calling out to nobody. Or maybe Toby was standing on the other side of the door now, listening to her plead her way in, open sesame.

"Toby?" she knocked again.

He wasn't there. Why had he left when she had not returned and did not have a key? Where *was* he? Didn't he care that she wasn't with him? What was she supposed to do now, just sit here in the hallway? She didn't want the concierge to know more; he seemed to have already pieced together enough.

You're being paranoid. But what would he think, me asking for the key, looking like this, without Toby? You're just going to have to suck it up, she thought. *Just pretend you didn't do anything wrong, like there's nothing strange going on.*

So she turned and slinked back down the stairs. Before she turned into view of the front desk she stopped, took a deep breath, and tried to stand up straight. She turned the corner and headed for the balding man in glasses.

"*Buon giorno,*" she said.

"*Buon giorno,*" he said.

The corners of his mouth seemed a little tense. What could he see?

"Ah, uh, I, uh, forgot the key to my room. Room eight."

"I see," said the concierge, unsuccessfully masking his irritation. "Just a moment."

He went into the back room, then emerged a few moments later with a ring of keys.

Without a word, he started up the stairs.

July turned and followed him up the stairs, about half a flight beneath his jangling. When she turned into the hall, he was already at the door putting the key in.

"Your husband, he has the key."

"Oh! Uh ... he's—he's not my husband."

"Mm." The concierge turned his face toward her, one eyebrow raised slightly. Just what sort of melodrama was going on in his hotel? "But he has the key."

"I ..." July shrugged helplessly. "I would think so."

"Yes, he has the key. He come in this morning, three or four asking like you to let in the room. I let him in, he take the key, go back out again! What you doing so late in the night?" asked the concierge impatiently.

"I ... don't—know."

The concierge turned his head back to the doorknob and July could swear that he rolled his eyes. He jangled the key a few times, unable to open the door. He pushed against it with his shoulder and turned the knob left and right.

"Oh, you have to—pull up," said July.

The concierge looked at her, then peevishly stepped out of the way and motioned for July to do it herself. She turned the knob and pulled up and the door opened.

"Thanks," said July, sliding into the room.

"*Prego,*" said the concierge dryly as he removed the key from the door.

July shut the door as soon as she could and stood with her forehead against the cool, hard wood. He had gone out and come back and left again. Was he avoiding her? She looked in the corner and saw that his suitcase was still there. He hadn't left. Not permanently, anyway. *Where are you, Toby?*

A weasel had crawled through Toby's belly button and burrowed itself between the folds of his intestines to die. It was rotting, polluting his body with his every breath. The Jenny carcass crawling with Kevin maggots.

He was paralyzed. Earlier in the morning, around three or four, when he had gone back to the hotel, he thought his viscera would burst through his skin like the final measures of a Beethoven symphony. So he kept moving. The concierge, soured from interrupted sleep, had unlocked the door, but as soon as he had seen the stillness and solitude of the hotel room, Toby fled. He needed to be alone, but only inside himself. At least outside, he would know that others existed while he retreated from function.

He went back out under the awning and back into the night. It was cold, but Toby decided not to notice as he tunneled back through the hovering, leaning Florentine shells. He just walked.

And walked.

But soon his function began to give way. The noxious stench of carrion inside him spread through his body like toxic gas; he could walk no more. So he stopped in the middle of the street.

What are you doing, Toby? it asked. *Why are you stopped in the street? What good will this do? This isn't a Tennessee Williams play—howling in the street won't fix anything.*

His body had disconnected, as though his head and spinal cord were floating three paces behind the rest of his body, which had stopped in the middle of the not-day not-night street.

Without warning, he began to cry.

Big boys don't cry, said his brain, which simultaneously told him that at least no one was looking.

He was hunched over, staring at the pavement, crying louder, his mouth open, drool coming uncontrollably over his bottom lip.

You're drooling, said his brain.

But his mouth could not close, nor his throat swallow.

I am helpless. His knees wanted to fall to the pavement, but his brain willed him not to—*You'll never get up. This isn't a movie. Don't be melodramatic.*

Why hadn't the separation, the divorce, made him feel this way?

Now Jenny was really gone.

July had been his upper hand, but now Jenny was going to marry Kevin. Jenny was supposed to feel this way, while Toby was supposed to take the divorce as his new lease on life.

She was gone. She wasn't coming back. She wasn't thinking about him. Toby didn't matter anymore. He had lost his privileges. There was no one else to have his back except for him.

She was gone. And Toby was alone on a street in Italy crying like— like Jenny.

Pull yourself together, man.

He picked a spot on the pavement and stared at it hard, concentrating on what it looked like. A chicken. A chicken. A chicken, a chicken, a chicken.

His tears stopped, his shoulders un-hunched themselves a bit. His brain was stuffed with cotton balls, like the morning after a night of heavy drinking.

Walk, his brain said.

Where am I going?

Just. Walk.

So he walked, like a robot, a mannequin, a man with no brain, no heart, no home, no nerve, and blood of novocaine. Novocaine Man, who felt so much he ceased to feel anything at all.

He walked the same places many times; the Ponte Vecchio, to the Duomo, down the Uffizi, back to the Ponte Vecchio and over and back again, up and down the Arno. There were too many places he recognized. Suddenly his brain had remembered everything he and Jenny had done, everywhere they had gone. And he could see himself, feel himself, there twenty years ago, remember exactly what he was doing. It was like some sick opposite version of Alzheimer's.

He passed the corner where he and Jenny had ordered pasta and she had dropped a forkful all down her shirt. And he had taken her picture at that fountain, her sunglasses pushing her hair up and back and down in waterfalls, her tank top riding up so he could see a wedge of skin. They had stood there once figuring out how to get to the Accademia. Another American had taken their picture in front of that statue and cut the statue's head out of the frame. They stood right there and kissed. And there. And there.

Those steaming, decaying remains sent indignant shivers up his throat and rattled his ribs as he remembered she had lied; he hadn't mattered to her for a long time. The warm hiccups of betrayal just wouldn't leave him.

Then, as the sky began to drain of night, he noticed another person, the first since the sour concierge. It was a young man, tallish and so skinny, hosing down the walk front of a café. The water slid over the grimy cobblestones, which were still slick from the night's frost.

Why is he hosing in the middle of the winter? thought Toby. He realized that this had been his first coherent thought in hours.

He didn't know what his body wanted to do. Sit, drink coffee at the same table all day, speak as little as possible? Walk, try to function as normally he could, return to the hotel?

Toby didn't know how long he stood thinking non-thoughts as he tried to decide what to do. Novocaine Man. Novocaine Man had already started walking by the time his brain caught up. One foot in front of the other, time heals all wounds.

When he went to put one foot in front of the other, he found that the other was no longer there for one foot to go in front of. And his brain, three paces behind him, watched as his body turned parallel to the earth. He felt his body hover for a minute, like in cartoons where characters run off cliffs and linger in the air, looking helplessly at the camera before falling in a white puff of dust.

His body slammed onto the cobblestone and suddenly he was looking up at the draining sky. *Like a bad movie,* he thought, *where the main character will have a revelation by virtue of being flipped on his back.*

Oh look, another coherent thought.

His brain moved on as he tried to figure out just how to move, and if he really wanted to move anyway. *Maybe I'll just stay here,* he thought. *Maybe I'll just lie here and go to sleep, or stare at the sky until I come to terms with my life.*

Yeah, right.

The novocaine began to wear off; the cold was seeping through Toby's jacket and his pants. He pictured the fish at the grocery store, dead and sitting on blocks of ice. The cold was beginning to get painful, but moving seemed less desirable than discomfort.

Whatever, it doesn't matter—

"Porca Madonna!" came a deep Italian voice, and suddenly the very skinny man was leaning over Toby, his face looking frightened and concerned. He kept speaking in rapid Italian.

Then the man grabbed Toby's arm.

I guess he wants me to get up, Toby thought.

So he tried to prop himself up but a searing pain stabbed through his spine.

Toby must have cried out, because he was instantly back to flat on his back and the skinny man was visibly panicking. Toby thought he heard him say, *"Mamma mia"* and then the man was running away; he came back again, this time with a man and a woman, fatter, in their pajamas, Toby's age. They looked worried, like the skinny man, and looked into Toby's eyes with intent concern as they spoke to him in Italian.

They looked at each other in worried silence. Did they realize that Toby's silence was a language barrier, not an injury?

I should have learned this damn language, he thought.

He tried to move again, to sit up, but it felt like someone was cracking his spine like a whip. Best stay on ice.

What if they have to take me to the hospital? thought Toby. *What if they have to bring me to the damn hospital and then I can't talk to the doctors and then they have to call July and she'll have to come get me and see me all laid up like an old man? What if I can't get up? What if I can't walk? I'll be stuck in a wheelchair. That's all I need. What If I never walk again? Oh my God, what if I'm paralyzed? July will have to feed me, to help me to the bathroom, bathe me. This is what I get. I had it coming.*

The fat couple left and came back again with a short man with a moustache. The three of them were talking, shouting, really, and gesturing frantically, periodically pointing down at Toby. The skinny boy watched them helplessly, like a dog hoping for a walk.

"It's okay, it's fine," said Toby. "Just let me lie here awhile. *No problemo.*"

Moustache and Fat Couple shut up and looked down at Toby.

"*Americano,*" murmured one of them.

They exchanged glances for a moment, then went back to arguing.

Toby sighed and closed his eyes. His pants were turning damp against the ice, but he didn't care. The colder he was, the better it felt. It seemed only fitting that his body be as comfortable as his mind.

He pretended he was floating in a lake, in a cold, ice encrusted lake in Alaska, surrounded by black water and snowy mountains. Alone, away from anything, where it could just be him and his wounded ego.

Or maybe instead he was eight years old again, lying in the snow in his front yard making a snow angel. Soon he would go inside and his mother would remove his wet clothes for him, and then he would do whatever the hell he wanted like eat a cookie or watch TV because he was eight and didn't have to worry about adult things like insurance or the mortgage or a job or ex-wives or taxes or whether he would ever find someone he could share his life with and whether that was even a good thing anyway.

There is someone I can spend my life with. Three someones.

My girls. I wish they were here. Well, not here, here. They don't need to see their dad splayed out like a crime scene outline. They don't need to see the old man they'll have to take care of in thirty years or so.

Maybe I'll just make Kevin take care of me, he thought with a snort.

Moustache and Fat Couple turned to him. He must have snorted out loud.

He imagined himself from their perspective. This graying, softening American lying helpless on their street and now he was their problem. *Just leave me,* thought Toby. *I'll be fine.*

Part of him wished July were here, to translate, make him feel better. But if she were here—well then she'd see him for his age, his slowly dying body that couldn't recover after a little slip on the ice. He was supposed to be the one taking care of her, not the other way around. *Poor July. She's too young to be saddled with the likes of me. Poor me—I'm too old to saddle the likes of her!*

Yes, thought Toby, this was perhaps the worst thing about getting older—there were so many younger people, so many desirable younger people, and once you crossed that threshold, either marrying and having kids or somewhere around thirty-five, there were a lot of people who became almost off limits. A whole section of the population was out-of-bounds. How unfair.

Then Toby noticed that the skinny man was at his head.

"We will araise you," he said, lifting his hands in illustration.

Moustache was squatting by Toby's chest; Fat Couple were at his feet.

"No, no," said Toby. "It's fine, don't move me, I'll be fine."

But there were already hands beneath his shoulders, under his back, raising his feet,

"*Uno, due, tre!*"

His back was off the ice and he was moving, hovering over the earth, rising with the sun. He remembered how, when the girls were small enough, he would hold them in his arms, parallel to the earth, and fly them around the house like superheroes. Grace was just barely small enough to still do this, but with his back—and the fact that he may never walk again—she may have taken her last flight.

The four Italians shuffled across the icy cobblestone, Moustache grunting slightly.

Just watch them slip on the ice, thought Toby. *Then we'll have a five-car pile up.*

They brought him inside the café, which smelled like coffee and baking sugar. They were shouting at each other again, and Toby hoped they didn't forget they were holding his body and resume gesticulating. All he needed was a second impact.

Instead they brought him over to the bar, which wasn't quite long enough for Toby's body, but all the tables in the place were small and circular, perhaps just large enough for Toby's ass.

The men grunted as they lifted Toby onto the bar, then draped his legs around either side and let them dangle.

"Okay?" asked the skinny man.

This was probably worse than the ice. But at least here he wouldn't get run over by any cars.

"Okay," said Toby.

Then Fat Man made some coffee, and the four of them sat, drinking and nibbling some biscotti and talking about who knows what, probably the dumb American lying across the bar like a mummy and what was he doing out at that hour anyway?

Eventually, Moustache left and Skinny and Fat Man went into the back room. Fat Woman came over to Toby and stood at his bar side.

"*Come stai?*" she said.

"*Molto bene,*" said Toby, because that was the only response he had learned.

Fat Woman laughed, a deep, hysterical laugh, and she threw her head back and her bust jiggled around. She put one hand on her hip and the other on Toby's shoulder, then said something that he didn't catch.

"Thank you," said Toby. "*Grazie.*"

"*Oh, prego prego,*" she said waving him away. Then she asked another question, which Toby decided was, "What the hell were you doing outside at sunrise the day after Christmas?"

"My ex-wife," he said. "She told me she's getting remarried."

Fat Woman cocked her head and furrowed her brow.

"*Mon mari,*" he said, and then he realized that was French and maybe not even right. For all he knew, he may have just said, "My husband." *Oh well, fuck it.*

But the woman nodded.

"Ex-*mari,*" he said, and mimed a ring coming off his finger.

"Ohh," clucked Fat Woman.

"She's getting married," continued Toby. "To another guy. Kevin."

"KE-vin," said Fat Woman.

"She's getting married again. It's only been two weeks since we signed the papers! Did the last seventeen years mean nothing to her that she's already with someone else? Didn't I matter at *all?*"

As he spoke, he thought that these were probably the same things Jenny had been asking herself when she found out about July. Oh.

Toby looked at Fat Woman's face. Her brows slanted outward in sympathy, but she obviously had no idea what he was saying. She probably thought he was crazy, mourning the divorce from his French husband Kevin.

She patted his shoulder again, then called out something in the direction of the back. After a moment, Fat Man came out. She talked at him and gestured outside, and Fat Man left obediently. Fat Woman turned back to Toby and said something in a reassuring tone of voice.

After a few minutes Fat Man came back with something rattling in his pocket. He reached his hand in and handed Fat Woman a small bottle.

Fat Woman opened the bottle and shook two white pills into her hand. She held her hand towards Toby and cooed.

"No, *grazie*," said Toby. He didn't want painkillers, especially if he didn't know what they were.

Fat Woman pushed them at him again, motioning back to Fat Man, who smiled and nodded with satisfaction as he patted his back.

He took a deep breath, reached out for the offerings of Morpheus, and swallowed the pills.

Fat Woman stroked his head, then followed Fat Man into the back room. So now it was just Toby and the newly risen sun on the day after Christmas, alone and half of him lying paralyzed on the bar of a strange café in Florence, the contents of an unknown drug coursing through his blood.

What time was it? It must be somewhere around seven, if the sun was up. What was July doing now? Was she asleep in the hotel room? Had she come back just after he had left? Or was she somewhere else, sleeping on the street? Sleeping with Massimo? Or *not* sleeping with Massimo?

Don't get all worked up, he thought. *You're acting like you're in high school. But if Jenny could, couldn't July? No.* Toby mattered to July. He could tell, the way she looked at him, how her eyes and the right corner of her mouth were always smiling at him. It was in the eyes, the way they moved in slow motion, how the eyes moved away from him with reluctance, looked at him when there was no reason to look. Did he look at her like that? At least if she were here, he would have someone to care about him. He needed that reassurance.

The woman came out of the kitchen with a cup of coffee. She stopped next to Toby and smiled. Then she pulled out a straw and put it in the coffee. Toby turned his head a bit and Fat Woman put the straw in his mouth. Toby feared it would be too hot, but when he sucked and the coffee hit his mouth, it was hot but just cool enough not to burn.

"*Grazie,*" he said between sips. "*Grazie mille.*"

When a few of the first customers came in, they tried to move him, but his back would still not agree. Fat Couple were unexpectedly gracious about it, serving coffee over and around him. But sometimes a new customer came in and he was subject to another "What-the-fuck?" stare, and Fat Couple had to explain just why there was a middle-aged American draped across their counter. For the most part, the customers ignored Toby, or pretended to.

Fat Woman, who worked the counter most of the time, tried her best to pass pastries and coffee over the large glass case, but ended up spilling two cups of coffee over the front of the display, so she switched to passing coffee over Toby instead. Each time he watched the bottom of a saucer pass over his chest, he almost hoped it would spill, just so that it would happen and then he wouldn't have to worry anymore. Besides, it would make a better story. But instead, Fat Woman's hands were steady; she barely even looked at Toby as she sent brimming brews across him.

It's better than a hospital bed, at least, Toby decided.

He imagined what would happen if, in a truly sick twist of fate, Massimo happened to come in. *Of all the cafés in all of Florence in all the world ... and he walked into mine. What would I do? Maybe I could roll myself off the bar fast enough for him not to see me. But probably not.*

"To-by?" he would say in that devastating Italian accent, and he would cock his head and raise one eyebrow.

He would be frozen for a minute, all words icicles hanging from his brain.

"Massimo," he would manage with his tongue, his lips unable to move.

"What are you doing?"

There would be no way to answer that one. Then his face would be frozen too, and he would only be able to move his eyes around uncertainly. Toby would smile weakly, but there was nothing that could cover this up, no jokes to be made. That would hurt worse than the fall.

"Well, I—just—I'm just having a little problem with my back."

Massimo would make that face, that knowing "okay-I'll-pretend-I-believe-you" face. Then he would probably ask Fat Woman what had happened. She would animatedly tell him the story, maybe embellishing, but how would Toby know? As she was talking, Massimo would look from Fat Woman to Toby a few times. *This* is what July was with? An old man folded onto a small counter because he couldn't walk, playing spill guard to cappuccinos?

It would be like one of those naked dreams, only much, much worse.

What would Massimo do then? Maybe he would order a coffee served over Toby. He would take a sip, mop the foam from his upper lip with the inside of his lower lip and flippantly bid Toby *Ciao*.

Or maybe he would insist—*insist*—on calling July. Maybe he would go get her himself. *I bet he'd love any excuse to be in the hotel with July*. And bring her here to help him, but really it would just be another exposition strategy.

Or maybe he would call a doctor for Toby, or bring him to the hospital himself. Massimo's pervasive good manners had seemed a little sinister to Toby last night, like Massimo had some ulterior motive, to show that he was better. Why wouldn't that continue this morning?

Luckily the chances of Massimo coming in were slim. But what if Astrid came in? *Oh God, I don't know which would be worse. Well, she'd probably feel sorry for me, actually. She would come in and see me sprawled on the counter and she'd say ...*

"Toby? Is that you? What has happened?"

She would bend over him, concerned, her face close to his, that deep but fleeting perfume around her hair. Maybe she would put a concerned hand on his chest or his forehead.

And he would lie there, poor Toby, and he would tell his story, and Fat Couple would probably chime in too, and Astrid would take pity on poor Toby, aging as she was but not nearly as well. Somehow she would manage to get him back to her apartment, which would be neat and modern but still like a home. She would put him on her bed and tend to him, and he wouldn't have to worry about being old in front of her. She already understood what it was. Maybe she would even make him something to eat, like a soup or a sandwich or something to soothe his body, and they would spend the day together telling stories of their lives. She sure seemed to have a lot of interesting stories, and they could commiserate on divorce and the way love goes.

Maybe they would come to a point of mutual understanding or agreement, and there would be one of those moments where they lock eyes and Toby's face would start to glow like each of his pores was an individual light bulb. Maybe their hands would touch, or touch other spots. Maybe more, because in this daydream there was no July, only Astrid.

But Astrid was one of those women who should never be caught. She was too good. She would be bored with Toby in a month. Probably less. She was one of those women who seemed as though she didn't need a man; it was rare a man who didn't want to be needed a bit.

Isn't that what was so great about July? Sure, she didn't *need* Toby, not in the grand scheme of things, but she did kind of need him. She wouldn't be here without him; she wouldn't get to do most of the things they did together without him, and she knew it. Consciously or not, she made up for it in other ways. The Thanksgiving apple pie. Doing little things around his house that she didn't need to do, like hand washing her drinking glass along with everything else in the sink and then drying everything. Or making the coffee, or letting him have the last bite at dinner, or making the bed when they got up, or staying in bed an extra fifteen minutes at his request when she was already late for class. Didn't she do all that for him? That's why this would work—she could need him just enough.

But do you need her? he thought. *Shouldn't you? Like you needed Jenny. I don't want to need another woman. It's better to have the upper hand. It's easier not to need.*

Toby closed his eyes and tried to clear his mind. These were not thoughts to have when someone was ordering a cappuccino over his nose. He just wanted to get back to the hotel room, to see the look of relief on July's face when he came in the room, to have her hug him and help him feel better. She would need him and he would matter again.

Eventually Toby realized that his back felt as though it had been coated in a warm fuzzy blanket, and he thought of that scary bear in Downy commercials. It was time for him to get up. He wasn't sure how long he'd been lying there; it felt like all morning, though it couldn't be later than ten. When there was a lull in coffee passing, he started fidgeting and moving his elbows into props. Fat Woman immediately started clucking and holding his shoulders, but she didn't try to force him back down.

Soon Toby was sitting up, his back against the case of pastries and panini. He sat like that as Fat Woman passed a few more coffees over the counter. Then she helped him swing his legs over one side of the bar, and for the final step, she called out Fat Man to take one of Toby's sides as they helped him down from the bar. Though his back was crackly and achy, Toby could stand. When he took a few steps across the small café, Fat Couple clapped their hands as though he were a toddler taking his first steps.

How old age has turned me young again, thought Toby.

He told Fat Couple *Grazie* a thousand times, tried to pay them, at least for the coffee he had sipped through the straw, but they wouldn't take it. Instead, Fat Woman pressed the small bottle of pills into his hand, cooing at him reassuringly once more. He didn't want them but put them in his pocket out of good manners, then hobbled out the door and stopped on the sidewalk, trying to regain his bearings. He was east of the Duomo, thirty minutes at least if he could walk like a normal person. With his spine in his heels and no sleep to power him, a taxi seemed a much better option.

So this is what living in a monastery would be like, thought July. *Looking at the same place forever, the only change of scenery taking place in your thoughts.*

Though she had only been waiting in the hotel room no more than an hour, the knowledge that she couldn't leave made the hour feel much longer and the room seem smaller.

A monastery. Or maybe prison.

She tried the distraction method—television, pacing, reading, but nothing held her interest or suspended her thoughts. All she could focus on was the fear gnawing inside her. Where was Toby? What would she say when he asked where she had spent the night?

But then her thoughts shifted to Massimo—where he was, what he was doing, if he was thinking about her, if she would see him again, and if she did, what it would be like.

She pictured Massimo at work in the bookstore serving coffee like he did every day, like nothing had happened. But nothing *had* happened—or had it? It must all be in her head. Maybe he was chatting with another American girl now—blonde and beautiful and unattached. Maybe that's what he always did, and July was just another girl.

She realized that she probably didn't matter to Massimo, but that she wanted to. But, mattering should only matter with Toby. So why had nothing happening suddenly mattered so much? She thought back to the night before, on the walk to the Indian restaurant, when she and Massimo had been protected by the distance of at least five paces and shielded by speaking Italian.

"After you return home, what will you do?" he asked.

"Finish school," she replied flatly.

"And then what?"

She sighed, "Everyone always asks me that, and I still don't have an answer."

"It is the logical question."

"But I don't like the logical answer."

"The logical answer is the one you'll like."

July was silent.

"It's okay," he continued. "I am still trying to learn the logical answer as well. It is different for everybody. The problem is that you have no quick answer."

"No," she shook her head. "It's that the answer changes every day, and everyone tells me the wrong answer is right."

"Is Toby trying to give you answers?"

"He's only giving me more questions!" she laughed, without thinking about it.

"That's not how it should be," said Massimo. "He should give you questions, but only if he can lead you to answers as well. That's what people who matter should do, help you answer questions but create a new question with every answer."

"Hm," she agreed. "Yeah. I think that people—people that matter—should improve you in some way, not by forcing it on you, but by creating the desire to improve."

"*Esattamente*! For example, meeting you, I want to speak better English."

"Well I don't mean trivial things like skills—I mean things like habits, philosophies, goals."

"I don't think learning English is so trivial. English is communication; we could talk about such habits and philosophies."

"But we can talk about that in Italian."

"But it is different in one's native language. Perhaps in Italian it won't be quite what you mean."

"Perhaps in English it won't be quite what *you* mean."

"*Si*," he conceded. "Astrid, she improves me, makes me think twice about my beliefs."

"How?"

"Astrid, she is full of contrasts, you can see it just by looking at her. Very beautiful, yes, but if you look closely at her eyes, you can see she is always questioning the meaning of things and if it is what she wants. If she does not want it, she will change immediately, but at heart she wants to be able to want one thing. It's very difficult, this contrast, but it's what makes people worth knowing, and what makes her beautiful, no?"

"I guess," replied July. She hadn't had a close enough look at Astrid yet.

"When I first saw you, I saw the same thing. An American girl reading an Italian book about Indian food. That's why I talked to you."

July was silent. She felt unworthy of any favorable comparison to Astrid, but her heart fluttered from flattery all the same. How could he see so deeply at first glance? No one had done that before. Was she transparent, or was he just different?

They walked in silence for a moment. July could hear Astrid behind them, her intonation like iambic pentameter.

"You are really only twenty-two?" Massimo asked.

"Yes."

"Hm. You don't seem so young."

"How old do I seem?"

"I think, twenty-six, twenty-seven."

"Oh."

"It's good, this contrast."

They turned the corner and he pointed to the sign for *Ashoka*.

"It means," he said after checking over his shoulder for Toby and Astrid, "that we can, I think, improve each other."

They stopped outside the restaurant, and Massimo opened the door, stepping aside to let July in first.

By now July had curled up on top of the bed, as though folding into the fetal position were the only way to contain and concentrate any conscious energy left inside.

Possiamo, penso, migliorarci l'un l'altro. We can, I think, improve each other.

His words tumbled down July's spine like smooth pebbles. Why hadn't Toby ever said anything like that? She tried to imagine him saying those words, but she could hear either Massimo's rolling marbles or only silence.

And then, for real, she heard a rattling, clacking sound crunching through the walls.

Is someone throwing rocks at the window? She wondered for a split second. And then she realized that it was a key churning in the doorknob.

Goddamn this motherfucking piece of shit key.

It had been a long hobble from the taxi to the door of his hotel room; for what seemed like an hour, he had listened to the schkt, schkt, schkt of his shoes against the floor and the kachik, kachik, kachik of the pills in his pocket. His spine ached when one foot moved forward, then ached again when the other moved forward in response. His thoughts had been contained solely to his body; he imagined the muscles in his back, the crook in his spine, the blisters on his heels. And now he couldn't get the door open.

The last thing he wanted to do was answer when July asked, Where were you? What happened? Why did you disappear? like a wife would do.

And he wasn't in the mood to hear her answers when he asked the same things of her. He just wanted to slide into the room and slowly, silently, fall into the bed and take back what he had lost in the past twelve hours.

He jostled the key around some more. July should be back—couldn't she at least come open the door for him?

"Motherfucker!" cried Toby loudly into the hallway.

He immediately closed his mouth in sheepish surprise—since the girls were born, he had managed to reduce his swearing to almost never. He looked around, hoping no one had heard him, hoping July had heard him so she would come open the damned door.

July heard Toby curse in the hallway.

He locked me out, thought July. *He can unlock himself.*

But she stood up anyway, moving slowly to the door. She couldn't leave him out there, even if part of her wanted to.

Now that he was back, she didn't really want him to come in. She didn't want to have to explain herself, like she would surely have to. She didn't want to have to assure Toby that nothing had happened when she couldn't quite assure herself of that. Would it be a lie, a half-lie, a white lie?

It was the first time lying, doing so by omission, seemed to be the best—and only—way to mitigate a problem. Was this being an adult—recognizing the necessity of lying?

She yanked the door open.

Toby stood there, stiff and hunched, one hand on the small of his back, the other out in front of him where the doorknob had been just before. Gravity seemed a bit stronger than it had before, pulling him like an anchor. His gray hairs seemed more obvious, his face less elastic, like a deflated red rubber ball.

He looked at her, his eyes surprised, confused, suspicious? His mouth opened slightly, like he wanted to say something, but he just cocked his head to the side and stayed silent. Then his eyes changed clicking off like they were disinterested, disengaged, condescending even, so July decided not to say anything.

Let him speak first. Just let him—he who had left her alone and locked her out—accuse her, question her, interrogate her. She was not in the wrong.

Toby shuffled past her, as though he were wading through waist deep water. Why was he walking like that? He looked like her father had last summer when he threw out his back loading a cooler of fresh Alaskan fish into the trunk of their rental car.

He shuffled over to the other side of the bed.

"What happened? Are you okay?" she asked.

"Ngh," he grunted.

"What is *that* supposed to mean?"

Without answering, Toby lowered himself stiffly, awkwardly onto the bed beside her, and within a minute he had already begun that nasal, heavy breathing that would soon sound like a vacuum cleaner clogged by a penny.

All he has to say to me is "Ngh"? she thought, still standing by the door.

Well fine, then. If he didn't want to talk, then neither did she.

July spent the next two hours in agonizing silence. Toby was asleep and hadn't moved a hair since he had lain down. What the hell was she supposed to do, keep pacing around, wondering if something had happened—to Toby, with her and Massimo, to her and Toby—without explanation or relief? Was she supposed to just wait around for him all day? And just how was she supposed to get any lunch doing so?

The way Toby had been hobbling around, she suspected that even after he awoke, if he ever did, that he wouldn't want to—or be able to—go anywhere. She would have to go fetch dinner for him, eat a cold panino covered by a thin film of slightly congealed olive oil, help him sit up, fluff his pillows.

She didn't come to Italy for that. She didn't come here to wait around, to wait for someone to wake, to wait on him after he did. He hadn't seemed willing to do the same for her the night before. She looked around for the room key and found it on the floor next to Toby's side of the bed.

As she bent down to pick up the key, she looked at Toby, his mouth slightly open, breathing in the same Darth Vader rhythm as he had for the past two hours. She felt a sudden pang of tenderness for him. Or perhaps it was pity. He looked so worn, so beaten. Aside from the lack of foot long facial hair, he looked a bit like Rip Van Winkle, having awoken to find that he his no longer young.

"Inside I still feel like I'm twenty-two," he had said to her more than once before. But it seemed that now his brain and body had set off on divergent paths, and she suspected those paths would only drift further apart until they crashed into each other and he finally acted as old as he felt.

Could I still love an old man? she wondered. *I would rather get old with him, so I wouldn't have such a clear idea of what to expect when I get old.*

She looked closer at him. He would take care of her, show her the world while keeping her safe from it. He was a man with stories, experiences, accomplishments. He was beautiful. Maybe he would be old, but couldn't he still be beautiful?

Holding the key, July stood up straight. She needed to get out of the room. She went to put on her coat and saw Massimo's trench coat on top of her own green one. She thought better of wearing it now, so she folded it into her suitcase. She could give it back later and Toby wouldn't have to know. For a moment she thought of her mother, who routinely bought shoes she didn't need, hid them from July's father, then wore them weeks later so as to claim that they weren't new, she just hadn't worn them in a while. Two things true independent of context, but combined, not so much.

She was an adult now.

Tying her scarf around her neck, July walked out of the room and closed the door quietly behind her. She would be back by dark, in time for Toby to wake up. Maybe.

She didn't have a place she wanted to go, she just knew she wanted lunch. Lasagna, ideally. And today seemed like the right day for some gelato. So she started walking to see where her legs took her.

The streets were still fairly quiet, but more shops were open, a few more people out and walking. She focused her thoughts on her exhales, the white puffs that came from her "O"ed lips.

That Toby probably didn't love her hadn't seemed like such an obstacle before. Somehow, part of her had believed that he would have an epiphany and would realize how happy she made him, and love for her would follow. He would understand that he wanted her in his life, in his daughters' lives, that she belonged. He would see—he *would* see—that she was it, and with time, he would want to get married—to July, this time—again.

But now July felt that his just liking her for today, for Italy, when the girls were with Jenny, wouldn't be enough to sustain her. She could love him all she wanted, but if he didn't love her back, then what was the point? It would be wasted.

She thought again of what Massimo had said.

"We can, I think, improve each other."

Improving meant mattering, that something of that person had stuck with you. She wasn't sure that any part of her had stuck to him, or if he saw anything worth improving in himself.

She would have to talk to him, but she felt that she wasn't supposed to speak with him about such serious, long-term matters. She wasn't supposed to fall in love with him in the first place. She surmised that Toby was looking ahead no further than their return home on January fifth, and then after that no more than a week at a time. She didn't know what it was he wanted—and she guessed this was because neither did he.

But what about what I want? she wondered. *What about me?*

She stopped in the middle of the sidewalk.

What do I want?

She looked to her right and saw a little bistro. She could get lasagna here. A serious question required serious food, and there wasn't much more serious than lasagna.

She sat alone at a table by the window and gazed out at the people outside. Did they know what they wanted? Did they have it? How was one supposed to plan now for forever?

Maybe she would come back to Italy, find a job waiting tables, see what happened. Or maybe she would mimic Massimo, move where her dreams, her brain itches, told her to go, or where she told her dreams to go. She tried to imagine, realistically, what she would want, where she would be by June, but the calendar seemed blank after graduation day, black, a void, like uncharted galaxies outside of the universe. There was no formula, no law to help her calculate the arc of her projection. It may not be an arc at all.

Then she was lost in the layers of lasagna, noodles so thin and fine, so close together, there must have been a dozen layers in her one piece. At the bottom everything melted together in a cheese tomato sauce, cheese harmony. This was all she needed—for her life to fit together like lasagna, where each part of it would come together at the end to form the resolving end chord of her life.

Maybe what she wanted was to make lasagna, open a small bistro, just live with sauce and noodles and cheese. Her father would like that. Her mother definitely wouldn't. Maybe her lasagna bistro would be printed in Florence guides, word would spread, her lasagna would be a destination.

Right.

She scraped the tines of her fork against white ceramic dish, scrounging every bit of sauce and cheese that she could. It was perfection. It's too bad she didn't know how she got here; she had only followed her legs. Perhaps that's what she would need to do come June—follow her legs instead of telling them where to go.

She left the bistro and looked around. This street seemed familiar—hadn't she seen that statue before? But from a different angle ... she walked towards the statue, which was surrounded by benches made of wooden slats, and realized that she had seen this statue on the way to, or from, the *gelateria* last night.

She looked down a few of the streets until she found one that looked familiar. After only a minute or so, she came to the small *gelateria* hiding between two residential looking buildings. It seemed empty, and not obviously open. July stopped outside the door, hesitating, then pushed tentatively. It was unlocked; a bell jangled as she walked in.

July waited for a moment, but no one came to the counter.

"Uh, *buon giorno?*"

"*Enh? Che?*" came a deep voice from the back.

After a moment, Gianni came out, his sleeves rolled up past his elbows, his apron smeared with a rainbow of color, like a child had used him as a finger painting canvas.

"*Ah, bella! E ritornato!*"

"Yes, I'm back," she replied in Italian. "Your gelato was like a dream."

"No, no, no, it's just gelato," said Gianni modestly, though she could tell he was pleased. "Please, have some more! What would you like? What is your favorite?"

"Well—"

"Try the *nocciola*, it is, I think, very good. Ah! And it goes perfectly with the *crema*."

A moment later, he handed her a cup of mouse ears—one brown, one a yellow-tinted white.

"*Grazie.*"

"*Prego, prego.* Please, sit! Enjoy it!"

July sat at a table and Gianni watched her from behind the counter.

"Is it good?" he asked.

"Oh, yes," said July. "I wish I could eat this every day."

It was more than good. Alone, the flavors were intense and pleasing, but together each flavor seemed different; it improved by complementing the other.

"Me too!" laughed Gianni. "That's why, when I was young, I decided I would make gelato—so that I could eat it every day. So I do! Sometimes, it is all I eat. And maybe a little pasta, sometimes."

July looked at him, short, skinny Gianni, who was over fifty to be sure. His skin, though a bit worn, was still so smooth; she imagined that he hardly looked any different than he had when he was thirty.

"I have been making gelato since I was twenty-three," he continued. "That's over thirty years."

"You don't get bored with it?"

"Bored? How could one be bored with gelato? It's like falling in love every day."

"Sounds … tiring," she smiled.

"I had my first gelato when I was very young, on a Sunday after church, during the season of anticipation, when spring has left but summer has not quite arrived. Warm enough to want something cold, cool enough not to melt it before you can eat it."

Gianni leaned forward against the counter, looking past the present, speaking like a poet. He must have practiced this story many times.

"As she did every Sunday, my mother stopped at the butcher's on the way home to get a rabbit, or sometimes a duck, or a leg of lamb or something for our supper. Across the street was the sweet shop. For some reason, one day my mother decided to let me buy some sweets, so she gave me some money and sent me across the street. I thought I must have been a good boy that day in church, but later I found out that she was having an affair with the butcher! No, no! My father had been dead a few years; my mother was not that kind of woman to cheat, though the butcher's wife was not especially pleased. Anyway, I went across the street and carefully examined all of the things I might buy. So many chocolates and hard candies. I was about to pick out a chocolate bar when I saw one of the older boys in the neighborhood buying something from the counter, something round and green and served in a cup."

He continued, "Wanting to be like him, I decided that I wanted a green round ball, too. If he was eating it, it must be good, and if it was in the shop, it must be sweet! I was a very smart little boy. So I went to the counter and watched as the owner scooped it carefully, and he molded it into a perfect little ball, setting it tenderly into the dish. I paid him and went over to a corner to taste the mysterious concoction. I was so surprised when the first thing I tasted was cold. The first flavor! And then the cream, the smooth, the thickness that coats the mouth. And then the deepening, rolling mist of pistachio, and then, finally, the sweetness, like a hug."

July laughed.

"It's true!" he cried.

"I know!"

"That is how gelato—real gelato—good gelato—should be. Like a staircase, going somewhere. Or a striptease, revealing itself slowly," he paused. "From then on I used most of my pocket money to buy gelato. I became a sort of apprentice to that shop owner. When I went to university my mother, she made me go to school to learn medicine, but

I much preferred the science of gelato, so after I graduated, I instead left and came here. It's very romantic, really."

"Wow. What did your mother say?"

"Ah, well, she was not very happy. Every time I returned to Torino she reminded me of how noble, how respectable a profession medicine was, how I was wasting my abilities, how this would not have made my father proud, but then she also never liked sweet things anyway. Practicing medicine would have darkened my soul and ground it into a fine dust. Gelato, it is the fountain of youth!"

He spread his arms wide and smiled.

"I am sorry, I am boring you," he said, lowering his arms.

"No, no you're not," said July, who had finished her gelato.

"There are not many people who like to listen to me talk about gelato."

"If there were, you would never want to talk about it."

"No, one never gets tired of telling a love story. Or hearing one, for that matter."

A timer rang in the back.

"*Mamma mia!*" exclaimed Gianni with melodramatic flair. "I have to work on this batch in the back—the pistachio, she is very fickle."

He sprang back from the counter, then picked up the scoop again.

"Here," he said, scooping from the tubs again. "Please, have some more for the walk home."

"Oh no, I couldn't," said July, even though she could. She could eat the entire counter's worth if given the chance.

"No please! Massimo had told me he would bring someone here who would appreciate the gelato, and it was a shame you had to leave so early last night. Enjoy some now—I'm sure the gelato in America is worse than the coffee."

He handed her a packed cup of chocolate and strawberry.

"Please come back if you get a chance. I will show you around the back."

July barely had time to say "*Grazie*" before Gianni had leapt into the back room.

She pushed the door open with her hip and ate the gelato as she walked back in the crunchy air.

I probably shouldn't eat this, she thought. *My pants are already getting tighter on this trip.* She looked at the cup of beckoning gelato.

Oh well. Adding grains of sand to the beach.

A few minutes after she finished the second gelato, July had wandered into the proximity of the bookstore where Massimo worked. Just one more block over and she would be there. Should she go? What would she say? Wouldn't it be weird? It would look a little questionable for her to walk in, after the night that just passed. But she kind of wanted to see him.

Maybe he would be off work soon, he would want to get dinner or coffee or something, they could talk some more about lucid dreams and life dreams. Maybe, after seeing him, things would seem a little clearer. Maybe last night she had been clouded by ... something. His Italian-ness, Toby's behavior. Maybe if she saw him now, she would realize that she wasn't in fact attracted to him at all, she was just lonely, worried, confused. Maybe if she saw him, she would come to her senses.

She started walking toward the bookstore. What would he say when he saw her?

I'm glad you came.

What are you doing here?

One of the two. Or maybe both.

Her heart beat a little faster, a steady drumbeat keeping time, speeding it up. She saw the bookstore in the distance. She imagined Massimo inside; maybe he was busy, didn't have time to talk. But it was the day after Christmas, it was probably dead, he was probably bored out of his mind. Maybe he was reading a book to keep himself occupied. Maybe he was looking at his hands and asking if he was dreaming.

Am I dreaming?

July looked at her hands. They were still, but they felt like they were shaking. *Don't be nervous. What am I doing?*

She thought about Toby, the way he shuffled into bed, unable even to lift his feet and walk heel-toe heel-toe. Maybe he was awake now, stuck in the bed, waiting for her to come back.

What if he's waiting for me?

July stopped a few stores down from the bookstore. What if Massimo came out right now? If he came out and saw her standing there like an idiot deliberating whether to go in or turn around and run. Then what would she do? Laugh and say something stupid. Pretend she didn't know where she was, like she was lost.

She knew where she was, but she was lost anyway.

Go in or go home.

What if, if I don't go in, I never see Massimo again? How would I feel then?

Well then, you could make a fool of yourself now, or wonder for the rest of your life what would have happened if you walked in that door.

She would walk in. She would see Massimo at the counter, the smooth buzz cut of his hair, the moving blocks of his body. He would see her immediately, or maybe he wouldn't see her until she reached the counter and he looked up from whatever he was doing. She would sit at the counter, they would say nothing, just smile and know. Know what? Or he would say 'July, what are you doing here?' And he would look puzzled; what was this desperate girl doing here, after having rejected him the night before? Either way, she wouldn't know what to say. She would open her mouth, and nothing would come out.

July exhaled sharply, turned around, and walked away from the bookstore. Ignore the voice that says go in. Instead she would stop at a café or something, buy some food for Toby. That's what she should do. She could always come back to the bookstore tomorrow, or the next day, or the next. But Toby, he needed her now.

XIX

WHEN TOBY AWOKE, IT WAS DARK. FOR THE FIRST MINUTE OR SO after he opened his eyes, he experienced the dull suspension of not knowing where or when he was, what had happened before, like opening a book to the middle and trying to follow the story from there. But then his brain flipped back the pages—Massimo, Indian, Kevin, ice. He preferred not remembering.

He tried to sit up but a jagged knife slit up his spine. Then he felt hands guiding him up, adjusting a pillow, sitting him upright. The pain abated somewhat as he relaxed against the pillow at his back.

"Hi," he muttered, his throat coated in heavy sleep.

"Hi," he heard July say, and then a light on the other side of the bed came on.

She sat next to the light, in her pajamas, hair pulled back into a ponytail.

"What time is it?" he asked.

"Almost eight."

"Shit."

"Are you hungry?"

He thought about it. "Yeah, but I can't go anywhere."

She reached from the bed to the floor and lifted up a bag.

"I brought you some food," she said.

She shimmied the plastic bag down. Inside were a few apples, some chocolate, and some cheese and bread.

"I also got some wine," she said, pulling up a small green bottle from the same place beside the bed.

"Thanks," said Toby, ripping an end off the loaf of bread.

"Sure," she flattened her lips in a half-smile.

The bread crackled in his mouth. July opened the cheese, broke off a piece, and handed it to him. Toby took the cheese obediently and took a few more moments of silence to eat.

"So," July ventured tentatively.

Here it comes, he thought. *Here's where she asks me what the hell my problem is, why did I leave her all alone like that.*

"What happened to your back?" she asked. "Are you okay?"

"I slipped on some ice this morning," he said. "It kind of hurts to do anything, I guess, except for sleeping."

"How did you get back here?"

"I walked about a block, then I took a taxi."

She raised her eyebrows and looked to the side.

"It was a long and rather painful block," he added.

"Do you want to see a doctor?"

"No, I'll be fine."

"Are you sure? It seems like it's pretty bad."

"I don't need to see a doctor. I'll be fine."

Toby listened to the sound of his own chewing. He didn't want to have this conversation. Just get it over with. Like getting a filling at the dentist—open wide and get it done.

"So," he tried to sound as evenly as possible. "Where did you sleep last night?"

There was a pause as she drew in a breath and held it slightly.

"Massimo's couch."

"Ah."

Massimo's couch. Was Massimo on that couch, too? Or was his couch his bed? How much would she explain? The more she explained, the more she had to hide. Unless she doesn't try to explain anything. Then she has even more to hide.

"I—I got lost. He came back and found me. I was freezing, we were close to his apartment. He took me back for an extra jacket, but first he made me a hot drink, then I got sleepy and fell asleep on his couch."

Toby tried to assess her answer. How much of it was true?

He nodded.

"Why didn't you call?" he asked.

"I did. Well—Massimo did. After I fell asleep. He said you didn't answer."

"What time was that?"

"I don't know."

Pause. She shifted her weight and crossed her legs.

"So—where did *you* sleep last night?"

"I didn't," he answered quickly, perhaps rather harshly.

"Oh. Well—then what—?"

"Where did I go?"

"Yeah."

"I went for a walk."

"All night?"

"I had a lot to think about."

"Oh."

She pursed her lips and looked at her hands.

"Is everything okay?" she asked.

He took a breath. *You can say it*, he told himself.

"Jenny's—she's—"

July's eyes got a little wider and her face froze. What did she expect him to say?

"She's getting—married. *Re*-married."

July's neck fell forward and her eyebrows raised higher.

"Whoa."

"Yeah."

"To who?"

"I don't really want to talk about it."

She frowned.

"Oh. Right. Sorry."

Silence again. July picked at one of her nails and bit her lip.

"What is it?" he asked.

"Nothing," she said, shaking her head. But she didn't look him in the eye. Then, after a moment, "How do you feel?"

"Like shit," he said sharply. He could practically see her retreat into her shell. "Well how do you *think* it made me feel? Happy?" It came out of his mouth before his brain had a chance to stop it. He had planned to only think that.

"I don't know, not happy, but I mean—" he heard her say.

"You mean what?" he snapped. There it was again, his brain behind the times. "You mean that two weeks after you sign divorce papers you should get *engaged*?"

Though her hair was pulled back, she tried to tuck it behind her ear, "I didn't say that—"

Why are you saying this to her? What's your problem? Well what does she expect, asking such stupid questions.

Finally his brain managed to bite his tongue and they sat in silence again, tenser, like someone had pulled the air around them taught and stretched it thin.

"I didn't say that," she said again, with a bit more firmness than he had anticipated. Time to take the heat off of himself.

"Well what about you? How was spending the night with Senor Massimo?"

Her eyes flicked a bit.

"It was—fine. I slept on his couch."

"Right. I bet he loved that."

"Well what else was I supposed to do?" her voice had the wobbly, tearful sound with a new sharpness. "You practically ran away from me!"

"I had to talk to my daughters."

"Yeah, and you *forgot* about *me*."

"I didn't forget …" he said.

"Yes you did," she said. "You couldn't have walked a bit slower and made the phone call five minutes later."

"You knew I had to make the call at eleven."

"Did I ever tell you not to? Did I complain when you rushed us out of Gianni's gelato shop? Not only were you rude, but that was the best gelato around."

This wasn't going well. How did she get so good at turning things around? She should be a lawyer, he thought bitterly.

"I don't see why you had to stay at Massimo's. Why didn't you just tell him to bring you back here?"

"I spent over half an hour wandering the streets *alone*. I was freezing; I could hardly move."

"Would you really have contracted frostbite if you had just hauled it back here?"

"Is this really about my homeostasis?" she cut in. "I was tired, I was cold, I was disoriented and upset and you left me."

She sounded angry, really upset. It couldn't have been that awful; he suspected she was being a bit dramatic. What was going on here?

"The simple question is, why didn't you make Massimo bring you back here after you warmed up?"

"It was well after midnight—I was tired! I practically fell asleep in my mug!"

"It was only a ten-minute walk away."

"How was I supposed to know that? I didn't know where the hell I was!"

"Massimo knew that."

"Well then he didn't tell me!"

"What happened at Massimo's?"

"What are you talking about? Nothing happened!" She crossed her arms and turned her face away from him.

"Did he put the moves on you?

"No!" she cried a bit too emphatically.

"He did!"

"Nothing happened—I fell asleep on his couch!"

Nothing happened—the excuse of death. Jenny had used that one quite a few times, and it looks like nothing had been something. Something enough. She was omitting something; he could tell. His daughters did this sometimes when they would conveniently neglect to mention their homework assignments or that Jenny had said no to something they wanted him to say yes to.

He looked closely at her. Her arms were crossed in front of her chest, her eyes in a fixed gaze at the sheets. The corners of her mouth were pursed in, she was biting her inner lower lip, she wasn't blinking, her eyes were glistening. He was about to have a crying female on his hands. Great. Women cried when they wanted to avoid the whole story.

"You act like this is all my fault," she said. "Like I planned this just so I could stay at Massimo's. I didn't do anything wrong."

"You should have come back last night."

"Why? So I could sit around waiting for you to get back from your all night sojourn?"

"If you had been here I wouldn't have left."

"I would have been here if you hadn't left me! And you shouldn't have locked me out so that when I came back this morning I came back to an empty room, wondering where you were, why you didn't care that I wasn't there! Making me think you ditched me, like you lost me on purpose!"

The tears started falling down her face. Part of Toby wanted to reach his arm around her, wipe her tears away, assure her it had just been a bad situation and that mistakes had been made but it was okay now. But the other part of him was stubbornly pissed. A night in Massimo's apartment? Massimo seemed like the type to try something. How could he *not* try something on someone like July? Toby himself would have tried something.

Then he thought of Jenny, of how much something she must have withheld from him about Kevin. He wasn't going to let that happen again.

"I just don't understand why you didn't make Massimo take you back here."

"Oh my God!" she cried, slapping her hand against the mattress. "Don't you listen? Can't you understand how I was feeling?!"

Now she was getting hysterical, and part of Toby enjoyed it. He would have liked to see Jenny squirm a bit. Women and their feelings.

"I bet you were feeling pretty good. A young, handsome guy like Massimo—how could you resist?"

"Are you totally *blind*?" she yelled. "Haven't you noticed that I'm in *love* with you?"

Well that shut him up.

She was in love with him? How—it had only been a few months— he was so old—what—*love*? Did she know what that was? How could she love him? He was so wrapped up in everything Jenny–he didn't realize she was taking this so seriously. He tried to think back to what he had missed, all the things that would have told him she was in love with him, or was about to be.

The way she practically lit up, glowed, when she was around him, how she smiled, how she touched his face sometimes, tender, wispy touches like the wind's fingers, or twisted a section of his hair around her finger, how she dropped plans for him, the apple pie, her favorite children's book she brought for his girls, the brownies from a "new bakery" that she made once and left in the kitchen for his girls, and all the other things, but it hadn't occurred to him then that it was love. *That* was love, not lust? He just thought it was—what? Him? That she recognized him, understood him. All those years with a woman and he was still blind. *Shit, Toby. Nice work. Good fucking powers of observation.*

He felt hot. He couldn't say he loved her back—he didn't love anyone except his daughters right now. She should know that. After watching him go through all that shit. He thought she knew that. Hadn't he told her that? Didn't she know? Didn't she know he nearly hated women before he met her and that it was a miracle that he even liked July at all?

She was looking him straight in the face. He was supposed to have an answer? For *this*? Now?

Say something, his thoughts begged her. *Say something and give me a hint as to how I should respond.*

But she didn't say anything. She just raised her eyebrows higher, her eyes filling gradually with worry. Or fear?

Still she said nothing. Damn, she was playing tough. His tongue searched for words, dug through his brain, all the way down his throat, but he had nothing.

He should say something. *Some*thing. *Any*thing.

"I—"

She tilted her head forward.

"I—"

Nothing. He had nothing else. Well, one word was better than nothing. He tried forming a thought in his head first:

July. July, I—July. You're a great kid, I love spending time with you.

July. You're a great person. I love being with you.

He could launch into all that divorce bullshit, but she knew all that. And it didn't really matter anyway, did it?

July. You're a great person; I love being with you. But.

But.

I don't love you.

That didn't sound very nice. She would probably get really upset. She would probably leave. Break up with him. He certainly didn't want that. It wasn't that he didn't like her, it was just that—well, he didn't really know what. *What? God, I'm too old for this.*

I don't know when I'll be ready to love again?

Well wait a minute, that's not fair, he thought. *How come Jenny gets a monopoly on my feelings here? What does she have to do with July? Nothing. Couldn't I love July? If I just got past this Jenny shit—I mean it's practically over, she's getting married, there's nothing. I just get past it, deal with it separately, then I can still have July, right? And then we see what happens, right?*

Why did silence seem the better answer?

July wanted desperately to shake Toby, violently pull him back and forth, force a sentence out of him.

Answer me! she cried in her head. *Answer, answer, answer!*

She got it—he didn't love her. She got it. If he had, he would have said something. Her eyes felt ready to pour out her face. Was she supposed to sit here all night, across from a silent Toby, waiting for him to respond? Was she just supposed to pretend she had never said that? Was she supposed to leave? Humiliating.

Say something, Toby, she thought. *Say something so I know where this is going.*

"July," he finally said.

Her eyes flicked back up. *Oh my God, here it comes.*

But he was silent for a long time.

SPEAK! She tore though her body. *Please speak!*

"July," he said again.

"What?" she said with all the control she had left.

"I don't know."

Breathe. Think of the horizon, July.

"You don't know?"

What the hell did he mean he didn't know? *What kind of an answer was that? Q: I love you. A: I don't know.*

"I—look, it's very complicated."

Yeah, no shit, she thought, but she kept her mouth shut.

"It's just that, I—I—I don't know. I don't know what—you want. What you want me to say. I just divorced; I'm still hurting. I—don't—love you. Yet."

Yet. Yet? Did that mean that he would? That he could? Or was he just trying to soften the blow?

"Yet?" she repeated. "What does that mean? That you will?"

"That I—might?"

"You might."

"I might."

She frowned. He might. So he might also *not* love her. *What am I supposed to do with that?*

"Well," she said, trying to be patient. "Where do you see this in a few months?"

He sighed, "Honestly, I've given up trying to see. It hasn't worked well for me; it ends in disappointment. At first, I didn't see my marriage ending, but it did. So I could see one thing but it could end up being a whole slew of different things."

No shit, she thought. *That's such a non-answer.*

"Well, you may not want to look ahead but I have to. I can't just hang around until graduation, make plans, only to find out that you *might* love me or *might* not or that you *might* move to Mexico."

"I'm not going to move to Mexico."

"Well, how do you know? You just said you gave up trying to see into the future."

"Oh come on, July."

"No, you come on. Am I just supposed to hope around, waiting and seeing until graduation? Maybe we're still together at graduation. Then what? Do I stay around, hoping every week that you don't change your mind and totally remove the floor beneath me?"

"You should do what you want."

"But what if what I want includes you?"

He was silent.

"Don't you think I should know if you also want to be included? Or does waiting and seeing entail staying together until graduation while I make other plans and then either saying goodbye or trying to get me to change my plans at the last minute?"

I need to calm down, take a breath, count to ten. He probably doesn't want all this flung at him at once, right now, after he's just woken up with a busted back in Florence the day after Christmas and the day after his ex-wife of two weeks told him she's getting re-married. Not the ideal timing. Nice job, July. Cosmopolitan would have a fit with this one. Way to be a horror story.

But she couldn't stop pushing. Even if she'd never reach the top, she couldn't just let the boulder roll back on her now.

"You haven't thought about this at *all?*" she said.

There was a long pause. What was that man's brain *doing?* Like it was processing thoughts on Jupiter.

"I guess—not as much as you've been."

"Obviously."

"Well come on now, July, I've kinda been going through a lot here. Heartbreak, divorce, single fathering, and now Jenny is getting *married*—"

"So what am I? Just a little side pleasure?"

"No, of course not.

"Then what am I?"

"You're—my girlfriend."

"Yeah. And how long was it going to stay that way?"

"July, I don't really know what you want from me here."

"I want you to answer my question! I want you to tell me what this relationship means to you!"

Oh, God, she cringed inwardly. *Did I really just say that?*

"July, look, I'm tired. I'm in pain. I have a lot to think about. And I feel like this subject requires a bit more thought on my part."

"Yeah, a bit," she thought and said before her brain could put down the barrier.

"Look," he said a bit more tensely. "Let's talk about this later."

"Fine. Tomorrow."

"Okay ... tomorrow."

He didn't sound happy about it.

I think he was hoping later meant never, she thought.

"Fine."

She stood up and went into the bathroom. She didn't want to be around him right now; she wanted to be alone. She sat down on the toilet seat lid, pulled her knees to her chest and put her arms around her legs.

So Jenny was getting married. Already? She wasted less time than it appeared Toby had; it must have been going on for a while. Toby must have known something about the guy, it couldn't have come as a total shock.

He had July, but she didn't matter like Jenny used to. She didn't even matter like Jenny *still* did. If she left Toby, would he be equally as hurt? Would he spend a sleepless night wandering the city, thinking of what had gone wrong, how much he missed her?

No. Probably not.

Part of her wanted to keep loving him, but there was another part that was growing bigger. She had hardly noticed its introduction. It warned her to stop, stop while she was less behind, or else it might blow up bigger.

What about Massimo? it said. He's different; it's like you've known him for years. And the sparks he sends through your body—you felt every vein in your body by sheer contact with his skin. Maybe it wasn't quite as simple as leaving Toby for Massimo, but wasn't it at least an option? In theory?

She needed to talk to someone; she needed guidance, but there wasn't really anything she could do; she wasn't about to do what Toby did last night and spend the whole night outside. She couldn't call her parents; they would just say I told you so. She didn't talk to any of her friends about Toby; they thought it was too creepy and weird. So she was stuck. She was stuck in the room with a bedridden Toby and if she wanted to be alone she would have to sleep in the bathroom.

Unless.

Unless I go to Massimo's, she thought. But that would be a bad idea for too many reasons. But Massimo. He would make her feel better. He wouldn't ask questions. When they said goodbye this morning, he had said, "You have a problem, you tell me."

She had a problem.

He had written something in her passport—what was it?

She opened the door and walked out of the bathroom before she could think about it too much, hoping Toby wouldn't notice her grabbing her passport.

But when she glanced over to the bed, she saw that Toby was asleep again. *How was he asleep? He just slept all afternoon! Doesn't he want to think about us at all?*

July pushed the thought from her mind and rummaged for her passport in her purse. She pulled it out and flipped through it.

It was in the front pages, on the page that had a big number five at the bottom and was entitled "Important Information Regarding Your Passport". It shouldn't invalidate her passport, but she would erase it later anyway. At the bottom of the page, Massimo had written:

Se trovarci nei miei sogli lucidi non è abbastanza
If meeting in my lucid dreams is not enough
Followed by his name, address, phone number, and email
And then,
Spero di non. I hope it is not.
I should have gone into the bookstore.

*I shouldn't call him now. But what else am I supposed to do—sit here
and stew waiting for a bedridden man who doesn't love me to wake up and
tell me so? This is totally unfair. I don't have to stand for this. Stand up for
yourself, July. What do you want?*

I want to call Massimo.

She marched out of the bathroom, took the key from the night
table, and went out into the hallway. She closed the door as quietly
behind her as she could and walked swiftly down the hall, admiring
how softly she could walk. She glided down the stairs and stopped at
the reception desk.

"Can I use your phone?" she asked the concierge.

"There is a phone in your room."

"Well he's sleeping and I don't want to wake him."

The concierge tried to hide his exasperation behind pursed, taut lips.

"Okay, fine," he said.

July moved to come around the desk.

"No, no, there is one in that room over there," he pointed jerkily to a
room adjacent to them.

"*Grazie,*" said July.

He didn't respond.

July opened her passport and picked up the phone. She was suddenly very aware of her heartbeat. What was she going to say when
she heard Massimo's voice at the other end of the line?

"Hi Massimo, Toby's mad at me and doesn't love me, will you make
me feel better?"

Well that sounded stupid. What could she say? What could she say
that wouldn't make it sound ten times worse than it actually was?

The dial tone persisted in her ear. She felt like she was in a play
and had forgotten her lines. Or like no one had given her the lines
in the first place and she was acting in a play she had never read or
seen before.

I feel so unprepared for life.

Wasn't college supposed to have readied her for the real world? She
was four months away from graduating and she still had no idea how
things really worked, how people really felt and reacted. How was a

class on the Sociology of American Mass Media supposed to help her become a functional adult?

She was totally frozen.

"*Eh!*" came the concierge's voice from without. "Are you done yet?"

July was jarred back to the dial tone. What could she say? She hadn't had any practice—she hadn't read the book—she hadn't studied!

College had never seemed such a meaningless, massive waste of time.

"*Eh!*" came the concierge again. "Don't tie up the line!"

She put the phone down. She couldn't call. She stood up and walked back out to the foyer.

"*Grazie,*" she mumbled without looking the concierge in the eye. She shuffled back up the stairs and trudged down the hall. Time to face down the lock, and do it without waking Toby.

She slipped the key in carefully, pulled up on the knob, closed her eyes, and pushed. If he awoke, asked where she had been, she would have to lie even more, it would fall apart like a paper plate seeping through with a heavy serving of watery baked beans. This could give at any moment.

The door opened, but loudly. It creaked and moaned as it swung open, and July spent far too much time and noise jiggling the key out. Then the door hit the jamb with a definite clump. She heard Toby rustle and she dived for the chair near her. Sitting still in the dark, as though he could sense her movements, she held her breath, praying he wouldn't wake up.

Toby awoke sometime in the dark. It could be three or four, but it could also be one, it could be six. There was no clock in the room, and his watch was in his bag.

He felt wide awake, due most notably to the constant, dull ache that pulsed in his back. If he thought about it, he thought it felt a bit better, but supposed that lifting himself out of bed would be the best idea. Well great. What was he supposed to do now—just lie here staring into the dark?

Apparently so.

But then he realized that he really needed to go to the bathroom.

Oh no, he thought. *I don't know if I can get up by myself.*

Shit. What was he going to do? How was he going to get up?

He would have to wake July, which he really didn't want to do given the discussion they'd had earlier. What if she didn't even want to help him? What if this played out like that book *Misery*? *No, July wouldn't do that. Stop being over-imaginative.*

He'd still have to ask for her help. He felt like such an invalid. But there was no choice. He'd better get used to it.

He looked to the other side of the bed for July, but she wasn't there. Where was she? Did she leave him again? Great. Good going. Thanks a lot. So much for being in love with me.

"July?" he called out, though it felt as useless as yelling "Taxi!" at a moving cab.

Did he hear a stir? He leaned his head forward, as if that would help him hear better.

"July?" he called again, a bit louder this time.

"Mm," he heard. Unless he was hallucinating. That would be a bad sign.

"July," he said louder.

"Whuh?" she croaked.

So she was here—she hadn't left him. Maybe she really did love him. But why wasn't she in bed?

"July?"

"What!"

"I—uh—I have to go to the bathroom."

"That's great."

"No, I—I can't get up. I can't get up alone."

Silence.

"I need your help."

There was more silence for a minute, and he may have heard a scowl. But then there was rustling and he heard footsteps. Suddenly the light beside him came on, the yellow burning, searing light.

She didn't look happy—she looked grumpy. She rubbed her face with her hand and inhaled deeply, then huffed it back out.

"Fine. Let's go."

After a lot of finagling and a few spasms of protest up Toby's back, he was bent over July and shuffling to the bathroom.

I feel like I'm in a nursing home, he thought. *Like I'm eighty. This is what I have to look forward to? Someone push me in front of a moving truck before I am reduced to using a bedpan. Or worse, a catheter.*

It must have taken ten or fifteen minutes from bed to bathroom to bed again. When July had finished laying him down again, he didn't feel like sleeping. She had tucked him in just like he usually did for his daughters. Suddenly he felt younger than July, like she was the mother, the caretaker. How strange.

The light turned off and he heard July's steps, which seemed to stop at the foot of the bed.

"July."

"What."

"Are you sleeping on the floor?"

"No," came her voice from beyond the bed.

"Yes, you are."

"No, I'm in the chair, though I'm currently not sleeping anymore."

"Come up here."

"I'm fine."

"Come on, it can't be comfortable over there."

"No, it can't."

"Just come up here."

"I don't really want to."

Ouch.

"Come on, July," he said as tenderly as possible.

But she didn't respond.

What time was it? How long until it got light? Not that it would matter, he couldn't go out anyway. He would probably be stuck in this bed for most of the rest of the trip. *Fuck.* The flight back would be a delight. What if his back didn't improve? The airlines might have to transfer him in a wheelchair. Oh, *God.*

He wondered if July would leave him. He was pretty sure she still loved him; she had helped him to the bathroom. And he knew first-hand that love usually didn't just go away when you wanted it to—too often it was the opposite.

How did my life get like this? he thought, *the middle-aged man with a beautiful twenty-two-year-old in love with me. Life is tough.*

Toby reached into his head, his heart, his stomach, trying to find the part of him that would tell him how he felt. When he sighed his breath out as far as it would go and tried to look down into the empty space that was left, he admitted it.

It's not that I can't love her. It's that I just don't want to be in love right now.

There it was.

It's not that I don't want to stay with you, not that I won't or can't love you in the future, but I just don't want to deal with love right now, waiting for the other shoe to drop.

Well if you don't deal with it now, there's a chance that, even if you want it, you'll never have the chance to deal with it again.

He didn't want to break up with July. That would only make his life worse. She made him happy. But he was rather nearsighted at the moment. It was all he could do—the future only made him despondent.

But the future was a gaping crater, and he didn't want to try and fill it only to find that it has a hole at the bottom that drains without warning. He didn't need a whirlpool like that again. So it seemed better to fill it just a little every day, or every week, so that if he lost, he lost small, not big.

Toby was no longer a gambling man.

He lay in the dark for hours, days. Had nights always been this long? Had he been missing out on all this time for his whole life? There were so many things he could have done if he hadn't slept. He could have expanded his business, or relearned Spanish, or hell, learned Italian. He could have spent more time with his daughters and worked at night. He could have spent more time with Jenny. Maybe he could have saved their marriage.

But now that he was awake in the middle of the night, he couldn't think of a single thing he could do at the moment. July was asleep.

In a chair! How childish. Even when he and Jenny had had their worst fights, they had still shared a bed. It was theirs, and even when he was steaming, raging mad at Jenny, he always slept next to her, and she next to him.

He dared not move anyway. So he sat and stared at the moving particles of darkness, dancing before his eyes in different shades of dark and light, whatever colors those were. He thought about his daughters, imagined coming home, hugging them and hearing them shout, "Daddy! Daddy! What did you bring me?"

I wish I could go home a new man.

They still had over a week left in Florence, but it was beginning to seem like too long. He would need at least three days of relaxing his back. He didn't want to just sit here with Italian TV. July would want to go out, but he would need her to stay with him just in case. To help him down the stairs to breakfast, to take him on short walks, then help him rest in bed. Now he needed her, just when he had told her that he didn't love her, he needed her.

What would she say if he changed their tickets to go home early? She probably wouldn't be too pleased; she'd probably think it was her, the argument they'd had, that he wanted to end things.

It would certainly be a convenient way of ending things, he thought. *It'll probably end anyway, sometime or another. Wouldn't it be doing her a favor to end it now?*

What if, after he ended it, he found that that wasn't what he really wanted? He didn't much want to end it now, either. July was so beautiful, sexy, young, great to be with. He could see his life back home without July: an endless cycle of kids and solitude. The solitude wouldn't be so bad at first, maybe, but with Jenny's impending wedding and no one to take his thoughts off of the new emptiness in his life, he would probably just feel lonely and depressed.

Maybe he would find a new girlfriend, someone closer to his age. Maybe, probably, she would be divorced too, or have a kid, or *kids*, and Toby would have to learn to be a father to complete strangers, and his girls would have to learn to be their sisters. Or if she hadn't been married before, she would either be one of those independent women who didn't *need* and he would have to learn to be married to someone who hadn't wanted to be, *or* she would be one of those women who had desperately tried to find a man but, through bad luck and circumstances, had never been married and had been bitter and resentful for at least a time. The women like Astrid—single, beautiful, closer to his age—were like century plants in bloom. You were lucky to see one in a lifetime.

Or, the other alternative: he wouldn't find anyone else. Maybe he'd cycle through a couple of girlfriends but never find anyone suitable for him or the girls. And then, well, what would he do with his life? Once the girls left for college … what would there be? His life would be an endless calendar of empty days.

His prospects weren't looking good, which did nothing to abate the soreness in his back.

Was that reason enough to stay with July—fear of loneliness? It wasn't that he would never love her, he just didn't know if he would. That was fair, right? Isn't that what relationships were about—seeing if it worked or not? He was just going to take a little longer to make up his mind.

He may have drifted in and out of sleep, but his sleep was the same color as the darkness of consciousness. Once or twice he thought he saw the light of the sun beginning to inject itself into the sky outside, but after endless minutes of waiting, the sky got no lighter. Had he lost all sense of time? One day he was twenty-six, the next, forty-three. He slipped between the ages but he didn't notice. Forty-three was the same feeling as the weight of twenty-six, back injuries excluded. He never knew the difference.

When finally the dawn had lightly grasped the sky, Toby felt a sense of relief. So the night had an end, the day had a beginning. Toby wasn't usually so philosophical. It must be the darkness, the paralysis. A lack of sight made everything more visible, more serious, more meaningful, like light is only there to show you what a fool you are.

July stood outside the door to the bookstore where Massimo worked waiting for the mail. It was hot and sunny, and July was in Massimo's trench coat and she was hot. Sweating. Where was the mail? Why wasn't it here yet?

She looked up and down the street but it was empty. Where was the mail? She knew Massimo was inside, but she didn't know if she could go in until the mail came.

Her mother walked by on the other side of the street.

"What are you doing in Italy?" she called to July.

"I'm waiting for the mail," July called back.

"The mail? But it's Sunday!" yelled her mother.

"What? It's Sunday?"

"I told you yesterday that today would be Sunday! You never listen! I told you so."

"No you didn't."

"I told you so, July."

Oh no, today *was* Sunday! But she needed the mail today—she was leaving Florence tomorrow and she needed to see Massimo.

Forget it, I can't wait for the mail anymore, she thought. *I'm just going to have to go in anyway.*

She turned around and pulled on the door to the bookstore.

But it was locked.

She looked inside. She could see Massimo, making coffee, talking and laughing with customers. She had to go in and see what would happen. What he would say.

Then she looked at the doorknob—it was a Magic 8-Ball.

"Should I go in?" she asked it.

She shook the ball.

A little triangle bubbled to the top of the blue liquid, but she couldn't read the answer. She tried to look closer but it was like part of her eyes had been removed—that section remained obscured. She tried moving the Magic 8-Ball around, but no matter where she moved it, she couldn't read it. Like Toby and his reading glasses.

She turned to Toby, who was lying on a patch of ice on the sidewalk next to the bookstore.

"Can I use your reading glasses?" she asked.

"I don't know."

"You don't know?"

"I don't know."

"How can you not know?"

"I don't know."

July grunted in frustration and turned back to the Magic 8-Ball door. She pushed and pulled but it wouldn't open.

"You have to pull up on it," said the concierge.

July pulled up and the door opened. She went inside the school cafeteria where Gianni was working behind the counter.

"Where's Massimo?"

"He is in New York with Astrid," said Gianni. "But tomorrow they will dream about China."

XX

BY THE TIME JULY HAD AWOKEN, TAKEN TOBY TO THE BATHROOM, and dressed herself, breakfast at the hotel had already closed.

"I've been craving a coffee since at least six this morning," said Toby when he realized that the time to eat had come and gone.

It felt like a passive aggressive form of criticism—she had quite the nerve sleeping when he was in such a state. Did he expect a full breakfast in bed?

"I had wanted to finish that bread and cheese you bought," he said. "But they're on the floor on the other side of the bed. I couldn't reach. I'm starving."

While July was skeptical that he couldn't even reach the other side of the bed, a small corner of her brain felt a bit triumphant. But soon she was crossing the river in search of a grocery store for ...

"Peanuts, chips, maybe some chocolate and cookies, all the things I like," he had said.

"Just cross the bridge, turn right, and you're there," said the concierge, whose directions seemed so deceptively simple that July momentarily contemplated doing exactly the opposite.

But now she was walking across the bridge in the blinding December sunlight. They hadn't had a day this clear since coming to Florence. It was cold and bright blue, like the particles of sunlight interacted with the cold, wrapping the chill in a glittering afterthought of warmth, memories of May.

I can't believe I'll be stuck inside on a day like this, she grumbled as she reached the other side of the Arno. There didn't appear to be much here—some small shops, which were all closed, a small *gelateria* across from a café on a corner. She turned right, expecting to find a street as dead as those around it, but instead she saw a supermarket, just like the concierge had promised.

She entered and immediately got lost among all the foods. The fruits and vegetables were the same as those she bought in the States, but they seemed somehow different here. Buying nuts and chips and things that Toby usually ate at home seemed so boring. Look at the prosciutto, the tomatoes, even the pre-made gnocchi looked appetizing. She wandered the aisles, putting the things Toby had requested in her basket and agonized over a few things she wanted to buy herself. Bread and olive oil, some shortbread cookies, mozzarella ... but she couldn't eat it all on her own, and Toby probably wouldn't want them, and then they would go to waste.

This is how it would be if we stayed together, she thought. *Me helping him out with his shopping, getting his things and mine.*

She tried to decide how that made her feel. For all these weeks she had wanted to be part of his life. She had wanted to slide right in, be the perfect fit. But it didn't seem fair if he didn't want to be part of hers. At least when he and Jenny had first met, neither of them had lives yet; not established ones, anyway. If July came in now, wouldn't she have to fit into what Jenny used to do? Maybe July was failing already. Yet there was something so reassuring about a life that had already been set up, and if she had to make a few compromises—like buying potato chips instead of bread and olive oil.

What good is a compromise if I'm the only one doing so? He doesn't want me anyway, she reminded herself. *I'm doing everything in vain.*

She decided to stop at the corner *gelateria* on the way back to the hotel. It would only be a few extra minutes; Toby wouldn't starve to death.

For the millionth time, July rolled their ages around her head— 50:29, 61:40. When would Toby start needing closer care? She could become a caretaker by the time she was forty, after being a step-mom throughout her twenties and thirties. Maybe it would be fun, but when would he slow down more? What would happen when his skin sags, when he succumbs to late life pudge, when the lines become his face's most noticeable attribute, when he can't drive? What then?

Maybe one day she would be driving one of the girls to sports this or music that, seeing the road but wondering about Massimo, where he was, what he was doing, if he had designed that building under construction downtown, what would have happened if she had just walked into the bookstore all those years ago in Florence when she had had the chance, if she had said something, just shown up, just been there, and for the thousand millionth time she was looking at that red light and scripting what she would have said had she gone in, and every week or so she would change the lines slightly, an if to a then, a would to a could.

After a few minutes, July willed herself to stand and begin the walk back to the hotel.

Maybe she would leave Toby, stay in Florence, not return to school and travel the world with Massimo wherever whenever they wanted to go, and then maybe they would be leaving one place for another, packing the suitcases again, but she would be wearied of living a life of transition, of eating in restaurants every night, of making friends only to leave them, or not making friends at all, and as she was folding her worn pair of jeans she would wonder about Toby, where he was, what he was doing, if the first man she had been in love with missed her, thought about her, if he was with someone new, what her life would have been like if she had settled down with the man she loved, worked through the bullshit and just made it work.

She would never be free. The ghosts of endless possibilities would always haunt her.

She had dawdled as much as she could, but all too soon she was passing beneath the Hotel Ariele awning. The grocery bag bounced against the side of her shin with each step up. Before putting the key in the lock, she stood in front of the door and took a deep breath.

Toby was in bed reading and looked up when she came in. The lights were on and the blinds were closed. It looked like a terrorist's lair.

"Hey," he said. "Did you find the store okay?"

July held up the bag of groceries, "Yep."

"Great, I'm starving."

Toby split the book open face down on the bed, "Help me sit up, please?"

July came around to his side of the bed and helped him up, placing all the pillows behind his back. Though he moaned and huffed and puffed a bit, he seemed to be able to do most of the movement himself.

"Is that okay?" asked July.

"Can you put the pillows up just a little higher?"

July rearranged the pillows, "Better?"

"Um, actually a little lower now?"

July moved them down a bit, "Now?"

"A bit higher?"

Was he kidding with this shit?

"That's good," he said. "Did the store have the chips I like?"

"No," she replied. "I got these instead." She tossed him a bag of chips.

"I guess that'll work," he said, and pulled the bag open with a squeaky plastic twreak.

July took off her scarf and coat. "It's really lovely outside today," she said. "There's so much sun. If you looked out the window you'd think it was June."

"Mm," said Toby, crunching on the chips.

July sat on the edge of the bed. Toby ate for a few more minutes. The only sounds coming from his mouth were the crunches from the potato chips. Didn't he want to talk? Yesterday he had said they would talk later. It was later.

"So," said July.

"So," said Toby.

They were silent. It seemed Toby was waiting for her to continue, and she was waiting for him to do so.

"So ...?" said July again.

Toby raised his eyebrows expectantly, "So ... do you want a chip?"

"No, I mean, so, it's later."

He frowned as if pondering the depths of the ocean.

Was he just trying to avoid this? He couldn't possibly have forgotten what had happened last night.

"Toby. Where are we going?"

"What?"

"Where are we going? What happens when we get home? When I graduate?"

He stuck another potato chip in his mouth.

Stalling. Great, thought July. *So he hasn't thought about it at all. He doesn't care about anything that's going on here.*

"I—" he blinked, and his mouth opened in a few phantom words, "I—don't know."

July looked at the floor, the grout between the tiles that separated them all in a perfect, predictable grid. Now she didn't know either. She had tried repeatedly not to imagine herself with his daughters, becoming their friend. She tried not to fantasize about living with him after graduation; about what it would be like to have a husband who was sixty-one when she was forty; what it would be like to be the youngest step-mom at school fundraisers and plays; how safe and happy she would feel knowing that she could be next to Toby every day, that every morning she could stare at the folds of his eyes, rest her head in the nook of his chest and shoulders, fit her hips between his like the last two pieces of a puzzle.

But she couldn't do it. When she awoke early that morning before dawn, as angry as she had been, she had still spent a good portion of it looking at Toby, wanting to absorb him through her chest and keep him behind her rib cage forever. And she didn't want to tell him any of this because she didn't want to hear him explain all the reasons that what she wanted wasn't possible. But she didn't know what he *did* want. Her mind was an oval track, and she kept doing lap after lap, passing the same thoughts, never knowing where the finish line was or when the race ended.

"What do you want?" she forced the words up her throat and over her tongue.

Toby sighed and looked ahead into the mounds of frozen color.

He swallowed his chip, ran his tongue stickily along the outsides of his teeth, and licked his lips.

July built a dam with her lips to hold back the thousand follow up questions. Instead, she tilted her head so that her hair veiled her face from Toby's view as those questions formed hot tears against the lower rims of her eyes, pushed their way down her cheeks and splatted on the floor.

She tried to blink them away before Toby noticed.

Was there even a future in his head? JUST TELL ME WHAT YOU WANT! she shouted in her head.

"July? Are you okay?"

"Yeah," she said, uniting every muscle in her throat to cover the oppressing bubble of despair.

July wished that Toby would draw her hair back like a curtain and tuck it behind her ear and say something reassuring, put a hand on her back or around her or something. But they both remained still, him in bed, her at its foot turned away from him using her hair like chainmail.

When she finally looked at him again, she saw his face was cloaked in an anonymous relaxed tension. She didn't want to pry into him, but if she didn't say something now, he may not answer her for hours, maybe even for the rest of the trip.

"Please tell me what you're thinking," she said, hoping she hadn't sounded like she was pleading.

His shoulders fell about half an inch, the only indication that he had heard July.

He sighed.

"It's just that—it doesn't really come down to what I want. It comes down to my daughters, and how I can be happy with what's best for them."

July frowned, perplexed.

"So you're telling me that even if you liked me, it doesn't matter because I'm not good for them?"

"Well, I don't know," he said. "You haven't spent any time with them."

"What's your biggest reservation here, Toby? Is it me? My age? Or is it really your daughters? Or Jenny? I'm going crazy here because I don't know how much I should keep feeling if you're just going to unload me."

"I'm not going to *unload* you."

"Well, were you just going to let this keep going until you decided it was time to change? Were you just going to let me graduate and move on?"

"Well, I—"

"Don't say I don't know. You *do* know."

Toby finally looked at her, his brows contorted like calligraphy strokes.

"All I know is," he began. "I like you. I love spending time with you. I feel like we could do anything together and it wouldn't feel awkward, like I could kiss you forever and not get tired of your lips, like life is easy when you're around. I know I have baggage and issues, and that what you want when you're young may not be what you want fifteen years down the road."

"So does that mean that you should not get what you want now because you might not want it later?"

"Well, I—no," he sighed. "I guess—not."

How was it, she thought, *that this man who had lived a chunk of adulthood, who was so much more aware than any college boy, could be so clueless? He had had forty-three years to figure himself out.*

"What about you?" he asked.

"What *about* me?"

"Well, what do you want? Did you plan to just graduate and run off with Massimo?"

"No!" she said, a bit more suddenly than she'd like. "Didn't I already tell you I love you?" But what was she supposed to say now? *If you ask me to stay, I'll stay because I'm in love with you and if you let me I'd love your daughters, too.*

He doesn't want me like that, she realized, as gravity seemed suddenly stronger through her shoulders, the hollows of her eyes, her throat. Her eyes folded inward and her mind went blind.

"I—would like our relationship to continue. For ... as far as ... it can," she said instead.

He stayed silent.

"I'm the only one that wants that, aren't I?" she finally uttered.

"Well," he began.

The first time Toby had told a girl he loved her, he was sixteen and utterly, hopelessly horny. It was Valentine's Day and he and his first girlfriend, Mary, had been together for three months. Even though it was a school night, his parents let Toby take Mary out for dinner. He wore a tie and even bought her flowers. Or rather, his mother took him to buy her flowers, proclaiming that no man could take his girlfriend out on Valentine's without flowers, but Toby couldn't recall ever seeing his father give her flowers. That night over chocolate cake, when Mary was smiling and happy, she told him she loved him. She was a freshman, he was a junior, and even though he wasn't sure what love was, he was pretty sure that this wasn't it. But, listening to his hormones, he told her he loved her too, and that night got more action than he had previously.

He continued the charade for a few more weeks until something didn't seem right, until he got restless, and until he developed a crush on another girl. When he broke up with Mary after school by the closed snack bar, she cried and cried, and then asked didn't he love her? He shrugged and stuck his hands in his pockets and had to look almost immediately away. Her pupils seemed to dilate to the size of quarters and come at him like a 3-D movie. It was all he could remember afterward, those pupils, shiny and infinitely round.

When he saw her at school the next day, she refused to look at him, walked away from him, and her friends gave him looks that froze every muscle in his body. He felt like a cold, scaly snake had slithered slowly down his throat.

The next time he said it, a few months later to the new girl he had developed a crush on, it was just after he had lost his virginity, and he thought it was the appropriate thing to say. She said it back, and maybe she meant it. But after that he began to notice that he didn't feel any different, didn't feel the attachment that he thought he should if he was going to be in love. He broke up with her at the end of the school year in his father's car, after they had had his house to themselves and he was driving her home.

At first she cried, but then she got angry. She, too, asked him if he had loved her. When he answered with a damp, sinking silence, she stormed out of the car, slammed the door, and egged his house the next night. He knew it was her because he heard her and her friends laughing outside his window in the middle of the night and then the flat crunch splats against his window. His parents called the police and filed a report, but Toby didn't tell them who had done it. Instead, he wordlessly scrubbed the dry, stubborn yolks from the front of his family's white house. He vowed that from then on, he would mean those words whenever he said them.

He kept that vow, but soon learned what it was like to be lied to when he heard himself asking the question, "Did you love me?" to his next girlfriend when she was breaking up with him. When he was met with that same piercing silence, he felt like the world's biggest fool. Which, strangely, was quite similar to how he felt when Jenny told him about Kevin.

Now he was in a position to do that to July. But he had told her the truth—that he didn't love her yet. Even if she didn't now, she would, in the future, appreciate his honesty.

"Well," he said for a second time. "Look July, I've been thinking. It doesn't look like my back is going to get better in time for me, for *us*, to enjoy the rest of our time here. I was thinking about changing our tickets and going home early."

Her face froze and her jaw fell open slightly.

"It's not because I don't want to be with you, but I don't think either of us wants to spend eight days cooped up in this hotel room while you tend to me. It's not fair."

She clenched her jaw shut.

"I thought that maybe, once we get back to the States, back home and into the swing of everyday life, that we'll be able to better—assess what's best for us."

"So—" she cocked her head to the side and frowned, almost as though the middle of her brow and the peaks of her top lip would meet together like two parabolas. "When were you—thinking of going back?"

"I called the airline while you were out. They said they have some free seats for a flight back tomorrow night, so I booked them."

"Tomorrow! Can't you see a doctor here? They may be able to help you!"

"No, I don't need to go to the doctor. I just need to rest."

"But won't you be really uncomfortable on the plane?"

"Maybe, but it would be worth it to me to be home sooner."

"But—I don't have anywhere to stay if we go back tomorrow," she said. "The dorms are all closed until the seventh ... I was going to stay with a friend for those two nights, but she's in Mexico until the fourth. What am I supposed to do?"

"I'll pay for you to stay in a hotel. Or you could fly home and see your family."

"What makes you think I want to go home? What if I don't want to leave Italy early? Didn't you think about that? Doesn't what I want matter, too?"

"Well, I mean, July, I'm a little incapacitated here; the trip is essentially over. And let's not forget who's paying for everything ..."

"So I'm at your mercy because *you* invited me here and *you* paid for my ticket because *you* wanted to?"

"July—"

"I don't believe this!" she interrupted. "What am I supposed to do? I don't want to go home! Do you know what my family will say to me? After all the shit they gave me about being with an older man and going abroad and not coming home for the holidays and then just crawling back with my tail between my legs?"

"I told you—I'll put you up in a hotel until you can go back to school."

"I'm not even welcome in your home anymore? What am I supposed to do for a week and a half in a hotel? And what happens when you decide I need to check out because *you're* paying for the room and *you* don't want me staying there anymore?"

"July, that's not going to happen."

"You really can't look into the future, can you? You tell me you don't know what's going to happen but you seem to know what's *not* going to happen!"

"July—"

"And then I go and tell you I love you and then you decide to ditch me! Once you find out I love you, you go and end everything, time to pack it in and move on."

"I'm not breaking up with you July."

"Well what *are* you doing? Or can you only tell me what you're *not* doing? Because it sure feels like this is you ending the relationship."

"All I'm saying is that maybe this will be easier to solve once we get back home."

"I don't think that our current geographical location has any pertinent effect on the future direction of this relationship."

July was the only person he had met who used larger words when she got angry.

"July, I just don't think it's a good idea to make big decisions when I'm cooped up in bed and you're tied to taking care of me."

"Does changing our departure date to a week earlier than planned not qualify as a big decision?"

"July, you're not listening to me."

"I'm not listening to you! No, the problem is you aren't listening to me or to you. You're just going along without taking into consideration my emotions, my state of mind, and then you're just manipulating what you say into a non-response."

"Whoa, July, you need to calm down. If there's anyone manipulating words here, it's you."

"I don't believe this. I *don't* believe this."

"Look July," said Toby, taking a deep breath. "If I'm going to have to be restricted to my bed, I'd at least like to have my girls around."

"I thought they were with Jenny until after the New Year. What are you going to do for those few days when you're home?"

"I'm going to call Jenny and explain the situation and ask her to come home early."

"Yeah, I'm sure she'll be quite receptive to that request."

"There's no need to get bratty."

"Now I'm a brat? Tell me Toby, do you really want to go home early because of your back and your girls, or because your ex-wife is getting remarried and you've got a wounded ego?"

"That was really uncalled for."

"Are you hoping that Jenny will come rushing to your bedside and that she'll suddenly realize how she still loves you? That suddenly you can put your old life back together because of your back? You're living in the past, Toby. Your marriage ended—you're *divorced*. It's over."

"It's never over!" he yelled before he could think about it. "The past is never over. It always matters. The past is still the present!"

"Well what about me, Toby? You don't have to love me, but you should at least care. I should at least matter, and right now it doesn't seem like I do."

"Oh come on, July," he said, because he had no better retort.

"No, you come on, Toby. You brought me to Italy, one of the most romantic countries ever. Doesn't that mean you're supposed to care about me, that we're supposed to have some romance? Or am I just filling the void?"

"July, stop making all these accusations."

"Well, what am I supposed to think when you can't even tell me how you feel about me?"

"You sound just like Jenny," he said before he could stop himself.

"Well, maybe she was *on* to something," sneered July like a filet knife.

"You know what? Right now I'm feeling like you're acting like a spoiled, bratty bitch."

She stood up abruptly.

"And I'm thinking you're acting like an obnoxious, self-absorbed prick who's living so far in the past his ass is ten years behind his eyelashes."

She grabbed her purse, her coat, her scarf, the room key. Toby would have laughed if he weren't so angry.

"Where are you going? You can't leave me here—I can't move."

"I guess you should have thought of that before you called me a bitch." She moved swiftly for the door, flung it open, and slammed it shut.

The room echoed with silence as the words from their fight vibrated around the room. Had he really just called July a bitch and lumped her in with Jenny? Did she really deserve that? How come after all these years, he still hadn't learned to control his tongue when he was fighting with a woman?

"Maybe she was *on* to something."

The words felt branded across his chest, hot and sore and burning. How was *he* the problem here? This all made perfect sense to him; July was grossly overreacting, misinterpreting everything he said. Jenny had done the same thing. Maybe it wasn't him; maybe it was the women he chose. Like alcoholics tended towards each other or abused women kept picking abusers, maybe he was just attracted to the wrong type of woman, to the irrational woman who didn't listen.

He hadn't pinned July as that type. But then, he hadn't pinned Jenny as that type either.

Why are you always blaming them? asked a small voice beneath him, but he smothered it quickly. The voice only made him feel worse.

When would July come back? Probably not for a while. Probably not until night time. He would have to go to the bathroom eventually; could he stand by himself?

I guess I'd better get started before it becomes an emergency, he thought.

Slowly, carefully, he began shifting his weight, the rustle of the sheets magnified in the room's stillness. He propped himself up and though a crackling pain skittered momentarily up his back, he managed to shift himself upright with comparatively little pain. Perhaps he was, as July suggested, using his injury as an excuse to go home and cradle his wounded ego, which seemed to lay a culturing, festering compost pile deep within him. He admitted it was possible he was playing up his injury to gain sympathy from July, from Jenny, and from himself.

But at the moment, he wasn't inclined to drag himself from the comfortable seat of despair that was his self-pity.

He grabbed the bag of groceries as he staggered toward the bathroom. Though his stride was a bit stilted, he considered his back to be a source of intense discomfort rather than considerable pain, which could only be an improvement.

Is it me? came the voice again. *What if it's me? I can't divorce myself.*

He slowly leveraged himself down to the toilet, grunting as his back sputtered a bit.

Oh my God. What if it's me?

What if it's me?

July strode heavily down the street, trying to vent her anger through the heels of her boots as they clacked against the pavement. She felt only anger, pure heat sizzling off her chest and out her throat, only try to move to stave off the overwhelming roasting inside. Her jacket and scarf swung jerkily from her arm according to the movements of the her body.

"You sound just like Jenny."

She had heard Jenny; she didn't want to sound like that. But now she was beginning to feel that maybe Jenny may have been just a little justified at some point during her marriage to and divorce from Toby.

Why couldn't he just give her a simple answer about their relationship? And this bullshit about the tickets— thinking about it again caused her anger to double, and she looked to see if she could actually see steam rising from her chest like the breath huffing from her mouth.

A car honked in her ear, and she stopped abruptly, realizing that she was crossing a road and hadn't bothered to stop for the car. It whizzed past her, inches from her skin, the passing breeze tickling her skin. She could practically feel the side view mirror snap against her arm.

She looked left right left, then jogged across the road.

How could he just switch the tickets like that, without asking her? *Tomorrow?* He wanted to leave *tomorrow?* July wasn't ready. She wasn't prepared for tomorrow. What about Massimo? What about her last meal, her last lasagna, last gelato? She still had to buy presents and take pictures of everything. There wasn't time to leave tomorrow.

This wasn't the way these things happened. This was supposed to be the beginning of a great love story, one that would defy the odds, one that would show everyone that it could work even though everyone said it wouldn't.

Failure was not supposed to happen to her; that happened to other people. Her life was supposed to be different. Being with him was supposed to be a layer of protection against failing, against the stumbling years of early adulthood, but he still seemed to be tripping. Wasn't that supposed to fade with age? Grown-ups were supposed to have it figured out, right?

July's parents weren't stumbling, at least not to her knowledge. They had been married more than half their lives. Her father had been in the same job for over twenty years, and while he complained about work occasionally, he seemed happy enough, even with that brief bit in the car at Christmas last year about travel. Her mom had changed jobs once or twice without much drama, she had had the same core of friends since before July was alive. Their lives seemed perfectly stable and functional. What did they know that Toby didn't? How was July supposed to figure those same things out?

Where was she going? She didn't know.

July stopped in the street and looked around. She saw the red curved roof of the Duomo and headed instinctively towards it.

What was she going to do? Even if she were willing to go home tomorrow, at this point she didn't want to sit next to Toby for those eight or so hours.

She could remember her parents arguing only once, when she was no older than twelve. Ansel had been in the hospital for over a week with pneumonia and her mother's parents were coming to help watch July and Iago. July's father wanted them to stay in a hotel, her mother wanted them to stay at their house. Her parents were in the kitchen, thinking July was outside.

"It would be so much easier to have them around. My father can drive the kids around, my mother can take care of dinner. It'll be such a load off."

"Jill, your mother is a terrible cook—"

"Oh, she is not!"

"We won't have any privacy with them around. We'll have to take care of them, play host and hostess. Your parents are not low maintenance. Your mother rearranges things to her liking and your father steals the crosswords from the newspaper."

"He does not *steal* the crosswords."

"He does them before I can get to them! He knows I do the crossword every morning with my eggs!"

"Gray, our son is in the hospital and all you can think about are your crosswords?"

"He deliberately burns his toast and then scrapes off the black part into the sink and then I'm late for work trying to clean it out!"

"You don't want my parents here because of how my father eats *toast*?"

"That man has no respect for a copper sink!"

"It wouldn't ruin the sink if you just cleaned it out later. You paid through the nose for it because it doesn't stain or scratch."

"Don't make this about the sink. Your parents will only add to our burden, Jill."

"Excuse me? You brought up the sink! God, you are being so selfish! You've never managed to get along with my parents, you've never even *tried* to, you always make yourself scarce when they're around, you just don't *try*! You don't care! You don't care that they're my parents, that I need them here to help me. And now our son's health is at risk and you can't get past your goddamn copper sink to let them help?"

"This isn't me being selfish, it's me being practical! You aren't *practical*, Jill, and you're being completely irrational!"

"I am *not* being *irrational!*" she screamed.

"You're not looking at this objectively …"

"Don't get all holier than thou on me, Gray! This is about our son. We can't do this alone, we need help! I'm hanging by a thread here, Gray, a *thread*. This is my *son* we're talking about!"

"He's my son too, don't you dare forget that, Jill! I suppose you think it's easy going for me, I just make myself scarce, right! Like I don't have feelings, like this isn't a tough time for me too! Well guess what, Jill, I'm hurting, too. I love our son just as much as you do. But having your parents living with us indefinitely is more than I can handle right now!"

"Well forget what *I* need, let's all bow down to your needs! What about me? What about what July and Iago need? Ansel needs someone at the hospital, and they need someone here when they come home from school, someone to cook their dinner, to reassure them. That's why we need my parents!"

It went on like that for a while as July watched, crouched behind the couch, knowing this was something she wasn't supposed to hear. After a very silent dinner and a tense next morning, when her father had pointedly not done the crossword, her parents had worked it out, and her grandparents stayed at their house until Ansel came back from the hospital, when they moved to a hotel.

But they hadn't called each other names like she and Toby had. She couldn't even fight clean, she had to go calling him a prick. *But he called me a bitch first.*

They were like children, but July was much closer to being a child— that gave her more leeway, right? He had no excuse—he had been an adult for much longer. He should have learned, he should be setting the example.

Was that really how it should work in a relationship, one person leading the other? What if he led her in the wrong direction? They should both be navigating, moving in accordance to each other. Twin compasses. Moving in accordance with each other, not following. She thought of John Donne:

Thy firmness makes my circle just,

And makes me end where I begun.

Something she learned in school finally had meaning in real life, but it had different meaning in her life.

I don't want to go back to where I began, thought July as she stopped in front of the Duomo. *I don't want to go back to America, back to school, back to a life of books and papers and no one to care about. I want a twin compass—moving with someone, a life of making spirals, always expanding, circling around where I've been but never to quite the same place. And I want a twin directional compass, where he, someone, is north and I am north to him, where we are moving but always in reference to each other, always pointing back.*

Toby's life seemed to be going in a circle. But after going once around with him, what was the point of going round again?

July closed her eyes and tilted her face to the sun, letting its weak warmth seep inside her. She pointed herself north, opened her eyes, and found that she was looking at the bookstore, Massimo's bookstore, just a block or so away.

Well, how's that for poetry?

Toby still hadn't moved from the toilet. How long had July been gone? An hour, maybe two? It felt like longer. He had forgotten to bring his book in with him, so he sat staring at the tiles and snacks. He must have read the cookie box label a hundred times. Or tried to—it was all in Italian.

Never too late to start learning, I guess.

He had been thinking himself into circles. He didn't like the cycle that his life seemed to be going in, though this one seemed to be much shorter than the first. How was he going to fix this—or should he even bother? Would things just end with July anyway?

I guess that's kind of up to me.

It seemed he had the veto power in this relationship. If he wanted to stay with July, she would stay with him. If he wanted to end it, then it would be over. It didn't seem like *she* wanted to end it, so it seemed that it was pretty much his call, which would be great if he could figure out what the hell he wanted. He was past forty—he was supposed to know this already. He was supposed to have figured it out when he was eighteen and applying for college.

Part of him was unsettled by this power. He didn't want July to depend on him, to live her life following him. It wouldn't take long for her to realize that he didn't know what the hell he was doing.

How did he get himself into this mess? It had all been so simple before this, just two people who liked each other, and suddenly they were all caught up in life, life had caught up with them.

He really just wanted to go home tomorrow. Italy seemed like a curse on him, his memory, his present. Italy was supposed to clear his head, set the world right again, but it was more like a haunted house filled with ghosts and skeletons and vampires sucking his blood. Would that go away when he got home? Would things seem clearer, would he realize that July fit—or didn't—into his life? Sure, it was a bit unfair of him to leave her hanging, but how could she expect him to make a future now, again, when the future he had worked to make before had totally gone to shit.

Looking at the way his life was pointing now, he thought, *Is July really so bad? Maybe the point of your life being smashed to pieces was so that you could meet July and put them back together.*

Oh for Christ's sake, just make up your mind already!

No, that was that. He was going home tomorrow. And July was going to have to come with him.

But how was he going to make her do that? Here he was, barely able to walk the ten feet between the bathroom and the bed, and he was going to force July back here and force her on the plane tomorrow night?

He could hope she came back tonight. She has to, right? Where else is she going to stay?

Massimo, said a heavy hand as it wrenched the bottom of his stomach. *She'll go to Massimo. She doesn't have anyone else. Besides me.*

There were a whole range of things he could do, it was just a matter of how drastic he wanted to get, how much more dramatic he wanted his life to become.

He could always just let her do whatever she wanted, run away like a kid, trying to avoid things she didn't want to deal with. Let her run away, he would still leave tomorrow. Let her deal with how to get back, a real lesson in growing up. How she would pay for a ticket home, where she would stay, how she would get her things back once he had checked out of the hotel. Let her deal with the consequences of running out. But that would be irresponsible of him. Hadn't he assured her parents that she was safe with him?

It's not my fault she's acting immature. Buck up, take life as it comes. Way to take your own advice.

Or he could go the extreme route, involve the police. Tell them July was missing. Tell them where she might be. He would work his way slowly from bathroom to bed, plop himself down with a grunt, pick up the phone and call the *polizia*. Ask for someone who spoke English.

"My girlfriend is missing," he would say. "She went out and hasn't come back and I haven't heard from her. She's got pretty reddish hair, wears a green coat, brown eyes, these great lips that'll knock your socks off. We had dinner the other night with a fellow named Massimo, who took her back to his apartment and tried something on her. I think they might be together. No, I don't know his last name, but he works at the coffee bar at the *Libreria* in Piazza della Repubblica. He's tall with very short hair, handsome of course, perhaps twenty-eight. He lives on the north side of the Arno somewhere, near a *gelateria* run by a guy named Gianni who probably knows where Massimo lives."

Sure he didn't know much—anything, really—about Massimo, where he lived, who he was. But the police would find him, right? And thereby July. And it wouldn't be at all humiliating to have to call the police to find his girlfriend for him, he wouldn't lose the least bit of pride when the police knocked on the hotel door and he had to hobble over, answer the door hunched over to see them standing with July, who would probably be shooting poison darts out her eyes and probably never speak to him again except to call him some perhaps rightly deserved horrible name.

Or he could involve the mafia. But he didn't really know how one would go about finding a *mafioso*.

Perhaps that wouldn't be the way to go about it. If only he could walk with a bit more ease, he could go out and find her himself, maybe even make things right, change his present situation from a bad soap opera to the end of a bad romantic comedy. He could see a doctor to see if he could give him anything—

Toby stopped. The pills. From Fat Woman. He had completely forgotten about them, what with the naps and the fights and the fact that he didn't much like medicine anyway. But this—this was a special circumstance. The pills hadn't made him feel funny yesterday, they had just warmed him, dulled his pain, made moving and being just a bit more bearable. He had only taken two. He could take three now, wait and see how he felt, and then head out in search of July. It didn't matter if his back got worse tomorrow—by tomorrow he would have found July and they would just kill time until their flight, and then he would just have to sit on a plane for a few hours. No heavy lifting tomorrow.

Maybe his back would get a little worse, but he could sacrifice a bit of pain for July, to get her back here, see if they could, or couldn't, talk things out. They couldn't just leave things hanging like *this*, could they? So it was necessary—indeed, required—that he go out and retrieve her, because he doubted that she would come back on her own in time.

Once, Sophia had taken out her suitcase, packed a few stuffed animals, and gotten halfway around the block. She didn't actually want to leave; she just wanted someone to follow her. But Sophia had broken his heart nonetheless. To think that part of him, someone he had started from scratch, would, at least momentarily, hate him enough to leave him, never want to see him again—of course she wasn't gone. He had found her on the corner, standing helplessly with her suitcase sniveling and crying quietly. But it had the potential to turn into one of those horror stories on the cover of *People* magazine.

When he first saw her standing there, he wasn't quite sure how to approach her. Run up to her and smother her with hugs and kisses and pick her up and carry her home? Let her stand there and make her way home herself? Just walk up to her and say, "Sophia," and then stand there until she said something? Was she in trouble, or was all forgiven? Could he really ever forgive her for wanting to leave him?

But when she turned and saw him and he walked over and scooped her up in his arms, he left all his selfish anger on the street corner, along with the suitcase full of stuffed animals, which he had to go back and retrieve after. His anger had run away, but the hurt, all these years later, still had not subsided. Maybe that's why he always kept sugary cereals in the house—to keep his daughters there as well.

He fished the bottle of pills from his pocket, screwed it open, and looked inside. There were at least eight pills, plenty. Maybe even enough to cover him tomorrow. He tapped three pills into his palm and swallowed them dry. They stuck to the insides of him as they inched slowly down his throat, swift as a glacier, smooth as balls of sandpaper.

Now he would wait.

He lay himself down on the bed, staring at the old, browning ceiling, the anachronistic fluorescent light, waiting, waiting to follow, to go out there and find July standing on a street corner, not sure where to go or whether to go back to where she had left.

XXI

July stood outside the bookstore. what if massimo wasn't there? What if he *was* there? What would she say?

No more thinking, she told herself. *Just go.*

She opened the door and headed for the coffee bar. At first she didn't see Massimo, and couldn't decipher whether the twinge in her stomach was due to relief or disappointment. But between the heads of a few customers she saw Massimo's nearly shaved head bent over some coffee concoction. Her writhing stomach twitched so hard she thought it may have smashed into her brain.

She didn't want to make a huge entrance, so she wordlessly took a seat at the bar. It took a few moments for Massimo to look her way.

"*Che cosa desiderate?*" he asked from the corner of his eye.

She thought this would be the perfect time to say something meaningful like they did in movies, something they would say in *Casablanca*, but she couldn't think of anything. Not a single thing.

So she said nothing.

"*Che cosa desiderate?*" he asked again, an irritated edge to his voice.

But then he turned and looked at her. His face stayed in the same expression for a moment, then his eyebrows flicked up and his mouth dropped slightly open.

"July, what are you doing here?" he said, sounding genuinely perplexed. "Is everything okay?"

Her eyes started to burn hot and wet. *Don't cry, don't cry, don't cry.*

"No," she said blinking them back.

"I—I am not off until five o'clock," he said looking at his watch.

"I'm sorry," she pleaded. "I just didn't know where else to go."

"Did he hurt you?" he pressed.

"No," she shook her head. "I mean, not physically."

"What has happened?"

Her brain flashed to formulate what to say, *He slipped and hurt his back and can't move and then we got into a fight about our future and he called me a bitch and then switched our plane tickets to leave tomorrow.*

On split-second review, this sounded pretty minor and fairly stupid. She came all the way here for *that?* She's crying over *that? It's called a relationship, sweetie—deal with it.*

"We got in a huge fight," she said. "He called me a bitch, said I reminded him of his ex-wife. And then he told me that he had changed our tickets home to leave tomorrow night."

Massimo didn't move. He was smiling very faintly but stayed silent for an agonizing length. *What was he thinking?* Perhaps she needed to elaborate on the problems.

"I—it's just—if I go back to the States, I don't have anywhere to go. My dorm's not open, I can't fly home, I can't afford to stay in a hotel, but I can't buy another plane ticket back to the states either ..."

Was she talking too much? Probably.

"And if I left tomorrow I—I wouldn't get to—see you. Or say goodbye," she finished quietly.

Massimo still hadn't moved. He must be thinking, but his face was a placid mask.

"*Questo è un problema,*" he said finally.

"*Si,*" she sighed.

He stayed still and silent a bit longer, as though hiding from a predator.

"Does Toby know where you are?"

"No."

"Where is he?"

"In the room. He hurt his back. He can't walk."

"Mm."

He squinted, as if peering into his brain.

"This problem calls for *puttanesca.*"

"Oh ..." said July, frowning.

He looked at his watch again.

"I must work this afternoon."

"Of course."

"Have you eaten lunch?"

She shook her head no.

"There is a café around the corner, they have wonderful gnocchi. Get a magazine or a book, go have lunch, relax, maybe have a macchiato. Tell them Massimo sent you, they will let you stay, perhaps they will give you a *corretto* as well. I will be there after work, and then we will talk."

"Right," she said. "Okay."

It was just past one—that would be a long lunch.

He gave one firm nod, "*Ciao.*"

"*Ciao,*" she said, then stood up and walked towards the door.

She bought a magazine on her way out—far too expensive since it was in English—and headed around the corner to where Massimo had pointed. The restaurant was very small, and though July had walked this way before, she had never noticed the place. There were no more than ten or so tables; bottles of wine were racked against the back wall and framed old black and white photos peppered the ochre walls. Even though it was midday, it was rather dark inside.

"Massimo told me to come here," she said to a waiter in Italian.

"Massimo?" he repeated, raising an eyebrow.

"Yes, from the bookstore around the corner."

"Ah, Massimo! Of course. Sit down."

She ordered the gnocchi and removed her coat. A few minutes later, the waiter brought her a *corretto.*

"*Grazie,* she smiled, and immediately took a sip. She soon felt herself relax a little bit. There wasn't much a bit of coffee and liquor couldn't fix. She listened to the sounds of the kitchen for a bit, some quiet clacking and the low rumbling of a gas burner. There were only two other people in the restaurant: an old man and a young one, both sipping coffees. The young one read a newspaper, the old one stared out the window.

After a few minutes, the waiter came and sat down across from the young man, who looked up from his newspaper.

"How's life?" asked the waiter in Italian.

"Eh," replied the young man flicking his wrist outward indifferently. "My wife's father died and now her mother, she wants to come live with us."

"*Che merda,*" said the waiter.

"I, of course, would rather claw my eyes out through my nose, but my wife accuses me of being selfish, of not loving her mother."

"Why are women always the source of our problems? My girlfriend, she wants to get married."

"Ah," sighed the young man knowingly.

"She tells me she wants a ring or she's gone. It's not like I want to leave her, but I don't want to get *married*. There are too many beautiful women out there, why limit yourself until you know for sure?"

"*Esattamente!*"

"So I broke up with her."

"*Non, devvaro?*" asked the young man in surprised awe.

"*Naturalmente*," shrugged the waiter.

"But don't you love her?"

"How can I love someone who wants to force me to do something I don't want?"

"Sounds like marriage."

The waiter shrugged, "*Esattamente.*"

"Eh, Bruno!" came a voice from the kitchen.

The waiter stood up and crossed the restaurant. A moment later he emerged from the kitchen with July's plate of gnocchi. He smiled at her, then returned to the table with his friend.

"You see?" he said, thinking he was out of earshot. "Why get married when there are girls like that all around?"

"You know her?"

"No, Massimo sent her."

"Lucky bastard."

July kept her eyes to her plate, and though she knew she shouldn't, she couldn't help but smile a bit.

"He's the one that comes in here with that beautiful blonde woman sometimes, right?"

"That's him. Oh, it makes my day when she comes in. She hasn't been in in a while though."

"What does one man need with all that beauty? Share the love!"

She ate her gnocchi slowly, mushing each one on the roof of her mouth with her tongue. She had plenty of time, there was no sense in rushing. The waiter let her stay when they closed down between lunch and dinner, and after he had cleared tables, he came over with a macchiato.

He nodded and went into the back. July tried to read her magazine, but her brain was tired; she had been thinking and worrying so much that all she could do was be. She stared blankly out the window, sipping her coffee every once in a while.

Time dripped by. It was just half past three and somehow it had been only ten minutes since July had last looked at her watch. Usually she could picture time in her head. She pictured the calendar like a loop, Monday over Tuesday; December next to January; July next to Toby. But now she couldn't see past five o'clock.

Four o'clock?

Toby gasped at his watch. How was it already four o'clock—he had taken those pills around one. He must have fallen asleep. Slowly he sat up. His back didn't hurt, and any remaining discomfort had been suspended somewhere in a cloud in his brain. If he was going to go out, it needed to not hurt. He would have to hurry now. He had lost time. How had he fallen asleep? He hadn't even closed his eyes, he had just been waiting for the pills to take effect.

He lifted himself from the bed one degree at a time, like an angle in a protractor. He scooted himself to the bottom corner of the bed and did a half-roll half-slide off the bed, hoping that muscle memory in his legs would help him stand. For a moment he was caught in an awkward squat hunch crouch, but soon he had straightened himself upright to appear as though he could stand. He felt a bit like Ariel in *The Little Mermaid*, which he had seen many times with his daughters, when she first tries out her new legs and teeters around naked even though all you really see are her legs from the knee down and her shoulders.

Okay Toby, rein it in, here. Perhaps he was a little fuzzy after his nap. His back was still a little creaky, so he decided to take another pill. He had only taken three, and really it's pretty hard to take too much medicine. Once when he was giving Chloe, who was eight at the time and suffering a massive fever, two Tylenol and Jenny was worried he was giving her too much he went and calculated just how much Tylenol it would take for her to reach mild toxicity and by his math, she would need to take at least 12 normal pills just to break into the toxicity range. That shut Jenny up.

So he figured that now taking one or two more of the pills probably wouldn't kill him. It's not like he had a whole supply to continue taking, and it had already been three hours and he needed to make sure he was feeling good—or at least not so shitty—for when he found July.

This time he looked around for something to wash the pills down with. He didn't see any water, just the bottle of wine July had bought the night before. He knew pills and alcohol were a bad combination, but swallowing them dry was just so unpleasant. One small mouthful of wine wasn't going to hurt. So he swallowed the pills and a gulp or so of wine. There, see? He was still alive. Time to find July.

Not that he knew exactly where he was going to find July. He figured the bookstore would be a good place to start. Hopefully Massimo would be working. But he couldn't just ask Massimo if July had been in—Massimo would probably just lie to cover for her. Women always pretended they didn't want to be found when they were angry but it was such a lie. That was just something years of living with a female, and for a time four of them, had taught him. Unless they ask you to leave—that's when they really didn't want to see you. Especially if she has a baseball bat behind the door.

Okay now it was really time to go. He checked his pockets and around the bed but didn't see the key. Well of course July had taken it; she didn't think he'd be up and about, did she? Well, shows what she knows. She was obviously grossly underestimating him. He was still young, still lively. Just because he was old didn't mean he was *old*. Age was just a number—like the number of people you'd slept with. How many had he slept with? He thought back and counted. Certainly not more than twenty—he wasn't *that* easy. No, it must be less. Eight sounded right. Jenny, July, a smattering in the middle, plus that girl in high school, some in college, a couple before Jenny. His precision was lacking just now, but he was sure it must be less than twenty. Or maybe thirty. *Was that a lot?*

Toby! Focus! What was going on? It was only one sip of wine. And maybe five pills. He was fine. This is what he got for never trying painkillers—no tolerance for this sort of thing.

Okay, to the bookstore.

He walked out of the room, though his form of walking was more a ginger, tentative placement of one foot in front of the other than it was in normal circumstances. His modified tender walk took him slowly onto and off of the elevator, past the terse concierge, and out into the chilly air. The light had already turned sunset orange; July said earlier it had been sunny today, and part of him wrenched a bit when he thought how he'd missed it. When he went back to the States it would be gray at home for at least three more months. Why was he wasting his time? Wasting the precious time he had with July, worrying about Jenny when there was nothing more that could be done. They were divorced. It was over. It was time to stop hurting. Time to move on.

Oh July. She loved him. She had put up with so much, even though she didn't need to. She didn't need to be concerned about his divorce, yet she was. She had stayed around. She had said yes to the old man's request for a drink three months ago. He seemed to have lost sight of the reasons he had asked her out, asked her to Italy in the first place.

You silly old man. You're a fool to let her go. Go get her, bring her home with you tomorrow, ask her to stay with you until she wants to move back to school. If the girls meet her, so what? They know Kevin, so they can know July. What was I so afraid of, being replaced by Kevin? They're still my daughters, and they'll love July so maybe she can just replace Jenny. So take that.

Wow, these pills really did make him feel great. Why had Fat Woman only given him two? Five was obviously the magic number. They really put divorce in perspective. This was a good thing. His life wasn't ruined—it was just beginning. *Oh Jenny. Jenny Jenny, you thought you'd won. But you've never met July. Well, you have, but not really. You just think she's a silly little college student, but she's so much more, plus she's graduating in a few months and she loves me, which is more than I can say for you.*

Eventually Toby came to the Duomo. Last time he had been here, with July, he had forgotten to remember how beautiful it was. How perfectly it seemed to fit right in the middle of everything, like a perfect game of Tetris where everything fit just so.

He looked at his watch. Ten to five. Which way was the bookstore? Let's see, they had been at the Santa Croce and went looking for someplace warm, and they came over this way, but not to here.

Away from the river, he decided, and headed in. He saw the store a bit ahead. Yes, that was it. That was where everything had started to go wrong. If they hadn't gone in there in the first place, he wouldn't have hurt his back and he wouldn't be out here hopped up on some mysterious painkiller looking for July, who just may be seeking solace in the arms of another man.

Damn books and the places that sell them. They'll only get you into trouble.

When he was about half a block away, the door opened and Massimo came out. Wait, that was Massimo, right? He wasn't just hallucinating, was he? No that was definitely Massimo. Well this was unexpected good luck. He would just follow him. It would be like a Bond movie. Alder. Toby Alder. Erh. That didn't sound quite as good, even if he did try it with a British accent, which he did.

Massimo turned left—well, Toby's right—outside the bookstore. Toby tried to walk a little faster, but by the time he turned the corner, Massimo was gone.

What the fuck? That little fucker can't have known I was following him; I was only following him for half a block. Unless he saw me. I wish I were invisible.

Toby walked a bit along the street down which Massimo had turned. The next street was too far down for him to have turned, so he must have gone in somewhere. *See? I still have my wits about me. I may be old but I'm not old.*

Toby walked slowly past the store fronts, most of which were closed, and then came to a small restaurant on the left across the street.

He must be in there; everything else was closed, unless he went into the mechanic shop right there. And Massimo doesn't seem like the mechanics type of guy. Too oily and metallic.

Toby had to figure out his plan of action from here. Should he go in now, burst in on them and reclaim July? Or maybe he should wait and see. But if they leave and start walking fast, he may not be able to keep up for long, and he didn't know where Massimo lived. It could be a mile away or more. He would have to take more pills for that, and that may push him past his loopy threshold.

But then Massimo came out of the restaurant. He held the door open and July came out behind him. There she was, she *was* with him, Toby had been right. Though he kind of wished he hadn't been. She was going to someone she hardly knew instead of, because of, him?

Massimo put his hand on the small of her back to steer her left—Toby's right again—out of the restaurant.

Hey, that's my move, thought Toby. *That's my back, that's my place.*

They started walking down the street, a bit too fast for Toby's liking. He shuffled after them, doing a sort of stiff limp and hunch sort of thing, like he was walking against a strong gust of wind. Despite his Frankenstein walk, he felt that the movement was beneficial, loosening and warming his muscles, even though it was difficult to keep pace and occasional twinges of pain reminded him not to get too confident.

You're killing yourself, he thought. *Just wait till the pills wear off.*

Shut up, he thought. *You obviously need more pills.*

Well it has been four hours since you took the first ones, so now it's like you're running on two, not five. Hm. Was another pill overdoing it?

He looked ahead at July and Massimo. They were walking in step, like they were in the army, he was looking at her, she was talking, gesturing with her hands. Probably telling him about what had happened, what a jackass Toby had turned out to be, an invalid jackass, dwelling on his divorce, calling her a bitch, somehow resentful that she could love him so easily and he couldn't give it back.

Yes, that was it wasn't it? The young not only had nimbler, newer bodies, but they had newer, nimbler hearts, so much easier to fall in love. They were unscratched and unworn, like a bright white pair of sneakers, not yet tainted by dirt, still sturdy, no holes or busting seams or split soles or split souls.

For a few years it had seemed as though it was impossible for anyone to love him, or if it was possible, it was a task, a chore, an unpleasant undertaking that could only be accomplished on certain days. He had been wearing his shoes for so long, he had forgotten just how new shoes felt—so pillowy that you couldn't feel the road below anymore; so clean and white he had forgotten that his old pair had once been that white too.

The distance between him and July and Massimo had grown; he would have to pick it up a bit or he could lose them, which was not an option; he couldn't be all the way out here like this and then just lose track of July. She may not come back to the hotel, she may not come back to the States. But if he got to her now, then she would. Right? She wanted to be followed, she had been followed, he found her, time to bring her back and take things from there.

Toby willed his feet to move faster by counting time on them, like a metronome. Pick a fast song, walk in time. What song? Um. *YMCA.* What an irritating song, but it was fast, that would get him moving, if only so that he would get there, wherever there was, and then he could stop singing it. *How did it start? Young man, something, something, something, I say young man, something, something, something.*

Toby picked up his feet, tried to move in time. He might have to sing just a notch under time, but so far it was working.

It's fun to stay at the Y-M-C-A ...

July and Massimo turned a corner.

It's fun to stay at the Y-M-C-A-a ...

Two–three–four ...

He was falling out of time. *Come on, Toby.*

You can have a good time something–something–something ...

He was gaining a bit.

Something hang out with all the boys ...

Massimo stopped at a street corner and grabbed a hold of July's hand as he looked both ways.

Hey! What the fuck? Don't let him do that, July, you love me.

But July did nothing, and didn't look as though she minded very much. Oh come on.

It's fun to stay at the Y-M-C-A ...

Massimo stepped out into the street and July followed him, still holding his hand. They crossed the street, Massimo tilting his head from left to right to left. They went down another street, and Toby followed. Suddenly there was an angry braaaaaeeeeennnp as a car stopped short in front of him.

Blame it on the pills, he thought, and walked on in front of the car and across the rest of the street.

It was mostly dark now, and his middle-aged eyes started blurring July and Massimo in with some of the other pedestrians. Without the light to make July's green coat stand out, he had to pay closer attention.

Young man, something something, something ...

How was it that he couldn't remember the words to a song he had heard well over a million times?

They must be getting close to Massimo's apartment; the neighborhood was quieter, there were fewer shops, more buildings that appeared to be housing. And Toby was getting sleepy, still contemplating that extra pill but trying to hold out.

Massimo, still holding July's hand – or was that an imagination of the dark? –stopped outside a building, and after a moment he was holding a door open for July.

Toby moved closer. So this was where he had his bachelor pad. Well now, what was he going to do? The outside to the building was locked. He looked at the buzzer outside, but he didn't know Massimo's last name. It looked like he was just going to have to press every buzzer until Massimo answered. But he wasn't going to do that just yet. He had to figure out his plan of action here.

Ring the bell. Massimo answers.

"Massimo," he says as gruffly as he can, channeling Dirty Harry. "It's Toby. Let me in."

Hm. He couldn't decide if sounding angry would be effective or just pathetic. It was a fine line.

How about: ring, Massimo answers.

"Hello, Massimo, it's Toby. I'd like to talk."

"I'd like to talk." What the hell kind of nonsense was that?

How about: ring, Massimo answers.

"Trick or treat."

Toby chuckled. Massimo would probably just get confused. Or Toby would come off sounding like a jackass thinking he was funny.

Ring, Massimo answers.

"It's Toby."

Leave it at that; they'd know what he wanted. It wasn't like he'd be ringing the bell just to hear the sound.

So he would wait for the right time. He didn't know when that would be. A few minutes. Until he couldn't take the cold anymore, until his back started to cramp again, for the pill to take effect.

"Oh no," said July as she stepped into Massimo's apartment, "I forgot your trench coat. I should have brought it. I just remembered."

"Don't worry," said Massimo, throwing his jacket across the back of one of the kitchen chairs. "You know how to make *puttanesca*, yes?"

"Uh."

"Is very easy. Is no need to go to the store or find the fancy ingredient. You can chop the tomatoes."

He took some tomatoes from a bowl on the top of the fridge and put them in front of July. He pointed her towards the knives, then went rustling in a cabinet.

"So," he said after he had retrieved a can of olives and a tin of sardines. "You have this fight with Toby, he wants to leave tomorrow. I see this. Now, tell me."

He looked at July. She put down the knife.

"Why did you come to me?" he asked in Italian.

"I—well, I—I guess I just didn't know what else to do."

"You could have called your parents."

"No," she shook her head.

"You could have had a quiet lunch, cooled off, gone back and tried to talk with him."

She looked at the cutting board, at the bleeding tomato turning the wood a darker shade. That probably would have been the mature thing to do.

"But I was just so angry and upset," she began.

"It's not that you are wrong," he said. "It's just that, well. I think you know that I think you are very, ah, attractive."

He spoke slowly, like he was explaining high level physics and he wanted to ensure she grasped his meaning.

"And I think, and maybe I am wrong, but I think that, maybe, you feel the same away about me, perhaps, and you are confused. And these few days you have been confused, yes?"

July was still looking at the tomato seeds swimming in a pool of congealed tomato insides. She felt almost embarrassed that Massimo could talk so plainly about his feelings.

"And so I wonder," he continued in English. "Is this mean you are to leave Toby? That it is over?"

Well. Is that what it meant? In coming to find Massimo, had she ended things with Toby? It suddenly seemed as though her life could split in two right here.

Once again, it came down to Toby. But what if she misinterpreted him? What if she decided that he should be all in or not in at all and left him now only to find out later that he wanted to stay with her? What if he was laying in bed right now wishing that she were there so that he could apologize, give her an answer one way or another?

Now July was facing a question, she who was unable to give a clear answer, just as Toby had been unable to give one to her.

But she loved him. She loved him, she really did, but she didn't want to love him if he didn't return it, or if he didn't want it in the first place. Love always seemed so much easier in the movies. She had seen too many Disney movies, too many classical movies where the characters meet and decide twenty minutes in that they are made for each other. Part of her always believed that the real thing would just happen, and she would know, and that would be that, and she wouldn't have to spend the rest of her life wondering if the next man was The Man.

With Toby, it had seemed to happen. But her screenwriter had forgotten that it was supposed to happen for Toby, too.

But her more imminent problem was Massimo. What was she supposed to say—"I came to you because I thought you could be my back up?" Just thinking that she felt despicable, like a doctor was pressing a tongue depressor just a hair shy of her gag reflex.

"I—don't know," she replied, employing the despised Toby response.

"Hm," said Massimo, turning to the sink and filling a red pot with water. "So you want what to happen now? You will go back to America anyway, no?"

"I guess," said July, even though she was thinking, *If I had an excuse, the right reason, I would never go back at all.*

Toby would be her reason to go back, maybe Massimo could be her reason to stay. But she couldn't tell him that. That was a bit much a bit fast.

Be my reason.

Massimo set the pot of water on the stove and turned on the gas and switched to English.

"There are many stories of the, how you say, skirt chasing?"

July nodded.

"Skirt-chasing Italian men, who love to yell '*Ciao, bella*' and have the short romances with the tourists."

He put a pan on another burner and poured in some olive oil.

"I am not one of them," he said, punctuating that by throwing some garlic and anchovies into the heated pan. "I am different. Perhaps you know this already. If I wanted a brief romance with you, it would have already happened."

Really? she thought, perhaps a bit disappointed. He did seem awfully sure of himself.

He took the tomatoes from her and began cutting them himself.

"Is not that I have never done this, is that ah, well, the last time I did this, she was here for a month, a summer art student."

He chopped rapidly and slid the tomatoes into the pan with the garlic and anchovies and switched to Italian.

"We agreed that we liked each other, but that it could not be for long. We agreed that we liked each other then, that it would only be for then. I thought I could do this."

He stirred and ground in some pepper.

"I thought I could do this, told myself *non chè problema*, I will just not love her. I would enjoy her for the time we had, and when she left, I would be sad, but it would not be serious, and I would be a better person. Is never bad to know more people."

He stood straight and looked past the burbling pots.

"I was wrong," he said plainly. "I was wrong. Two weeks before she was to leave, I found that I was in love with her. I wanted her desperately to stay, not to leave me. I could see she did not want this, so I said nothing. And when she left, I was broken. Perhaps is not *maschio* to say this, but what is more *maschio* than loving a woman, yes? I cannot love someone for this short time. My heart, it does not work like this."

How would her heart work if Toby officially ended it? Would it work at all?

"Ah, *Luglio*," he said, turning to her putting a strand of hair behind her ear.

His hand was warm, soft and rough at the same time. His fingers had traced a permanent line of light in that small area of her face.

He cupped his hand around her ear and drew his face close to hers. Their foreheads and noses touched. For a moment July kept her eyes open and watched as Massimo's face came towards hers, his eyes moving closer together, his nose disappearing into hers. They huddled like that for a moment, their breaths warm between them, their lips so close and so far, touching in imagination. Her body was blank, because all that was in her existed in a line from her forehead to her lips.

They stayed that way for a minute, and then Massimo leaned back and smoothed her hair.

"But you see, now it seems we are both the ones who will leave."

"Huh?" she murmured.

"I have told you, I am ready to leave Italia. I have finished up my classes this month. I will leave Italia now."

"What—when?"

"I think at the beginning of *febbraio*."

"Where?"

"I booked ticket to New York. Astrid, she says she doesn't like New York, but I think it will be a good place to start."

"Oh," said July, falling. "When did you book the ticket?"

"Yesterday. I decided it's time to go, to do what I say I will do."

He was leaving too. Even if she stayed forever, he would be gone. But she had known that—he had told her.

July, don't you see you're being so silly, she thought. *Yes, and I can't help it.*

So now she had to confront reality: she would have to go home tomorrow. There was no avoiding it. She was acting how she did when she was young, when she would be at a friend's house and she would hide when her mother or father came to pick her up and bring her home, thinking that if they couldn't see her, they couldn't bring her home.

What was it she was running away from? Not America, not Toby, not school. No, it was the realization that now, it seemed she had nothing waiting for her there. America hadn't seemed so bad when she had thought and hoped that Toby was there for her too. With Toby, she felt a connection, the starting of a root, of a reason for life, not just drifting or wandering. Like there was a semblance of a home. And wasn't going home the point of traveling? Seeing something new and having a place to return?

"July? Are you okay?"

"Yeah," she replied faintly.

"New York is very close to your school, no?"

"Close enough," she said. "A few hours by bus or train. I go there on the weekend sometimes with my friends if we ditch class on Friday."

"Perhaps our paths will across in New York."

"Sure," said July.

Yeah right. New York was a big place. You don't just come across people you know there. She would probably never see him again.

"Perhaps," he continued. "Perhaps we will have a chance there."

He cocked his head to the side and leaned in and kissed her. She should have expected it, but she hadn't. After being so used to Toby's lips, Massimo's seemed strange, a new city she had not yet mapped in her mind. Where kissing Toby made her body ignite in fire, kissing Massimo sent shivering shocks down her spine.

Massimo pulled away, smoothed her hair again, then turned back to the stove.

"You know, two years ago I would have already moved you to the bedroom," he said, pouring dry pasta into the boiling water. "It's not that I don't want to, is now I can distinguish between thoughts and actions. Is must be this growing up thing they talk about."

July gave a weak half-laugh, but her mind may as well have been boiling with the pasta. Growing up might be the dumbest invention ever. She was torn between wanting to kiss Massimo more, wanting him to pull her into the bedroom anyway, and wanting to be back with Toby like it was before. Part of her was planning a New York weekend; another was banning all forthcoming New York trips.

Whatever happened to Disney romance, where love was unquestioned and everlasting?

It was time, Toby decided.

He had been waiting outside Massimo's apartment, standing in the clinging darkness, and now he was getting cold. He had taken another pill to stave off the aching of his back and also to feel the blanket of warmth envelop his body again. It was cold, after all, and avoiding frostbite was high on a man's list of priorities when he was trying to win back his girl.

So now he stared helplessly at the buzzer list outside the door. What was Massimo's last name? Had he ever known it? There were eight names listed. Time to start buzzing away.

He randomly picked number four, "Mirabella," and pressed the button.

No answer.

He pressed again. That better not be Massimo getting too busy with July to answer the buzzer.

"*Che?*" came a harsh, crackly male voice.

"Massimo?"

"*Che?!*" followed by a lot of Italian that Toby didn't catch.

Not Massimo.

Let's try lucky number seven. He pressed the buzzer.

After a moment, as he was about to press the button again, a woman answered. She sounded old.

"*Si?*" and some more Italian chatter.

That wasn't July, unless she knew it was Toby and was disguising her voice. But Toby didn't think she could do it so convincingly. He didn't answer and let the woman ask who it was a few more times before she gave up.

Which ones had he already tried? That one was number …six? No, seven. Lucky number seven? So what was the first one he had tried? Crap. He tried five. Also no.

He pressed the last one, "Giovaninni".

A man answered. Could be Massimo. Maybe.

"Massimo?" Toby asked.

"Massimo?" the voice said. Then something something *numero due*.

Due? Like the number two?

"*Due?*" Toby repeated, cringing at his own bad Italian. The pills should have made it better, more free flowing, not worse. Maybe he needed more pills.

"*Si, si, numero due!*" shouted the man's voice, and then the speaker crackled as he hung up.

Okay, so what was he going to say? Just his name, right? It's Toby. They would get the idea. No need to explain too much, to seem over eager or anything. Right. Because it wasn't over-eager for you to hop yourself up on pills, trudge across the city with a bum back and follow them back to Massimo's apartment. He needed to be the Sultan of Subtlety. Hm, Sultan of Subtlety. That had a good ring to it. What was that called? Proliferation? Annotation? No, no. Damn, he really should have paid attention in school. He'd have to ask July. She read books and she was still in school, she would know.

He pressed button number two and waited.

Come on, answer.

The silence hung around him like the darkness. He pressed the buzzer again. And again. *Come on. What were they doing that was taking him so long to answer the buzzer?*

Then it clicked on.

"*Si?*"

That was definitely Massimo. *Okay, Toby, play it right.*

"I know what you're up to!" Toby yelled. "Stop trying to steal her away from me, she's *my* girlfriend."

"I believe it is Toby," said Massimo away from his speaker.

Toby heard a faint cry in the back, sounded like July saying, "What?"

There was a pause.

"Toby?" came July's voice.

"July!" said Toby rather loudly, "July, let me in."

"What are you doing here? How did you get out of bed?"

"I'm not so feeble, I'm the Sultan of Subtlety," he replied.

Wait, what? came what was left of his rational thought. *Where did that come from? What are you saying?*

"What?" said July, totally befuddled, "The Sultan of *Subtlety?*"

"What is that?" he asked her.

"What is *what?*"

"The Sultan of Subtelty."

"What is *with* you? Are you drunk?"

"No. What is it, the Sultan of Subtlety?"

"I don't know what you're talking about!"

"The Sultan of Subtlety. It's not annotation … is it assonance?"

Another crackling pause.

"Do you mean *alliteration?*" she sounded thoroughly disgusted.

"Alliteration! That's it! I knew you'd know."

The speaker stayed silent.

Toby waited for her to say something but she didn't. Was she waiting for him? What was he going to say? It seemed fairly clear to him that he was waiting to be let in.

"Well?" he said finally, after waiting for what seemed like hours.

"Well what?"

"*Well*, are you going to let me in yet?"

"Let you *in*?"

"I will let you in," said Massimo.

"Thank you!"

Why did this have to be so complicated? he wondered. *Isn't that what he had been clearly communicating from the start?*

A moment later the building's main door opened and Massimo stood holding it.

"Please," said Massimo, motioning Toby in.

"Trying to leave me to freeze to death?"

Toby walked through the door and into the dingy foyer. There was one apartment on either side of the door and stairs leading to higher floors. Toby automatically headed for the stairs.

"No," said Massimo, pointing to the apartment on the left. "This one."

He pointed to an open door on the first floor.

Toby gave him a defiant look and walked into the apartment. It was a nice place, he'd give Massimo that much. Someone had probably helped him arrange things; the apartment looked cohesive, not like Toby's pre-marriage apartment filled with unmatched castoff furniture from various family members and acquaintances. It smelled good, too. Were they cooking? Oh no. That was the thing to do with July—cook for her. Aside from pancakes, Toby hadn't made anything for her. He was obviously sorely behind. Massimo was a step ahead and twenty years behind.

Massimo came in after him and closed the door. July stood about five feet from Toby, her arms crossed, her face a cocktail of anger, annoyance, curiosity, expectation, hope? Who could tell what a woman's face was really saying? It was like trying to determine the color of water.

Massimo was behind Toby, and July in front, so he couldn't decide which way to face. He was feeling a bit monkey-in-the-middle. Both of them looked at him expectantly. They wanted *him* to talk first? Didn't *they* have some explaining to do?

"Toby," July finally ventured, her voice like marble, "what are you doing here?"

"I should ask you the same question."

"How did you find Massimo's apartment?"

"I followed you."

"So you can get out of bed?"

Toby shrugged and smiled mysteriously.

"I have my ways."

"Are you drunk?"

"I already told you, no."

July went silent and continued to give him the water colored stare.

Massimo moved past Toby and over to the stove.

"We were about to have dinner," he said, leaning over a steaming pot.

"Would you mind leaving us alone for a few minutes?" said Toby.

"The sauce will overcook."

"This is *his* house, Toby."

If Massimo had any manners, he would have voluntarily walked out of the room by now, but, Toby noted, he stayed planted over the stove, stirring, trying to blend in and listen in simultaneously. *Oh, fuck it.*

"We have to talk," July.

"About?"

"Uh—us."

"What about us?"

"I—I don't want to lose you."

"Really," she said skeptically, but it sounded for a second as if there was a crack in her marble. "Well then what *do* you want?"

"Wh—" He had to be very careful about how he phrased this. *Think, Toby, think.* And then he thought of the perfect answer.

"I would like this relationship to continue for as far as it can."

Repeat what a woman says. It's safe and it seems romantic, like you were listening.

"And what exactly made you come to that conclusion, when only hours ago you couldn't regurgitate such a response?"

Uh oh. Her words were getting bigger. ALERT. ALERT.

"Well, I had time to think."

"You had time to think all last night. What brought about this sudden change in perspective?"

"I—you left."

"Yeah."

"And I—realized I didn't want you to leave me."

He was groveling. He *hated* groveling. Wasn't one of the benefits of divorce supposed to be the cessation of groveling?

She frowned, absorbing.

"So what *do* you want?" she finally asked.

Oh no, not that question again.

"I don't know," he answered before he could formulate a better response. As soon as it left his mouth, he knew it was the wrong thing to say.

"Well what *do* you know, Toby? Do you know *anything*?"

"Oh, stop acting like a teenager," he said.

"Well you stop treating me like your second choice!" she yelled. "Stop treating me like I don't matter as much as Jenny does! Like I don't matter at all! This whole trip you're moping over Jenny. If you're not over her, why did you bring me? Why are you *with* me, letting me fall in love with you?"

Over July's shoulder, Toby saw Massimo turn his head towards them, no longer pretending he wasn't listening.

"And then you go and end our trip. I knew I shouldn't have told you I loved you."

"Loved?"

"Oh what, you want me to tell you again just so you can hold it over me? To boost your ego?"

"Wh—? No ..."

The back of Toby's neck prickled.

"What do you *want*, Toby? Why are you here?"

Toby's mind suddenly turned to cotton puffs. Why *was* he here? He should have let her come back on her own instead of chasing after her like a five-year-old on the playground.

"I—I came to bring you back."

"To bring me back *where*?"

Talk about the third degree. This was getting ridiculous.

She continued, "To—the—hotel room? And then what?"

"Why do you always want me to predict the future?" he retorted rather loudly.

Massimo snapped to attention and came to stand next to July.

"Toby, perhaps you should go."

"Oh, fuck you," said Toby. "Stop trying to steal my girlfriend."

"Excuse me, but *she* came to *me*."

For a moment all three of them were silent. And then, like spontaneous combustion, July burst into tears.

Toby and Massimo looked at each other, sending "Oh my God what do we do now?" brainwaves. A crying woman was like chemical titration. But there was no litmus test for her pH and she was highly reactive.

Toby and Massimo stood there as July cried and heaved and gasped. She hunched her shoulders, covered her face, but she didn't leave the room. Toby remembered when Jenny used to cry, how if she wanted him to rot in hell she would lock herself in the bathroom, but other times she wouldn't. He was going to have to titrate. In a split second glance, he saw that Massimo was about ready to do the same thing. *Oh, no, no, no. MINE.* Toby had to get there first. No more Massimo getting in the way. Toby had to get to July first. It was time for him to stop fucking up.

Just as Massimo's arm started a wisp of movement, Toby held out his arms and said, as tenderly and as he could muster, "Oh, July, come here," and moved towards her.

Or rather, he tried. But when he moved his right foot to take a step, his back crumpled like a cardboard box. He put his right hand on his back to brace it and reached his left out to steady himself on the couch, but miscalculated the height of the armrest and wrenched his back to the left.

He let out an awkward, consonant laden guttural noise, which seemed to echo around the small apartment, bouncing off the walls and sticking in everyone's ears. He had left time behind and the room passed vertically by as though on a strip of film. Suddenly his nose was inches from the carpet that was too expensive for a kid Massimo's age and July had hiccupped into a shocked silence and Massimo just stood there like an idiot—an amused idiot—as Toby succumbed to gravity with the grace of a belly flop.

Then he was looking at the feet of a coffee table, and Massimo's and July's feet behind those. There was a moment when everything hung, like moments of silence between movements of a symphony when no one was sure if they should clap. He remembered standing, and now he was on the ground, but the process was a blur of back and arms and spine.

Then time fell on Toby, slammed into him, not like pain, but like impact, as though a giant fist had punched his entire body. Sound seemed to have come slower, he thought, but then he realized that July and Massimo hadn't said anything; their shoes may have been pasted to the floor. How long were they just going to stand there? How long had it been?

It occurred to Toby that, embarrassing as the situation was – and it was nothing more serious than a simple loss of balance – it could work to his advantage. Garner a bit of sympathy, maybe add a taste of wounded hero to the mix. If this became a more serious injury in July's eyes, their departure from Italy, and Massimo's, became obligatory.

He was surprised at the general lack of pain, aside from the throb in his arm, which seemed to have broken his fall.

"Oh my God, Toby, are you okay?" called July.

She was at his side. He could see her knees on the floor in front of him, her hand on his shoulder rolling him carefully from his side to flat on his back and then a hand on his and another on his head, thumb on his forehead.

"Are you okay?" she asked again urgently.

"Yes," he grunted. "If I don't move."

"Oh, God," she said. "Are you sure you're okay? Should we call a doctor or an ambulance or something?"

"No, no, I don't think so."

"What, are you just going to *lie* there?"

"Yeah. I think that's the best thing."

"O—kay," she said.

He wasn't going to move. He wasn't leaving July alone with Massimo anymore. He didn't like the way Massimo had looked so surprised, a bit hurt, when July had mentioned she loved Toby. He was going to plant himself right here and turn himself into Massimo's new rug if he had to.

Only the day before, Toby had imagined that the humiliation of Massimo seeing him like this would set his skin afire and char his pride. But now, he felt aflame with defiance and possessiveness. Starting now, in Massimo's apartment, on his floor, Toby was going to stop fucking up his life. He was going to stop letting things get out of hand, stop giving women reasons to leave him, stop giving them reason to find better, to leave him alone and obsolete, a forgotten gray area. He was going to leave with July, even if he had to pretend to be an invalid, and if she didn't want to, then he would stay here as she stayed with Massimo.

"Do you want a pillow or something?" she asked helplessly.

"Yeah, I guess, for my head. Please," he said.

She rocked to her feet and straightened out.

"Can we have a pillow?" she asked Massimo.

Massimo stood, his arms crossed just as he had been, as though July were still next to him, as though nothing had happened.

He raised his eyebrows.

That's right, Massimo, thought Toby. *I'm not so disposable anymore.*

"Yes, yes," he said slowly after a moment.

But he stayed where he was, as if examining a chessboard before his next move.

"Don't let the sauce burn," he said, and then turned and walked down the hallway. A light came on at the end and spilled across the floor to Toby's right. Toby turned back to July, who was looking at him with a slight frown.

"What were you thinking, coming here?"

"I could ask the same of you," he said evenly.

"But you followed me."

"You left me."

"I didn't *leave* you."

"Yes you did."

She was silent.

"July," he began.

"I'm so confused!" she blurted out.

"Wh—about what?"

"Everything! You don't love me, you want to end our trip a week early, but then you come here drunk or something and chase me down and say that *I* left *you!*"

"July," he said again.

All right Toby, he told himself. *It's time to say the right thing. It's time to stop fucking up already.*

"I know that you're frustrated because I can't tell you where I see us, because I don't know, but that doesn't mean I see us ending. I really care about you. I don't want to go home early because of you—I want to go home early for you, and because of me. Back at home you'll have more freedom—cars and kitchens, no hotel rooms. I'll be in a comfortable place with doctors and television programs that speak my language. Remember those days before we came here, how great that was, just us in the house? It can be like that. And I know you're disappointed to leave early—so am I. But July," he said, trying to stay with her eyes, "I'll bring you back here."

Her eyes frowned out.

"I promise you, I'll bring you back here. And we can go to Rome, or Venice, or anywhere else. But I'll bring you back. I promise."

She looked at him, her face softening slowly.

"I promise," he repeated.

Her eyes flicked to the ground beside her.

"I know you want me to tell you the future, but in any relationship, that's something you'll never know," he said.

Where was this sage sounding knowledge coming from?

"I will bring you back, that's the only future I can tell you."

Her eyes stayed fixed on the ground.

"What is it?" he asked. "What are you thinking?"

Did she realize that he was, perhaps in a way, bribing her? He remembered that time last year that he had to go to the accountant's office before filing his taxes, since the divorce was screwing with his finances, and had to bring Sophia and Chloe along for what turned out to be a two-hour meeting. He told them that if they were good, he would take them out for McDonald's and buy them a toy of their choice. He didn't hear a peep out of them the entire meeting.

Perhaps this promise was a stalling tactic. So what if it was? His intentions weren't devious; he wasn't using her. He just wanted to buy his feelings a bit more time so that he could figure out what they actually were.

"But—" she said.

"What is it?" he asked again.

"You're not going home because of—Jenny?"

"No," he said, trying to sound just convincing enough to sound like he wasn't lying about it.

"I—am I a bitch?"

He sighed. He wished she had forgotten about that. He didn't particularly care to revisit his words. Not that she was innocent, but if he pointed that out to her, well, she might not take that so well.

"You aren't a bitch," he said. "Maybe some of the things you said were bitchy—"

Her face began microscopic changes into indignation. Hurry up and say the last part of that sentence, buddy

"— but then I pretty much sounded like a prick."

The indignation halted and hung a bit on her face, and then she sighed heavily and her face relaxed.

"I guess," she said quietly.

"I'm sorry, July," he said.

The apology was a valuable strategy. Not only did it usually diffuse things, but then, if they were both in the wrong, which was the case, she would pretty much have to say it back. When the apologies became soliloquies instead of dialogues, it was almost always followed by the exit of one of the two players.

This would pave the way for things to be right.

XXII

HE LOOKED SO PATHETIC LYING ON THE FLOOR, AND SHE FELT SO BAD for him. And yet, part of her enjoyed seeing him so helpless. This would give her the chance to take care of him, to show him that he needed her, to give him reason to love her. This was the way she could make it work. She could take care of him, too.

"I'm sorry, too," she said, then smiled at him tenderly.

He reached out and put his hand on top of hers. Lots of long, thin strands of angel hair traveled up her arm and tickled her heart. There it was—how much she loved him. It was still there; the sun had come from behind the clouds.

She lay down on the floor next to him and situated herself in that spot that was hers. Like a bed with foam that molded to fit her body, this spot along Toby, her head beneath where his collarbone met his shoulder, and she could turn into him and run her body along his and rest her hand right in that groove in his chest. She closed her eyes and turned her head into his body, smelling her way inside him, taking his warmth and giving him hers.

It didn't matter that he was splayed on the floor—he would care for her, protect her, look out for her. That's what this meant. It meant, finally, that she would matter.

He promised he would bring her back. It made her feel better, like collateral on their time together. It now seemed more guaranteed, more assured. They would still be together. It didn't really matter when they would come back, as long as they did, and Toby stayed true to his promise. He seemed to mean it; that meant he wanted to stay with her. Maybe he *would* love her after all. Someone's got to love the other first.

"Would you like the pillow?"

She opened her eyes and turned. Massimo stood next to them, a colorful throw pillow in his hand. Her scalp flashed hot as she remembered they had kissed not an hour before. She felt a bit like he had caught them doing something wrong, like she didn't want him to see her with Toby.

Toby crunched his neck up.

"Yeah," he grunted.

Massimo walked a few steps forward and stopped in strange hesitation. Then he tossed the pillow down and it landed next to July. He stood watching as July sat up and tucked the pillow under Toby's head.

July sat back, her knees in front of her and glanced up at Massimo. His face was blank, like he was looking staring off into space, but his eyes seemed to have screwed into her. She expected to see maybe anger or jealousy, but instead he looked at her with cold indifference.

I know how he feels, she suddenly realized, but the thought so unsettled her that she banished it, as though pulling up her collar against the cold.

She remembered what he said the other night—how she didn't look like who she was. It was like some people looked like their names. Her friend Rachel looked like a Rachel, whatever a Rachel looked like. But Massimo—well, on first glance, perhaps he looked like a Massimo. But he didn't seem like one. Is that what she was like as well? What— who—did she look like?

Massimo's eyes ticked to Toby, and July thought she saw his right upper lip curl just a bit, like someone was tugging it up with fishing wire but he was fighting it as best he could.

July turned and looked at Toby, who was looking back at Massimo, his eyebrows slightly raised, smiling faintly, as though he were resisting the pull to smile more broadly.

All they needed was Jenny and there would be a quadrant of awkwardness, the fourth dimension of the social Bermuda Triangle.

Massimo inhaled sharply through his nose and blinked rapidly.

"Well!" said Massimo, looking nowhere and all around.

His word stuck to the ceiling and clung to the air like a thick mist. No one seemed to know what to say. Were they supposed to leave now? Would Toby be able to get up, let alone walk? And was Massimo going to let her try the dinner? Because she was kind of hungry. But she couldn't ask him for food now; she felt too—something. Too of indeterminate feeling. She had the overwhelming desire to be gone. She couldn't stand that look on Massimo's face.

"So," she cleared her throat and turned to Toby. "How do you feel? Are you going to be able to go back to the hotel?"

He raised his eyebrows.

"Well—I mean, I certainly can't walk."

"I can call you a cab," said Massimo.

July felt like she had swallowed icy Jell-O. He wanted them gone.

"I'm going to have to get off this floor first, and as it is, that's not looking good."

"We can help you."

"Well, if you want to *try* ..." said Toby, sounding skeptical.

"No! I know what we will do! No need to call a taxi—I will call Astrid. She has car. She will drive you back to hotel."

July frowned involuntarily.

"Why trouble Astrid?" she asked. "We can just call a taxi."

"No, no, Astrid, she has the bigger car, Toby can lie in the back seat."

July looked at Toby, who wasn't grinning anymore. In fact, he looked a bit worried.

"Well then shouldn't we get me off this floor?"

"I call Astrid first," said Massimo, walking towards the phone, which was by the stove. "She can help to lift you. It will be easier with three people."

"I'm not *that* heavy," said Toby.

"Is safer this way," said Massimo dialing. "Less chance of dropping."

He paused for a moment.

"Astrid!" he said into the phone. And then he began speaking in very rapid Italian and using a lot of words July didn't understand. Was it a dialect? She wondered if he was doing this on purpose, saying something to Astrid that he didn't want July to understand. She caught a few words here and there, but not enough to piece together what he was saying.

She turned back to Toby, who had a hand over his eyes.

"What's wrong?"

"Oh God, I don't want her to *see* me like this," said Toby.

"It doesn't matter," said July. "It's not like she's going to laugh at you or anything."

"I know, but still."

"Why do you care?"

"It's humiliating!"

July was annoyed that Massimo was calling Astrid. July liked Astrid just fine, but she wasn't the sort of woman she wanted to be around in the presence of men. She made other women disappear. Toby was supposed to be caring about July, not fearing how he appeared in front of Astrid.

July wondered if Astrid had any female friends. It seemed to her that few females would want to be friends with someone like her, out of sheer competition. No matter who her friend was, Astrid would always be a caste unto herself, unless maybe her friend was Sophia Loren. And yet, part of July wanted to be just like Astrid. She suspected that many women would want the same, as isolating as it would be.

Maybe her memory was exaggerating. She must be idolizing Astrid—no woman was that perfect.

"Ah!" cried Massimo. "She will be here in thirty minutes."

"Should we eat while we wait?" suggested July, trying to sound as not hungry as she could.

"Ah, the sauce, it is ruined," said Massimo, waving his hand dismissively as he turned off the gas beneath the sauce's burner.

The sauce didn't smell ruined to July. Nothing smelled burned or overcooked or off. In fact, it smelled wonderful. Was he denying her food just to spite her? Well part of her didn't blame him—too much.

They sat around and waited in astounding silence for a few minutes—Massimo at the dining table, looking through a magazine that had been thrown there. July sat on the floor next to Toby, shifting her position occasionally and staring off into space. Toby lay on the floor, looking bored but indifferent to it.

July prayed that someone would say something, but she didn't know what could possibly be said—Hey, Massimo, I know we kissed and everything, and I'm still with Toby, but hey, you know, no hard feelings and let's still be friends? And then maybe if it doesn't work out with Toby things will be different?

This time tomorrow she would be on a plane back to America. All she could conjure when she pictured America now was gray: a sprawling prairie of overwhelming gray—in the skies, in the earth, in the water. Not even any black or white—just a world of shades of gray, where not even contrast could survive. Here it was red and deep yellow and black—and she was willingly going back to gray?

Then what? Assuming things would keep going with Toby, well, then she would still be there, wouldn't she? Not at school, but right near it, watching from the sides, trying to find some real life endeavor to give her life a bit of the color it needed. Because of his daughters, they could never move elsewhere. Unless Jenny moved. Unless Toby *wanted* to move. Maybe not far away? An hour or two away. They wouldn't stay in the same city for the rest of their lives. Would they? Well, they would travel.

That was so far in the future. Who knows what would happen, right?

For a moment, July was disturbed that maybe life after graduation was a little less free and wide open than it had seemed before. But she had Toby. That's what mattered.

The three of them were still silent. How long had it been? She almost wanted Astrid to get there just so that life would resume. This silence was excruciating.

"Massimo's going to New York," she said to the room. Though technically it could only be directed at Toby, she put it out there for Massimo to elaborate on as well.

Instead, Massimo just looked at her and flicked his eyes up and down, acknowledging that she had spoken.

"Nhg," sighed Toby.

The silence fell around them, heavier than it was before if only for the previous presence of sound.

"Right."

She could hear Toby breathing lightly through his nose, Massimo fiddling with his fingernails, drumming them lightly on the table to some indiscernible but definite melody in his head. It could be anything from Ravel's Bolero to some Beyoncé song. She wondered what music he listened to. Probably something she would never expect. Jazz? Opera? Or eighties bands? Or maybe something really obscure, like folk singers from Brazil. Or maybe he didn't listen to music at all.

She found that pondering the answer to this question occupied much more of her time than it should have, because suddenly the door opened and Astrid blew in, keys dangling from her hands, making a grand entrance by existing.

She had her own set of keys? For some reason, the keys made July's stomach flip like a pancake in a skillet. How often did she come here? And for what?

She was dressed simply in gray slacks and a gorgeous white coat that showed not a smudge of life or dirt. Her hair was pulled back into a simple loose bun, a style so devastatingly minimal that July would never be able to copy its effortless precision.

"*Buona notte!*" she sang, closing the door behind her. She twirled to face Toby. "*Mamma mia,*" she cooed softly with just the right amount sensitivity and tenderness without making it seem like he was a total invalid, like a mother cooing to a child who had just thrown up.

"What happened?" she said to Massimo in Italian.

He began speaking in the rapid Italian with that heavy accent again. July watched Astrid's face, trying to read it for translation. Astrid's eyes flitted to July briefly, then back to Massimo. It was like when her parents used to spell out words before she learned how to spell.

"What a shame!" cried Astrid when Massimo had finished speaking.

She turned to Toby.

"How terrible! And on *Natale!*"

Toby tried a horizontal shrug.

"It's not a big deal," he said. "You know, these things happen to all of us."

"But to fall twice! Such bad luck! I have many times hurt my neck just by sleeping! For many days, I cannot move. Is not as bad like this, but is make you realize just how delicate is our bodies."

He did a horizontal shrug again.

"I'm sorry to bother you like this," he said. "Massimo thought that – with your car—"

"No, no!" she said, waving the hand holding the keys so that she tinkled. "Is not trouble!"

"*Come possiamo fare questo?*" asked Massimo.

Astrid sighed and put her hands on her hips.

"*Non so …*" she bit her bottom lip. "*Credo que solo lui ascensore e, se si fa male, egli sarà sopravvivere.*"

Her hands mimed the action of turning something up straight.

"What's that?" asked Toby, looking to July and raising his eyebrows with mild concern.

"We will just to lift you up," chirped Astrid before July could speak. "It will be not a problem!"

"She said if it hurts, you'll survive," said July.

Astrid looked at July, moving only her eyes, not the rest of her head, but she said nothing.

"Well that's reassuring."

"Is not problem," Astrid cooed again. "Perhaps not as good as the *paramedico*, but, you can walk, yes?"

"I—don't know. Once I get up, I guess."

"Now we must just decide how to get you up!"

"Well we can't pull him up," said Massimo in Italian. "We have to lift up and then set him upright."

"*Sì, sì,*" said Astrid. "That will be hard since he'll be heavy."

"Well there are three of us," he said, gesturing to July but not looking at her.

"*Sì, sì,*" twittered Astrid.

Astrid put her hand up to her mouth in thought, the keys jangling quietly.

"Maybe we girls take a leg each and you take the shoulders and then just—vppt!" she said, raising her hand quickly into the air. "It won't be comfortable for him, but there's no other way."

"*Così credo,*" said Massimo. "You understand?" he asked, turning to July.

"*Sì,*" she replied.

"Okay, Toby, what we will do is lift you," sang Astrid as she moved to his feet.

Massimo moved to Toby's head and July moved down to Toby's left leg. She and Astrid positioned themselves so that they had one hand on either side of his knees, and Massimo grabbed just under Toby's shoulders.

July looked up at Massimo. He reminded her of Ansel, who used to spend the whole day pouting silently when their mother made them clean their rooms on a Saturday.

"*Uno, due,*" said Astrid, "*tre!*"

On three, they all lifted. Toby let out an "Oof" as his legs and shoulders rose before his middle and his butt sank, so that his body was curved. Astrid immediately moved to put a supporting hand on his back, and then Massimo pushed so that Toby's body became more and more perpendicular to the ground. Astrid and July bent around, planting Toby's feet on the ground.

"Agh," gurgled Toby, wincing and sinking into Massimo.

Massimo wasn't ready for the weight and stumbled beneath Toby, and the two of them would have fallen over had Astrid not moved in to take some of the weight from Massimo. July stood back and watched as Astrid and Massimo balanced the weight between them like two crutches.

"Okay?" asked Astrid, her left shoulder under Toby's arm and her body turned against his.

Toby, his head only inches from Astrid's, nodded and exhaled sharply.

"Can you walk?"

"In a sec."

"Is like the old man! How do we get this old?" Astrid laughed, and Toby laughed with her.

If I'd said that, it wouldn't have been so funny, thought July. She looked up and caught Massimo's eye—how long had he been looking at her? She felt a bolt of sheepish lightning go through her, and for that flash, she wondered if she had made a mistake.

Then he rotated away, the three of them like a kick line and headed towards the door. July watched as they moved together, feeling as useful as a hairless paintbrush.

"The door?" said Massimo.

July moved quickly for the door, tore it open, and stood aside as the three of them inched slowly out the door, turning their backs to July and sliding out single file. Massimo first, then Toby hanging between them, and then Astrid, swirled in vanilla and gold and spring. July inhaled through her nose as many times as she could before Astrid was out of olfactory range. She would have to start wearing perfume.

"The door!" shouted Massimo from the hallway.

July jerked to attention and ran to the door leading outside. She pulled it in and held it open as they filed past her again, like they were doing the *Hora* at a Jewish wedding.

Toby's head was turned towards Astrid, his nose inches from her neck. He must be just as intoxicated by her perfume.

Before she passed through the door, Astrid caught July's eye. July couldn't name the look in her eyes. It could have been pity, caution, disgust, contempt, or all of them. Was there really a difference? But July suddenly felt very ashamed of being so young, as if it were a handicap.

Astrid's car sat parked about ten feet down the street. It was a standard four-door sedan, not, as Massimo had claimed, a larger car. Toby would have to either half-recline in the front seat or lie on the back seat with his knees pulled in. July didn't know which would be more uncomfortable.

"The door!" yelled Massimo as he arrived at the car door.

July rushed over to the car.

"Back seat or front seat?" she asked.

"Back seat?" said Massimo.

"*Sì,*" said Astrid.

"But we won't have Massimo to help us get him out," said July. "Won't it be easier to help him out from the front seat?"

Astrid and Massimo looked at each other over Toby, and then Astrid shifted her eyes to Toby.

"What you think?"

"I can lie down in the back seat."

"I think back seat too," said Astrid. "Open the back door."

So July did as Astrid said, opening the door and stepping out of the way.

Massimo ran around to the other side of the car, crawled across the back seat, and guided Toby into position as though in a mosh pit, carrying him overhead. Toby grunted and huffed a fair amount, and Astrid gave Massimo instructions. When Toby was successfully packed into the back seat, Astrid ducked out of the car first, heading intently for the front seat and starting the car to warm it up for Toby. Massimo pulled out of the car as Astrid started it, shut the other back door, and looked intense.

Then the passenger's side window rolled down.

"Go and grab your things," Astrid called in Italian.

Obediently, July turned around to go back inside, but the door back into the building was locked.

"Massimo!" she called.

He looked up at her.

"It's locked."

"Ah, *si*," he said indifferently.

He stuck his hands in his pockets, bent down to the driver's window and, after a few moments, popped back up and walked calmly, lazily, over to July. He pulled the keys out of his pocket, unlocked the door, opened it, and went in first, pushing the door as he walked through so that it would stay open just long enough for July to push it back open as she came through.

She followed him into the apartment, the door to which was still ajar.

"Don't forget any of your things," he said, keeping his back to her and walking over towards the stove.

"Why are you acting so strange?" said July, hardly believing she had spoken the words she was thinking.

"Strange?" he asked with feigned innocence.

"You just said you didn't want anything temporary."

"Nothing is temporary. Is only each person's idea of forever."

She frowned, "What?"

"Forever is temporary."

"You almost sound like Toby."

"But temporary is forever. He does not understand this."

"What do you know about Toby?" she snapped. "What was all this philosophical dreck? Talking and saying nothing."

Massimo shrugged. "He is not so mysterious a person. Is a thing you see with time."

"You're almost as young as I am!" she said, a bit louder than was necessary.

"Is not about age," he said simply, then turned to the stove and turned the heat back on under the sauce.

"Stop being so condescending!" she yelled louder.

"Is not your age. Is his."

A car horn honked outside.

"Make sure you have everything," said Massimo. "Don't forget his coat."

July picked up her purse from the couch, and her coat and Toby's coat. She walked to the doorway then turned around.

"Bye, Massimo," she said, her arms crossed in front of her, the two bulky coats dangling down like armor. "Good luck in New York."

"*Ciao, bella Luglio,*" he said just loudly enough to float to her ears.

Outside, she climbed into the front seat of Astrid's car. Astrid wordlessly put the car in gear and drove away. That, thought July with equal parts sadness and relief, would probably be the last time she saw Massimo. At least for a while. Or maybe forever.

But forever was temporary.

XXIII

TOBY WATCHED THE SECOND-FLOOR WINDOWS OF FLORENCE SLIDE BY. There was the occasional light, or maybe the white fluorescent sign of a trattoria or a bar, but he saw only the shades of dark brown that hung over everything.

In terms of dramatic, humiliating falls, this one had gone quite well. Not only had he successfully intervened in the whole Massimo-July ... *whatever*, he also got July back on his side and got to put most of his body weight on Astrid. Though in an ideal world he would have liked to change the circumstances under which all these came about, particularly the latter, since it was an ideal world, he was certainly in no position to complain.

"You are okay, Toby?" came Astrid's voice from the front.

He could imagine her batwing eyes peering at him in the rear-view mirror.

"Just fine, thanks."

July looked back at him from the passenger's seat and gave him a reassuring smile. He smiled back. That's what he liked to see.

The car swerved around street corners and roundabouts, but Astrid seemed to be driving quite conservatively, which Toby appreciated since the last thing he needed was to prove Newton's Law and go flying from the back seat to the floor.

His thoughts turned to all the good things about home—his kitchen, his television, his bed, all that familiarity, the familiarity that had once seemed strange due to the absence of his family. But now it was his, it was what he lived, and he wanted to be back. July could cook something for him, maybe even bake another pie or cookies, she liked that. Then, when the girls came they would have cookies. And maybe they would see July again, under less antagonistic circumstances.

Hm. Maybe. She seemed so separate from them, a totally different life, different world. He imagined trying to introduce her to his friends or hell even trying to *tell* his friends about her existence. There would be a lot of slightly-too-long pauses, raised eyebrows, fake smiles and whispers when he was out of earshot. What would she talk about with them? Well hell, what did *he* talk about with her? Daily stuff. Maybe food. What did he talk about with Jenny? Before the girls? He couldn't remember that much either. He had never really been one to stay up late into the night talking, debating the finer points of philosophy or politics or ethics or things like that. What was the point?

But what did he talk about with his friends? Pretty much all of them were other couples, and then they'd talk about kids and school and maybe if they'd had a lot of wine and the kids weren't around they'd talk about sex or what they would do if they didn't have kids and what they'd use all that extra time and money for. He hadn't seen many friends since the divorce, since before the divorce.

When was the last time I went out with friends? Well let's see, I started seeing July in late September—I haven't seen anyone since then.

Oh lord, really?

What about before that?

Okay, well there was ... summer vacation. He had gone to a few pool parties with the girls and seen some parents then, and they had all tactfully tried to avoid the subject of his divorce and Jenny's name. But they weren't really friends per se ...

Okay, so friends. Real friends.

There was the Super Bowl party at Matt's house. That was definitely a friends situation, so February at the worst. Matt's wife had been the only woman there and let's face it, she didn't really count since she was one of those kind of thick women with a stomach that reached as far out as her boobs and that fry died hair and a face beyond makeup and, more importantly she was kind of a bitch and they had all wondered just what this woman had up her sleeve. But that afternoon they had had beer and nachos and all the things you're supposed to have at a Super Bowl party and that had been a good time. Few of them watched the actual game and spent most of the time complaining about their wives.

"Man, Toby, I can't believe you're actually getting out," said David.

"Just watch she doesn't take half of everything you got," added Jack.

Toby raised his eyebrows and sighed, "My lawyer's going out of his way to show how much Jenny's made from the ballet company, especially with lessons and stuff. Plus, she's actually been remarkably civil about it. I mean, compared to some of the stories I've heard."

"My brother got a divorce and his ex-wife not only got custody of the kids so he can only see them every other weekend, she moved to a city six hours away, took half his money and takes half his monthly salary as alimony," said Matt.

"That is so fucked up," said David. "He's just as much their parent as she is."

"Is Jenny trying to do that to you?" asked Jack.

"Not that I know of."

"Just sign the papers and go find yourself some twenty-five year old, have a good time, and forget about Jenny," said Jack.

"If it were that easy, I'd walk out the door right now," said Matt, who started laughing.

The rest of them laughed just as hard, even Matt's wife. But Toby was pretty sure each of them wondered whether they could actually attract twenty-five-year-old women anymore.

What would those guys think of July? He couldn't keep her a secret forever, but any one of those guys could be her father.

Well, so could I, but that's different. July and I just work. Usually. But they'd look at her like guys looked at a Victoria's Secret catalogue, treat her like the hot babysitter. They'd ask her placating questions—what's your major? Make jokes about if she was old enough to drink with them. They were good guys, but could they ever be around her without tagging her as Toby's twenty-something? What if they tried to go out with a couple? Say they went out with Jack and his wife, Lynn. She was a nice woman, a great mom, and she and Jack were pretty happy as far as Toby knew.

They'd be sitting at a table with a white tablecloth and there would be introductions and handshakes and Toby and July would sit across from Jack and Lynn and Toby and Jack would probably make some small talk at first, probably about kids. July would sit quietly by, her elbows on the armrests of the chair clasping her hands in front of her, smiling but out of context.

Then the conversation would reach its first little lull. Lynn would turn to July.

"So, July ..." she would start, trying to be inclusive but wondering just what to ask. "Toby tells us you're still studying. What's your major?"

"International Relations and Italian," July would say.

"Oh," Lynn would say with a trill of socially required interest. "So, what, exactly does an International Relations major study?"

"Oh ... history, economics, government, politics, sociology. It's pretty much the major for people who can't pick one of those." July would say exactly that, just like she said on her first date with Toby.

Then the conversation would probably turn reminiscent about their college years, how long ago that was and wouldn't it be great to be in college again, and July would sit quietly by, her wrists clasped in her lap, smiling and still out of context.

They might ask her where she was from, if she had siblings, what do her parents do?

They would mention Andrew.

"Who's Andrew?" July might ask.

"Oh! Um, our son," Lynn would answer, not used to having to recount their family roster around Toby. "He's our youngest. Jaime is our oldest, Kelly is the middle child."

"How old are they?"

"Andrew is eleven, Kelly is thirteen, and Jaime is fifteen."

Everyone would silently calculate that July could not be the mother of even their youngest.

After her second glass of wine, Lynn might mention Jenny accidentally, or recall something that she and Jack had done with Toby and Jenny. And then she'd get that "oops" look on her face, and Jack would put a hand on her forearm to remind her about the divorce, and they would look at July and Toby sheepishly.

They would bid each other goodbye in the parking lot, pairing off and exchanging handshakes and nice-to-meet-yous. On the car ride home and the rest of the night and probably a fair portion of the next day, Jack and Lynn would be hissing about how *young* she was, she could be *our* child, would you ever date a twenty-two-year-old if *we* got divorced? To which there was no right answer, not even an answer that wasn't wrong.

Soon David and Matt and their wives and all their friends and their mutual friends would all hear about the twenty-two-year-old that Toby was dating and whenever Toby got invitations to see his friends and their wives or girlfriends, July would be thrown in as a curiosity or an afterthought. He would have to marry her before they even started to take her seriously. And, let's face it, probably not even then.

Of course there was a chance that July would click with people. Maybe someone would have a May barbeque in the early summer weather, and July would make an apple pie or cookies or something to bring along. And maybe they just wouldn't mention how old she was, decide to play a game together and let them guess, wonder amongst themselves. Her pie or cookies or something would be a big hit, other wives might ask for the recipe, and maybe they would all see past her youth like Toby did. But probably not. If she were anything else to him, they would love her. But as his girlfriend—she was the loathed, dreaded younger woman.

This was almost as complicated as the divorce. When did everything get so hard?

"Here we are," sang Astrid as the car stopped. She turned her head back to look at Toby. "Now how will we get you out of this?"

"I was just wondering the same thing," he replied.

"We need a big strong man like Massimo."

"What about the concierge?" said Toby, looking over to July.

She rolled her eyes, "I'm sure he'd love that, given his service oriented nature."

"Well I'm the only other big strong man here, so ..."

"Tomorrow'll be his second Christmas since we're checking out a week early," she said, getting out of the car. She forcefully swung the car door closed behind her.

Astrid craned her neck back around to Toby again.

"You are okay?"

"About as well as can be expected."

"*Si* ..." she sighed, as though there were more she wanted to say.

Toby didn't want to know. He had enough to worry about.

A moment later, the back door opened. Toby lifted his chin to see the surly concierge stooped over, peering back at Toby.

"I don't think I can help."

Astrid opened her door and got out.

"*Per favore, signore,*" she cooed, then said something else in her rolling Italian, like Bingo tiles in a rotating basket.

The concierge stooped down and looked at Toby then stood up again.

"*Signora,*" and a whole bunch of stuff he didn't understand.

Astrid countered with more sounds.

She was a beautiful woman and a lawyer. It was pretty apparent who would win here. Finally it seemed that the concierge agreed. Astrid opened the door by Toby's head.

"He will help us get you out," she said, "and to the elevator."

"Great."

First Toby scrunched his way along the back seat, feet to butt, push. Feet to butt, push. The concierge came around and grabbed Toby's shoulders as Toby continued to scrunch his way along the back seat.

I feel like I'm being born again, Toby thought, *the backseat birth canal.* He promptly tried to push the thought from his head. Perhaps he was taking this production a bit too far.

As more of his body came over the end of the seat and out the door, Astrid grabbed his back and—Hello! — his ass. Not bad. July came and got his legs and all three of them grunted Toby into bipedal perpendicularity. He leaned on the concierge and Astrid, but Astrid was better looking and smelled fantastic, so he leaned a bit more on her and turned his head in her direction.

Butterscotch. Was that what she smelled like? Butterscotch that was alive underneath, like an instinct. The kind of scent that filled his whole head, obscured his vision, crowding all his senses into his nose. The whole deception was almost worth it just for her smell.

July went inside first to get the elevator and Toby moved slowly in, his feet walking but it was like he was on the moon, Astrid and the concierge taking all his gravity.

They shuffled through the lobby, past the reception desk, maneuvering around the dark wooden table and over to the closet elevator. Astrid and Toby moved into the elevator and then the concierge ducked out from under Toby's arm.

"Okay," he said, stepping back.

July moved to enter the elevator.

"Wait!" started Astrid. "Will you please go close and lock the car?"

She tossed the keys to July, "We will see you upstairs."

"Oh. Um, sure," said July, frowning a bit, as the door closed.

And then it was just Toby and Astrid in the elevator. It whirred and squeaked upward.

She sure had gotten rid of July fast. What was she going to do—profess her love? What would he do? What would he say? Could he really ditch July after what had just happened? Women.

"What do you really want from a girl like that?" said Astrid suddenly, shaking Toby from the butterscotch forest.

"I don't *want* anything from her."

"No? She knows nothing. She is baby."

"She's not a baby. She's a smart woman."

"Then what is she doing with you? If she is so smart, she should see you will hurt her."

He had not expected that.

"Excuse me?"

Astrid shook her head and sighed, clicking her tongue in her mouth.

"Where do you get off telling me what I'm going to do? Do you think you're a psychic or something? I care about her."

"I see men. I *see* men my whole life. I can tell."

"You can tell *what?*" he said, with all the scorn he could summon.

She took a deliberate breath and looked right at him.

"Is men like the beautiful girl, and then she loves him, but he doesn't love her, but he no break up with her. And she doesn't want to see he no love her."

"Wh—why would I break up with her? She's a great gal."

"Is not want. Is will. Is should."

"And why *should* I break up with her?" he scoffed, trying to ignore his nagging genuine curiosity.

"For to be free to live."

Who did she think she was, judging Toby's relationship with July like that? She had probably fallen in love with an older man herself when she was younger, and he had broken her heart, and so now she was super sensitive. Well, not all men are the same.

The elevator stopped and the door opened. July was standing about five feet away, straddling the hallway and the elevator waiting area. She hurried over and tucked herself under Toby's free arm. He had almost forgotten to be hurt.

As they exited the elevator, the door started closing on them and July hastily tried to push it back in with her hips.

Like running a four-legged race, thought Toby.

They slid down the hall and, finally, back into the hotel room. July and Astrid helped Toby gingerly down onto the bed and swung his legs around so he lay properly.

"Hahhh," Astrid exhaled with accomplishment and relief. "Is okay?"

"Yes. Thank you, Astrid. *Grazie mille,*" he garbled in bad Italian.

"*Prego prego,*" she waved away. "Is no problem. You have my keys?" she turned to July.

"Oh! Yeah." July fished them out of her pocket and tossed them to Astrid.

"Okay! Then I go."

Astrid came over and gave Toby a kiss on each cheek, then did the same to July.

"*Ciao!*" she called, waving the hand holding her keys so she jingled like a bag of coins.

The last thing he saw of her was her shadow of butterscotch and bronze trailing behind her.

For to be free to live.

What the *hell* was that supposed to mean?

The next day, despite Toby's obvious handicap, the concierge insisted that they still check out of their room by noon.

"Is policy," he shrugged, and refused to listen further.

Toby generously gave July some money and told her to go splurge on a final Italian lunch before they went to the airport to sit around until their flight left at seven that night.

Though Toby had intended for her to go someplace nice and get antipasto, *primi, secondo,* and dessert and whatever else she wanted, July wasn't in the mood. So she crossed the Arno and wandered for awhile, trying to notice everything—the green shutters, the pink and ochre buildings that radiated warmth even in its absence, the cobblestone grids, the darkness in the narrow blocks, how it felt like the buildings were propping themselves on her shoulders against the brown hills flooding the buildings—to hold it in her memory.

You'll be back, she thought to herself. *You'll be back.*

But she felt as though she would never see it again, so she tried to will her eyes as big as they could go.

Somewhere along the way she came upon a small neighborhood pizzeria tucked a block or so behind the Arno, with paper menus and cannoli in a display case. There was a patio but the tables had been tucked inside against the cold. She slid through the spaces between tables, her thighs squeezed between the edges. She sat with her back against the wall and looked at the table, where the paper menu was displayed beneath glass.

She could smell the pizza dough, the yeast and heat and grain permeating from the kitchen. A pizza it would be. After a bit of hesitation, she ordered the *marinara,* a simple pizza, if one could call it that, of dough, a thin layer of red tomato sauce, garlic, and olive oil. She ate it much faster than she should have eaten her last meal, but it seemed too perfect to stay out in the cold winter. The dough was delicate and thin, crisp but soft and so—bready. The olive oil slid off the edges of the dough and slathered her fingertips, turned her paper napkin sheer as tulle. And the slices of garlic, so thin they were practically translucent, tasted a foot thick.

She would come back here, she decided. When she and Toby came back, they would come here, and she would order three of these and eat them all. And then she would try the other kinds, too.

She could try to recreate this pizza. And a *puttanesca.* She had the time—she could make lasagna. Maybe she could do some reading, and lucid dreaming if she remembered.

After she paid she decided to keep walking with the general aim of finding gelato. She was about to put the change from the pizza in her pocket when she realized that she was holding more than eighty Euro in her hand. Even if she bought all the gelato her stomach could hold, which didn't sound like a bad plan, she would still have sixty or seventy Euro left. It seemed silly to change it back to US dollars and not use it. She could buy something. Would Toby mind? Would he ask for change, or ask how much the meal cost?

She bought a gelato and pondered what she would buy, if she bought anything. She didn't have room in her suitcase for anything big. Maybe something leather—the leather was good here. Or paper. She didn't have enough money for any of the pretty jewelry or any of the Italian designer clothes in all the display cases. She would buy gelato if she could take it back on the plane with her.

Standing on the street corner licking her gelato, she noticed a small store selling edible goods. It was, she decided, a sign. So she finished her gelato and went inside. It was a bit dark and musty, but it smelled fantastic, a fusion of everything. Beneath a curved glass case there were tubs of assorted cheeses, olives, and meats, and on the wall opposite there were baskets of different kinds of bread dusted in flour dandruff.

She looked at the things in jars: peppers, olives, capers, bottles of wine and *limocello*, balsamic vinegar and olive oil.

"The *balsamico*," July, she could hear her father saying. "Get the *balsamico di Modena*."

But something else had caught July's eye—a clear bottle of deep, vibrantly green olive oil. She had seen this in Massimo's kitchen. She picked it up and tried to read the label.

"*Castello di Poppiano Laudemio*," called a man behind the counter in Italian. "You know it?"

July turned around.

"You must," he said. "It is the olive oil of olive oils. Those who know olive oil use this one the most."

Of course Massimo would know.

"I don't know much about olive oils," she replied.

"It's made just south of Florence. It's made from the *Frantoio*, *Pendolino* and *Moraiolo* olives. Only harvested when they're perfectly ripe, in November."

That seemed like an important fact.

"What kind of a taste does it have?" she asked.

The man came around the counter, excited into discussion.

"It's very fruity, very strong olive taste with a hint of fresh cut grass—"

Did he say grass? wondered July. *Or is it my Italian?*

"—a bit of almond, a twist of artichoke with a peppery finish to round it all off. It's very Tuscan. It goes wonderfully with a *Bistecca alla*

Fiorentina, Ribollita ... " he trailed off. "Or one could drink it straight from the bottle."

July looked at the square bottle and its simple white label. For this, she would consider abandoning a pair of shoes to make room in her suitcase. The oil could be drizzled on her pizza, on vegetables. Hell, if it was as good as this guy said, she would drizzle it on ice cream, or gelato if she could find it, and maybe even drink it from the bottle, like she suspected he had done at least once himself.

July looked for the price tag on the shelf.

"Thirty-five Euro," said the man. "A small price for perfection."

Thirty-five Euro? That was an expensive bottle of olive oil, considering it couldn't be more than two cups. But she had enough money—of Toby's money. He would understand the irresistible nature of olive oil, and know that it was the best souvenir of their time here that his money could possibly buy. She should buy a second one for her dad. He would like that. She cradled the bottle a bit more tenderly. Every time she used it she would think of Massi—Toby. She would think of *Toby*. He was the one who bought it.

She bought two bottles, along with two sandwiches made from the prosciutto and cheese under the glass and some bread from the baskets. On the way back to the hotel, she stopped for gelato again and ambled across the bridge, relieved at the absence of thought or worry in her mind. At least for now, her brain had gone on hiatus, silenced between layers of pizza and gelato.

When she turned the corner back to the hotel, she saw a man with a shaved head about twenty feet ahead of her. Her heart shot up her throat—Massimo. Massimo had come looking for her, trying to find her before she left. What did he want? What would he say? What would *she* say? Her heart was beating so hard she could feel it pulse through her teeth.

The man turned into a café and in a split second she saw his profile. It was enough time for her to see that it was not Massimo. Her heart slumped halfway down her throat and fluttered like a hummingbird. False alarm, but she was baffled to find that her hands were shaking.

She had to stop for a few moments, regain her breath, regain control of her hands and legs. Of course it wasn't Massimo—he was probably at work right now.

Soon she started walking again, a bit slower than she had before. She was hungry again. That rise in blood pressure must have sped up her stomach. So she turned into the same café as "not Massimo" which she realized was the café she had come to in a blinding hunger her first day here.

How long ago it seemed, and like yesterday. She had been here forever and no time at all, and now she would be gone. A chill hovered above her shoulders.

This time she ordered a *panino* with roasted eggplant and mozzarella, olive oil squeezing from the supersaturated eggplant. After finishing the sandwich, she felt as though she was the one supersaturated with oil.

Reluctantly, she wandered or rather, waddled back in the direction of the hotel, past the anonymous buildings that had originally disoriented her so but now seemed familiar, like she had seen them every day for years and was meant to see them every day for years to come.

Places this beautiful should not be limited to a few jet-lagged days of vacation, she thought. She could see why Toby always came back here. There were so many other places to see, certainly, but this city just seemed made for living as a human. It had been only slightly more than a week, but she felt that she had already put the oppressive blandness of America in a box labeled past life.

July wandered into the hotel, past the front desk where the concierge seemed to deliberately avoid eye contact, and into the sitting room, with its large window and fancy looking chairs. Toby was sitting in one by the window, his arm propped onto the arm of the chair, his head in his hand, sleeping when he was supposed to be watching the luggage that surrounded him like a Lego fortress.

She went to her suitcase to put away the olive oil and saw a corner of Massimo's coat peeking out from under a blouse. *Oh God! I still have Massimo's coat. Shit.*

Toby was sound asleep. She quickly pulled the coat out of her suitcase and took it to the farthest corner of the room leaving it casually draped over the back of a chair. *Someone is going to inherit a very fine coat.*

After putting the bottles of olive oil in the suitcase she slipped into a chair across from Toby. She pictured *Whistler's Mother* and smiled. The rustling of the bag with the sandwiches must have stirred him, because a moment later his head sprang up like a robot rebooting.

"Hey," he inhaled groggily. "How was lunch?"

"Great," she said. "Here, I got you a sandwich."

She reached into the bag and handed him the wrapped sandwich.

"Thanks," he said, then unwrapped it and took a large bite.

"Good," he said, chewing and raising his eyebrows.

She watched him eat his sandwich in large, bread tearing bites, a few crumbs spilling from the sandwich and raining into the white wrapping paper. She wondered if his taste buds had had time to notice the delicate tissue prosciutto or the mellow sourness of the mozzarella. At least he could tell it was good.

She heard a clacking suitcase roll along the floor and instinctively looked to her right, where she saw a man and a woman squeeze into the elevator with their suitcases. She wondered if they were moving into what had been her and Toby's room. She wondered what had happened in the elevator with Astrid last night, when she had assigned July to locking the car, which July discovered was already locked. She wondered idly what had become of the Rothmans, but decided she didn't much care.

The look on Toby's face when the elevator door opened had been—confusing. He looked a bit irate, a bit pensive, and a lot confused. Astrid, of course, acted like nothing happened—she was unflappable. But Toby had remained quiet the rest of the night, and she was pretty sure he didn't fall asleep until well after she did.

Had Astrid told him what had happened between her and Massimo? But how would she know?

Of course, she realized. *He must have told her. She has the keys to his apartment; he probably tells her everything.* Shit. And now Astrid had told Toby. What about sisterhood? Didn't she know how to keep her trap shut? Women were such gossips. Apparently Massimo was no better, kissing and telling. He had probably told her all about their kiss the evening before—or maybe that's what he had told her last night when they started in their rapid, heavily accented Italian dialect. Maybe *that's* what Astrid had told Toby in the elevator.

Oh my God, thought July. *What if she told him everything?*

She looked at Toby, who seemed pretty focused on the sandwich. If Astrid had told him all that, wouldn't he have reacted last night? He had gotten mad at her when he only suspected something was off, so wouldn't he go ballistic when he *knew* something had happened, or was he just biding his time?

Maybe Astrid hadn't said anything. Maybe she didn't *know* anything. But what could have caused Toby to look like that, like Astrid was the ghost of imminence?

She looked at Toby to see if his face was hiding something, but he was always so preoccupied with all that Jenny shit that his face may as well have been in Russian.

"There are just some things that go beyond language," her father had said.

She had called him the night before, after waking at one o'clock, sitting in the dark as Toby snored lightly on the other side of the bed.

"I'm coming back tomorrow," she said like marbles in her throat. "Toby hurt his back and can't walk. So we're going back and I'm going to stay with him and take care of him."

Her father inhaled, like he was about to say something.

"Don't say it," said July. "Don't say I told you so."

"I—I wasn't. Who could have predicted he would hurt himself? It's a shame, though. You're missing out on a whole week of eating."

"Yeah," she said emptily.

"Is something wrong?"

Should she tell him? What would he tell her mom? They would shake their heads and click their tongues. They didn't understand.

"No, it's just ..." she twirled the phone cord. "It's just, well, Jenny is getting married and Toby's a bit ... preoccupied."

"Who's Jenny?"

"The ex-wife."

"Ah," said her father. "Well. That's rather fast, isn't it?"

"Yeah, he's been acting really weird about it."

"Well I can imagine that it's really weird for him."

"Yeah."

"You know, July, if you're going to be—involved with this guy ... you're going to be involved with Janie."

"Jenny."

"You don't just get the person. You get all their people: parents, siblings, friends. In this case, ex-wives and children. You're going to have to be ready to handle that."

"Dad—how did you know that Mom was right for you?"

She could practically see her father jerking his head back in shock. He didn't talk about things like this. But she needed an outside opinion.

"Wh—uh ..." he stammered, "I mean, I just knew."

"But *how?*"

"Well, things just seemed—right."

"But *how,* Dad?"

"Well, I mean, it was a—gradual ... mutual ... comfort. We wanted the same things out of life—a home, a family, and the timing was right ..."

"But—what about your travel?"

"Well, that's what being young is for. We make more compromises the older we get."

"But—"

"July. There are just some things that go beyond the confines of language."

She sighed. He was obviously going to be of no help.

"Everything's—okay—right?" he ventured.

"I dunno," she mumbled.

"He's not—pressuring you to—do—things you don't—want—is he?"

"No, Dad."

Just the opposite, she thought.

"You know July, men my age—we—they ..." he trailed off.

July waited for him to continue his thought, but instead the silence buzzed across the world.

"Well," he said abruptly, after a long pause. "Your mother will be upset that she missed her call."

"Hm," grunted July, "She'll probably be more upset that she couldn't say I told you so."

"Okay then. Have a safe flight. Don't forget to let us know when you're back."

"Okay."

"All right. Bye, kiddo."

"Bye."

Thinking back, July was glad that her father didn't finish his thought about men his age. She didn't need him to compare himself to Toby. She didn't want to be one of those women who dates her father.

Toby crumpled the butcher paper decisively, "Well, should we get ourselves to the airport then?"

"Yeah."

"Okay, well, why don't you let the concierge know he can call us a cab then."

July stood up. Toby held out the ball of butcher paper, and she took it from him.

"He's been giving me the evil eye all afternoon," said Toby. "This will be the high point of his day."

Soon they were in the taxi rushing away from the Ariele, from the Arno, from Astrid and Massimo. July didn't look out the window. Instead she looked at the spot where her knees met the back of the front seat while Toby stared blankly out at the buildings, as though he saw them every day and had forgotten what they were.

July stared at her knees as they sat and waited in the airport for three hours, and then again on the flight to Paris. She stared at her feet as she walked through the endless terminals of Charles de Gaulle, the airport worker walking next to her pushing Toby in a wheelchair, and back at her knees again as they flew over the Atlantic.

What was wrong? Why did she feel so empty inside, like her stomach had been squeezed as long and thin as her spine, like her organs had been crumpled up and thrown away with the butcher paper from Toby's sandwich? She didn't understand. What had she lost? And where had she found it to begin with?

XXIV

THE WHEELCHAIR WAS A SURPRISINGLY GOOD WAY TO TRAVEL. TOBY got to board the plane first, and he didn't have to haul his luggage around everywhere. He didn't have to worry about walking fast enough to catch the plane, or taking a wrong turn to the terminal. He wasn't traveling—he was being traveled.

He had thought that once the plane landed back on home turf he would feel an enormous sense of relief. When he didn't feel it, he thought maybe it would come once he got off the plane. When that didn't happen, he thought maybe once he got to the luggage carousel. When, in the back of the cab home, he still felt the tense worry, and then a twinge of guilt as he worried that maybe it was his theatrics, not his location that was the problem. But surely he would feel better once he got back to his house. Back to familiarity. Routine. Ownership.

When they arrived back at his house, it looked the same as when they had left it. It was the middle of the night now, so the neighborhood was coated in the same icy black puddles as before. There was still snow on the ground—maybe more than before—and Toby's walk wasn't shoveled. A man with a hurt back couldn't shovel snow. He would have to ask July to shovel it in the morning. He would have to ask really nicely.

They left the bags by the curb as July helped Toby up the walkway, through the front door, up the entry steps and then up to the bedroom on the second floor. As they groped through the tunnels of the house, he turned on lights, hoping to be struck by that sense of coming home that he loved so much. Instead, he felt like he was touring the home of someone who had died so long ago that they had ceased to matter.

The house was cold. Of course—the heat had been turned way down for over a week. And the water was off. Maybe the pipes were frozen. Why had he come back to all these things to worry about—and when he couldn't even deal with them? Keeping up with the pretense of his injury was harder work than he'd anticipated. While his back was still sore from his first fall, he was mobile. And it wasn't as kingly as he thought it would be, lying in bed, describing to July where the switch for the water was, how to turn up the central thermostat, and the water heater. She had trouble locating everything and had to come and go several times before she did it right, as Toby lay in his bed, drifting in and out of sleep as she clomped up the steps, asked him a question, and clomped down again.

She didn't complain, or huff, or seem resentful, which Toby appreciated, but she seemed so indifferent and checked out that it made him almost more unsettled than a scowl would have. Even after July had locked the doors and helped him to the bathroom and they were lying in bed—his bed—he still didn't feel like he was home. It was too quiet, too empty, like it had been abandoned for years.

Maybe it was that his daughters weren't there. Or maybe it was that, after more than a year of living in "his" house, not "their" house, it still felt just a little bit temporary, like maybe he would go to sleep and wake up back in "their" bed, where there had always been a family instead of just every other week or select weekends. Maybe he hadn't realized that until he had been away, until he had wanted to come home and realized he still didn't have a home.

Did Jenny ever feel the same way? Didn't she ever go down to the kitchen in the morning before the girls were up and wish that he were standing at the coffee pot next to her, someone to share that moment of calm with, that moment before you're Mom and Dad to just be Jenny and Toby? But she had that now. She had Kevin.

He thought about the time he lost his wallet. Jenny had had a stressful week and needed some quiet time. Walking out the door, he put it in his back pocket. He and the girls got in the car and went for McDonalds, but don't tell Mom. The yellow cheeseburger wrappers sat like mutated dust bunnies next to bits of fries, errant salt and ketchup drips.

"Daddy, can I have an ice cream?"

Why the hell not? He reached for his wallet to give them money, and it wasn't there. He stood up, looking all around him, feeling his pockets over and over again, as though it would reappear. He had had it to buy lunch, and sometime between the counter and the ice cream, it had evaporated. Jenny rolled her eyes and sighed heavily when he got home and called the credit card company to cancel their cards.

It was there, and then it wasn't, and he didn't know how it got that way, but he drove himself crazy trying to figure out what had happened and what went wrong. This was kind of like that.

He woke the next day never realizing he had fallen asleep. July was still sleeping—it must be early. And then he looked at his watch and saw that it was three in the afternoon. If his eyes could have bulged from his sockets like in cartoons, they would have. Three p.m.? That was impossible. Had jetlag really fucked them up so bad? But then he looked at the clock on his nightstand, which read seven o'clock.

Oh, he realized as his body calmed down. His watch was still on Florence time, and he was somewhere in between now and there.

He really had to pee, but didn't want to wake July, poor thing looked exhausted just sleeping, so snuck to the bathroom himself. Maybe his back had already healed from the initial fall. Maybe they should have stayed in—

Let's check phone messages! Toby decided. Surely there would be quite a few.

He hobbled over to the phone and computer, which sat by a window looking out front. He turned it on, picked up the phone to check messages, and saw their luggage sitting out front, in the snow, huddled together like kids waiting for the school bus.

If Jenny had done something like that, he would have rolled his eyes, sighed heavily, perhaps cursed. But this poor kid was stuck taking care of him, resetting the house on their return. She had hardly said a thing since Florence. He couldn't blame her for forgetting the luggage. If it were his marriage, he might have begun a game of wills, waiting passive aggressively for her to bring in the luggage. Had he more faith in his present condition, he would have gone outside himself and retrieved the luggage. But as he thought about it, his back was getting crankier, and now that he noticed, he was hunched over, leaning on the desk. Maybe he was hurt after all. Or maybe he felt pain to assuage his guilt for pretending to be worse off than he really was.

He carried the cordless phone over to the couch and sank into it with relief. Maybe after a rest he would restore his energy and his mind.

He listened to his messages, most of which were crap, then dialed Jenny's parents' house. They would be up now—Sivertsens were early risers. He wanted to see the girls.

The phone rang three, four times. *There's no way they were still sleeping, and they wouldn't be out this early. Why weren't they—*

"Hello?" a man's voice answered the phone.

Who was that? It wasn't Jenny's dad. There were no other males in the household.

"Hello?" said the voice again.

"Uh—I'm looking for Jenny—Sivert—sen?" he said tentatively, wondering whether he had accidentally dialed the wrong number.

There was a pause.

"May I ask who's calling?"

Who was this guy? Did they have company over for breakfast?

"The father of her children."

"Oh—sure," said the man rather hesitantly.

"Jenny!" he called far away. "It's—Toby."

How did he know Toby's—

"Kevin?"

"Uh, yeah. Hi, Toby," said Kevin, trying to smooth himself over.

Excuse me? thought Toby. *A week at her parents' house and he's already answering their fucking phone? What the fuck?* This was almost as mind boggling as the disappearing wallet, but this time he couldn't blame Ronald.

Toby couldn't speak. His mouth was open, his lips moving in incensed "Oh's," but his vocal chords had gone the way of that wallet.

"Jenny!" Kevin called again with an edge of urgency, like Toby had done when Jenny made macaroni and cheese and left it on the stove so long it started to smoke, an occurrence with which he was too familiar.

"Hang on," he heard Jenny yell distantly.

"Just a moment," said Kevin into the phone, his tone compensating with formality.

"Yeah," said Toby dryly.

The silence stretched between them, staring at each other nose-to-nose, ear-to- ear, through the wrong end of binoculars.

What the fuck are you doing there? said Toby's silence.

None of your goddamn business, said Kevin's.

Back the fuck off.

Make me. Kevin's silence stuck its tongue out.

Toby's silence flipped Kevin's the bird and lunged at him, aiming for Kevin's face. Or maybe he should go for the toes, break them one by—

"Hello?" said Jenny.

Later, sucker, said Kevin's silence just before he hurriedly hung up.

"Hi, Jenny."

"Hi, Toby," she said, as though she had already heard everything he could ever possibly say and would say. Women.

"What is it?" she asked.

"I'm home," he said. "And I want to see the girls."

He could swear he heard her silence laughing: Ha-*ha*!

"Home so soon? What's wrong, things didn't work out with your oldest daughter?"

"No, she's with me. I fell and hurt my back. Can't walk. So we decided to come back early."

"Huh," she said disinterestedly. "Sure."

"Well, you can talk to her if you want, but I'd have to wake her up. She's still upstairs sleeping."

"The girls and I aren't coming back till after New Year's."

"Well, come back early. I'm sure the girls will want to see their dad."

"You're just going to have to wait. We still have plans to keep here."

"Well, break them. I haven't seen the girls in almost two weeks."

"That's not *my* fault."

"The only reason I left for Italy is because you hijacked them to your parents' for the holidays."

"And I still *have* them for the holidays, which aren't over until January second, which is when we're driving back."

"That's almost a week away!"

"I don't *control* time, Toby. That's not my problem."

"Jenny, come on. We both know the girls are better off when they see *both* of us. We agreed on this when we drew up the divorce. They have two parents, not one."

She was silent.

Ooh, he was playing the civilized-adult card. This could work. He should have thought of this sooner.

"Look, I know you love visiting your parents," Good, good, sympathize ... "and that they love seeing their grandkids ..." Sympathize with her parents, "and that the girls love seeing their grandparents ..." Compliment plus arguing for the girls' best interests ... "and that it's not fair to make you drop everything and come back just because I'm here."

Personal appeal. This was like a cigarette ad or something. He should have gone into advertising.

"But when the girls hear that I'm back in town, which they will, because I know you're not the kind of person or mother to deny her daughters a phone call from their father ..." Appeal to her as a good mother, as a decent person, and prevent her from denying just by saying she would never do such a thing.

"I think they'll probably want to see me."

Jenny was silent.

"And you know I love our girls …" *Our.* Good, good, "and that holidays are better spent as a whole family."

Family values. That always got her.

"So, I thought maybe we could spend New Year's Eve together, as a family, like we did with Thanksgiving."

Wait. When did he *think* that? When did he *ever* think that, let alone think that that would be a good idea? What was his mouth *doing*?

"Would your little plaything be there?"

"Will *yours*?" he said in a condescending adult tone of voice, temporarily called for departure from maturity.

She was silent for a moment.

Was this—working?

"What about my parents? They're part of the family too."

This is working. She's negotiating! But—oh shit. He hadn't thought about her parents. Maybe that was because he hadn't *thought* in the first place. *Damn. She has you cornered. Think, think, think.*

He started to see the only plausible solution. But he didn't like it. He didn't want it. No no *NO.*

"Well," he said, hardly sounding convincing to himself, "maybe they could come here too? They haven't visited town for a while …"

"I don't think my parents are up for a last-minute car trip at the end of December."

Oh she was wiggling. There was only one way, and it she sounded like she knew that but she wasn't going to say it, and she didn't think he would either. He was going to have to prove her wrong. But she was going to make him lay his balls on the cutting board.

Oh God, he thought. Heat rose around his cheeks. *Mature adult. For your kids.*

"Well—"

Don't sound unsure. Don't let her win. Cigarettes are cool.

"Well, I hate to be presumptuous, but what if—we—came down there?"

He closed his eyes. He had said it. Like passing a fucking kidney stone. Here comes the cleaver—

"We?" she asked.

She was probably doing that face where she's trying not to smile and ends up puckering her lips like a pompous lemon. She was taking immense pleasure in undercutting July.

This is going to be a tough play. How can I invite myself and my half-my-age girlfriend to the home of my ex-in-laws for New Year's Eve? This is what you get for not thinking, asshole. There had to be some mature adult argument in there somewhere. Come on, mature adult. Come on.

"Look Jenny, we both have to accept that we're moving on with our lives. We have to act like grown-ups here, even if we don't want to. This isn't a one-time situation. This is what it's going to be like from here on out."

Where was this shit coming from? "Now I know it's going to be uncomfortable, for pretty much everyone except, I hope, the girls. Now all four of us are adults here—"

"Barely," she cut in.

"Hey, the only one not acting like it right now is you," he said.

"T-uh," Jenny clicked like a teenager. "Please, Toby. Why should I agree to let you bring your little child along? Can't you see how I might find that a little insulting?"

"Well, can't you see how I might find it insulting to learn that a few weeks after our divorce is finalized you're engaged to a man we had a few issues over when we were married?"

"*We* did not have issues. *You* had issues."

"And obviously for good reason."

"*Excu*se me, but—"

Clean up fast, this is getting far too messy.

"Look," he interrupted. "The point is, neither of us is looking like an angel here, okay? It remains that we're all intelligent adults with the best interests of the girls at heart. Plus, I know that your parents are warm, caring people who also want what's best for their granddaughters."

Okay, that last bit was actually true.

"So if there's a way we can work it out where ..." He was about to say, "I could see my daughters over the holiday," but changed his mind at the last minute, "... we could all be together for the holiday, well, I think it would be worth the discomfort. And I bet our daughters would think so too."

Throw that last bit in there for effect.

How come he couldn't talk like that at work? He would probably sell a lot more houses if he did. Hell, how come he couldn't talk like that when he was married? Then maybe he would still *be* married.

His heart was fluttering a bit, his cheeks still hot. It was a good speech. There wasn't anything more he could say. Though he didn't like that Jenny was judge and jury. How come she got all this control? There was no way *he* could take the girls away for two weeks.

Unless I have them for her honeymoon. Fuck, don't think about that now! Don't lose focus.

"I don't know," she finally said, oozing reluctance.

She was waiting for him to plead further, to say something stupid. She had done this all the time. How come he hadn't seen it then?

"Well, there's nothing more I can say, Jenny."

"Let me talk to my parents," she said after a moment.

"Fine. Let me talk to the girls while you talk to your parents."

Of course, the first thing he did was tell the girls he was home. They were, to his joy and relief, ecstatic.

"Daddy's home!" shouted Sophia back to Chloe and Grace.

"Daddy! Daddy!" they shouted in a chorus.

Beautiful. The most beautiful thing he'd ever heard. They'd never shout for Kevin like that. And fabulous to manipulate Jenny just a little further.

After he finished talking to all three of them, being sure to get them just a little worked up over his return and expressing his enthusiasm to see them, Jenny got back on the phone.

"You can come on the thirty-first. At four."

"Great," he said.

"But you have to stay in a hotel," she said.

"Of course."

"And no hanky panky."

Or what, you'll divorce me?

"Same goes for you."

"It's my house."

"They're *our* children. Just because they're at your parents' house doesn't mean they're less mine. I'm still Dad. I still have a say."

"Four o'clock," she said tightly. "Sarah and Ryan and the kids will be there. And bring a dessert."

She hung up.

Though he was about to walk into the biggest sinkhole of socially awkward situations, Toby was elated. Not only would he get to see the girls three days earlier than planned, hug them and tickle them again, but he had won. If you could call this winning. And July could make a dessert.

She wasn't going to like this much. After all his talk about coming home to comfort and bed and no hotels and quiet, he was taking her on a road trip to stay in a hotel and spend New Year's Eve with his children, ex-wife, her parents, and her new fiancé.

What if she refuses to come? No, she couldn't do that. He had fought for her to come. He couldn't show up without her. Especially not when Jenny would have Kevin there. Even with July along he was going to be outnumbered, but at least with her he had some support.

She was not going to like this. At all.

This called for another visit from mature adult. And probably the best pancakes he had ever made. Right after July went to the store—Toby was out of everything.

July watched as Toby, sitting on a stool, beat egg yolks with a whisk, switching hands every few moments and grunting faintly. He had sent her to the store earlier for those eggs, and for everything else he was using, too. If he had been able to get up and come downstairs without help, when not even forty-eight hours ago he had been lying helpless on Massimo's floor, then why had he insisted on coming back home so soon? He could have been up in Florence. Who knows how he'd be tomorrow. They could have been walking around, out at a restaurant celebrating New Year's in Italy.

When she woke up this morning—well, perhaps it was technically the afternoon—Toby had insisted he would make her his pancakes as the first part of a thank you and I'm sorry. She was glad—his pancakes were quite delicious—until he told her that she would have to go to the store since they were out of everything, and that she'd left the suitcases outside all night. She had brought them in and gone to the grocery store as quickly as she could, but grocery stores usually distracted her, and since she would be passing a lot of the next week in the kitchen, she needed to make sure she got what she needed.

But now here Toby was, at three twelve in the afternoon, making pancakes. He was just pouring the first batch into the pan.

"Can you do me a favor and put the syrup in the microwave?" he asked, spatula poised inches above the pan.

She got up wordlessly and poured some syrup into a glass measuring cup, then stuck it in the microwave.

"Make mine runny in the center," she said to Toby.

"Yes, ma'am," he said cheerily.

A few minutes later they were sitting at the counter eating pancakes. Or rather, she was eating pancakes, but he just used his to mop up syrup when he wasn't looking at her.

"What's wrong?" she asked.

Oh, God, were these breakup pancakes? Oh no, she would never be able to eat pancakes again.

"There's something I want to—talk to you about—ask you."

"Okay ..."

He rubbed his beard stubble with the insides of his hands and then ran them through his hair.

"What is it?"

"Well, I—talked to Jenny this morning."

Oh God, she thought. *I don't know what's coming but I don't think I like it.* Except for her butterfly heart, her body froze, her ribs like icy iron claws around her.

"I—I wanted—want—to see the girls."

"Yeah."

Oh God, he's kicking me out, she thought. *The girls are coming and he wants me to leave. He promised I could stay with him! Where am I going to go?*

"And Jenny, um, refused to come back."

"Okay."

Okay, then … what did he want to tell her? Why was he keeping her in suspense? *Just spit it out already!*

"So she um, I—invited—"

July raised her eyebrows in curious anticipation.

"I managed to get her … to … invite us … over there to visit the girls."

She put down her fork, as though that were obstructing her hearing. "You invited us where?"

"To—to her parents' house."

"Her parents' house. So—wait. You want us to go to your ex-in-laws' house?"

"Yyyyeah."

"To see Jenny and your girls?"

"And—Kevin."

"And Kevin."

July looked into her plate full of maple syrup, "And you want me to go with you?"

"Jenny asked us to bring dessert," he said helpfully.

July frowned into the ochre pool in front of her. His girls. Toby wanted her around his girls. He wanted her to come with him. In front of Jenny. And Kevin. Like a real couple. Like his real, serious girlfriend. *He really does care. He really does take me seriously. I must matter.*

July looked up and saw Toby looking at her intently, a bit afraid, as though she might get angry. Was *this* why he had insisted on making the pancakes? To butter—or batter, she laughed to herself—her up? She swallowed a gulp of laughter with a dose of sticky pancake. For all these weeks she would have practically *begged* Toby to do something like this. This would be her chance to show him, to prove that she could work in his life. It would be something like this that would help him realize that he loved her.

July could win them over. She wasn't a bad person. She was friendly and fairly smart. They would like her. It would be fun. *And* she could make dessert—what better way to win people over than with sugar? What would she make? What said New Year's with the former family? Something to win the kids over first. Nothing fussy. Like cheesecake, or cupcakes, or maybe something with nuts and chocolate ...

"July?" said Toby.

"Is anyone allergic to nuts?" she asked.

Toby frowned in confusion.

"Is that a—yes?"

"Huh?"

"Is that a yes? You'll come?"

"Of course!" she said. "I'd love to."

"Really?"

"Why not?"

"Well—I mean—it's—no. No one is allergic to nuts," he said, putting another pancake on her plate. "But Jenny and Kevin watch their weight fairly strictly, since they dance."

"Oh," she frowned, thinking *that's no fun.*

"So you should use as much butter as possible," he said.

She smiled, "So for what, nine of us?" she asked, counting on her fingers.

He counted, too, "Oh. No, thirteen. Jenny's sister Sarah and her husband Ryan and their two kids will be there. But one of their kids is barely two. He won't eat anything."

"Any dislikes?"

Toby's face compressed in thought.

"Uh," he sighed. "It's been a while ..." He shook his head and looked at her with a crooked half-smile. "Is the only reason you're coming is so that you can make dessert?"

"Maybe," she said, rolling her eyes around sheepishly.

"You do realize what you're up against, right?"

"There's nothing a little butter and sugar won't fix."

"A lot of butter," he nodded. "And I'm not going to try to convince you otherwise."

"Likes or dislikes?"

"Um. Chocolate's always the hit. Miriam loves caramel, Alan eats whatever you put in front of him, but I think for his sixty-fifth birthday he had a huge cheesecake. Jenny had a cheesecake at her thirtieth. She likes peanut butter. And each time she was pregnant she would go out and buy jars of Jif and spoon it out, sometimes eating half a jar in one sitting."

He smiled and huffed a laughing breath, "One day when I came home from work I kissed her hello and she had that clinging smell of peanut butter. That's how I knew she was pregnant with Grace. But I think that since then she'd had so much peanut butter she can hardly stand the smell anymore. Oh, and she hates mint. If that matters."

I wonder if he could name my likes like that, thought July. Did she dare make anything that reminded him of her? But if she wanted to win them over, prove she wasn't some silly kid, well. She'd have to hit them where it counted.

"Oh! Miriam hates raisins. *Hates* them. No raisins."

"Well, caramel, chocolate, cheesecake. That's easy enough," said July.

"Oh," said Toby in surprise. "I guess—you can do that?"

"Sure," she shrugged. "Anything else I should know?"

"Bring a thick skin."

She smiled. *He wants me there. He knows I can handle it. I matter.*

She called her father that night for advice on a chocolate caramel cheesecake.

"Keep the heat pretty low," he said. "Stir the dry sugar with a fork. When it melts and it's a light brown, keep cooking but don't stir. Just swirl the pan until it's a really deep golden color. Add in some heavy cream *off* the heat, then put it back on the heat after it hardens and cook it till it dissolves, then just stir in the chocolate."

"Right."

"Bittersweet chocolate!" he added quickly, "and don't even think about using anything other than full fat cream cheese."

"I *know,* Dad."

"I'll email you my recipe for crumb crust. I like to double it. Everyone likes chocolate cookies. And make sure it's still a little wobbly when you take it out of the oven."

"Okay."

"And don't under mix. Make sure it gets all incorporated."

"Duh, Dad."

"Well, sometimes people have problems with the simple things."

"Oh, Gray, that was over twenty *years* ago," said her mother, who was listening in.

"We had a batch of molasses cookies with white stripes because she didn't mix the molasses thoroughly."

"They still tasted *fine.* You still *ate* them."

"Of course I did. I was still trying to impress you back then."

"Well, thank *heavens* you've stopped doing that," said her mother a bit bitterly.

July ran through the ingredients once more with her dad.

"What are you making this cake for, dear?" asked her mother.

July winced. Her father, taken with the idea of a chocolate caramel cheesecake, had neglected to ask, and her mother had joined them in the middle of the conversation.

"Uh, it's just for, you know, I missed having a kitchen in Italy so I thought I'd do some baking."

"Oh! Well I have a great recipe for some spice cake with ginger and raisins—"

"No, Jenny's mom doesn't like raisins."

"What?" said her mother.

Oh, God, she had done it again. Where was that think-speak filter when she needed it? Stop telling your parents everything!

"Nothing."

"No, not nothing," said her mother sternly. "I'm your mother. Just because you're with some older man doesn't mean I didn't carry you around for nine months and change your diapers and clean up your vomit."

July sighed and rolled her eyes, but recounted everything anyway. Where was her spine? Had her mother forgotten to give her one when she carried July around for those nine months of which she regularly reminded July?

"July," said her mother. "You're getting too involved in this. You're getting too involved in his life. It's time to stop this nonsense. You're graduating in six months. You have the rest of your life to think about. Haven't you been thinking about what you want to do?"

"Yes," she mumbled.

"Well? Regale me!"

"I dunno," she grunted.

"July, we have been talking about this for weeks, months! You need a plan! Remember your father's friend Dave Gold? He can help you get a job here! Talk to him over spring break, meet with his boss, give them your resume … this is a golden opportunity, honey, the economy is not what it used to be."

"I *told* you I *don't* want to work at a *bank*."

"Well what *else* are you going to do?"

"I don't *know!*" said July, raising her voice.

"July! We keep going in circles! You're supposed to be *thinking* about this! You're supposed to have a *plan!*" said her mother, matching July's rise in volume.

July was silent.

"July Jocile Van Buren," continued her mother, just as sternly but back in safer decibel range. "Toby is at a totally different point in his life, he has *children*. I know it's been—fun—" she conceded, "—but you need to face reality. You are investing too much in this."

July still did not respond.

"Once you graduate, you have nowhere to go but here. And when you come here, you'll have a job at the bank if you just go see Dave Gold. Work there for a year or two until you find something— or someone—better."

"You can't flounder, July," said her dad, finally participating. "You can't just wander around looking for things. You have to go seek them. Even if the bank isn't your ideal job, you'll be working for something. The Van Burens do not flounder or wander. You figure out what you want by doing. Life doesn't just fall into your lap."

"Look at Ansel!" chimed her mother. "When he graduated he got a job at that e-something place."

"Mom, he *hated* it there."

"Her point is that Ansel used that experience and knowledge to find something that he *does* like."

"But he was miserable for a year."

"July, you can't always be happy," said her father. "It's not a constant state. Sometimes you just have to be content with being alive while you're finding those moments of happiness."

July did not want to listen to this. What did they know? She didn't want the kind of life they had. She did not want to be her mother, answering phones in the main office of her children's middle school long after they had moved on, playing the same roles she had played for more than twenty-five years. Her father had abandoned any yearn to travel he may have had, seeing the world only through his kitchen. Did they ever have moments of happiness anymore, or had that gone stale? Did they keep waiting for the next moments, wondering when they would come, though the moments had gotten fewer and farther between with time?

"You'll come home over spring break and talk with Dave Gold," said her mother with finality. "You'll have a plan, a job, a direction."

There was nothing she could say to make them hear. So instead she just hung up the phone slowly, putting it down softly, as though in doing so, her parents wouldn't hear the click of disconnection.

A plan, a job, a direction. Isn't that exactly what Toby had had before it ended up totally overturned? Maybe Toby was right—there was no point trying to make the future. It would happen no matter what you did.

July spent the next two days shuttling between the grocery store and the kitchen. She practiced making caramel a few times, and when she got it right they put it in a bucket of ice cream, eating from the carton in bed. She made two kinds of cookies, peanut butter cookies and oatmeal dried cherry, instead of raisin, extra butter, just in case someone didn't want cheesecake.

Since they were going to be traveling with the cake and the hotel may or may not have a refrigerator, July made the cake late on the night of the thirtieth, starting around ten o'clock and finally getting to bed after one, having dried the last mixing bowl and triple checked the cake's setting and the refrigerator's temperature. They left before six on the morning of the thirty-first, the cake secured safely in a cooler belted into the back seat.

While Toby said his back was better and he could move around, she didn't want him to take chances, so at July's request he spent most of his time on the couch or in bed.

Now he lay reclined in the passenger seat as July drove his car the whole nine hours to Virginia. The roads were icy and she clenched her jaw and the steering wheel like doing so would give the car more grip on the asphalt. Toby slept most of the way, so she spent the time listening to the monotonous blend of the wind passing around the car and the highway underneath it.

She felt like she was driving through a cartoon, where the background moved behind her in a repeating loop. Endless black, naked trees passed, domed around the road like when she learned to square dance in school and people held hands, making a tube of arms for each boy and girl pair to pass beneath.

They stopped for lunch in the middle of nowhere, where the only choices were drive-thrus or Cracker Barrel. They chose Cracker Barrel, much to July's dismay. She would have preferred a drive-thru, mostly so that she could stay in the car next to the cake.

"July, it's Cracker Barrel. There are tons of people around. No one's going to break into the car, and if they did, they wouldn't steal the cake."

"Well, it's the only thing worth stealing," she replied.

"Besides the car itself."

"Oh God, what if they steal the *car*? With the cake inside?" she gasped reflexively.

"July, are you *listening* to yourself?"

She thought for a moment, listening as her words played back from the felt walls of the car, "Oh God, I'm worse than my father." She put a hand over her face.

"Come on, July, let's go, I'm hungry."

July requested a table by the window, necessitating an extra fifteen-minute wait and driving Toby crazy with hunger and an inexplicable passion for their chicken and dumplings.

After eating an entire plate of chicken and dumplings, fried apples, hash brown casserole, fried okra, and mashed potatoes, Toby reclined his seat and fell asleep as soon as July started the ignition. It was the other end of the spectrum from Italy, and she could hardly finish half her turkey sandwich. July found herself wishing for a simple loaf of bread with tomato, mozzarella, and olive oil, maybe a leaf of basil. But there were no roadside Italian trattorias in rural Pennsylvania.

When at last they crossed the state line into Virginia, her stomach started fluttering like a flag in the wind. What would they think of her? Would they all be cold and begrudging, speaking to her only when necessary? She almost wouldn't blame them if they did, but it wasn't her fault things were the way they were. She hadn't even met Toby's parents and already she was spending a holiday with his ex-wife's parents.

Well you should get used to this, she thought. *This is how holidays will be with him, split between him and Jenny.*

But what about my family? she wondered. *What if we stay together and I want to spend the holidays with my family? That would mean taking the girls across the country with us.*

Which was fine with her, if it was fine with Toby. And, of course, her parents. What would her parents think of the girls? They're just kids, it's not like they could resent them; they'd have no reason to. They love kids. Her dad could show them how to make cookies, or heck, even recruit them to help with brioche if they visited on Christmas. How strange, to think of Toby and his daughters at her home, in the house where she had grown up, to watch his daughters in the places where she had once been their age. Looking at things from the adult perspective, floating in the purgatory between being daughter and being mother.

She felt like she was still in the child's role, still turning to Mommy and Daddy when things got rough, or even when they weren't. How could she possibly play the other side? How do parents know what to do?

What would her parents do when they met Toby? Maybe they would all go out to dinner when her family came for graduation. They would go to a steakhouse, probably, so her father could see how Toby ordered. Maybe they would get on like old friends reunited after years apart. Or it might be worse than when Chris just ordered a baked potato. Could Toby order a steak big enough to win her father and mother over? What would they talk about? And even as awkward and torturous as the specter of Toby meeting her family seemed, she wanted it badly. Meeting in person could affirm how right they were for each other, how much they cared about each other. Her parents would see that, they would accept that. Eventually.

She looked at the clock. It was already three and they were twenty miles from the town where Jenny's family lived. They might not have time to go to the hotel first, but she didn't know where she was.

"Toby," she said, squeezing his arm.

"Mm?" he sat up.

"I don't know where to go."

After consulting a map and calling the hotel, they decided they didn't have quite enough time to stop at the hotel first. So instead they spent about fifteen minutes sitting in a Starbucks recaffeinating and using the restroom. July brought her makeup bag from the car and tried her best not to look like she had been driving for nearly nine hours. She had spent a long time—too long—last night figuring out what she would wear today, wanting to appear confident but not overly confident and definitely not too young.

As she leaned over the sink and inches away from the mirror, applying mascara, she thought, *Show them. Show them you're just as good. Show them you're better. Show them that he's happier.*

She put the mascara wand down and looked at the mirror. What did it matter? Nothing would convince them anyway. They were all on Jenny's side, and yet she wanted so badly to impress them all. *They've already formed an opinion about you. You're already out.*

You're still in with Toby, she thought, looking into the sink drain. *You're here for him.*

Wait, she thought. *Why am I here? He doesn't need me here. What does he need me to see his girls for? He knows Jenny already hates me. Her family probably does too. What good can bringing me along do? Am I just there for him to show off—Ha, see what I got, I can move on, too?* For a moment, she wished she hadn't made that cake. Or the cookies. Why was she trying so hard?

Because, she thought. *I can't not try. If I can't try, there's nothing else I can do.*

A tube of dread rammed itself down her throat. There was nothing more that she could do.

XXV

"OKAY, RIGHT AT THIS NEXT STOP SIGN," TOBY SAID TO JULY.

It had been three years since he was last here, but Toby still remembered the neighborhood perfectly.

"All right, third house on the right," he said as July turned right up the hill.

There was the house with the pillars and red door, there was the one with ugly yellow shutters Jenny commented on every year, and there was the Sivertsens' house, looking exactly how it had the first time he had come. The gray-blue siding blended in with the clouded sky, the white shutters standing out like pockmarks. The icicle lights hung from the trim, turned on and blinking faintly in the early dusk. They had some new lawn ornament outside, some giant rebar fish that stood at least eight feet high. He would never put something like that outside any house, especially if he were trying to sell it, but then the Sivertsens had always been a little arty.

He recognized Sarah and Ryan's white minivan in the driveway.

"Just park in the street," he said.

July did so and turned off the car.

They sat for a moment in silence as the four o'clock darkness pulsed into the car. Was he really going to do this?

He sighed through puffed cheeks and put a hand on July's thigh.

"You ready?"

She looked into her lap, "Yeah," she said almost inaudibly.

She had been pretty quiet; they would have to talk that night, probably. Great. That's just what he would need after this circus of exes.

He unbuckled his seatbelt and opened the door. He got out a bit stiffly and opened the back door to take out presents for the girls. July hadn't moved. Great. Now was not the time for a pep talk. Hell, they were all probably watching him from the windows, waiting for a glimpse of her, waiting to pick apart every little thing they did. All they needed was to see that she was insecure.

"Hey," he said over the back seat. "Look, don't worry about this. It'll be fine. You're an amazing gal, and if they don't treat you like one, it's not because of you."

"Yeah, I know," she said sullenly as she unbuckled her seatbelt.

She got out and opened the other back door to take out her cake. She really did look amazing. If he were going to bring any girlfriend, especially a young one, to this "reunion," he'd want it to be someone this gorgeous and smart. Maybe he should say something like that, just to get her head back in the game.

"Look," he said, looking at her over the seat belted cooler, "it doesn't matter what they think anyway. You're important to me, that's what matters."

Half her mouth smiled, but he could see her face relax a bit.

She took out the cake container carefully, and then the bag of cookies. They closed the doors and locked the car, then he waited as she came around his side of the car. He leaned in and gave her a half-second kiss on the lips, then put his free hand on her lower back and walked with her up to the door. He hoped they *were* watching.

They stopped in front of the door, that black door and the golden knocker, which somehow seemed bigger in his memories. He pressed the lit orange doorbell and listened to the muffled chime inside. He was sure Jenny was standing right on the other side of the door, counting how many seconds until she could open the door without seeming like she had actually been standing there. He had seen her do it before.

But he heard footsteps, so maybe no one had been there after all. There was the clackety fidget with the lock. His heart was beating hard. He looked over at July, whose eyes kept moving around, not sure where to look.

The door opened and there stood Chloe in faded jeans and a red turtleneck sweater, her light hair frizzy as usual. She was beautiful, and he felt like someone had wired a bucket of warm water to the top of the door and it had just fallen all over him.

"Daddy!" she made to lunge at him but stopped short, instead gingerly wrapping her arms around his waist.

He could swear she had gotten taller.

"Chloe! Hiya, kiddo!" he cried, putting down the bag of gifts and kissing her through that frizzy hair. She smelled the same, the same as she had every night that he had tucked her in since she had been born.

"Daddy! Daddy!" he heard high pitched yells from inside the house. A moment later, following some thumping footsteps, Grace and Sophia were there too, tugging at his arms and shouting, "What'd you bring me?"

Jenny popped her head into the entryway from the kitchen.

"Girls, close the door, you're letting in all the cold air!"

Then she disappeared again.

For a moment he felt like it was five years ago and he had just come back from the store, like time had doubled back.

"Daddy look at the watch I got for Christmas," said Sophia, sticking out her wrist and displaying a bright blue watch with fake diamonds around the face.

"Very nice," he said enthusiastically. "I guess you were good this year!"

"I got an iPod!" shouted Grace.

"Me too!" shouted Chloe and Sophia in unison.

"Mine's purple! Mine's pink! Mine's blue!" they continued shouting, but Toby couldn't tell which color came from which girl.

"Wow," he said, his enthusiasm a bit more forced this time. "Girls, you remember July, say hello."

July greeted them with enthusiasm, and Grace gave a broad smile and a loud "Hi July!" But Chloe and Sophia showed a bit of reserve, giving a quick "Hi" before returning to the subject of their Christmas gifts.

Toby slipped his boots off and put them by the pile of large and small boots next to the door.

Then the girls pulled him inside, shouting, "Daddy we're playing Candyland, come play with us! They turned into the living room, where Ryan sat in a green armchair with his and Sarah's kids, their daughter Violet and their youngest, Mike.

Ryan stood up when Toby came in.

"Toby, long time no see," he said, sounding genuinely happy to see him.

He and Ryan had always gotten on well, but hadn't spoken since the separation. Ryan was almost ten years younger than Toby, as was Sarah, and Ryan looked to him just as a young dad should. Frazzled and a little traumatized.

"Ryan, it's great to see you," he said as they shook hands.

"Yeah, yeah, you too man. I'm—you know, I'm—sorry about, everything," Ryan gestured around vaguely.

"Yeah," said Toby with equal vagueness, "yeah, me too."

"Daddy!" called one of the girls from the coffee table across the room.

"Just a minute, sweetie, Daddy's saying hi to Uncle Ryan."

"Where's uh, where's Sarah and ...?" trailed Toby.

"Yeah, uh, I think they're all in the kitchen," Ryan replied. "You know, huddling over their coffee gossiping while dinner cooks."

"Right," said Toby as the girls called him again. "I'm gonna—" he motioned to the girls.

"Yeah, yeah, we'll catch up later," said Ryan, sitting back down on a chair next to Violet.

For the moment, he could pretend that things hadn't changed.

July stood in the entryway holding the cheesecake. The girls had been so ecstatic to see Toby, and vice versa, that she ended up just floating awkwardly in the foyer.

This feels like a high school dance, she thought, her face burning with the same frustration of not knowing where to stand, where to go, what to say, afraid of the upperclasswomen.

She stood for a few moments longer, just to see if Toby would remember that she was here and come back out and get her and introduce her or something. But he didn't. She hadn't really expected him to pay much attention to her, but she still felt forgotten. The kitchen seemed the only logical place to go.

She took off her boots then crept forward, afraid that her footsteps would alert the predators that prey was in the vicinity. What was she going to say to them? *Oh, God.*

On her left was the staircase, and just beyond that, on the right, was the living room where Toby sat cross-legged on the floor playing Candyland. On the left, she saw, was the kitchen. She hunched her shoulders a bit and moved in tentatively.

The kitchen smelled like warm bread, coffee and chicken. It was a very cool kitchen too, she couldn't help noticing. Gas stove, two ovens, island counter, black marble countertops and light wooden cabinets. Her father would approve. The tile floor was slick under her socks.

Two blonde women stood leaning on the counter, reflected in the shiny black stone, coffee mugs in hand, heads huddled. She recognized the one on the left as Jenny. She was impeccably dressed, same expensive-looking jeans as last time, but this time in a drape-y blouse thing and her hair blow dried perfectly straight, her nails French manicured. *Crap. I should have gotten a manicure,* she thought.

The woman on the left was noticeably younger but obviously Jenny's sister. Her hair was a bit darker, she was a bit heavier, and her nose was different, but the resemblance was clear.

They both straightened at the same time as they noticed July's presence.

"Hi," she said, trying to smile.

Jenny and her sister looked at each other with sidelong glances, then back at July.

"Uhhm, I brought dessert," said July, lifting the cake a little. "Can I put it in the refrigerator?"

"Yeah," said Jenny coolly, motioning with her thumb to the steel fridge behind her.

As July made room for the cake, Jenny and her sister stayed silent behind her. They were probably making faces at each other, but for all she knew they were sneaking up on her with a fillet knife.

July closed the fridge door and turned back to them. *Okay*, she thought. *Just be relaxed.* "I'm July," she said, smiling the best she could and extending a hand to Jenny's sister.

Jenny's sister's upper lip curled just slightly as her eyes slid quickly to Jenny and back again.

"I'm Sarah," she said flatly, extending her hand flaccidly.

July shook it, then turned to Jenny. "Jenny. Nice to see you again."

Oh God, she thought. *Kill me NOW.*

Jenny smiled tightly and briefly, like a blink with her mouth.

July took a breath in but couldn't think of anything to say, so she stood there, frozen. Silence wafted through the kitchen, hanging in the air as thick as the aroma of bread. *Oh God. Oh God, God, God.* Her temples were on fire. She didn't even know where her eyes were looking, or if they were open at all.

"Let's go check on the kids," said Sarah, and the sisters picked up their mugs and sauntered out.

Now July was alone in the kitchen with the quiet hiss of the gas stove, the happy squeals of the kids in the other room. For some reason, she remembered the way the other girls teased her in sixth grade when they saw she hadn't started shaving her legs.

"You're supposed to shave that you know," said a girl named Sharon, who wore lip gloss and whose mother already let her highlight her hair and wear dark sparkly eyeliner, pointing to the hair on July's exposed legs.

The girls and boys around her had laughed and teased. That night when she got home, July stole her mother's razor from the shower and tried to shave but ended up with cuts around her knees and ankles and along her shin bones. Her mother saw July walking from the bathroom back to her room, the towel not long enough to hide the icicles of blood trickling down her legs.

She sat down on a stool at the counter just across from the stove. The window over the sink looked into the back yard, where there was a hill and a grove of leafless trees and a wooden swing set shivering beneath a layer of snow. To the left of the fridge was a door into the back yard, and against the wall opposite her there were glass cabinets filled with cookbooks above a desk, across which were littered papers and magazines and some files. Taped along the edges of the cupboards were family photos, some with Jenny and Sarah at different ages, and plenty of the grandkids.

July walked over to the cabinet to see what sorts of cookbooks they had. She was a bit dismayed to find seven years worth of *Cooking Light* compilations. There was the standard *Joy of Cooking*, *Vegetarian Cooking*, *The Moosewood Bible*, twenty or so issues of *Gourmet*, and a few *Betty Crocker* books on how to cook Italian, Mexican, and Chinese food. Her father judged people on their cookbooks. If he were here, he probably would have shrugged and said, "Meh."

She walked back to the counter and drummed her fingers. The girls squealed with delight in the other room. *Well, this is fun, being the group leper.*

The back door opened behind her and she turned around quickly, startled as two men walked in. One was tall and graying slightly. He wore a simple black jacket over a red flannel shirt. The other came in after him and *whoa*. July's heart jumped a bit. She had never actually seen a man that handsome before. Not up close, anyway. He was a bit short, but even beneath his clothes she could tell he was buff, and his face, was—*like an underwear model*, she thought. *Holy crap.*

That must be Kevin, she thought. *Oh God.*

"They should take all those bankers out and shoot them is what they should do," Jenny's dad was saying.

As he was taking off his jacket he turned around and saw July.

"Oh! Hi," he said with surprise.

"Hi," said July, unsure.

"You ... must be ... uh ..."

"July," she said, trying to smile.

"July! Yes, yes. I'm Alan, Jenny's father," he said, coming over with his hand outstretched.

"Nice to meet you," she replied, shaking his hand.

"Hi, I'm Kevin," said the underwear model, smiling.

They stood silent for a moment, then Alan cleared his throat.

"Did you just get here, July?"

"Uh, yeah, we got here about ten, fifteen minutes ago."

"Oh, great, great," said Alan, nodding his head.

"Where is—everybody?"

"I think they're in there," she said, motioning to the other room.

"Right. Excuse me, I'm going to see if I can find my wife and ask her what she wants me to do with this," said Alan, holding up a paper bag. "Excuse me."

July smiled as he walked out of the room, leaving her and the underwear model. They caught each other's eye and smiled flatly, awkwardly.

So he was who Jenny had moved on to. Well, there was no denying it was certainly a step up in the looks department, but everyone was a step below this guy. Poor Toby.

"So," Kevin started, "Um."

He opened his mouth and raised his eyebrows.

July raised her own eyebrows, waiting for him to finish—or start—the thought.

"You ... you must have more guts than a plate of haggis," he blurted.

July guffawed.

"Sorry, I—" he stammered, shaking his head, but he was interrupted.

"Kevin!"

July, trying to straighten her face, turned around and saw Jenny in the doorway.

"Dad said you were back. Come on in here and say hello."

Kevin smiled a brief apology at July then walked past her over to Jenny. They disappeared into the house, leaving July alone in the kitchen. She sat back down at the counter and traced her finger along the slick black countertop.

Great. Just fucking great. A plate of haggis would probably be more popular than she was right about now.

"Alan," said Toby, standing up stiffly, hands on his knees.

"Toby," replied Alan, warmly and coolly at the same time.

"It's great to see you again," Toby held out his hand.

Alan nodded and shook Toby's hand, his eyes kind but distant, "How was the drive?"

"Oh, you know, a lot of road," Toby said, laughing weakly.

He had responded that way every year when Alan asked the same question. It was their routine, and he was grateful that Alan had acknowledged that. Had it really been three years since he had last seen Alan? Except for looking a bit older, as they all did, Alan looked exactly the same. Still wearing the same flannel LL Bean shirts that the family gave him every year for his birthday in varying colors and patterns. He wouldn't be surprised if some of those shirts were older than Jenny.

Jenny came back into the room, her arm around Kevin. *Oh, fuck.* It hadn't been too weird to see Jenny—they saw each other multiple times a week. But seeing Kevin again, Toby felt a flash of anger like a mirror reflecting the sun. He wondered where July was.

Jenny cocked her head to the side and smiled with what Toby sensed was a rather vindictive edge.

"Toby, you remember Kevin."

"Hi," said Toby, cocking his head to the side and sticking his hands in his pockets. It felt like yesterday that he was waiting in the dark hallway for Kevin to come out of the bathroom.

"Toby," nodded Kevin.

That prick still looked like a model. How was it that he wasn't gay? That would really make Toby's life a whole lot easier. Who the fuck could compete with a guy like *that*? Hell, Kevin was barely human. And an asshole.

Everyone stood around silently, looking to the walls and floors for escape.

"Is Mom back yet?" Alan asked Jenny.

"Not yet."

"Where is she?" asked Toby. He wanted to see Miriam; it had been a long time.

"I believe she's still at the hospice," said Alan. "She should be back soon."

Toby had forgotten that she volunteered there, and always signed up for holiday slots.

"I'm going to go put this where it belongs," said Alan, holding up a bag. He nodded to excuse himself and walked out of the room and up the stairs.

Toby sat back down on the floor with the girls but found that they had already abandoned the Candyland board and were playing instead with their iPods. He looked at the Christmas tree behind them, still poured in tinsel, the same netted butterfly on the top of the tree.

Ryan was still in the green chair and Sarah sat next to him on the arm. Jenny and Kevin were sitting on the couch now, and Toby was alone on the floor. Again he wondered as to July's whereabouts. While he couldn't blame her for avoiding the awkwardness, he had hoped she'd be a bit more proactive in socializing.

Kevin was leaning back on the sofa, his arm around Jenny. *You asshole,* Toby thought. *You've probably been waiting years for this day, to rub it in my face. Ever since the bathroom incident. Thanks, jerk off.* He needed to get away from this.

"Hey girls, wanna go play in the snow with Daddy?"

They looked up, white earphones in their ears like alien tentacles.

"Yeah!" shouted Grace.

Thank God for the four-year-old attention span.

He managed to convince Chloe and Sophia to join too, and after a few minutes of putting on snow clothes, he was out in the cold being pelted with snowballs, though declined to bend down and make his own, should his back choose to stop cooperating. Eventually they moved around to the side of the house, where the snow was untouched and a bit deeper, for the girls to make a snowman. As the girls started rolling the body, he leaned against the house for a breather.

He wanted to see Miriam. He had always considered Miriam to be a real friend, and had hoped that she had felt the same way. There had been one time, when Chloe was two and Sophia was two or three months old, when she and Alan were visiting and helping out. Toby was worn down—it seemed that with twice the children he had quadruple the worry and work.

One night, Toby had been too anxious to sleep. It must have been well past one in the morning, but he was still awake and had gone downstairs into the kitchen for some of the cookies that Miriam had baked. He had been sitting alone for a while, in an island of light in the dark kitchen, eating most of the cookies and reading the newspaper, when Miriam came in. He didn't know if he had woken her, or if she couldn't sleep either, but she sat across from him and smiled knowingly.

"You know, Toby," she said after some chitchat. "After Sarah was born, I was a total wreck. I had been fine after Jenny, and everyone says it gets easier the second go-round, but I was a mess. Everyone always says what a blessing children are, but I didn't feel blessed; I felt awful. I felt like I should be elated to welcome another daughter to the family. Instead I was sad, I was stressed, I was lonely."

He didn't say anything, but thought that she must be able to read his face like a tarot card.

"I'm going to tell you what I told Jenny when she was eleven and afraid to go to sleepaway camp."

She picked up a pen from the table and reached her arm across to the newspaper.

"For some reason we think we should always feel like this," she said as she drew a happy face on the top of the paper above a picture of Bill Clinton.

"But no one tells us that most of the time, we feel like this."

She drew a sad face.

"Or this."

A face with a squiggly mouth, which Toby interpreted as scared.

"Well I'm telling you, Toby, it's okay to feel like that. And you have every reason to feel like that now. A second daughter is a blessing, of course. But I think maybe it will take longer to feel like that."

"How long?" he uttered.

She sighed and sat back.

"Well, that I don't know. It took me six or seven months, until I got into the rhythm of things. You know I always say that life is like a symphony. It sounds corny, and it is, and the girls always laugh at me for it, but it's true. There's more than one movement and a lot of key changes. Well, you not only just started a new movement but the key changed and the conductor fell into the orchestra pit. But that's what life is all about, dear. Pushing through the fright and worry and finding the new key. You're just lucky your life is still in a major key!"

Toby didn't know much about classical music, but he felt better anyway. He had always remembered that conversation and the simple faces she had drawn in the newspaper. He wondered if she still remembered that now.

He didn't know where his life was right now. He still couldn't figure out what key it was in, or if he was feeling happy, sad, or squiggly. Maybe all three. The three faces of Toby.

Before they finished the snowman, the girls got wet and cold, and since it was nearly dark out anyway, they headed back around to the front door to go inside and warm up. Toby was surprised to see Miriam's car in the driveway; he hadn't even heard her drive in.

July had been sitting at the counter alone when she noticed a burning smell. Or rather, that slightly carbon-y smell, like a marshmallow just set aflame—sweet turning to bitter—that indicated a dish just about to burn.

She stood up quickly. What was cooking? She lifted the lid to the simmering pot, but she knew that wasn't it. It must be in one of the ovens. She opened the top one, but it was just some rolls in tin foil. She closed the door and opened the bottom oven.

Inside was a large glass baking dish filled with bubbling cheese and red sauce. It looked like chicken parmesan, but it had been left in so long that the red sauce was crusting and the bottom of the chicken was about to char. Had there been a timer set? She hadn't heard it. She scrambled for some potholders, looking in the drawers just next to the ovens, in the drawers in the island just across from the ovens, and along the counters, but she couldn't find them. So she snatched a towel lying next to the sink, got it wet, and grabbed the dish out of the oven.

When she was mid-turn between the oven and the island, the heat came, gradual but quick like a spike on a heart monitor.

"Owowow," she said, but managed not to drop the baking dish.

She closed the oven door and shook her hands around. How long had that been in there? She had been alone in the kitchen for at least twenty minutes, so it must have gone in before that. But the oven was set far too high – to four hundred and fifty degrees. That chicken should have been done in fifteen minutes, and it must have been in at least three times as long.

She plucked a spatula from a large holder beside the stove and investigated the damage. A little burned, but if there were some extra sauce that would help cover the taste of carbon.

She started opening cupboards, craning on her tiptoes searching for a jar of sauce.

"Can I help you find something?" she heard a woman's voice say with confusion.

July flattened her feet and turned toward the voice. This was Jenny's mother; there was no mistake about that. Her face was a slightly rounder, a more old fashioned version of Jenny's. Her hair, an odd yet appealing combination of yellow and silver, was combed carefully into a bun. She was standing by the back door, wearing a black over-coat and holding a pair of purple gloves in her hands and looking at July with her eyebrows raised in bewilderment but the corners of her mouth pulled in amusement.

"Oh! I, uh, the—chicken was—burning," she managed. "So I took it out. I thought maybe if there was a jar of sauce or something to help—resuscitate it?"

"I'm afraid we don't use jarred sauces," said Jenny's mother.

Wow, thought July, impressed. Perhaps the bland collection of cookbooks had led her astray.

"There might be some leftover sauce in the fridge," Jenny's mother moved toward the fridge. "How long has that been in the oven?"

"I don't know. I've been in here alone for at least twenty minutes and it was already in the oven when I came in."

"Hm," said Jenny's mother, her head bobbing between the shelves of the fridge. "Someone didn't count right. Math was never this family's strong point."

July remained silent.

"Well," said Jenny's mother, closing the fridge door. "No sauce. Is it burned badly?"

"No, I don't think so. I think I got it before it got too charred."

"Well, we'll just have to make do," she sighed. "I'll just cover it with some foil and keep it warm in the oven,"

July looked at the counter, the chicken parmesan reflected in the marble.

"You must be Toby's new lady friend," said Miriam, yanking foil over the dish.

July looked up. "Oh, um, yes. I'm July," she said, extending her hand and trying to smile.

"I'm Miriam." She shook July's hand, her face neutral and friendly.

"And how old are you, July?"

"Twenty-two," July replied a bit glumly. She thought everyone knew already. But Miriam moved on like she didn't even care.

"And you say you've been alone in here for twenty minutes?"

"Yes."

"And the family knows you're here?"

"Yes."

"Well, that's very rude. No one's offered you anything to drink?"

"Oh, no, that's okay, I'm not thirsty."

"Nonsense," said Miriam, moving into the kitchen. "What would you like?"

"Really, I'm fine."

"Well I was just thinking how I'd love a glass of wine. Let me get you one. You like white wine, don't you?"

"Oh, uh, yes. Thank you."

Why was she being so civil? Wasn't the mother supposed to side with her daughter against the ex-husband's new twenty-two-year-old "lady friend"? Maybe she was going to spike one of the wine glasses with poison and play mind games while July chose which one to drink.

"Here you are," she said handing July a glass of wine. "Happy New Year," she chimed, moving her glass forward and clinking it with July's.

"How did you enjoy Italy?" asked Miriam over the rim of her glass.

"I loved it. I wish I could have spent longer there."

"I've always loved Italy. I once spent an entire afternoon at a café in Rome just sipping coffee and enjoying the sun. It was one of the best afternoons of my life."

"I believe it," replied July. "Everything seems a bit more vivid over there."

Miriam cocked her head slightly and smiled.

"Why yes it does."

They were quiet for a moment. July could swear she could still hear the chicken sizzling.

"Should we go join the others in the living room?" Miriam said finally.

July wished she could just curl up in the oven, but she followed Miriam out of the kitchen anyway.

Kevin and Jenny were sitting on the sofa together, with Jenny's sister on the floor with a little girl in a purple dress, and a man, who must be Ryan, sitting in a green armchair with a young boy on his lap.

"Hello, dears!" cried Miriam as she entered the room.

"Hi, Mom!" said Jenny, turning around and smiling.

Jenny's gaze froze momentarily on July, but she decided to continue pretending that July wasn't there.

"Jenny, it seems you forgot about the chicken. It was supposed to come out right at quarter to five."

"Oh, shoot!" exclaimed Jenny, moving to get up.

"No, no, July rescued it," Miriam motioned Jenny back down. "Good thing she has a good nose, eh?"

"How was the hospice, Mom?" asked Sarah quickly.

"Oh, fine, fine. July, have you met everyone?"

"Uh, no."

As Miriam introduced the family, each adult nodded, eyes averted, as though she were Medusa.

"July, please sit, make yourself comfortable," Miriam said, motioning to the free spot on the couch next to Jenny.

July sat as far against the armrest as she could, wishing she could disappear into the corner cracks of the cushion. She could feel the tendrils of Jenny's disgust coiling around her.

"Where are the girls?" asked Miriam.

"Playing outside with Toby," answered Jenny with strained indifference.

A hollow silence echoed around the room. July was tempted to clap her hands just to make sure she could still hear. Everyone's head seemed tilted away from her, like if they didn't look at her she would disappear. She couldn't take it. The kitchen alone was better than this.

"Excuse me," she said quietly, standing up and turning to Miriam. "Where is your restroom?"

Miriam's lips flattened with a very slight twitch of sadness. Or maybe pity or disapproval or triumph.

"Go ahead and use the one upstairs. First door on your left."

"Thank you," said July as she set down her wine glass.

She walked out of the room as fast as she could. She stopped at the staircase to catch her breath, and, when she was out of the sightline of the living room, listened to see if they said anything about her.

"She's a child," said Jenny scornfully.

"You're not being a very good hostess," said Miriam.

"That's not my *job*," Jenny scoffed with disdain. "And you don't have to be so nice to her."

"Haven't you ever heard to keep your friends close and your enemies closer?"

So that's why she's being so civil to me? thought July. *I'm the enemy.*

She felt her eyes swell and pulse with tears. Oh no. No, no, no crying, that would only make their case stronger. But she couldn't help it as a few tears rolled down her cheeks. She sniffled, perhaps a bit too loudly, and ran up the stairs before anyone could see that she was there.

She shut herself in the bathroom quickly and steadied herself against the counter.

How was she an enemy? She hadn't fought this war. Hadn't the peace treaty been signed?

This wasn't the way to deal with things, hiding in the potpourri sprinkled bathroom and crying. She couldn't stay in here all night—then she really would be a child. Yet all she wanted to do was stay there, still and alone and teleport herself back to the hotel. Even better, back to Italy. Back to Massimo's apartment with a plate of *puttanesca* and a glass of red wine. Back to that couch, lying with her legs across his lap, his body against hers, leaning closer. There were no bitter ex-wives there, only Astrids with keys.

She stood up and looked in the mirror to clean herself up. As she opened the door out into the dark hallway, she felt choked by those coils of hate that came from all directions.

She stood at the top of the stairs, watching Toby and the girls taking off their snowy, damp clothes and laughing. Toby told the girls to go change and they ran up the stairs to their rooms. Chloe and Sophia ran past with faint smiles and small waves, and Grace straggled behind them and stopped briefly to describe their snowy sojourn. By the time July looked up, Toby was in the living room saying hello to Miriam. So as the family, or former family, recalibrated in the yellow light of the living room, July staggered quietly down the stairs and slid into the kitchen.

She wished she hadn't made any dessert at all.

XXVI

"MIRIAM," SAID TOBY. HE WAS SMILING BROADLY AND HE COULDN'T help it.

"Hello, Toby. It's nice to see you again," she said politely, if remotely.

He would have hugged her, but instead he shook her hand. "It's very good to see you, too."

"I presume you had a nice time in Italy?"

"Yes. It was lovely. Though I hurt my back and decided to come back early to recuperate."

"I heard. Though you seem to have bounced back quickly," she said, smiling with closed lips over her wine glass. She looked at her watch. "Well look at this, it's past five o'clock, we're late for appetizers. Where's your father, dear?" she said to Sarah.

Sarah shrugged.

"I think he's upstairs," offered Kevin. "Would you like me to go get him?"

"Yes, thank you, dear. Tell him it's time for appetizers. And grab the girls while you're at it."

"Sure thing," said Kevin cheerily.

Asshole, thought Toby.

"How about helping me in the kitchen, girls?" Miriam said to Sarah and Jenny.

They got up obediently and followed her into the kitchen, pointedly not looking at Toby, leaving just him and Ryan.

"Well this is fun," said Toby dryly as he took a seat on the couch.

"Tell me about it," said Ryan, leaning forward. "I've been forbidden from talking to you. Which leaves me with what? Alan and his model airplanes or Prancer Boy?"

Toby smiled, "You call him Prancer Boy?"

"Well, Sarah and I do, but Jenny doesn't know that."

Toby laughed.

"Shh, shh," said Ryan, patting his hand downward and leaning in closer. "I'm not supposed to be fraternizing with the enemy."

"So now I'm the enemy?"

"Well to *them* you are."

"Why, because Jenny asked for a divorce and got it? What, is it contagious now?"

Ryan rolled his eyes slightly and licked his lower lip, leaning further forward. "How did you *meet* her?"

"Who, Jenny?"

"No, the girl."

"July?"

"Yeah. How did you *do* it?"

"She worked at my Starbucks."

"Man, I always heard stories about this shit but I thought it only happened to rich and famous dudes or, like, Denis Kucinich."

Toby didn't know what to say, so he nodded slightly and raised his eyebrows.

"Well, I'm a happily married man; I hope that never changes. But if it ever does, I hope my unhappiness looks like that," he said simply.

"So," said Toby after a moment. "What about Kevin?"

Ryan shrugged, "Well, apparently he's not gay."

"Yeah, how 'bout that," said Toby.

He heard the girls running down the stairs and turned his neck toward them. Sophia and Chloe came clomping down first and then, behind them, Kevin with Grace on his shoulders.

It felt as though someone had pressed a white-hot branding iron to his heart, searing him with the words get-away-from-my-daughters. The words simmered into his chest and bubbled up through his throat, waiting to explode out his head.

Seeing Grace, a miniature of Jenny, on Kevin's shoulders, was more than he could handle. Kevin already had Toby's first Jenny—how dare he get the second one and, if Toby did say, the better one. She was half him, too.

Part of him stood up, walked to meet Kevin at the base of the stairs, tore Grace off those insultingly sculpted shoulders and carried her under his arm out the door like a rushing football player. But what hurt him more than seeing Grace on Kevin's shoulders was seeing that she was laughing. She looked ecstatic. Like she was having the time of her life.

So instead the brand encapsulated his heart, charring and shriveling it into coal that broke into pieces inside him.

"Let's get some cheese and crackers onto plates, put the nuts in the bowls, arrange some veggies on the tray, and nuke those pizza rolls the girls like real quick," Miriam instructed as she, Jenny, and Sarah swooped into the kitchen.

July was sitting at the counter again, looking through a copy of *People* that had been left lying about. She lifted her head as they came in.

"Oh! July," she said with surprise as she stopped at the door of the refrigerator.

"Can I help?" asked July, standing up.

Sarah and Jenny froze behind Miriam, exchanging glances and then looking at Miriam.

"No, no, you're a guest. Please, go relax in the living room."

"No, really, I'd – I'd love to help out."

"Oh! Well," said Miriam, looking over her shoulder at her daughters, "why don't you arrange the cheese and crackers."

Miriam took out a block of cheddar, a wheel of brie and camembert and placed them on the counter in front of July, followed by three different boxes of crackers, two plates, and then a knife.

As July opened the block of cheddar, the blonde trio moved about the kitchen in silence, communicating through glances from the same set of eyes. For a moment, it seemed like July was seeing triple.

When July had finished arranging the first plate of crackers and cheese and had just started on the second, Kevin came in with Grace on his shoulders. He walked over to Jenny and gave her a quick kiss on the lips.

"July, look how tall I am!" Grace called happily.

July smiled, perhaps for the first time that evening.

"Even taller than I am!" July replied.

"Mommy!" Grace squealed, pointing to July, "she's the one who showed me peanut butter and honey!"

"Oh, really," said Jenny, turning to look at July.

She ran her eyes almost imperceptibly up and down July, and then turned back to Grace.

"I want some peanut butter and honey!" called Grace.

"Not now, honey, we have all these other yummy snacks."

"No, I want peanut butter and honey. And milk!"

Grace looked at July, who smiled again.

Jenny looked helplessly at Kevin, who probably would have shrugged if he hadn't been weighted down with Grace. She glanced at her mother, who raised her eyebrows and shrugged.

"There's some peanut butter in the fridge, Grace," said Miriam after a moment. "Why don't you get it yourself like a big girl?"

Kevin knelt down and Grace scrambled off his shoulders. She took the jar of peanut butter from the fridge and came and sat on a stool next to July.

"How about peanut butter and honey on a cracker?" asked July.

"Okay."

"Which cracker do you want?"

"Um," said Grace examining the boxes. "That one."

She pointed to the box of wheat crackers. July pulled out a sleeve, opened them, and set them in front of Grace.

"Here's the honey, dear," said Miriam, setting the honey in front of Grace.

Grace opened the jar of peanut butter and started to dip the cracker inside.

"Oh! How about a knife?" said July. "That way we can spread it all over the cracker."

"Yeah," said Grace with such a tone of seriousness that July couldn't help smiling even broader.

"Miriam, where are your knives?" she asked with all the politeness she could muster.

"Right by Jenny," said Miriam, nodding her head.

Jenny opened a drawer and handed a knife to July. Wasn't that all July needed.

"You'd better spread it for her," said Miriam.

July picked up the knife and spread some peanut butter over the cracker.

"Do you want to pour the honey?" she asked Grace.

Grace nodded and picked up the honey bottle.

The four adults had turned to watch with what July thought to be a rather unexpected degree of interest. They stood frozen, moving only their eyes, as though a sudden movement would break time in half.

Grace drizzled honey deliberately over the cracker, only dripping some on July's hand, which July licked off once she handed Grace the cracker.

"Mmm," said Grace, taking a bite.

"Do you want me to start another for you?" July asked.

Grace nodded.

Time resumed as Jenny and Sarah looked at each other and silently, suspiciously, went back to working on the vegetable platter. Then they froze again as Grace said, "Don't you want one?" asked Grace. "You should have one, too."

"I would love one. Do you think everyone else would like one, too?"

Grace nodded.

"Okay. I'll do the peanut butter and you can be in charge of the honey."

"Make extra ones for us," said Grace.

"You got it."

So that's why kids are cool, July thought.

Toby had been sitting on the couch with Sophia and Chloe when Jenny, Sarah, Miriam and Kevin came in with the same appetizers they had served for the decade or so he had been coming. Miriam never changed the menu.

"Dig in everybody," said Miriam as she placed the last bowl of nuts on the table.

"Where's Grace?" asked Toby.

"They're coming," said Miriam.

They?

After a moment, he heard Grace say, "Excuse me everybody!"

The room turned their heads toward the door to the kitchen, where Grace stood holding a tray in front of her. July stood behind her, trying to look invisible.

"Me and July made this special snack for you. It's called Ju-lace crackers," said Grace, nodding her head for emphasis. "That's a mix of our names, July and Grace."

She walked over to Miriam and held out the tray.

"Grandma gets the first one."

"Thank you," said Miriam, smiling her grandma smile and reaching for a cracker.

"Just one per person!" added Grace hastily.

Grace moved from Miriam to Alan.

"July!" she called, and motioned her head for July to follow her around the room.

July smiled sheepishly and took two long steps to stand behind Grace.

Relieved to see July since he'd abandoned her, Toby watched as July shadowed Grace around the room, serving everyone crackers. He didn't notice any words in his head, or really, any feelings in his body other than the strange shivering, swelling sensation as his heart unshriveled in rewind, the words *take-that-Jenny* uncurling and pushing against the brand.

They stopped in front of him.

"This one's for you, Daddy," said Grace, pointing to a cracker in the corner that seemed to be overflowing with honey.

"Thank you, sweetie," he said, taking the cracker.

Though he looked straight into July's eyes, he didn't know what he saw or how he felt. Except for his taste, which was overpowered by honey, his senses had turned to gauze.

To accommodate the crowd of thirteen people, Miriam had divided them into the adults' table and the kids' table. July got the feeling that there had been a lot of jokes about which table she belonged at, but maybe she was being over sensitive. She sat with Kevin to her left and Toby on her right, directly across from Sarah. The seating had obviously been carefully planned.

When everyone had filled their plates, Miriam nodded at Alan, who then stood up.

"I'd just like to say a few words," he began, then cleared his throat. "As the old year comes to an end and the new one begins—"

July could see Miriam subtly mouthing his words.

"—we have to look back and remember how many—" he paused almost imperceptibly "—blessings came with the last year. So, uh, as is the tradition, let's go around the table and have everyone share one of their blessings from this year."

Oh God, thought July. *Oh God, oh God, oh God.* She couldn't possibly say I met Toby, even though it seemed that was the biggest blessing. She couldn't say that. *Oh no, what would Toby say? And Jenny? It hadn't exactly been a year of blessings for them.*

"I'll start," said Alan. "This year we have all been healthy. Miriam and I were privileged enough to spend three weeks this summer in Oregon with the family and the grandkids, and I know I speak for both of us when I say it was probably the highlight of our year."

He smiled warmly at the kids, who stood beside the table, huddled next to their parents' chairs. "Miriam?"

"Well," she said, sitting up straighter and folding her hands in front of her. "As you mentioned, the trip to Oregon. But it has certainly been a blessing to continue doing my hospice work, and to be so lucky to see my children with fair regularity. Sarah?" she turned to her right, where Sarah sat.

What am I going to say? thought July. *What other blessings have I had this year, besides Toby? School is … school. What did I do this year? I broke up with Chris. I made some gnocchi.*

Sarah was saying something about her family, and then it was Ryan's turn.

What else had she done? She stared at the cooling, overdone chicken on her plate. She had been to Italy. But she couldn't say that, could she? It was Toby, essentially, but she didn't have to mention his name—he would understand. And so would everyone else too, probably, but at least she would *say* the right thing even if everyone else knew what she meant. Part of her wanted to say something totally insensitive just to give them reason to be scandalized and give them something to talk about. But she would probably have to see these people again if she and Toby were to stay together. Wasn't there anything diplomatic she could say to make them like her? What was it?

Jenny, who was sitting at the head of the table across from Alan, was after Ryan. July's stomach did a jumping jack.

Jenny raised her eyebrows.

"Well," she began, pausing and looking at the table out of the corner of her eyes. "I've had the privilege of raising my beautiful girls, who are healthy, smart, and wonderful, and I love every day I have with them."

All the parents at the table smiled except Toby.

"And I had the rest of my family here to be so supporting and loving when things got rough. And then, of course, that includes Kevin, but I've been blessed to have him in my life for a while."

July had to stop her jaw from splatting into her plate. Obviously Jenny knew what she was implying and didn't care. July looked to Toby, who kept his head straight and maintained a decent version of his poker face, but she could see his jaw was clenched and his eyes, like concrete, stared past the room. July slid her gaze across the table to Miriam, who was smiling evenly, like she were a judge maintaining objectivity. Alan was looking nowhere, but Sarah was smiling broadly and had her hand on her chest, looking deeply touched.

Kevin smiled at Jenny, who smiled back, and squeezed her hand.

"Kevin?" said Alan.

"Well, obviously my biggest blessing is being welcomed into such a wonderful family as this. My family was never so close or caring as this one, and I truly feel honored and privileged to be so warmly and unquestioningly welcomed into this one."

"It's our pleasure, dear," said Miriam, smiling genuinely.

July could see Toby's nostrils flare. Poor Toby. Indiana Jones may as well have been watching as his heart was ripped beating from his chest.

"July?" said Alan, who obviously strained not to change the tone of his voice.

The entire room pivoted its attention to her, though no one was looking at her directly.

"Uh, well, this year I was very blessed to travel outside of the country for the first time."

Jenny's eyebrows were raised slightly, as though she anticipated July saying something so inflammatory and inappropriate that Jenny could tell the story of Toby's tart child girlfriend and the scene she caused on New Year's Eve. July had to break the tension.

"And in doing so, I met two of the most interesting people I think I've ever met. Two people with whom, I hope, I can continue communication for the rest of my days."

Toby turned to her, his mouth slightly open in shock. She was not going to mention *them*, was she? After the problems they had caused?

"Martin and Susan Rothman," she said.

Toby burst out in laughter, putting his hand on her thigh without thinking about it. July smiled. She knew it wasn't really that funny, but with the beating she imagined Toby was probably taking inside, she had to lighten him up a little. Plus, she felt a little smug bringing up an inside joke in front of all the others, just to let them know that they could be outside, too, even though July was, as the song went, the one thing that was not like the other ones.

Everyone else around the table raised their eyebrows or slid their eyes sideways at each other as Toby continued laughing. She smiled broadly and looked at him, meeting his gaze for a moment. He had aged ten years and back just in the space of these few hours.

July looked at Jenny as subtly as she could. Jenny had bunched her tongue up over the incisors on one side of her mouth, that Mom's-not-pleased look July recognized from her own mother. A little swell of triumph spiked up July's throat like mercury in a thermometer.

"Toby?" said Alan, trying to maintain that evenness, when Toby had stopped laughing and caught his breath.

"Well," started Toby. "The biggest blessing in my life is and always will be my girls. I love being their dad, even when they do remind me of their mom."

July's eyelids bugged a bit involuntarily. Maybe that laughter had loosened him up a bit too much, because that was probably not something to say given the present company.

"Uhh," continued Toby, obviously realizing his gaffe as the words echoed back to his hears, "and uhh …"

"Thank you, Toby," interrupted Miriam, flashing a smile that, like a quality paste diamond, showed its fakeness only in a flash under the right light. "How about you, kids?" She turned halfway around in her chair and looked at Chloe.

Hey, thought July, the mercury spike plunging fast. *He didn't get to say anything about me.* Which was probably the point.

Toby shut his mouth abruptly, his eyebrows shooting up in surprise. Alan rolled his lips into his mouth so that they disappeared and all that was left was a line like those simple yellow smiley faces. Sarah pursed her lips. July guessed that Miriam didn't usually interrupt people.

She only half-listened to what the kids said—"my iPod, my princess doll"—they probably hadn't felt too blessed this past year anyway. *Why are we here?* she wondered. What was the point? Why was she trying? Why did she care? It was hopeless. She just wanted to ring in the New Year at the hotel alone with Toby. Why did he still cling to this family?

"Okay then," said Alan, when the children had finished expressing the blessings of their toys. "This year has clearly been one filled with blessings, even when it seems we have to look hard for them. So let's end this year with a blessing—a final meal all together."

He raised his glass, and everyone followed suit. "To the year that's passed, and to the one ahead."

There were a few mumbled, "Here, heres" and "Amens." The kids went to their table and everyone started eating. July took a bite of the chicken and had to refrain from sticking out her tongue and contorting her face like a cat with a hairball in its throat.

"Like eating a ball of string," her father would have said.

Did they always eat like this?

"Wonderful job on the chicken as usual, Jenny honey," said Alan.

"Thanks, Dad."

"Yes, great job," said Kevin, forking another bite into his mouth.

The others echoed similar sentiments. July managed a timid, "Quite good," figuring it was less rude to be disingenuous than to say nothing.

How had Toby survived for seventeen years on food like this? How had the girls eaten anything? Did they think this was how chicken was supposed to taste? Jenny had probably totally warped their palates. Those poor girls. July would have to try to fix that. She had already started with Grace.

The sound of clinking, scraping forks seemed magnified ten times. No one was saying anything. She would rather be eating cardboard pizza boxes with the Rothmans. Or *not* eating cardboard pizza boxes in the case of Mrs. Rothman.

She thought about her father and the smoker her mother had given him for Christmas. They were probably eating a delicious, thirteen-pound brisket that had been smoked all day long. She swallowed each desiccated bite with a drink of water, but she finished the water before she finished the chicken. She was too nervous to ask someone to pass the water pitcher, so mushed each piece around in her mouth like chewing gum until it was wet enough to slide down her throat.

XXVII

MAYBE SIX YEARS AGO THEY HAD HAD A PARTICULARLY ENJOYABLE New Year's Eve dinner. The year had ended well for everyone, so all the adults had a bit more wine and blessings than usual. They all joked and laughed the way families did during movie montages, and they all managed to stay up until midnight, playing charades and group solitaire and making fun of Dick Clark. They all counted down until twelve, passing smiles around, anticipating the blessings that a new number would bring them all.

When they all shouted, "Happy New Year," or rather, stage shouted it since the girls were asleep, Toby and Jenny looked at each other and suddenly Toby was twenty-six-years-old looking on as the waiter motioned towards him, the pretty blonde looking straight into the eyes of the mysterious man who had sent her a drink, and the shimmers that had run through his shoulders then ran through them again like an aftershock.

"Happy New Year," he said.

"Happy New Year," she smiled back.

They kissed on the couch in front of her parents and Sarah and Ryan, who was still Sarah's boyfriend and whom Toby had just met for the first time that holiday season. But it turned out that all of them were kissing, too, and paid them no mind. Then everyone stood up and exchanged kisses and handshakes and Happy New Years to the sound of Times Square in a box.

"Happy New Year, Toby," Miriam had said, holding his cheeks between her hands and looking at him with solid affection, her chunky ring a cool contrast against her warm palms.

"Happy New Year, Miriam," he said, and they exchanged kisses on the cheek.

"Happy New Year, Toby," Alan had said moments before or after. He held Toby's right hand firmly in his and clapped his left hand firmly on Toby's back, drawing him in a bit.

"Happy New Year, Alan," Toby replied, and they hugged, back claps and all.

"May this year be even more blessed than the last," said Alan, his left hand now on the side of Toby's head.

"And for you, Alan."

Alan playfully tousled Toby's hair, like a father.

Even Sarah hugged him, and he and Ryan shook hands.

Now they were sitting in that same living room, everyone silently digesting before dessert. Every time Toby looked across the room at Jenny, she was exchanging glances with Sarah or Kevin or Miriam, a dog whistle conversation only they could hear.

The girls were playing a board game on the floor, some really obnoxious thing with flashing lights and a computerized voice that came from a poor quality speaker.

Kevin sat on the couch, his arm around Jenny, who had her feet tucked beneath her and leaned into Kevin, her hand on his leg. Did she really have to flaunt it?

Ryan sat on the other side of the couch and just below him on the floor sat Sarah, their son in her lap. Ryan was playing absently with Sarah's hair.

Miriam and Alan sat in their chairs, the ones they always sat in, the ones that were always ceded if one of them entered the room. Once or twice he caught Miriam's eye, but she never held the gaze very long.

This year could not be over soon enough.

Everyone's attention was focused in the middle of the room where the girls were playing. But even with the terrible computerized box and the kids giggling or yelling at each other, the room was ear splittingly silent, like they all had to remain still and quiet, a living diorama. Toby could practically hear his skin shed.

After a while, Miriam sighed, "Well, July," she said, and the diorama snapped to life. "Why don't you go get your cake ready? I think we'll have dessert soon."

"Oh. Okay," said July standing up.

"I want to help!" cried Grace.

"Grace, you have to finish the game," said Sophia with irritation.

"I want to help July!" said Grace stubbornly.

Toby flicked his eyes to Jenny, careful not to move his head. Her mouth had twitched ever so slightly to the side. She was annoyed. *Ha.*

"But you have to finish the *game!*"

"Come on, honey, I'll play for Grace," said Toby, even though he had no idea what the point of the game was.

"Come on, Grace, let's go get the cake ready," said July, holding out her hand.

Grace scrambled to her feet and grabbed July's hand, and they made their way into the kitchen. Toby noticed that Jenny and Sarah exchanged another round of dubious glances and raised eyebrows.

That's right, thought Toby as he eased his way onto the carpet. He felt a little swell of triumph. *Sure, July is young, but look how good she is with the kids. Obviously her age is not a factor here.* She was proving to everyone that Toby wasn't just going through a mid-life crisis by dating some little sorority ditz. No, July was different. She was mature.

Toby heard Grace giggle gleefully from the kitchen. Whatever July was doing in there was working. Grace was a pretty happy kid, but to get any kid to sound that happy was a triumph. She was better than the babysitters they had used. Hell, she was better than Sarah had been when *she* babysat them. July could be trusted. She wasn't a kid. July was as good—no, way better than—the adults here.

Toby turned his concentration to the talking robot box. What was he supposed to be doing?

"No, Daddy, you're supposed to press *this* button," Chloe was saying, and then suddenly Jenny was leaping off the couch and Kevin was standing and everyone was looking with alarm toward the kitchen. What—?

And then Toby heard it, Gracie screeching and wailing. Oh God, that was her hurting cry. She was hurt—what happened? The kitchen, knives, ovens, *oh God* and Toby was scrambling to his feet as fast as his back would allow and he was suspended, trying to swim through time, slogging like he was knee deep in mud.

Oh God, Grace please be okay not Grace not Grace take me not Grace. Her screaming, her crying, she was hurting, something was wrong, wrong, wrong.

Toby hurtled into the kitchen and there was Jenny on the floor bent over Grace—Grace on the floor, what was wrong what happened?

In a passing glance he saw July standing a foot away, frozen.

"Oh God, what happened?"

Jenny turned around and he got a glimpse of Grace on the floor, her face red and wet, her eyebrows turned in like a Jack o'Lantern and her mouth open screaming and oh God was that *blood* coming from her mouth, running down her chin, dripping onto her white shirt with a pink flower?

It was like there was a strobe light going because one moment he was standing in the doorway and the next he was down on the floor across from Jenny.

"What's wrong? What happened?"

"Her mouth, she's knocked her teeth out!" cried Jenny. "Oh, baby, oh, baby."

Jenny cradled Grace into her breast, getting blood on her blue shirt.

"What happened?" Toby turned around and looked at July, who had turned into a statue of fear.

"I—we…"

"Tell me what *happened*?!" Toby yelled.

"I—we—I was—she saw me slide on the floor—" July pointed to her feet in black socks on the shiny tile floor "—and—she started too, and dancing—"

"You let her *slide around on the floor*?" yelled Jenny.

"I—I used to do it all the time when I was a kid—my brothers and I used to dance around like ice skaters …"

"Don't you know how slippery this floor is?" yelled Toby.

The world was blurry, warped like a Dali painting, like a dream, the cabinets running together and leaning over them, July standing there stupidly like she'd had no idea that a four-year-old sliding on a slippery floor in her socks would fall down.

"I—she—lost control and fell forward and hit her mouth—"

"Are you *stupid*?!" yelled Jenny. "Don't you know *anything*? What were you *thinking*? That's what you get for dating a child!" she shouted at Toby.

"I was—thinking it was—fun, when I did it—when I was a kid—"

July's mouth open wide, her eyebrows raised in permanent surprise, "It was an *accident*," she choked, and her eyes welled up with tears.

But Toby didn't care. All he could think was *Grace. Grace. Grace.* He turned to her.

"Let Daddy see, honey," he said as gently as he could.

Grace, still wailing, kept her head buried in her mother's chest.

"Come on, baby, you're okay, let Daddy see so he can make it better."

Grace, shaking and gasping for more breaths to cry, lifted her head away from Jenny, her mouth wide open and dripping drool and blood in gooey stalactites. But immediately Toby could see that teeth were missing.

"She's knocked out her two top front teeth," he said to Jenny.

"Oh God," said Jenny, struggling not to start crying herself, "It's okay, Gracie, you're okay sweetie." Jenny was stroking Grace's hair, and Toby leaned in too to hug Grace, closer to Jenny than he'd been in months, years.

"We're going have to take her to the hospital," said Toby over Jenny's shoulder, and looking straight into Kevin's eyes.

"Let's calm down, first," Kevin nodded reassuringly. "Maybe we should find her teeth?"

"Yeah," said Toby, standing up.

"I'm so sorry," said July.

Toby turned around and looked at her.

"What were you thinking?" he asked her again, putting his hand against his forehead. "Don't you know how dangerous that is?"

"But—I did it all the time as a kid, I thought—"

"No, you didn't think!"

"I—I'm sorry, I didn't know, it was an accident!" she wailed.

Ugh, the last thing Toby wanted to see was another hysterical child. Grace was hurt. She had lost her *teeth*. Oh, *God*. Gracie had been in danger. She had been in danger and Toby hadn't been there to protect her.

"You don't know anything about watching kids!"

"It was an *accident!*"

"If you had any perspective, any common sense, this would *not* have happened!" he yelled blindingly. It was all he could do. He didn't have the energy to defend her to everyone anymore.

"Her teeth, where are her teeth?" he cried, looking down and turning frantically.

"Here," said July, holding out her hand, in which were two little teeth, bloody pearls of Grace.

Toby's heart gushed into a million pieces as he took the teeth. Just minutes ago they had been part of Grace, part of her body, attached to her, and years before that they had been part of him, and now Grace was bleeding on the kitchen floor like a toothless hockey player.

"I'm sorry," July sobbed, putting her head into her hand. "I don't believe this. I should have known."

"She's just a *kid*, what did you expect?" spat Jenny with an edge of contempt.

But Toby found himself agreeing. All he could do was shake his head, fire running through his body.

"I'm sorry," she sobbed again, but he could hardly understand her she was crying so hard.

"What are *you* crying about?" he heard himself shouting. "You're not the one with teeth missing! You're not the four-year-old bleeding on the floor!"

This just made July and Grace cry harder.

"Toby, calm down, it's okay. It's her baby teeth, she'll be fine," said Kevin gently, putting a hand on his shoulder.

"It is *not* okay!" Toby screamed at July, violently shaking off Kevin's hand. "They aren't baby teeth, she lost those early. You should know that about her!"

July didn't have a child, she couldn't possibly understand or care nearly enough. He should never have brought her. He should never have introduced her to the kids. He should have kept her separate, where she belonged, never let it get out of hand like this. He had put his daughters in danger because he thought he had been too weak to resist his impulses.

"Hey, don't take all your anger out on me just because you screwed up your marriage and you can't get over Jenny and can't accept she's over you!" July shouted, as though jolted into reality.

"I should never have brought you here! I should have left you in Florence with Massimo."

"This isn't about Massimo and you know it! This is about you clinging to the past and cowering from the future!"

"I should never have talked to you. I should never have sent you that glass of wine!"

A strange hiccough of silence popped into the room.

"You never sent me a glass of wine."

"You sent *me* the wine," said Jenny.

Toby was confused.

"This is all your fault!" he yelled, pointing a finger at July.

"You're just afraid of your own life!" she yelled back.

"Just get out!" he shouted back.

He couldn't stand to look at her. Her crying disgusted him even though at the same time he knew it was an accident, there was nothing she could have done to fix it, things happen.

"What?"

Grace, his baby Grace, she was hurting and shrieking and his heart was breaking, falling from his chest like her teeth. He was holding part of her in his hands, and it was not okay.

"Get out!" he repeated.

July stopped crying and looked at him, frozen in horror.

"But—"

"Just! Go!" he said, pointing in the direction of the front door.

The room was silent but he couldn't hear it. All he could hear was the ringing buzz of anger torching through his body. He looked right into July's eyes and thought, *what am I doing?* Her eyes were filled with the same worry and sadness that he felt. And cooler waves of sorrow crashed from her eyes into his, and he almost slackened and shriveled and melted, melted.

Her face and body crumpled as she wiped her hands over her face and moved slowly towards the door.

"I'm sorry, Grace," said July, and then she walked out of the kitchen. She walked past everyone in the family, who had clustered in the kitchen along the walls and by the doors.

Grace let out another wail, but this time it was different. It wasn't her hurt cry. But Toby didn't care. He didn't want to look at July. He could only stand to see one hurt girl at a time. All he could think about were the two bloody teeth he held in his hands, the adult teeth from a child's body that had been knocked out because of a child in an adult's body.

Take my teeth, take July's teeth, take anyone's teeth, but don't take them from Grace. Take my teeth, he pleaded to no one. *Take mine. Take them all.*

July didn't know how she had found her purse, put on her boots, opened the door, closed it behind her, but she found herself standing in the snow outside the Sivertsen house, sobbing.

Just go, he had said—shouted. Just go, like a block of wood against her throat. It had been an accident, an *accident*. She and her brothers used to slide around the wood floor dancing to *The Nutcracker* all the time when they were young—they had never fallen or lost teeth or anything else.

"Be careful, Grace," she had said, just before Grace started twirling and sliding and then suddenly she was on the floor and bleeding and shrieking. July hadn't even done her fancy moves—she had even *thought* to herself that she should watch Grace like a hawk, and she had. There was only so much she could do. *It was an accident!*

She was sobbing, her teardrops falling into the snow, burning holes into it, she imagined, like cigarette stubs being extinguished against white paper. She could hardly move herself, her saliva fell from her mouth because she couldn't work the muscles to close it.

She wanted to fall down in the snow right there, curl up and just cry and cry and cry. Toby obviously did not want to see her, probably ever again. Not that she could bear to face him. She was so filled with shame that she thought she would overflow, burst forth and melt the snow away into immediate summer.

The only thing that stopped her from burying herself into the snow right there was the thought that soon they would head to the hospital. She did not want to be here when they left the house. She didn't want to see them, see Miriam give her a serious, cross look, or see Jenny's smug that's-what-you-get-when-you-date-a-child look, or Toby's who-are-you-I-hate-you look. That would almost be worse than what had happened, knocking July's heart completely out in exchange for Grace's two front teeth. An eye for an eye; a heart for a tooth.

She opened the car and started it, but then she realized that Toby's luggage was still inside. She shouldn't take it with her—she wouldn't be seeing him any time soon. So as the car was running, she went around to the back, opened the trunk, and removed Toby's bag. She left it on the curb in the snow. He would probably need it.

She went back to the driver's seat and realized she had left the trunk open, so she had to get out again and close it.

She needed to get somewhere so she could never leave again. But where would she go? If she just stopped at some random roadside hotel, who knows how long she would be there, and what if Toby reported the car stolen? The only way this situation could be worse. She would have to drive it all the way back to his house and go from there.

That's a long time not to cry, she thought as she put the car in gear and pulled away from the house.

For the entire drive back, she kept the radio off, driving through the tunnel of her head. It was not the road she saw in front of her, but Grace sliding on the floor, losing her balance, falling forward like a crash test dummy and that agonizing split second of silence as both their brains processed what happened, as her teeth shot across the floor, and then the blood started coming. Grace didn't make a sound until she saw her own blood.

Toby's face, contorted in rage and pain, Jenny's contempt and fear boring into her, and then the rest of the family crowded in silently, lining the walls, watching the aftermath solemnly with grim detachment. Miriam standing with her hand over her mouth, the way everyone watched her walk out after she had been banished.

"One day yes, the next day no. I go with the love."

Her skin still burned hot with embarrassment and regret and shame, and she could still feel everyone's eyes sizzling into her pores, chastising her, hating her, as though she may as well have ripped the teeth from Grace's mouth herself and absconded with them like a bank robber.

How long she drove, she didn't know. At some point she passed into the New Year, exiled from the previous one. She wondered how Grace was, if they had fixed her teeth. Surely she wouldn't be toothless for the rest of her life. Teeth were replaceable.

Hours, miles, blackness later, things started looking familiar, darkness the same from year to year. It was close enough to Toby's house—she could drive no longer, so she pulled into the first hotel she saw. Who knows what the concierge thought she was—a druggie, a prostitute, some poor woman with dried snot and mascara that had run and dried again, but by the time she finally got into the elevator, white plastic keycard in hand, she could hold back the tears no longer, and suddenly she was *Alice in Wonderland*, drowning herself, or drowning in herself.

The first day of the year was lost. This year there would only be 364 days.

The second day was found when she went downstairs for the free hotel breakfast. Sometime that day, her cell phone rang. She looked at the caller ID box. It was Toby, and she thought she'd throw up. She had resisted calling him because she didn't want to hear him yell at her again. The shame was too much for her to bear.

So she ignored the phone.

He called again later that afternoon. And then again. She would have to pick up. He would need his car back. Next time he called.

If there would be a next time?

There was, sometime that night.

She answered the call and thought she would vomit.

"July?"

Oh God, his voice, his voice, that short clip, like he pressed his lips together between every word. She slid onto the floor. If there hadn't been a wooden block beneath the bed, she would have crawled underneath.

"July?" he said again.

"What," she managed.

"Where are you?"

"The Holiday Inn by the library."

"Wait—you drove all the way back?"

"Yeah."

"Oh."

"I'll leave your car at your house."

"Oh. Right."

"Is—she okay?"

"She'll be fine."

"I'm sorry," she said, tears falling down her face.

"Me too," he said gruffly.

Sorry that it had happened, or for the things he said? They clung to silence for a few moments.

"We're driving back tomorrow," he said.

She stared at the floor, the diamond pattern of flowers and ages of crumbs.

"I'll leave the car at your house."

He sighed, "July—"

It sounded like the start of something—an apology, forgiveness, regret? Did he miss her? Want her back? Was he sorry? But he didn't finish. He sighed again, the air curdling in the receiver and rolling around like a bag of pebbles.

"I'll talk to you later," and he hung up the phone.

"Goodbye," she said.

With every day that passed, with every day that the phone stayed silent, she tried to reassure herself that tomorrow hope started all over again. But there was less hope to start with, and then there was none. She couldn't bear to call him first. She didn't want to grovel any more. She didn't want to hear that he didn't know.

How did he—would he—remember her? Did he ever think about her any more as the days grew to weeks? Why hadn't he called again? Had she ever mattered?

She wondered if she would ever see him again. Where she would see him, or if she would recognize him when she did? Would he look much older? Would his hair be white, his skin rippled with wrinkles, his body softened in golden years lumps, his skin translucent and eroded with time?

Has he forgiven me?

Just before graduation, a For Rent sign went up in front of his house. Toby's car was no longer parked in the driveway. Where had he gone? Why?

She spent many hours of her life wondering where he was, what he was doing, whom he was with, wondering if he wondered the same about her. She tried to remind herself what he smelled like, how he felt against her when he pulled her belt loops into his hips and the way he kissed her so long that the skin under her nose wore away like a river rock.

All she had left of him was a scarf she had borrowed from him one cold day and hadn't returned. After a few weeks, the smell of him had faded, but long after it did she continue to put her nose against the wool and breathe in, hoping to catch him between the threads.

Even after the sharpness of the pain had dulled, after she had graduated and moved away and found a few happy moments, she thought of him. Did he have a new girlfriend? He must. Maybe he was taking her to Italy. Making her pancakes. Pulling her belt loops.

She had stopped wishing for his calls to repair the damage, but hoped that maybe he would call, just to see how she was, where she'd ended up, because he'd like to know, and she had mattered for that short time. She wanted him to know she was substantial.

In idle moments, she imagined sometimes that she had gone back to Italy, back to Florence, walking around all the places she had first seen with him. Maybe it was in a few months, maybe it was years and years later. She'd be standing looking at the Duomo and by chance, luck, they'd both be there. They would both be at a café at the same time. They would both be staying at the Ariele. They would be anywhere and look at each other and then—it wouldn't be sad. They would be happy in their own new ways now, and their reconnection would be deep, and meaningful, and she would finally understand why.

She met Toby only in her dreams, and at first he just was, sitting nearby or walking through her night life like he belonged, like he was every day, every day like the sky or the sun. As time moved by his presence stayed poignant but became less pressing. The dream Toby turned progressively foggier. Sometimes he looked like he had the last day she saw him. Sometimes he looked like Clint Eastwood; other times like John Wayne, or Tony Blair; other times he looked like no one she had seen before, or like a smear of paint on a canvas—it was only him because she knew it was him.

When she focused, if she could admit she was dreaming, she could talk to him. Once she was in a bus station, or maybe it was a train station or an airport terminal, and Toby was there, looking younger, trimmer.

"Toby?" she said, half question, half statement, as he walked by her.

Am I dreaming?

"July," he said. "I'm on my way to Paris."

"Oh, wow," she said.

She only wanted to know how he was, there was no more sadness. Did he think of her, had she mattered at all?

"I'll talk to you later," he was walking away.

"Don't go," she pleaded.

But he went.

Her hands were webbed, the lights never went off, so she did the conversation again.

"Toby."

"July. I'm on my way to Paris."

"Oh, wow," she said. "We should get together sometime and catch up."

"Okay," he said. "I'll talk to you later."

And he walked away.

"Don't go," she shouted. "I'm sorry!"

I'm dreaming, come back.

And through the fogged window of dreams, *Don't you ever think of me? Did I matter?*

All he could ever reply was, "I'll talk to you later."

"Don't go."

He walked away through the faces of strangers that didn't exist.

But he stopped and turned around, the light of Charles de Gaulle bright around him, his bag across his shoulder, wearing jeans and a light blue shirt. Though he was ten feet in front of her, she felt his arm across her back and pinch on her left side. He looked back at her through his crinkly metallic eyes like a perfect candid photograph, calling her forward through customs into a new world like a ghost.

About the Author

ELLIS FRIEDMAN IS A WELLESLEY GRADUATE AND ARIZONA NATIVE. She spent four years living in China working as a teacher, magazine editor, and amateur gourmand. She and her husband currently reside in Phoenix.